Sheranchuk smiled to himself, his mind made up. He would go in and see for himself just what they were doing with Reactor No. 4. He was displaying his *paprushka* to the gate guard when the world changed around him.

There was a sudden orange-white flare of light, a flower of flame overhead, the shattering, hurtful sound of a vast explosion. "In God's name!" he cried, clutching at the guard's arm as the two of them stared up in horror.

The noise did not stop. A siren screamed inside one of the buildings. There was a distant sound of men shouting. "But this is quite impossible," the guard bawled accusingly in Sheranchuk's ear.

Sheranchuk's mouth was open as he stared up. The great ball of bright flame was floating away and diminishing, but behind it was a sullen, growing red glow. To the other noises was added the patter of a shower—no, a downpour!—but it was not rain that was falling. It was bits of stone and brick and metal, pelting down all around them.

"Yes," Sheranchuk said dazedly, "it is quite impossible."

But it had happened.

Chernobyl
by
Frederik Pohl

CHERNOBYL

A NOVEL

Frederik Pohl

BANTAM BOOKS
TORONTO · NEW YORK · LONDON · SYDNEY · AUCKLAND

CHERNOBYL

A Bantam Spectra Book
Bantam hardcover edition / September 1987
2 printings through August 1987
Bantam paperback edition / April 1988

Library of Congress Cataloging-in-Publication Data

Pohl, Frederik.
  Chernobyl.

    1. Nuclear power plants—Ukraine—Chernobyl'—
Accidents—Fiction. 2. Chernobyl' (Ukraine)—20th
century—Fiction. I. Title.
PS3566.036C54 1987   813'.54   86-47896
ISBN 0-553-27193-8

Published simultaneously in the United States and Canada

Bantam Books are published by Bantam Books, a division of Bantam Doubleday
Dell Publishing Group, Inc. Its trademark, consisting of the words "Bantam
Books" and the portrayal of a rooster. is Registered in U.S. Patent and Trademark
Office and in other countries. Marca Registrada. Bantam Books, 666 Fifth Avenue,
New York. New York 10103.

This book is dedicated to the hundreds of men and women whose courage and sacrifice kept a terrible accident from becoming far more terrible still.

From *The Revelation of St. John the Divine:*

And the third angel sounded, and there fell a great star from heaven, burning as it were a lamp, and it fell upon the third part of the rivers, and upon the fountains of the waters; and the name of the star is called wormwood; and the third part of the waters became wormwood; and many men died of the waters, because they were made bitter.

The Ukrainian word for wormwood is *chernobyl.*

CHAPTER 1

At this time Simyon Smin is an active, affable man of sixty-four years who looks rather like a former heavy-weight wrestler. He is short and quite stocky. He smiles often, with the kind of smile that other people instinct-ively return. He could not be called handsome, partly because he has a strip of smooth, almost glassy skin that extends across the left side of his face from his upper lip to where the back of his neck disappears inside his clothes. Still, there is a sweetness to his expression which makes his male subordinates feel free to speak frankly to him, and which women find attractive. That is one of the reasons his wife, Selena, married him, although at the time of their wedding he was nearly forty years old and she was only nineteen. Another reason is that he was a wounded and decorated war veteran, with special privi-leges in going to the head of queues and opportunities to buy things in special stores. It was also obvious even then that he was on his way up. He has succeeded well. He is the Deputy Director of the Chernobyl Nuclear Power Station, which supplies the eastern Ukraine with nearly one quarter of its electrical energy, a Party member of forty-three years' standing and one who has the privilege, from time to time, of travel abroad. Selena has been permitted to accompany him out of the country twice. Once it was only to East Germany, but the other time gave her five wonderful days when he was obliged to visit the International Atomic Energy Authority headquarters in the authentically western city of Vienna.

Immediately after lunch that day Smin received the three visitors from South Yemen in the plant's conference room. It was one of the showplaces of the plant, with its snowy white bust of V. I. Lenin gazing challengingly down from one wall and its deep-piled Armenian rug on the floor. His secretary had set up the long birch table with the things appropriate for distinguished foreign guests, who might (the people in Novosibirsk hoped) order an RBMK-1000 nuclear power plant for their own country. (Of course, for political reasons, it would be a long time before they ever got one, but still the nuclear power plant authorities wanted very much to have them ask.) There were opened bottles of Pepsi-Cola and orange Fanta, as well as ashtrays and packets of American Marlboros, and in the little refrigerator under the sideboard were unopened tins of Greek orange juice. (There was also a bottle of Stolichnaya vodka in the refrigerator's tiny ice compartment, in case the Yemenis turned out to be more Marxist than Moslem.)

The Yemenis were escorted in by Smin's secretary, Paraska Kandyba, her lined, lean old face impassive. Their translator trailed behind, deferentially seating himself at the very end of the table only after the men in the white robes were already sitting down. "I welcome you to the Chernobyl Power Station. I apologize for the fact that our Director, Comrade Zaglodin, is unavoidably absent, but he joins me in the hope that your visit here can add to the warm and friendly relations between our two countries," said Smin in his pleasing tenor voice, and waited for the translator to put that into the language of his visitors. It was the standard speech of hospitality and pride in the power plant, two sentences at a time and then a pause for the translator. He went right on with it as his secretary came in with a tray of coffee in small cups and a plate of sweet biscuits, which she handed around among the guests. They sipped and nibbled impassively as they listened to Smin's recitation of the virtues of the Soviet nuclear power system, the unflagging devotion with which they were carrying out the decisions of the 27th Party Congress, and their unfailing success in achieving their Plan goals.

The speech was nearly all true in what it said, though it said nothing of, for example, the stratagems and shortcuts that made the Plan at least technically attainable. Nor did it say explicitly what the other duties were that kept the Director from the honored Yemeni guests. (Which were primarily that there were other guests the Director thought more worth cultivating than a bunch of Arabs who chose to be born in the only country on the Arabian peninsula that didn't have oil.) Smin could have given the speech in his sleep. Sometimes he almost did. Normally in such conditions he used the fifty percent of time devoted to translation to study the visitors—Cubans and East Germans, Angolans and Campucheans, Vietnamese and Poles—and wonder what they made of this immense monument to Soviet science and technology. Of course, many of them had nuclear power generating plants of their own, or at least every expectation of having them soon. What they had, however, were generally pressurized water reactors. What none of the foreign guests had were the RBMK-1000s that powered Chernobyl. That particular model was not exported to the fraternal Socialist countries. The reactors they got were, no doubt, good enough to produce electrical power, but they were of little use for other purposes. (Of course. Who would trust Campucheans or Poles with the capacity to create plutonium?) Sometimes Smin tried to guess what the foreign guests would do if they actually ordered, and were allowed to receive, RBMK-series reactors. Sometimes he thought they would tamely return the spent cores for reprocessing inside the USSR without any unexplained shortages.

But he didn't think that often.

On this day he didn't play that game anyway. He had other things on his mind. When the leader of the Yemenis took his turn to respond to the speech of welcome, Smin, nodding in thoughtful appreciation at each translated fragment, took the opportunity to write on a piece of paper: "Experiment on schedule?" He passed it inconspicuously to the secretary when she came in to offer the tinned orange juice to the guests. No one seemed to notice what he had done. The head of the delegation was craning his neck to peer inside the refrigerator as the secretary opened it. He turned to Smin and said, *"Peut-être, un peu de vodka?"*

"Mais certainement," cried Smin affably. *"Et alors, vous*

parlez français? Très bien!" He waved the secretary off and opened the ice-cold vodka bottle himself, pouring a nearly exact one hundred fifty milliliters of vodka for each guest. If any of them noticed that Smin poured nothing for himself, no one commented. Thereafter the conversation continued in serviceable, if rather elementary French on both sides. It went much faster that way. Smin explained that each of the four reactors that made up the Chernobyl plant was rated at one thousand megawatts and could be refueled in operation, meaning that they were on line far more of the time than most Western models. He passed out glossy prints of the turbine room, the containment shell, the arc-shaped control boards with their four or five technicians always on duty, the bound book of aerial photographs taken during construction that showed the immense power plant as it grew, layer by layer.

"But why are you showing us only these photographs?" asked one of the Yemenis politely. "Can we not visit these places in person?"

"But certainly!" cried Smin. "Of course, there is a certain amount of climbing to be done—you don't object to stairs? —and it will be necessary, purely as a precaution, to wear protective clothing, but we can begin at once!" And do it very quickly, he added to himself, because the note the secretary slipped into his palm had said, "Yes, it is scheduled to begin at 2:00 P.M."

Chernobyl was not merely a power plant, it was nearly a city. Each RBMK-1000 reactor by itself was immense, with its tons of graphite blocks that slowed the neutrons; its nearly seventeen hundred jacketed steel pipes that carried water through the cores; its drying tanks, where all seventeen hundred tubes met to wring the droplets of water out of the steam and pass the energy-loaded steam itself on to the turbines; its huge macadam turbine floor, where the engines droned or howled away; its two feet of steel and six feet of concrete that surrounded each reactor—insurance against the wholly improbable chance that something, some time, should go wrong. And there were four of the RBMK-1000s already on line in the Chernobyl power station plant; and the plant itself was only one structure in a municipality of storage spaces and workshops and administration offices—and a medical center—and baths for the people who worked there—and cafeterias—and lounges for parties and resting after shifts—and everything else that Smin could imagine, and through begging or bribes manage to obtain, to make Chernobyl perfect.

That was the job of the Deputy Director, and the fact that a goal of perfection was impossible to attain did not keep Smin from continuing to try. Against all odds. In spite of all frustrations. There were plenty of those, starting with the workers themselves. If they did not drink on the job, they absented themselves without permission; if they did not do either, then they all too often drifted away to other jobs as soon as they were trained. In theory that was not easy to do in the USSR, since no one got a job without a report from his last employer and employers were supposed to discourage vagabonding of that sort. In practice, people who had worked at Chernobyl were in such demand that even a negative report was disregarded. And those were only the problems of personnel. If the workers were somehow placated and even motivated, then there were the problems of matériel. Materials of decent quality were always hard to get—for anything—and Smin was shameless and tireless in doing what had to be done to find unflawed steel and well-made cables and high-grade cement and even the best and freshest produce from the private plots of the nearby kolkhozists to go into the kitchens of the plant's cafeterias. Just weeks before there had been a story in *Literaturna Ukraina* that had harshly exposed the sordid history of incompetent people and defective materials; it had been a great embarrassment to Smin's superiors, but in the long run the story had added force to Smin's own dedicated routine of demanding and urging and shaming and even, when necessary— and it was often necessary—bribing. It was not how Smin would have preferred to do his job, but it was unfortunately the only way, sometimes, that the job could be done.

Because Smin was in a hurry, he didn't show the Yemenis everything. He skipped the oil storage rooms, high up over the reactors, where the diesel fuel was kept for the emergency pumps in case of power failure; he gave them only a quick peek through the heavy glass windows at the refueling chamber, where the huge, spidery refueling machine crept on its massive tracks from fuel tube to fuel tube as needed, lifting out the spent fuel and replacing it with new while the reactor kept right on generating power. He skipped the Red Room and the cafeteria and the baths, though he was proud of them all for the proof they gave of his constant concern for the four thousand men and women who worked at Chernobyl. He did not, of course, allow the visitors in any of the four reactor chambers, though he permitted a quick look, again through the heavy glass port, at No. 1, oldest of Chernobyl's reactors and still pouring out energy—with, he called over the noise of steam and turbines, the best safety and performance record in the USSR! He even let them look at the huge pipes of the water system, because they were in their line of travel anyway; and then they turned away and the leading Yemeni jumped back as he saw the hissing, spitting, eye-paining flames of the hydrogen burner.

"What is that thing? I thought atomic power meant you did not have to burn oil!"

"Oh, but it isn't oil," Smin explained reassuringly. "It has nothing to do with the steam, simply a way of getting rid of gases that might otherwise be dangerous. As water goes through the reactor, you see, a little bit each time is broken down into the gases hydrogen and oxygen through radiolysis. We cannot have this in the system, you know, it would be dangerous! So we flare it off here and burn it." Then he let them walk through the turbine room itself, with plugs in their ears and hard hats on their heads, because he knew they would not linger in that painfully noisy place, to get to the control room for Reactors 1 and 2.

While the interpreter was dealing with their questions for the chief shift engineer, Smin picked up a phone and checked again. Yes, the comrade guests were already gathering to observe the experiment, which was still on schedule. So, he found, checking his watch, was his tour. He had ten minutes yet to get rid of the Yemenis before going to the main control room, and so he approached them, smiling.

The shift engineer was not smiling. He turned away and muttered to Smin, "They are asking me about Luba Kovalevska."

Smin sighed and turned to the Yemenis. "Have you some questions for me, then?" he asked politely.

The older Yemeni gazed at him. It was difficult to read the man's expression, but he said only, "One has heard stories."

Smin kept his smile. "What stories are those?" he asked, though he knew the answer.

"There have been reports in your own press," the man said apologetically. He put on spectacles and took a paper out of his pocket. "From your magazine *Literaturna Ukraina,* is that how you say it? An article which speaks of poor design, of unsafe materials, of bad discipline among the workers—of course," he added, folding the paper, "if one had read such things in the Western press, one would understand they are not to be taken seriously. But in your own journals?"

"Ah," said Smin, nodding, "it is what we call *glasnost.*" He used the Russian word and translated quickly. "That is to say, candor. Frankness. Openness." He smiled in a friendly manner. "I suppose you are surprised to see such harsh criticism in a Soviet magazine, but, you see, there is a new time now. Our general secretary, Mikhail Gorbachev, has properly said that we need *glasnost.* We need to speak openly and honestly and in public about shortcomings and errors of all kinds. Mrs. Kovalevska's article is an example of this." He shrugged in humorous deprecation. "It is very useful to us to be called to account in public for any faults. I will not say it isn't painful, but that is how faults can be found in time to correct them. Sometimes it goes too far, perhaps. A writer like Mrs. Kovalevska hears rumors and she puts them in a newspaper—well, it is good that rumors should be aired, so that they can be investigated. But one shouldn't imagine that every word is true."

"Then this report in *Literaturna Ukraina* is untrue?"

"Not entirely untrue," Smin conceded, the shift engineer scowling as he hung on every word, trying to follow the French. "Certainly some mistakes have been made. But they are being corrected. And furthermore, please note, my dear friends, that these things Mrs. Kovalevska lists in so much detail refer principally to matters of faulty construction and operation. They do not suggest for one moment that there is anything wrong with the RBMK-1000 reactor itself! Our reactors are totally safe. Anyone can understand that this is true from the fact that never, in the history of atomic power, has the Soviet Union had a nuclear accident of any kind."

"Ah?" said the Yemeni shrewdly. "Is that correct? Then what about the accident in Kyshtym in 1958?"

"There was no accident in Kyshtym in 1958," said Smin positively, and wondered if he were speaking the truth.

By the time Smin had his guests out of doors it was already two-twenty. He had managed to find out from the control-room operators that Reactor No. 4 was still at full power, so the experiment was not yet ready to begin. That meant he had a little more time. He used it to be a gracious host. "See this lake?" he said, indicating the lake along whose borders they were walking. "It is our cooling pond. Six kilometers long, and, as you see, a beautiful thing in itself. And it is stocked with fish; our local sportsmen say the fishing is even better here than in the Pripyat River."

"Why is that?" the younger Yemeni asked politely.

"Because the water is warmed all through the year."

"But I see ice in it," the older one said dryly.

"But this is the Ukraine!" Smin said, smiling. "Of course our winters are terribly cold. But even in the worst of the winter the pond does not freeze over entirely here, and the fish love it. And now—see the trees, the flowers; it is spring." He stopped and gazed up at the towering buildings that housed Reactors 3 and 4.

"From here," he said, "you can see how large the Chernobyl Power Station is. Four operating reactors, each one producing one thousand megawatts of electrical energy, enough to light an entire city of one million people. And we have already begun construction of two new ones, even larger. When they are finished we will be able to supply a city of seven million."

"We don't have any cities of seven million," said the older Yemeni. "Also, we don't have any lakes."

"With such power you can create all the lakes you wish," Smin said grandly. "Come, I will show you where the new reactors are already being begun."

And when they were on the lip of the giant excavation where the core of Reactor No. 5 would soon go, busy with excavation equipment and dump trucks carting the soil away, the Yemenis seemed still unsatisfied. "These also will be RBMK-1000s?" the older one asked.

"No, no. Each will be even larger, fifteen hundred mega-watts electric rated output!"

"But still graphite reactors," mused the Yemeni. "Although some people say that this design is not as good as the pressurized water reactor, like those in the West."

"Ah, the West," said Smin good-naturedly, his mood improved since he had seen the dark-blue Volga car that would take the Yemenis away creeping cautiously toward them, among the rumbling trucks and bulldozers. "You see, in the first place, the Soviet Union also has pressurized-water reactors; we have both kinds in service. Each has its own special advantages. The Americans do not have this variety of choice. All of their nuclear energy comes from the submarine power plants."

The Yemeni looked puzzled. "What do submarines have to do with it?"

Smin smiled. "Do you know why the Americans stay with the pressurized-water reactors? It is because they are trapped in their own historical accidents. They are in a rut. The first power reactors ever built in America were designed for their nuclear submarines. Those had to be of the pressurized-water type, since nothing else would work inside the confined space of a submarine. Advanced models like our RBMKs simply cannot be used for submarine engines. So when at last the Americans decided to try to generate utility power with atomic energy, they simply built new and larger submarine engines. The RBMK is quite different, and by 'different' I mean 'better.' For one thing, it is extremely responsive. The American generators, like all pressurized-water generators, are only good for baseline power—they are very slow to start and very slow to stop. The RBMK is quick to respond. If there is a sudden need for power, an RBMK can be brought on line in less than one hour. And—well, I remind you of safety. Three Mile Island was a pressurized-water reactor, you know."

"If all that is so," said the older Yemeni suddenly, "then why have you not shown us Reactor Number Four?"

Smin shook his head compassionately. "Unfortunately, Reactor Number Four is about to be taken out of service for maintenance. So no one is permitted in the area because of some slight risk of radiation exposure, you see. It is a precaution very strictly enforced—you see, in spite of *glasnost* articles in the newspapers, we really are very cautious. What a pity! But perhaps you could come back tomorrow, when things will be tranquil again?"

"Unfortunately," said the Yemeni glumly, "tonight we

stay in the Dniepro Hotel in Kiev, and fly to Moscow in the morning."

"What a pity," repeated Smin, who had known that all along. "And now your car is here! I hope you have had an interesting visit with us, here at the Chernobyl Nuclear Power Station, and I look forward to our meeting again!"

Smin was still thinking of the Yemenis when he stopped, simply as a precaution, to make sure the experiment was still ready to go before going up to the main control room. But when he heard what the shift operator had to say he forgot the Yemenis. "Canceled? Why is it canceled? What are we going to do with all those people?"

The shift operator sighed. "If you figure that out, please tell me; they are still here. All I know is that the power dispatchers in Kiev say we can't go off line now. I didn't speak to them; you'll have to ask the Director. What? No, he isn't here; I think he's in the turbine room below."

Smin put the phone down, frowning. Now, that was a nuisance. There were almost a dozen observers on hand. They had gathered at Chernobyl from as far away as Leningrad, power-plant managers and representatives of turbine builders and electrical engineers, for the single purpose of seeing how the experiment in generating extra power from residual heat and momentum after a reactor was shut down would work. The experiment should be beginning right now, which would mean they would all be getting into their cars and bothering somebody else before dark.

But now what?

The only person who could answer that was the Director, so Smin went looking for him. Smin was meticulous about making sure his workers dressed for their work, and set them a good example by putting on the dosimeter badge and the white cap and coveralls and cloth slippers before he walked into the turbine hall.

He also fitted the plugs in his ears. The turbine rooms, particularly the big one that combined the output of Reactors 3 and 4, were the noisiest places in the Chernobyl Power Station. Perhaps they were the noisiest places in the world, Smin thought, but he welcomed the noise. The scream of the steam in the turbines was good news. It meant that the heat of the dying atoms was spinning the great wheels and magically turning steam into electricity to feed the lights and radios and television sets and elevator motors of a quarter of the Ukrainian Soviet Federated Socialist Republic—with enough left over to export electricity to their Socialist neighbors in Poland and even Bulgaria and Romania.

What was less pleasing, he thought, remembering, was that the Yemenis had asked unpleasant questions. The worst was the one about Kyshtym.

Was there any truth to the story about Kyshtym?

People had asked him the same question at the IAEA in Vienna. They hadn't been put off as easily as the Yemenis, either. They had even handed him a copy of a book by the renegade, Zhores Medvedev, with a worrying story. It said that in 1958 some nuclear enterprise had gone terribly wrong in Soviet Siberia. Nuclear wastes—or something!—had somehow, unbelievably attained critical mass. They had exploded. Lakes were destroyed. Streams were poisoned. Villages were made uninhabitable, and a whole countryside had become a radioactive waste.

Could such a thing be true?

Smin confessed to himself that he did not know. Yet even if that story were true, Smin thought rebelliously, what he had said—*most* of what he had said to the Yemeni about such questions—was demonstrably quite true. Soviet nuclear power had never had an accident. At least not one that was related to the nuclear reactors, and certainly not at Chernobyl!

Even with the plugs in his ears, the vast roar of the turbines made his head ache. He was glad to see the Director, Zaglodin, at the far end of the room. With him were the Chief of the Personnel Section, Khrenov, and the Chief Engineer, Varazin, talking with a fourth man. *Talking* was not the right word. The four men seemed to be having a sort of perverted flirtation, there under the towering half-cylinders of the turbine housings. The three high officials had their heads close together, and the fourth man was thrusting his own face in among them, shouting to be heard over the turbine scream.

As Smin approached, the fourth man broke away and, scowling, walked past Smin to the door. It was Sheranchuk, the power station's hydrologist-engineer, usually a friendly man, but he gave Smin only a short nod as he stalked angrily past.

An engineering work team, taking readings on Turbine No. 6 with checklists in hand, was more agreeable. They all gave Smin a hand wave of respectful comradeship as he passed, and he returned it, smiling.

Khrenov noticed the exchange. Smin was not surprised. As Director of the plant's First Section, Personnel and Security—which was to say, the section that reported to the KGB—it was Khrenov's job to notice everything. The Director, on the other hand, was scowling. He gestured Smin to go back, and all four of the senior officers exited to the comparative quiet of the hallway outside.

As soon as their earplugs were out, Khrenov observed, "You are very popular with the workers, Smin."

"Popularity is not what matters," the Director said testily. "Have you heard, Smin? What do you think the dispatchers in Kiev are telling us now? The grid needs our power; we can't go off line today."

"I see," said Smin, understanding. The experiment could be performed only when one of the reactors was being shut down. "And the observers?"

"The observers," the Director said with a glance at the Chief Engineer, "are now Comrade Varazin's pleasure to look after. He has just volunteered to take care of them."

"God knows how," the Chief Engineer said gloomily. "Perhaps tomorrow I can give them a little tour of the reactor chambers. None of them are nuclear; this is all interesting to them."

"I'm sure they'll enjoy it," said Smin, pleased to learn that he, at least, was not expected to give up his weekend. He added with a smile, "At least we will now be able to overfulfill our plan for the month of April."

Director Zaglodin looked at him speculatively, then allowed himself to return the smile. "At least," he corrected, "I can now leave to catch my plane. Is there anything you would like me to bring back for you from Moscow?—not that I will have time, really, for shopping," he added quickly, in case Smin intended to surprise him and actually ask for something.

"My wife would no doubt have a list, Comrade Director," Smin said good-humoredly, "but she isn't here. Have you orders for me for your absence?"

Of course Zaglodin had orders. He ticked them off on his

fingers, one by one. "The cement plant has already delivered five hundred tons for the base for Reactor Number Five. Well, naturally, we are not ready; and also I think the cement is not up to quality. See to it, Smin."

"Of course, Comrade Director." Smin caught the understanding look from Khrenov. He did not bother to comment. All of them knew that that meant that Smin now had the responsibility of either accepting substandard concrete or perhaps delaying pouring the foundation for the new reactor, which added up to a classical case of a no-win situation. How fortunate for Director Zaglodin that this weekend he was going hunting outside Moscow, with persons very high in authority!

"And then there is your man, Sheranchuk," the Director grumbled.

"I saw that he was talking to you," Smin said cautiously. "What did he want?"

"What does he always want? He is not satisfied with our power station, Smin. He wants to rebore all the valves again."

Smin nodded. It was understood between them that Sheranchuk, the hydrologist-engineer, was Smin's personal protégé, which meant that the Director had, and exercised, the right to blame Smin every time the hydrologist annoyed him. "If he thinks they need it, he is probably right. Why not let him?"

"Why not let him tear the whole plant down and build a new one?" the Director fumed. Then he calmed somewhat. "You will be in charge while I'm in Moscow," he said. "Do what you like."

"Of course," said Smin, not pointing out that in matters of running the station he always did. The Director was, really, only nominally Smin's superior. That was another thing of Gorbachev's, to put the man who really did the work in the second position, so that he could get on with it, while the putative chief of the project was free to entertain visiting dignitaries, represent the organization in formal meetings, go to receptions—in short, to be a figurehead. Only in this Director's case he seemed to want Smin even to conduct parties of Yemenis around the plant!

"There is also a soccer game tomorrow," said Khrenov, watching Smin.

The Director lifted his head loftily. He was a little,

sparrowlike man. All he needed was the little pointed beard to look exactly like the statue of V. I. Lenin that stood in the plant's courtyard. It seemed that he knew it, for Zaglodin even stood there exactly the way Lenin stood in all his statues and portraits—eager, chin thrust forward, hands half-reaching for—for whatever it was that Lenin was always trying to grasp. Perhaps the world. Perhaps, Smin thought, that was what the Director really wanted, too, in which case it was not likely that he would ever attain it from his present position as mere head of one single power station, and one that was not even located in the RSFSR at that.

"So," smiled Zaglodin, "you want your best forward excused from shift duty tonight so he can be fresh for the game? Why not, Khrenov? Still, you'll have to ask Smin here, since I'll be away." And then at last the Director remembered the afternoon's visitors. "How did it go with the Yemenis?" he asked.

Smin shrugged. "They asked about Luba Kovalevska's story. They also asked about Kyshtym."

"Nothing happened at Kyshtym!" the Director said severely. "As to Kovalevska and her disloyal stories, that's why I have to go to Moscow, to reassure our superiors that we are not, after all, totally incompetent here." He gazed at Smin. "I hope that is true," he said.

Before they parted, the Personnel man invited Smin to take a little steam in the plant's baths with him, but Smin declined. "I'd better get back to my office," he said. "Who knows what's gone wrong while I've been escorting Arabs around?"

As it turned out, nothing much had. Still, there was at least another centimeter of papers added to the stack on his desk that Paraska had brought in while he was lollygagging around with the Yemenis. There seemed to be nothing more urgent in the new batch than any of the other, older urgencies waiting for his attention, but the papers would not sign themselves. "Paraska!" he called. "A cup of tea, if you will!" And began to lower the stack, bit by bit. Acknowledgments of orders for structural steel, replacement bearings, fireproof cables, bricks, tiles, generator parts, window glass, double-thick reinforced glass, flooring, piping, roofing compound. Letters from suppliers regretting that, extraordinarily, the orders just placed could not be filled on the dates specified, but every effort would be made to ship a month, or three months, later. Party directives thick with reminders of the decisions of the 27th Party Congress to increase production, and production figures from the suppliers to show how woefully that was needed. Absentee and lateness reports from Khrenov's First Department—not too bad, those, Smin reflected with some complacency; the Chernobyl Nuclear Power Station was one of the best in the Soviet Union in those respects. As in most others. He found the little chit that excused Vladimir Ponomorenko from his duties on the four o'clock shift of the construction brigade at Reactor No. 5, and signed it with a little grin; the Ponomorenkos would all be busy practicing for the next day's football game and, after all, it did no harm to do Khrenov's First Department a small favor now and then.

The tea was cold before he tasted it, but he had gotten through almost a tenth of the papers on his desk. He sifted through the remainder. There was still nothing in them that seemed more urgent than any of the other urgencies. He sat back, thinking about the weekend. With any luck at all, he and his wife could get away to spend a little time on the plot of land twenty-five kilometers north, where their dacha had been growing toward reality for nearly a year. How fine that would be when it was finished! It was April now, almost the beginning of May; by July at the latest all the doors and windows would be in, and in August they could almost certainly occupy at least one of the rooms. By fall certainly they would be spending weekends there, and the ducks of the Pripyat marshes would learn that Simyon Smin knew how to use a shotgun.

He lit one of the Marlboro cigarettes thoughtfully, gazing at the old cartoon he had tacked over his desk; it was from an ancient issue of the humor magazine, *Krokodil;* it showed a bolt the size of a railroad car and a nut as huge as an apartment building coming out of a plant labeled RED STAR NUT AND BOLT WORKS NO. 1, and the caption read, "And so in one step we fulfill our plan!" It was not, Smin appreciated, an unfair jibe at Soviet manufacturing customs.

His workday was nearly over, and he even thought he might get home on time. He picked up the phone and called his wife to tell her so, but Selena Smin had news for her husband.

"We won't be going to the dacha. Your mother telephoned," she said. "She wants us all to come for dinner tonight. She says you didn't come last night, so at least you can come tonight. Do you know what she meant by that?"

Smin groaned. He did know, but did not particularly want to say so on the telephone. "But that means driving into Kiev and back!" he said, thinking of the hundred and thirty kilometers each way.

"No, we can stay over in our room in her flat, and then I can do some shopping in Kiev tomorrow morning," she said. "Perhaps we can visit the dacha on Sunday. Oh, also she says she has a surprise for you."

"What surprise?"

"She said you'd say that. She said to tell you that if she told you what the surprise was, it wouldn't be a surprise, but it's a *big* surprise."

Smin surrendered. When he had hung up he buzzed for his secretary. "I'll want my car tonight," he said, "but I'll drive myself. Have Chernavze bring it around and see that the tank is full, then he can go home."

There was one more thing for Smin to do before he left the plant. In a way, it, too, was setting an example. It was a visit to the plant's baths. He undressed in the locker room and, taking a sheet and a towel from the attendant, headed for the showers.

There had always been showers in Chernobyl because men who worked with radioactive substances needed them. But these baths were not only new, they were Smin's own. The slate slabs for each man to lie on, the shower heads above, the soap dispensers—those were Smin's. He stretched out, turned the water on to a trickle, and soaped himself. He lay back, bare, the glassy scar exposed for anyone to see if anyone had been there, but he was alone in the shower room. He closed his eyes, listening to the squeals and cries from the women's bath on the other side of the wall—some of the female workers were playing tag and ducking each other in their pool. He wondered absently if they appreciated the luxurious facilities he had provided for them. But, after all, whether they did or not, what was the difference? The extra care showed up in the plant's attendance, and the important thing was the plant.

When he had rinsed himself off, he wrapped the sheet

around his broad shoulders and headed for the sauna. It was almost time for changing shifts. There were eight or nine men in the steamy sauna. Four husky young men were tossing a knotted towel back and forth; one dropped it and kicked it to another, who rescued it and nodded apologetically to Smin.

"Don't mind me," Smin said, recognizing them. "Just do the job in the game tomorrow."

"You can count on it, Comrade Deputy Director," said the big forward, Vladimir Ponomorenko, the "Autumn" of the four related players they called the Four Seasons. They were two sets of brothers, and their fathers had been brothers as well; they all had the same surname of Ponomorenko. Arkady was "Spring," a slim, shy diffident man of twenty-three, just out of his Army service, who worked as a pipefitter in Sheranchuk's department, but on the football field he was like flame. Vassili, "Summer," was a fireman; Vyacheslav, "Winter," a machinist. All of them were on the midnight shift of the plant except for "Autumn"—Vladimir—the forward.

"So you are getting ready to practice for tomorrow's game?" Smin asked as he peered through the steam for a vacant place. He was never entirely sure which of the Four Seasons he was talking to. They were all strong-featured dark men of medium height, none of them yet thirty. Spring was the quick one, Autumn the one armored in muscle, Smin reminded himself; but the other two?

One of them said, "That's right, Comrade Deputy Director. Will you be there?"

"Of course," Smin said, surprising himself as he realized that, after all, he might as well; they would not stay in Kiev all day, he hoped, and the game was in the late afternoon so that the players on the midnight shift could get some sleep.

A man on the bench before him threw back the towel over his face and revealed himself as Khrenov, the First Department man. "Enough steam, Comrade Footballers," he said genially. "Now cold showers, and then practice!" And to Smin, "Thank you for excusing Autumn from the shift."

"Why not?" said Smin, shrugging. Absences for footballers to practice were always approved, for encouragement of sport was a directive from Moscow. The Chernobyl plant was not unusual in that respect. In some places, in fact, it was standard practice to give star athletes good jobs they did not necessarily ever work at at all.

It wasn't Smin's own way, of course, but in this he was willing to make concessions, since there were so many others he refused to make. He moved slightly to get past Khrenov, and the towel slipped off his shoulder.

Khrenov didn't get out of his way. He did, Smin thought, a very Khrenov-like thing. When Smin's towel failed to cover him in the baths, most men almost invariably averted their eyes. Not Khrenov. The First Department man reached out and thoughtfully touched the line of scar tissue at the back of Smin's neck, like an art collector appraising the patina on an old bronze. He didn't say anything about it, but then that was also Khrenov's way. He just studied the scar carefully every time he saw it, although Smin was quite certain that the Personnel and Security man not only knew its exact dimensions but very likely also knew the serial number of the blazing T-34 Army tank in which it had been acquired.

Smin shrugged away from Khrenov's touch. "So," he said, to change the subject, "will we win tomorrow, do you think?"

"Of course we will win," Khrenov said with pleasure, and began to explain the ways in which the Four Seasons would triumph on the football field. Smin heard him out patiently. It was a matter of policy with him to be as cordial as possible with the Security man, so that the times when confrontations were necessary would be eased. As GehBehs went, Gorodot Khrenov wasn't so bad. The men who were the organs of state security came in two main varieties—the ones who wanted you to know who they were, like Khrenov, and the ones who did not. The undercover ones were a nuisance sometimes, but as you could never be entirely sure who they were or what they were looking for, the way to deal with them was simply to guard your tongue and watch your actions all the time. The Khrenov variety was something else. They made themselves conspicuous. They were like the militiaman on the corner, whose principal job was not so much to catch violators of the law but, simply by his presence, to remind everyone that the Law was watching. It amused Smin to wonder, sometimes, if KGB training included, for people like Khrenov, lessons in how to look all-wise and sinister.

Yet Khrenov interfered less than other organs did in other

plants, and his interest in sports, if officially directed, seemed also sincere. The Personnel man looked as though he, too, could have been a wrestler at some time. He was shorter even than Smin, and not nearly as solidly built, but he had a driving energy that would have been troublesome in the ring.

"So," Smin said, to cut off the lecture on football strategy, "it should be a good game if the Four Seasons are in form. Why not let the ones on the midnight shift off an hour or two early, so they can get a little more sleep before the game?"

Khrenov smiled with pleasure. He said, "Thank you. I'll tell them," and left to find them at their practice.

Smin sat down and closed his eyes, inhaling the steam cautiously through his open mouth. He sat with his mind peacefully empty until he heard someone speak his name. When he opened his eyes he saw that it was his hydrologist-engineer.

"Good evening, Comrade Plumber Sheranchuk," said Smin. "And how are your sticky pump valves? Is it true that you intend to rebore every fitting in the plant?"

"Only a few at present, Comrade Deputy Director Smin," Sheranchuk said gravely.

"Yes, of course. You've done all the others already," Smin chaffed him. Sheranchuk was the newest addition among Chernobyl's senior employees, a stubby, red-headed Ukrainian, rescued from an old peat-fueled steam plant that was about to be decommissioned, and now gratefully lumbered with all of Chernobyl's water circulation problems. There had been plenty; every valve had come from the factory with only a rough approximation of the right dimensions, and Sheranchuk had been busy regrinding them.

Sheranchuk hesitated, then glanced toward the door through which Khrenov had just left. "I suppose," he said, "you are aware that Director Zaglodin ordered the automatic pump system turned off this afternoon?"

Smin frowned. He had not known. But he said, "Yes, of course, to prepare for our free-wheeling experiment. Since that was postponed, the shift chief will certainly turn them back on."

"I suppose so." Then, "I am sorry about this afternoon, Smin."

"Why? Our Director sometimes makes me sulky, too. The important thing is that you get your job done."

"I will come in tomorrow and check them once again," Sheranchuk promised.

Smin nodded. "So we will be in good shape for May Day," he said, and added judgmatically, "I would say that, in general, you have done well." He felt the hot air almost searing his lips as he spoke. One of the men had been pouring water on the hot ceramics again, and the steam had made the sauna oppressive.

Smin settled the thick, rough sheet around his shoulders and looked for a cheerful word to sweeten his engineer's mood. A joke? Yes, of course. The one he had heard that morning from one of the turbine men. He said, "Tell me, Sheranchuk, do you like Radio Armenia jokes? Here's one. Someone calls in to Radio Armenia and asks, 'What was the first People's Democracy?' "

"And what was the answer?" asked Sheranchuk, already smiling.

"It was when God created Adam and Eve, and then said to Adam, 'Now, select a wife for yourself.' "

CHAPTER 2

Leonid Sheranchuk is forty-two years old and looks like an ice hockey player, which he was for a time twenty years ago. He has two steel teeth in front as a result. Still, he is a handsome red-haired man. Women are attracted to him. As far as his wife, Tamara, knows, he does not respond even when their interest is made apparent, but all the same she wishes they could take their vacations together. She is a doctor on the staff of the hospital in the town of Pripyat itself. The town almost touches the grounds of the power plant, but its facilities are separate. This means that her vacations are at the summer resort of the hospital, four hundred kilometers south on a pleasant lake; his are taken at the resort of the power plant, on the Black Sea. She would like to be transferred to the medical staff of the power station, so they could be together, but the pay is better there, too, and the summer accommodations much nicer, and the competition for such posts is acute. Still, she knows that they are lucky. They have been in Pripyat for only a few months, since Smin recruited her husband into this much better post. She is aware that they have a good life. With Sheranchuk's three hundred rubles a month and her one eighty they are well-to-do. Their sixteen-year-old son is a dancer, an honor student and a Komsomol. Sheranchuk himself has a shelf of medals from his ice hockey days as well as all the diplomas and certificates of merit that made him qualified as a hydrologist-engineer in the Chernobyl Power Station. For he is, after all, not a "plumber." Nor would he smile at anyone who called him that, or at least not at anyone but Deputy Director Smin.

Sheranchuk left Smin in the baths. Feeling thoroughly refreshed the hydrologist-engineer decided there was no need to wait until morning to get at some of his paperwork; the evening was young and his wife would not mind that he was working overtime.

No one forced Sheranchuk to do that, least of all Deputy Director Smin. Sheranchuk imposed it on himself. As a senior engineer, he was scheduled to work management hours—nine to five-thirty on five days of the week. But he knew he had Smin's trust. He wanted to keep it, and spending an evening at home was less important than making certain that the trust was deserved.

So, long after five-thirty, Sheranchuk was back at his desk, in the office he shared with two assistants and the plant's sports director, writing notes to himself about what he wanted to do when Reactor No. 4 was at last down for maintenance. The experiment in getting extra power from the turbines then did not affect him. What he particularly wanted was to get a look at the inside of the great pump that forced the condensed water back out of the heat exchanger and into the plenum under the core of the reactor. According to the records he had inherited, that pump had been long since dismantled and checked by his predecessor, but Sheranchuk wanted to see for himself.

Going over the files on each component, Sheranchuk paid particular attention to the delivery dates of the parts. A valve fitting that had arrived at Chernobyl in the first week of any month, for example, had probably been turned out by its factory in the last week of the month previous. That was a warning signal. The last few days of any month were the frenzied, corner-cutting days of "storming the plan," the days when all shifts went on overtime in a last-ditch effort to meet the month's production goals that determined whether or not the workers would get a monthly bonus. Half of any month's production in a factory might easily come in the last few days of the month. Those were the days when machinists rushed their work and inspectors looked the other way, and the brand-new parts that arrived at their destinations might have to go right into the scrap pile because they could not be made to fit. Worse, they might be installed anyway.

Of course, the previous head hydrologist-engineer at Chernobyl had known that as well as Sheranchuk. Every part had been calipered for tolerances before it was fitted into place; all the equipment had been taken apart and, when necessary, reground or rebored or simply replaced with new parts. Sheranchuk knew this. All the same, he wanted to see for himself.

With a list of fittings to be checked in his hand he went to see if Deputy Director Smin had perhaps returned to his office. He was not there. The office was dark, as were most of the other offices he passed—though not that of the First Department. That didn't surprise Sheranchuk; Khrenov's Personnel and Security people were always somewhere about. He thought about going home, where his wife might, by now, be wondering what had happened to him, but went up to the main control room for Reactors 3 and 4 instead.

Smin wasn't there either, but Khrenov was, smoking a cigarette and chatting with the shift chief about how the football practice had gone. Behind them was the long, arced wall of instruments that displayed the condition of every part of the power station's systems. Most of the display, flashing lights and oscilloscope traces, had to do with things that did not much interest Sheranchuk, but automatically he checked the readings on the water and steam-pressure systems. The steam system was normal, the recirculation pumps were operating at normal pressure—all satisfactory enough, except that the pumps were under direct operators' control. The automatic systems were still switched off.

Sheranchuk scowled and looked around. Standing by the door, looking dissatisfied, was an operator Sheranchuk recognized, the half-Lithuanian one named Kalychenko. When Sheranchuk asked Kalychenko civilly enough if the automatic systems should not be switched back on, the operator said crossly, "How should I know? I'm not on this shift. I'm simply wasting my time standing here."

Khrenov looked up sharply, then came to join them. "Ah,

Kalychenko," he said, ignoring the hydrologist. "Are you still here?"

"Where else would I be? This is really too bad! I'm on the midnight shift, and here I've been ordered in early for this experiment that isn't going to take place. When am I supposed to sleep?"

"You could sleep," said Khrenov silkily, humorously, "in your own bed for a change, instead of spending half the night in some other bed."

Sheranchuk saw that the tall, pale man flushed, as though Khrenov had touched a sensitive point, but it was none of his business. "Excuse me," Sheranchuk said, "I was pointing out that the automatic pumping system is still switched off."

"Yes, yes," said Khrenov. "I'm sure the Chief Engineer is well aware of that."

"The directives say it should be left on at all times, except for special circumstances."

"You are very diligent in your work," Khrenov said, his tone admiring. "But these *are* special circumstances, you see. Chief Engineer Varazin is in charge. He has decided that at least that part of the experiment which is to observe how the pumps can be kept in order manually can be proceeded with, at least. Do you understand that? If you have criticisms to make of his procedures, I suggest you make them to him."

Sheranchuk gritted his steel teeth. It was not Khrenov's business to lecture the hydrologist-engineer on technical matters. It was only a way of reminding Sheranchuk, as well as anyone else around, that the Personnel man was well informed on every aspect of the work of the power plant even if he had nothing to do with running it. Sheranchuk shrugged, and kept silent.

Khrenov gazed at him affably for a moment, then turned to the shift operator. "Now, Kalychenko," he said, "since you're not on duty here at the moment, I suggest you get some rest. Alone, for a change, if you don't mind. So that you will be ready for your regular shift."

Sheranchuk did not linger to see how Kalychenko would reply. He turned and left the room.

He thought that probably Kalychenko wouldn't respond at all, in spite of the fact that his pale face was turning crimson and his scowl was ferocious. Sheranchuk sympathized with the operator. It was, after all, no business of the Personnel man's if Kalychenko was anticipating the privileges of marriage before the actual ceremony with one of the town girls.

The question was not so much where Kalychenko slept as whether Khrenov slept at all. Sheranchuk knew the man had been there at six that morning. He seemed always to be in the plant somewhere. Did he have a home? Did he sleep there? Did he, perhaps, have a cot in his office, and take short naps there from time to time, emerging to patrol the plant with those eyes that missed nothing?

That was a possibility, but no one outside the First Department was likely to know it. With any other boss, there would be a secretary or a file clerk to whisper the boss's secrets to some other secretary, and thus it would become common gossip in the plant.

Not with Khrenov.

Khrenov was First Department. It was called "Personnel and Security," but what it was, of course, was the organs of the state. The secretary to Gorodot Khrenov would not whisper to anybody, but if a whisper of any kind came to her ear, Khrenov would certainly hear it within the hour, and by the next morning it would be on a piece of paper in a dossier in a file in Dzerzhinskaya Square, Moscow.

As Sheranchuk left the reactor building, jamming into his pocket the list of parts to be checked, he was surprised to see lights on the top floor of the office block. That was where the special reception rooms for important functions were located— most of all the dining room for ceremonial occasions. It could mean only one thing, Sheranchuk thought as he showed his pass to the guard at the plant gate. The observers for the experiment had not gone away after all. The Chief Engineer was stuck with the job of feeding them dinner, and keeping them somehow entertained until, presumably, the weekend was over and Reactor No. 4 could at last be shut down for the experiment they had come to watch.

He put the visitors out of his mind. Entertaining visiting dignitaries was not among his concerns. Sheranchuk's concerns were pipes, pumps and valves that circulated water in the Chernobyl Power Station.

There was that much truth to the friendly nickname Smin

had given him. Sheranchuk's principal responsibility was plumbing. That is to say, almost everywhere that water flowed in the plant, Sheranchuk was in charge. He did not trouble himself with whatever water flowed in the baths and the toilets and the kitchens; he had assistants to deal with such minor things, and already he had made them understand that they would regret any complaints he received on any such score. Sheranchuk's direct concern was the waters that circulated in and around the generators and the cores. There were two main systems, kept quite separate.

One was the flow of water into the plant from the cooling pond at its border: that water was pumped in to condense the steam once it had left the turbines and was pumped out again, now a little warmer, back into the outside pond; there were not many problems with that. The other circuit was more complex and more critical. Its water came out of the condensing tank and was forced by mighty pumps into the plenum under the reactor core and thence up via hundreds of narrow pipes through the graphite and uranium of the core itself. There the heat of the nuclear reaction flashed it into steam. As steam the pipes converged into drying tanks, where the droplets of water were purged out of the steam, and thence used to turn the huge turbines themselves.

Thereafter the spent and cooler (but still very hot) steam entered the condensation tanks, where the looped pipes from the cooling pond turned it back into liquid water. Not one molecule of that water ever reached the outside world. That system was completely closed—and a good thing for everyone nearby, since in their passage through the core those molecules of water dissolved out particles of metals from the pipes, and many of those particles were radioactive. Only the radioactively clean waters from the sealed cooling circuit went back into the pond—and sometimes, when it overflowed in spring thaws and autumn rains, into the Pripyat River and the drinking-water supplies for millions of Ukrainians as far south as the city of Kiev.

Sheranchuk's responsibilities ended with the circulating water systems. His concerns, however, did not. He took Deputy Director Simyon Smin as his model, and what Sheranchuk did was what he thought Smin would have done in the same circumstances.

For Sheranchuk admired the Deputy Director more than any other man alive. It was not only that he owed Smin gratitude for rescuing him from a dead-end job on a peat-burning power plant almost at the end of its life. Watching Smin, he had seen how a skillful and determined man could overcome all obstacles and find a way around all problems to make this complicated network of systems called the "Chernobyl Nuclear Power Station" fulfill its obligations. He had learned a lot from Smin, and not the least thing he had learned was that the whole plant was the concern of everyone who worked in it.

It was a fact of life with the RBMK-1000 reactor that it was given to fluctuations in its power output. When they happened, they needed to be controlled. There were three basic ways of doing that. One was to thrust into the mass of uranium and graphite that was the core of the reactor rods of a metal that would soak up neutrons and slow down the reaction. That was the classic, time-honored way. More than forty years before, Enrico Fermi had controlled his first ever nuclear pile in Chicago in just that manner. Another was simply to flood the reactor with additional water to slow it down, or cut down the flow to speed it up; water, too, soaked up neutrons, and the more of it that was present, the fewer atoms would be fractured to release the heat that made the steam.

The third method was more subtle. Inside the thick containment shell of the RBMK, the graphite bricks, fuel rods, and water pipes that comprised the reactor itself were surrounded by an artificial atmosphere composed of two gases, helium and nitrogen. This was done for two reasons. One was that the helium-nitrogen mixture kept out the oxygen of the air, and therefore the hot graphite bricks could not catch fire. The other reason was part of the control system. The gases did not conduct heat in the same degree, so that by adding one or the other, the heat transfer capacity of that atmosphere could be changed, up or down as desired; the reactor would obediently run a little hotter or a little colder, and so the small glitches in performance could be smoothed out.

Usually.

Of course, no human being could watch the instrument readings carefully enough and calculate the necessary measures fast enough to take the right action every time.

It is the same with modern, high-performance aircraft. If

the pilot takes his hands off the controls of a conventional light plane, the thing will continue to fly itself reasonably well, for a while at least. If he takes his hands off the controls of a modern fighter, it will crash. Even if he stays on the controls, he can't fly the plane by himself. That is simply not possible. Too many things must be done too rapidly, and the human brain doesn't work fast enough to do the job. A computer flies the plane, the pilot only tells the computer what he wants it to do.

It was the same with the RBMK. The human operators only told the cybernetic system what they wanted. The built-in computers dealt with the moment-by-moment fluctuations. The operators could read the instruments, and they were wonderfully sensitive devices, most of them imported at vast expense from Western suppliers, but in any emergency the instant responses would have to come from the computers—which meant, really, that they were the ones upon whom the performance of the entire immense complex depended. Many others could help to make it succeed. But it was only they, and the handful of operators in the control room itself, who could, at any moment, make it catastrophically fail.

CHAPTER 3

Smin's mother, who has been a widow almost as long as Smin has been alive, lives in a four-room flat in an apartment building on the outskirts of Kiev. This causes a lot of talk among her neighbors. The official allowance for housing in the Soviet Union is nine square meters per person, and here this old woman, who does not even have a job, occupies nearly forty. It is true that old Aftasia Smin is a Party member from the earliest days, but it is also true that she has taken no active part for many years. So the talk of the neighbors is not about Aftasia's status as a veteran of the Civil War but about the real reason she has such a fine apartment. It is, her neighbors tell each other wisely, only because her son is in a high position; and in this the neighbors are right.

When Smin got to his mother's flat he discovered that the surprise was really a surprise. It was an American—two Americans, in fact, for there was a man and his wife.

Young Vassili Smin, who had been complaining for two hours about the prospect of sleeping another night on Babushka's folding Army cot, stopped complaining when he saw the American and the American's tall, young, blonde wife in the tailored canary-yellow slacks and the American's digital watch that told the time not only in Kiev but in Los Angeles as well. Smin saw that his son had fallen in love. He only hoped that

Vassili would somehow manage to refrain from offering to buy the watch from the American who, it turned out, was Smin's second cousin. "You remember," Smin's mother crowed, "I told you about my cousin Yerim, who went to America in 1923? This is his grandson! And this is his wife! He makes for television films about a black man!"

The second cousin's name was nothing like Yerim Skazchenko. It was Dean Garfield, but he was still family—family enough to have brought gifts for everyone, although he couldn't have been sure when he left Los Angeles that he would find any particular family members to give gifts to. So they were sort of all-purpose gifts. There was a silver tie clip with a Statue of Liberty on it for Smin, a cashmere sweater for his wife (it was too bad that it was so very tight on her, but apparently it had been cut for an American figure), a pocket calculator for Vassili, a box of liqueur chocolates for everybody, even a wonderfully thick, rich silk scarf which went to Aftasia. Best of all, there was a whole box of video tape cassettes for the whole family, and these were not simply American films which others might have. They were copies of the actual network television program Dean Garfield had actually produced—"Number three in the ratings," Garfield modestly announced.

What made conversation hard was that Garfield spoke only English, his wife just English and a little Spanish; neither knew anything of Smin's own Russian, Ukrainian, French, or German. Nor were Vassili's two years of English good enough for more than half of what Dean Garfield and his wife, Candace, said.

Smin's mother had provided for that problem. Aftasia had invited a young Ukrainian couple named Didchuk from the flat just below, both teachers of English in the local schools. Smin could see that they were both a little ill at ease in the presence of a senior Party member who drove a black Chaika with yellow fog lights, not to mention two actual Americans, and he put himself out to be nice to them.

While the young woman was helping Vassili's excited questioning of the glamorous American cousins, Smin chatted easily with the man about the relative merits of the Chaika over the Zhiguli, which he praised, the Moskvich (yes, a fine car, but it needs too much work to keep it running) and the Volga, which he declared in some ways was almost better than his own. The teacher listened intently and humbly asked Smin's opinion of the Zaparozhets, which he and his wife had thought of purchasing in a year or two. The Zaparozhets was the cheapest car made in the USSR, but Smin had praise for it, too. After all, he reminded the man, it was Ukraine-made and a very good value for the money—"Only, be sure you get one that was manufactured early in the month, before they storm," he said. The teacher nodded gratefully for the advice, though he did not need it. After all, what Soviet citizen did not know all about the merits of every Soviet car, even if his best hope of owning one lay somewhere in the twenty-first century?

In any case, Didchuk discovered, he had lost Smin's attention. The older man was gazing at his wife, and there was half a smile on his face.

For when Selena Smin got a good look at this blonde California goddess, she had taken the first opportunity to disappear into the flat's tiny lavatory. When she came out, her eyelashes were darker, her lips were redder, and she had even touched herself with the scent Smin had brought back from his last trip to Vienna; with affection, Smin realized his wife had decided once and for all to show these Americans that Soviet women did not necessarily have steel teeth and hairy armpits. It pleased Smin to observe that although Dean Garfield did not seem to notice any difference, his beautiful wife immediately did.

What Garfield was doing was listening to Vassili's stammering attempts to deal with the pitfalls of the English language. As Smin caught a few words of what his son was saying, he frowned. "Excuse me," he said to the teacher; and then, to his son, "Vassili? I do not know English, but I recognize such words as *neutron* and *uranium*. What are you telling our American friends?"

The boy flushed. "I was only explaining to them what you do, Father."

"Yes, that I am involved in the management of a nuclear power plant, of course. But what else are you saying?"

"Oh, our cousin Garfield did not understand how it was possible to control a nuclear reaction, so I explained to him what you taught me; that although most neutrons are released at once, there are a very few that take a fraction of a second longer, and it is because of them that there is time to adjust the speed of the reaction. Just as you have told me, Father. Did I get it right?"

"Perhaps too right," Smin said dryly. "I don't think Gorodot Khrenov would like you to be explaining nuclear matters to Americans. Go help your grandmother, please; she is getting ready to feed us."

So Vassili was drafted to put two tables together and find chairs to go around them, and young Mrs. Didchuk to help the formidable old lady put food on the table. In a few minutes they were all seated, one way or another, still talking.

Smin wondered what was going through the Americans' minds. The woman was, after all, very beautiful. She seemed exactly like one of those Western movie stars with their remarkable teeth and the figures of young girls—well, that seemed to be exactly what she was, to be sure. A movie star. From Hollywood. Who no doubt lived in one of those sprawling eight-room or nine-room mansions that clung to mountainsides and looked out over oceans—with, no doubt, a swimming pool in the immense backyard and two or three huge American cars in the garage. What could she be making of his mother's flat with its paper-thin carpet worn bare, its battered furniture, its walls with the paint chipping off in the corners?

He realized, with resignation, that before long there would be more said on this subject. From his wife. Who had been after him all along about his mother's "Khrushchev" flat, thrown up at great speed thirty years ago and decaying rapidly ever since, without even a telephone. "You must realize, Simyon," she would say patiently—again!—"that you hold a very important position. You should live accordingly. Not Brezhnev style, of course; no one does that anymore. But with dignity, even in your mother's apartment, since we often use it." And it would be no good telling her—again!—that the way his mother lived was his mother's own choice, because she would simply point out that old people did not always know what was best for them, after all.

Smin debated whether it was worthwhile to try to forestall some of his wife's remarks by explaining to the Americans just what kind of a woman his mother was. It seemed a daunting job, especially with old Aftasia sitting there and listening to every word. In any case, the conversation was going along very well without that. Garfield, through Mrs. Didchuk, was explaining to the whole group just why he and his wife had decided it was better to live in Beverly Hills than Brentwood, although, of course, Beverly Hills was much more expensive.

In the middle of it, Garfield broke off to stare more closely at what Aftasia Smin had set on the table. Then he grinned and spoke rapidly to his wife, who laughed and replied. Both were obviously discussing the food.

"What are they saying?" Smin asked the male teacher.

Didchuk seemed embarrassed. "It's funny, but Mrs. Garfield said"—he hesitated—"well, she mentioned that she was surprised there were no dishes of cabbage on the table."

Smin laughed. "Tell her, please, that cabbage does not agree with my mother. Was that all?"

"Oh, no." The teacher paused, obviously searching for the tactful words. "Mr. Garfield was saying to his wife what these foods are. He says that those are bitter herbs, and those biscuits are what he calls 'matzos,' and this is a real, pardon me, I don't know the word, it is something like 'cross over'?"

"Oh, my mother is at it again," Smin sighed. "This is the time of a Jewish holiday—what, the second night of Passover? Please tell him that we are not religious, but my mother—"

"Tell him nothing of the sort!" his mother called, setting down a great tureen of soup. "Even if our cousin from America doesn't know Hebrew, he's a Jew. I asked him!"

But it turned out, after a good deal of talk back and forth, that although Dean Garfield really enjoyed the Passover ritual, he said he was not much more of a practicing Jew than Smin himself, in fact was something called a "Unitarian," because his wife had been something called "Methodist" and they had wanted a "Sunday school" to send their children to; and then Smin's mother wanted to hear all about the children.

The chicken broth was excellent—Smin's mother boasted she had stood in line an hour to get the chicken. Then the food began—mushrooms baked in sour cream in individual pots, the meat of the stewed chicken that had made the soup, meat pies, sturgeon in jelly; when all that was done, there was fruit compote and small cakes with poppy-seed filling. The teachers were too timid to eat much at first, but then there was also Georgian wine and Armenian brandy, and at the end icy cold vodka.

By the time of the brandy, and long before the vodka, the teachers were stuffing themselves, and the Americans, though they ate very little, praised everything immensely and drank enough to make up. They even praised Smin's mother's two table spreads, overlapped to cover the round table that was pressed against the long one to make room for eight persons, and did not comment on the curious selection of kitchen chairs, armchairs, and other sittables that surrounded the tables. They obviously enjoyed impressing these relatives, and others, with their prosperity and the high ratings of Garfield's television show, but actually Dean Garfield was impressed with his second cousin too. "Director of a nuclear power plant!" he said through the female teacher. "That's a mighty important job."

"It is the most important job in the Ukraine," Smin's mother said severely, and Smin demurred.

"There are a lot of people who would be surprised to hear that," he told her, and then, for the Americans, told them what Chernobyl was like. Four billion watts of electrical energy derived from the smokeless, pollutionless power of fissioning uranium dioxide; enough to supply an entire city or run a whole countryside of factories.

It turned out that the American cousin had some views on nuclear power. He spoke of San Onofro and Three Mile Island, of earthquake faults and the China syndrome, of children's birth defects and future leukemias. The teachers gamely translated, though they had to consult each other frequently for some of the terms. "Yes," put in Vassili eagerly, almost falling off his seat—as the youngest, he had been given the hassock with pillows piled on top of it, "but our reactors are different. There was a report in a scientific journal years ago—I read it in school—which said that in the Soviet Union the problem of nuclear safety has been solved!"

"No, no," said Smin gently, "not *solved*. It is never *solved*. It is true that we know the solutions and embody them in our daily practice, but the solution has to be applied again every day, every minute. Forgive me—I don't want to say anything against American practices—" He waited politely for translation.

"Go ahead," smiled his American cousin in his turn, and added something that made Didchuk stammer as he translated: "I hate the bastards, myself."

Smin was slightly startled, but he went on with his remembered facts. "In America," he said, "it is the human factor that
causes nuclear accidents. I mention your Idaho Falls in 1961,
where control rods were removed by mistake and three people
were killed; in our reactor, the control rods are automatically
inserted if anything begins to go wrong. In your Brown's Ferry
in Alabama in 1975, a man looked for leaks in the shielding.
To find them he used a lighted candle! He set fire to the
insulation, and most of the safety systems failed because they
lost power—almost that was a total catastrophe. In your Se-
quoia plant in Tennessee in 1981, more than a quarter of a
million liters of radioactive liquid were allowed to leak out.
Just a few months ago, at Gore, Oklahoma, someone heated a
container of nuclear fuel and caused it to explode, killing a
worker and injuring a hundred others. And Three Mile Island—
well, everyone knows that at Three Mile Island it was nearly a
complete meltdown. It was stopped with only minutes to spare."

"Yes, exactly," nodded Garfield. "It is frightening."

"But all of these are human errors, Cousin Dean. We do
not allow human errors to occur. Our workers are not only
very highly trained—" Smin swallowed, thinking of the
Literaturna Ukraina report; but Dean Garfield would hardly
have seen that—"they are also taught to maintain vigilance at
all times. Nor are they allowed to work if they are not fit. It is
true, Cousin Dean, that in America, sometimes the reactor
workers use drugs on the job?"

"I've heard that, yes," Garfield conceded. "I think it was
just security guards and maybe laborers, though, not technicians. You don't have grass here?"

The teacher had to have that explained, and translated it
finally as "marijuana." Smin shook his head. "But," grinned
the American, "I suppose now and then somebody does drink
a little?"

"Never!" Smin declared. "No Soviet citizen drinks a little! We drink only very much—pass me your glass!"

Though Smin himself did not drink at all, not even the
wine, there was plenty for everyone else, and even the two
teachers were flushed and smiling. Smin's mother told over
and over how the letter from America had reached her only
that morning and she had at once telephoned the hotel and

sent a car for the visitors. Vassili Smin explained in detail the great importance of his father's work, and how he himself might someday be a nuclear engineer—or perhaps a helicopter pilot, like his elder brother Nikolai, now already a senior lieutenant (though no one mentioned exactly what country Lieutenant Nikolai Smin was flying his helicopter in).

The Americans told how greatly they had been impressed by Moscow (immense city, like one huge monument) and Leningrad (yes, really, certainly properly called the Venice of the North), and how this evening was, all the same, definitely the high spot of their trip, and they all agreed that it was a great pity that contact had been established so late, since the Garfields were scheduled to leave for Tbilisi in the morning. In the relaxed and friendly atmosphere, Didchuk daringly told a couple of Soviet jokes, his eye on Smin to make sure he was not being indiscreet, including the Radio Armenia one about the definition of a string trio (a Soviet quartet that has just returned from a tour of the West), and Dean Garfield responded with one about Aeroflot stewardesses. (In America the hostesses said, "Coffee, tea or me?" and on Aeroflot they said, "White wine, cherry juice, or go off in a corner, Comrade, and do it to yourself.") But that one, apart from requiring much agitated consultation about the translation, made the woman teacher blush.

Smin stole a glance at his watch. After ten, and they were still sitting around the dinner table. At least, he thought comfortably, it had been, what? three or more hours now when he had not had to think about the problems of the Chernobyl Nuclear Power Station. He thought, with amused sympathy—a little sympathy and a lot more amusement—of the Chief Engineer and the Personnel man, stuck with trying to get rid of the observers who had no experiment to observe. Not for the first time, he thought that his mother's old-fashioned ways were sometimes a convenience. If there had been a telephone in the house, he would have been tempted to call the plant. Since it was out of the question, he could simply relax.

It was not even difficult to keep up a conversation. Having explained America to his Soviet family, Dean Garfield was now explaining the Soviet Union to them. They had already done Leningrad and Moscow—had even, Smin was slightly startled to hear, managed to get tickets to the famous émigré

Vladimir Horowitz's once-in-a-lifetime piano recital in Moscow just a few days earlier. (And how many Soviet citizens would have given a month's pay for such tickets? But, of course, Intourist gave first priority to tourists—who could, after all, have heard him any number of times in America.) And in Kiev they had seen any number of tenth-century cathedrals, and the bones of the old monks in the Lavra catacombs, and the Great Golden Gate Moussorgsky had made famous with his *Pictures at an Exhibition;* in fact, they were staying at the brand-new Great Gate Hotel, just across from the Gate itself on the street called the Khreshchatik.

Garfield had funny stories about their pilgrimages: "So the guide showed us the footbridge to those beaches, you know? The ones across the river in Kiev? And I told her that in New York we had not only footbridges to islands in the river but cable cars. Then she showed us that Rainbow Arch that's supposed to commemorate, what is it, the joining of Russia and the Ukraine, and I told her that we had one that looked exactly like it in St. Louis—the Gateway Arch—only it's two hundred meters tall and it has little cars inside it that take you right up to the top."

"Yes, everything is bigger in America," Aftasia said dryly. "What, you're not eating the compote? Don't you like it?"

Then Smin's son, getting braver about practicing English, began telling his cousins about the four great football players on the team of the Chernobyl plant, the Four Seasons, and Dean Garfield responded with stories about his own team, something called the Los Angeles "goats," said Didchuk, although Smin could not quite believe that was the right name.

Smin yawned as his son went on explaining other things to the guests, until he saw the way the Americans were studying the glassy scars on his face and neck. From the expressions on their faces, distress and sympathy, he knew just what his son was saying.

Smin placed a gentle hand on his son's shoulder and addressed Didchuk. "Say for me, please," he said, "that Vassili, like all boys, is fascinated by stories about war. Especially he likes to boast about his father's heroic adventures, but in fact I was merely trapped in a tank when it burned. It was more than forty years ago."

"But you received four medals!" his son cried, distressed.

"And I hope for you nothing more than that you should never be in a position to earn such medals," Smin said firmly. "Now, whose glass is empty?"

It was turning into a long evening, and a wearing one after all, with this business of trying to carry on a friendly conversation with new-met relatives through translators. Smin was glad when the talk passed from him. The women were talking among themselves, the young teacher, Mrs. Didchuk, chatting in English with the glamorous American blonde woman, Mrs. Garfield. Aftasia Smin, on the fringes, asked. "So what are you telling her?"

"Why," said Mrs. Didchuk, flushing with remembered pleasure, "just that yesterday, when I went to the store, I saw that they had hundreds of rolls of bathroom paper. Imagine! All you could want! So I bought twelve, and the clerk scolded me, can you imagine, saying, 'There is no need to hoard, from now on there will always be plenty!' Do you think that is true?"

"I think," said old Aftasia Smin, "that that is not a proper subject to discuss with our guests at the table." Then, her eyes suddenly gleaming, "I have something else that is interesting. Will you ask my cousin's wife if she will come with us into my bedroom? There is something I would like to show her."

"She is at it again," said Smin's wife, frowning after her mother-in-law as she led the female guests away.

"I suppose she is," said Smin, and when the women came back, he was confirmed in his opinion by the new way the American blonde looked at Aftasia Smin. Aftasia had been showing off her war wounds again. Well, she had a right; not every old woman in Kiev had fought bravely in the Civil War, as well as owning a Party membership twenty years senior to Smin's own.

Surreptitiously Smin glanced again at his watch. Past midnight! And he had been up since six. Of course, the next day, he thought idly, would not be very strenuous. The experiment with trying to get power from a turned-off reactor would probably not take place on a Saturday. Perhaps they could even defer it until the Director came back? It was his baby, after all. But it was just like the Director to conceive the idea and then find "important business" somewhere else, so that

Smin was stuck with the responsibility of carrying it out. Important business! Shooting ducks outside of Moscow! When, really, if Director Zaglodin desired to kill a few ducks, there were millions of them in the Pripyat Marshes, just north of the plant. . . . But, of course, it was not the ducks Zaglodin wanted, it was the company; he was hunting powerful connections more than waterfowl.

Smin yawned and eyed the vodka bottle. But it was not yet time for the one drink he allowed himself each day. "Can I at least have some tea?" he asked his mother just as the male teacher, Didchuk, said eagerly:

"Can you imagine? Mr. and Mrs. Garfield say that their home is only a few kilometers from Disneyland!"

So it was a happy enough evening, and an interesting one for all concerned. It took Smin's mind off, or nearly off, the problems of Chernobyl and he forgave his mother for her surprises, even for her stubborn decision, at her time in life, to decide to observe Jewish holidays again. By the time Vassili was yawning and the old grandmother had dozed off in her seat, it was too late to try to get a taxi. Smin drove his new relatives back to their hotel, with Didchuk along to interpret.

Until they had crossed the bridge over the Dnieper River, they were almost alone in the streets of suburban Kiev. The officers in roving militia cars glanced at them as they passed, but few policemen would bother the driver of a black Chaika with yellow fog lights at any hour. Then, as they approached the center of the city, there was activity, even at this hour. In the main square, Army trucks with batteries of floodlights made the scene bright as new banners were hoisted into position for the May Day parade—WE WILL FULFILL OUR PLAN! and WE DEMAND PEACE AND FREEDOM FOR THE WORLD! As they crossed the square where the great old cathedral stood, Smin said to Didchuk, "Tell them that services are held there every Sunday; if one wishes to believe in God, one may."

"I already have," said Didchuk proudly. "They were very pleased to hear it."

The May Day parade would go along the Khreshchatik, of course—there was no more famous street in Kiev. They had to dodge around the Army trucks to get to the entrance of the Great Gate Hotel. Of course, the hotel doors were locked at that hour. When Didchuk had roused the doorkeeper to let them in, they all got out of the car and stood for a moment in the chilly April night air. "I wish," Candace Garfield said earnestly through Didchuk's translation, "that we had been able to get together earlier, Cousin Simyon. It's really too bad that we have to leave for Tbilisi tomorrow. We have enjoyed this very much, and if you ever come to Beverly Hills—"

"Of course," smiled Smin gallantly, reaching to put his arms around her. In his hug she was even slimmer than he had thought, and there was a scent of France and America that came from her hair. "Ah, well," he said to Didchuk as they drove away, "there is simply one more duty call we will have to pay next time we are in California. What a nuisance, isn't it?" But now that they were alone Didchuk appeared to have remembered that he was in the presence of a Deputy Director and senior Party member, and he did not seem to know how to respond to the pleasantry.

By the time Smin was back in his mother's flat everyone was asleep. He was careful not to wake his son as he poured himself the 150-milliliter nightcap of brandy that was all he allowed himself anymore and gratefully stretched out next to his gently snoring wife. It had been an interesting evening, if sometimes puzzling—what had Dean Garfield meant when he called his wife a "Valley girl"? And certainly it had been a pleasant ending to a day that had been full of irritating worries.

When the doorbell rang and someone knocked heavily at the same time, Smin woke up with a start. It was after three o'clock! Selena was upright next to him, her face strained. "No, no," Smin soothed, not having to ask what had frightened her because he knew, not having to reassure her that the bad days when a knock at three in the morning meant only one specific, hopeless thing were over, because she knew that too.

He almost persuaded himself to relax as he listened to the voices outside, until his son burst into the room, a blanket wrapped around him, crying, "Papa! It's the militia! They have brought an important message for you—you must go back to Chernobyl at once!"

CHAPTER 4

Leonid Sheranchuk knows very little of nuclear energy. In this he is like most of the engineers and managers in the Chernobyl Power Station. Sheranchuk's specialty covers piping, pumps, water, and steam, and his work experience has been confined to that outdated peat powered plant north of Moscow. For most of the others their experience has been in coal and oil plants, and what they know is turbines, transformers, and electricity. The mushrooming growth of nuclear power in the Soviet Union has gone faster than the supply of engineers trained in nucleonics can keep up with—though, of course, the problems of a nuclear power plant are known to be very like the problems of any power plant anywhere—you heat your water into steam, and you turn your steam into electricity—and the specifically nuclear questions, they are taught, have been solved at higher levels long ago. All the same, Sheranchuk wishes he knew more. He has even enrolled in an evening course in nucleonics at the local polytechnic, though it will not begin for another month. Meanwhile he reads texts when he can find time.

When Sheranchuk got home he thought of tackling the books again, but he was really tired. Maybe later, he thought. He ate something instead, with the nine o'clock news broadcast going on unheeded on the television set. His wife had, of course, eaten with their son, Boris, long since, but she sat companionably with him over a glass of wine. "Did anything interesting happen at work today?" she asked dutifully.

"No," said Sheranchuk; there was no use telling her about the annoyances with the proposed experiment on Reactor No. 4; she was already too likely to worry about the unknown dangers of nuclear power. "Some problems with one of the pumps, but it's all right now." He thought for a moment, and then said, "The Deputy Director said, in general, I was doing a good job."

"In general!"

"It's just his way. He calls me his plumber."

"Plumber!" But she knew how her husband felt about Deputy Director Smin. "Then you won't have to go in tomorrow morning?" she asked. "Because of your dentist's appointment, I mean?"

"I had forgotten all about my appointment with the dentist," Sheranchuk confessed. Then, grinning, "Do you know what she told me last time? She said, 'It's a shame you keep those stainless-steel teeth. Now we can make you much better ones, porcelain, even better than your own, so that the girls will turn and look at you.'"

"There's no need to have the girls look at you," Tamara said sharply.

"Not even just to look? If I don't look back?"

"They look at you enough already," his wife said. She began to clear dishes from the table in silence for a moment, then remembered to tell him about the young girl who had come to her clinic that morning for an abortion. "Imagine, Leony! She was only sixteen years old. No older than Boris!"

"At least our son can't get pregnant." Sheranchuk smiled.

"It is not a joke! She is destroying a life inside her, and so young."

Sheranchuk said reasonably, "But, Tamara, what else would you have her do? At sixteen she is certainly too young to marry, especially to have the care of a baby when she is only a child herself."

"I could never do such a thing," Tamara insisted.

"You have never had to," Sheranchuk said mildly. There was no reason she should; she worked in the clinic and had ample access to such things as diaphragms and sponges. But the look she gave him as she turned to get on with her household chores kept him from saying so. It was not an angry look, but it was definitely an exclusionary one, as if to say, *You are a man, what do you know?* If not something worse.

Sheranchuk turned off the television set and rummaged through their literary library for the works on nuclear energy he had set himself to go through. He found himself yawning as he opened his books. To help concentrate he put a *magnitizdat* tape on the player, and the soft sounds of a Vladimir Vyshinsky satirical song made a background while he tried to study.

Tamara Sheranchuk paused to listen. She knew the song. It was nothing out of the ordinary for them to play the tapes of Vyshinsky, or of Aleksandr Galich or Boulat Okudzhava—the balladeers who lived in, but not of, the Soviet system. Their records were never pressed by Melodiya. Their songs had no official recognition, but were known by heart by nearly every Soviet citizen, passed from hand to hand in the furtively recorded tape cassettes called "*magnitizdat*." "A little quieter, please, if you will," she asked. The tapes were not illegal, but all the same they were not what you would go out of your way to have your neighbors hear you playing.

Still—

She had met Sheranchuk at an Okudzhava concert. It was not in a hall or a stadium, or even in a nightclub. The concert had been out in the birch and pine woods, on a spring night not quite warm enough to be comfortable, and not even dry— little sprinkles of rain came now and then. Still, there had been more than two hundred people out there in the woods, listening to the Georgian balladeer play his old guitar and sing of trolleybuses and the road to Smolensk. All young. And among them had been this red-haired young man who had come by himself, and when he looked at her he did not smile. But as the listeners moved around under the trees, trying to stay dry if not warm, she had wound up next to him. She had left the little group she came with, and Sheranchuk had taken her home.

Tamara had gotten a cold from attending that concert, but she had also gotten a husband.

In order to be fresh for the morning, when he was determined to get in bright and early, despite the dentist, Sheranchuk gave up his yawning struggle with his studies and went to bed at ten o'clock. But now sleep did not come. He lay listening to the sounds of his wife, ironing Boris's white school shirt for the morning, with the sound of pop music from the television set faint in the background; and he heard Boris come in from his Komsomol meeting, specially called to plan for their May Day celebration, and head immediately for the refrigerator.

Just as he was dozing off he remembered that he had not checked to see if the automatic pumps had been turned back on after the afternoon's aborted experiment.

The experiment was not his business. The pumps, however, were. He thought for a moment, then rolled over on his left side, with his elbow under the goosedown pillow, curled up like a fetus in the position that always meant comfort and sleep to him. The duty engineers would certainly have restored the pumps' operation, he reassured himself. There was no point in lying awake and worrying. He tried to think of pleasant things. Of Tamara in the next room, for instance. He thought of calling her to bed; perhaps they could make love, and that would make him sleepy. But there was the boy, no doubt eating an apple at the table with his books spread out all around him, studying for his Saturday examination in geometry. If he had thought of it a little earlier, Sheranchuk mused, they could have taken advantage of the boy's being out of the house and it could have been just as it was when they were first married and in an apartment of their own ... He dozed for a moment, and then was wide awake again as someone in another apartment noisily flushed the toilet. He fumbled for the alarm clock and held it in the light from the window. Already after midnight. A new day; and the pumps were still on his mind.

Sheranchuk groaned and sat up, his feet on the floor, rubbing his chin. After a moment, he sighed, reached for his robe, and went into the living room to call the plant. Tamara passed him in the hall, on her way to the bathroom. "What, still awake?" she chided. He patted her on the rump affectionately as they passed, but did not stop.

Boris was already asleep on the couch, and Sheranchuk kept his voice down as he talked to Kalychenko, one of the shift operators. "The pumps—" he began, and listened in surprise as Kalychenko told him that the free-wheeling experiment was, after all, already in progress. "Without the Director present? But then surely, Smin—" But, no, Smin wasn't there, either. And was not missed, Kalychenko said, because, apart from small power surges, the experiment was going well. Sheranchuk frowned. "What kind of small surges? From six to eleven percent? But that's not small!" He listened for a while and then hung up. He opened the refrigerator and poured himself a glass of apple juice. He gazed thoughtfully at his sleeping son as he sipped the juice.

It occurred to him that Boris was not likely to wake, and Tamara would probably not yet be asleep in their warm bed.

Sheranchuk told himself that it was wrong for him to lose sleep over matters that were someone else's responsibility. He went back to bed. Tamara was already asleep on her side of the bed, and Sheranchuk put his arm around her experimentally. She made a faint, agreeable noise, but then turned away.

Ah, well.

He turned over and tried to sleep.

Half an hour later he sighed, got up and began to dress. At one o'clock he was down on the cold street, for there was no point in being awake at home, worrying about the plant, when he could just as well be awake and worrying about it on the scene. He was almost alone at this hour, the trolleybuses long since stopped for the night, only an occasional lighted window in the apartment buildings. There was a scent of lilacs in the spring night air.

In a way, Sheranchuk was pleased to be a part of the work at the power plant at such odd hours. It reminded him of the special importance of what they did. All over the country factories had long since shut down, people were turning off their lights and TV sets; electrical demand was dropping minute by minute. Oil powered turbine plants would be ceasing operations for the night. Coal and peat steam plants would be banking their fires; the hydroelectric generators would be slowing as the sluices were closed to preserve the heads of water behind the huge dams. But Chernobyl went on. Nuclear power was baseline power. You kept it going.

It was a warm night, with a few clouds among the stars overhead as he walked through the silent streets of Pripyat. He wondered why Smin was not on hand this night. True, the Deputy Director made a policy of leaving day-to-day operations to the people in charge of them. It was nevertheless also true that Smin had a habit of turning up when and where he was needed. He was a good man. Sheranchuk thought of the conversation in the sauna. When Smin had readjusted the sheet around himself, Sheranchuk could see the wide, pale, almost glistening burn scars that went from the left side of his face clear down his back; they were from the Great Patriotic War, Sheranchuk knew, but just how Smin had received them he never said. Sheranchuk wondered what it was like to be in a war. He was an infant in the Great Patriotic War; his own Army service had been in peacetime—a general sort of peace, at least, not counting a few skirmishes along the Amur with the Chinese, but Sheranchuk had been three thousand kilometers away from any fighting.

Sheranchuk's little flat was three kilometers from the plant, but this night luck was with him. An ambulance moved slowly past, and at his hail it stopped and gave him a lift. Sheranchuk half-recognized the doctor as a colleague of Tamara's, and the man knew who Sheranchuk was as soon as he gave his name. He had just had a call to attend a little girl who had swallowed something she shouldn't have, he explained—yes, yes, the child was quite all right, only a little sick from having her stomach pumped out—and he was now on his way back to the clinic. But there was no real hurry, and he was glad to go a couple of minutes out of his way for Tamara Sheranchuk's husband.

The ambulance circled around a man on a bicycle to take the engineer to the plant fence. He thanked the doctor and got out, fumbling for his papers as he watched the ambulance slowly start away. Although on the other side of the fence the Chernobyl Nuclear Power Station was almost as brightly lighted as in daytime, on this side it was a peaceful middle-of-the-night scene. The only things moving were the ambulance, the bicyclist, and some early-rising health faddist, it seemed, walking with great arm-swinging strides along the road and not even glancing at Sheranchuk or the gate guard.

The funny thing was, Sheranchuk discovered, that now that he was actually at the plant, he was beginning to feel quite drowsy at last. He could turn around and go back to bed easily enough.

He smiled to himself, his mind made up; no, he was this

far, he would go in and see for himself just what they were doing with Reactor No. 4. . . .

He was actually displaying his *paprushka* to the gate guard when the world changed around him.

There was a sudden orange-white flare of light, a flower of flame overhead, the shattering, hurtful sound of a vast explosion. "In God's name!" Sheranchuk cried, clutching at the guard's arm as the two of them stared up in horror.

The noise did not stop. A siren screamed inside one of the buildings. There was a distant sound of men shouting. "But this is quite impossible," the guard bawled accusingly in Sheranchuk's ear.

Sheranchuk's mouth was open as he stared up. The great ball of bright flame was floating away and diminishing, but behind it was a sullen, growing red glow. To the other noises was added the patter of a shower—no, a downpour!—but it was not rain that was falling. It was bits of stone and brick and metal, pelting down all around them. "Yes," Sheranchuk said dazedly, "it is quite impossible."

But it had happened.

CHAPTER 5

The Chernobyl Power Station contains four units, each of them an RBMK-1000 "pressure-tube" reactor. The RBMK is not the Soviet Union's only nuclear power generator, but it is the favorite. Across the USSR nearly two dozen such units are installed and operational, and the 1000-series models, each of them rated at 1000 megawatts of electricity, are the largest and newest in operation, though even larger ones are beginning to appear.

The fuel is uranium dioxide, which is encased in steel and zirconium tubes and inserted into a huge mass of graphite blocks. (The purpose of the graphite is to be a "moderator." Nothing is needed to make uranium atoms fission—that is to say, break apart—and when they do that they produce atomic energy in the form of heat. They do it naturally all the time; that is why uranium is called "radioactive." As each atom fissions, it releases neutrons which strike the cores of other atoms and cause them to fission too. However, the naturally released neutrons whisk through so fast that they only rarely cause fission in another atom; they need to be slowed down to make a reaction go at the right speed to be of use to human beings. Graphite, along with a few other materials, has the capacity to "moderate" or slow down these escaping neutrons, and so in a reactor the speed of the reaction can be controlled.)

Along with the fuel tubes, the slab of graphite is pierced by nearly seventeen hundred pipes containing water. As the uranium fissions, it gives off heat. The water carries away this heat, thus preventing a runaway meltdown of the uranium, and also providing the steam that turns the turbines that generate the electricity. Like every other nuclear reactor in the world, the RBMK-1000 is designed to be totally safe. And it is, as long as nothing goes wrong.

At ten o'clock that Friday night Bohdan Kalychenko was also trying to get to sleep, under circumstances less favorable than Leonid Sheranchuk's. He was in a bunk in the fire department of the Chernobyl Nuclear Power Station. Kalychenko had borrowed the bunk from a fireman friend—well, definitely a fireman and at least a sort of a friend—named Vissgerdis, who was a member of the plant's Fire Brigade No. 2. The bunk had been constructed for someone a lot shorter than a man with Lithuanian blood like Kalychenko—or like Vissgerdis himself for that matter. Kalychenko had difficulty in composing himself comfortably in it. It wasn't merely the bunk; it was his job, his boss, his boss's bosses like Khrenov, his girl, his approaching wedding—it was also the fact that before being allowed to get to sleep he had been wheedled into two hours of cards with the rest of the firemen. Now he was eight rubles fifty kopecks poorer than he had been that afternoon, and his fiancée, Raia, was sure to find out that he had been gambling again.

He pulled the thin, sweaty blanket over his head to shut out the noise from the card game. It didn't work. It made it dark for him, but also hot; it did not keep out the men's voices from the next room, or even the reek of tobacco smoke from the game. It was Kalychenko's pride that he did not, at least, smoke. In fact, he was quite intolerant of people who did, like his fiancée—except that in her case it was useful to have her possess at least one vice he did not. It would be particularly valuable after they were married, he thought gloomily. At least, that was when he would need it most.

The idea of getting married was not all joy for Bohdan Kalychenko. Sooner or later, of course, it was what one did. But he was not ready for that sort of surrender, especially since he considered that it was entirely Raia's fault that she had become pregnant. Of course, he reminded himself, when they were married and had a room to themselves in the families' hostel, it would be quite nice to share a bed together every night—at least until the baby came, when one room would no longer seem quite enough for the three of them. And even in Pripyat there was a three-year waiting list for flats. To be sure, first there would be the honeymoon. . . . But even that, Kalychenko told himself sourly, would not be without its drawbacks. Raia was determined to go to the Black Sea. Neither of them had enough standing to get the plant or the union to get them into one of the special "sanitoria," so that meant paying seven rubles a day to some Crimean robber, and lucky if they didn't have six other beds in their room anyway.

He pounded the pillow, threw the blanket off, and sat up angrily.

How could these other men sleep so soundly here? There were at least half a dozen bunks filled, and gentle snores coming from most of them. From the nearest bunk, not so gentle; Kalychenko knew that the fireman there was the football player they called "Summer," the best scorer of the Four Seasons.

Kalychenko was still trying to make up his mind whether it was worthwhile to lie down again, when Vissgerdis poked his head in the door. "Kalychenko? Telephone," he said. When Kalychenko mumbled a question about who would be calling him here, Vissgerdis only looked upward and jerked a thumb toward heaven before returning to his card game.

That could mean one of two things, either God himself or the organs—the GehBeh. And what in hell could *he* want? Sure enough, the voice on the other end belonged to the Personnel and Security chief, Khrenov. "Operator Kalychenko," he said, voice warm and intimate, "how nice that you sleep alone for a change, but if you can bring yourself to report to work a bit early, we need you. The thermal output on Reactor Number Four is dropping fast."

"With pleasure," snarled Kalychenko, looking at the clock. It was not even eleven yet! As he dressed he helped himself to half a cup of the concentrated tea the firemen kept for times they needed to wake up in a hurry. He pulled his clothes on rapidly. How like Khrenov to seek him out himself, instead of letting the shift chief do it! It was not that Khrenov interfered in the technical work of the power station—exactly—he was careful, always, to stay within his own sphere of authority.

But where did that sphere end?

Kalychenko didn't waste time resenting Khrenov's issuing orders, or in wondering how the Personnel man had known where to find him; of course Khrenov knew where to find anyone, all the time. What he did resent was Khrenov's continuing nagging little jokes about Kalychenko's relationship with the woman whom he was pledged to marry. Surely that was none of even the GehBehs' business!

It did not occur to Kalychenko to complain to anyone about Khrenov's actions. Who was there to complain to about the KGB?

Vissgerdis took time out from the game to look in on Kalychenko again. "What's up?" he asked. "There's a story that they're doing something strange with the Number Four Reactor tonight."

Kalychenko paused as he pulled a boot on. "Oh, of course," he said, remembering. "No, it is nothing strange, simply a test of a new energy conservation measure." They were friends, of a sort—Vissgerdis was half Lithuanian, like Kalychenko himself, and so they both stood out as tall and pale among the stubby Slavs, which had made them at least acquaintances. Nevertheless Kalychenko never forgot that he was an accredited power operator, while Vissgerdis was only a fireman. So he said, in rough comradeship, "A technical matter. Nothing important." But, he reflected, the trouble was that when something like that was going on, they would be busy all night. That was a nuisance. Normally Kalychenko actually preferred night duty. After all, the Chernobyl power plant pretty well ran itself. All the operators drowsed off from time to time on the midnight shift; oh, they were careful to see that there was always someone watching the boards and listening for the telephone in case of any messages from the load dispatcher in Kiev, but, really, there was not that much to do at night, when the bosses were all tucked away.

But tonight would be different, he thought glumly.

Reluctantly he left the fire department's comfortable little quarters, waving thanks to Vissgerdis, already back at the card table. The power plant was not quiet—it was never that, with the turbine scream always in everyone's ears wherever they were in the structures—but it was almost deserted. There were hardly more than a hundred people anywhere in the vast expanse at this time of night; construction had stopped for the weekend, and the three thousand workers who swarmed around the plant in the daylight hours were all back in their homes.

When Kalychenko got to the control room for Reactors 3 and 4, it did not look deserted. It was full. The four-to-midnight shift was still there, so were some of those who would take over at twelve, though it was only eleven-thirty by the big clock. And so was Khrenov, gazing thoughtfully at Kalychenko as he came in, and so, for a wonder, was the Chief Plant Engineer, Vitaly Varazin.

The Security chief gave him one of those intimate, understanding looks. "Are you just out of bed, then, Kalychenko?" he asked—it was his way of showing he was in a good humor, but what was he in a good humor about? "Did you also manage, this time, to get a little sleep?"

With someone like, say, Smin, Kalychenko would have managed some sort of retort to the effect that it was none of anyone's business whom he slept with, or when. Not with Khrenov. In a quite civil tone Kalychenko said, "Thank you, yes." He did not prolong the conversation. He relieved the other operator and took his seat before the big board, frowning as he saw that the main pumps were still disconnected. He called to the shift chief, "Shouldn't we turn these on again?"

It was Chief Plant Engineer Varazin who answered. "Not at all, Kalychenko. We've been allowed to take Number Four off line after all, so now we are able to proceed with the planned experiment."

And Khrenov, standing behind Kalychenko, said pleasantly, "Aren't you pleased?"

Kalychenko didn't answer. He didn't have to, because two more men were coming into the main control room. They were strangers to Kalychenko, but obviously not to Khrenov, who turned away at once to greet them.

Kalychenko scowled at the board. The best things about his job were that there was so little, really, to do, and that little could be done in comfort, without people standing around to watch you. This night was all different. Another stranger had just come hurrying in, looking as rumpled and sleepy-eyed as the first two. The shift chief whispered to Kalychenko that they were observers—from the turbine factory, from other power stations—but, whoever they were, they were not welcome to Kalychenko. Nor was Khrenov, who certainly had no business being present at this purely technical matter. As for Chief Plant Engineer Varazin, well, certainly the man had every right to be anywhere in the plant he chose, at any time. Still, Kalychenko had never before seen him in the control room after midnight before. With all these people present there would be no good chance to disappear for half an hour or so for a little rest from his duties.

Both Khrenov and the Chief Engineer looked freshly washed and shaved, and humorously apologetic to their guests for getting them out of bed at this uncultured hour. "Still, now you can see how hard we work here at Chernobyl," Varazin said affably. "In any case, you're just in time. We've already begun to reduce power on Reactor Number Four."

"Excellent," said one of the visitors politely, glancing around. "And the Director and Deputy Director?"

"The Director has left the entire matter in the hands of Chief Plant Engineer Varazin." Khrenov smiled. "As to Smin, I tried to call him, but he is off on some private errand. So when they come in to work on Monday, we will be able to give them both a pleasant surprise."

"Exactly," Varazin agreed, rubbing his hands together. "Now, as designated test leader, I must give a briefing." He stepped toward the board and raised his voice. "May I have your attention, please? As provided by the regulations, it is my duty to brief you all on the experiment we are conducting. But don't stop what you are doing. Continue to reduce the power; we don't want to be here all night!"

Kalychenko listened with half an ear. Most of his attention was on the tricky business of lowering the temperature of Reactor No. 4, though what the Chief Engineer was saying was certainly interesting. Kalychenko almost forgot to be sleepy as he heard the plan.

The basic intention of this experiment, Varazin announced, was to see if useful power could be generated from the heat usually wasted while a nuclear reactor was down for maintenance. The reactor never stopped being hot, of course; it never would until at last the plant was finally decommissioned, somewhere in the next century, and probably not for some time even then. But it was not the practice to try to use that heat while the reactor was being serviced. Now, perhaps Chernobyl could lead the way to new practices.

By the time he got to the new practices, more of the observers were drifting in, looking sleepy. Varazin nodded affably to them, and added, "This is how we will lead the way for our colleagues all over the Soviet Union. Also," he went on, looking serious, "these measures could be of great importance under catastrophic conditions. They could insure a steady supply of power to keep our operations stable until, for example, the auxiliary diesels could be started. Are there any questions?"

The shift chief raised his hand. "I do not quite understand what 'catastrophic conditions' we are preparing for, Vitaly Aleksandrovitch," he called.

"Who can say?" smiled the Chief Engineer. "A very bad storm? An earthquake? Or"—he frowned meaningfully at them—"a sudden nuclear attack from our enemies, perhaps."

"Ah," said the shift chief, enlightened. "Of course. But there is still a question in my mind. Why don't we simply shut down the reactor instead of trying to lower the output?"

"Because," said the Chief Engineer severely, "we must be quite *sure*. We will do this test a number of times, keeping careful record of the results each time. It is a matter of safety, after all—and we can't be too careful in a matter of the safety of the Chernobyl Power Plant!"

Kalychenko groaned silently. A number of times! They would be at this all night!—and, likely enough, well into the Saturday morning shift, too, the way things were going. With resignation he bent to his work.

The normal night shift in the control room was only half a dozen men, just a skeleton crew to keep things going. There was not much need for electrical power in the late night hours in the Soviet Union. Good Soviet citizens went to bed at night so they could rise, bright-eyed and refreshed, for the next morning's work.

Tonight was different. Besides Kalychenko's own crew, there were four men left over from the late evening shift, looking oppressed at being kept on overtime for which they were not likely to be paid, plus the observers, the Chief Engineer, and the Personnel man, Khrenov.

To lower the power on a reactor like the RBMK is not like turning down the gain on a radio set. To shut it off entirely is much easier. You simply thrust home all the boron rods, two hundred and eleven of them, piercing the graphite core from top and bottom and in all its parts. The element boron is poisonous to nuclear reactions. Boron soaks up neutrons; they cannot go on to make another atom fission, and so the reaction stops; that is the easy way.

To slow the nuclear reactor down is another matter entirely. There are three separate ways to do it. First, for a rough approximation, you shove a few additional rods into the core. Not too many; you don't want the reaction to die. (Once the reactor stops waste products begin to accumulate—the element xenon is the worst of them, since it is a worse poison to nuclear reactions even than boron. Then it is impossible to start again until weeks have passed and the xenon has decayed away.)

Then there is a certain measure of fine control that can be attained by varying the mixture of gases in the sealed space surrounding the core. Some of the gases soak up neutrons in the same way that boron does, though not as strongly; to slow the reaction a bit, you simply add more of those gases to the mix.

Finally, there is water. The water that flows up through the core to turn to the steam that drives the turbines also has the neutron-absorbing characteristic—as long as it is water. Once it has turned into steam, which is less dense, it soaks up fewer neutrons, and thus the nuclear reaction picks up speed. This condition is called a "positive void coefficient," a technical term which means only that the more steam there is in the tubes the faster the reaction will go. This also means that the faster the reaction goes, the more steam will be generated—consequently adding to the "voids"—consequently adding to the speed of the reaction—consequently adding to the steam. . . . It is a delicate balance to keep a reactor, any reactor, poised between dying and running away, and so controlling a power reactor is a constant dance of rods and pumps.

When things were going well, Kalychenko enjoyed his part in the dance. Most of it was automatic, anyway. There were heat sensors all through the reactor core. The optimum running temperature of the one hundred eighty tons of uranium

fuel was hundreds of degrees hotter than the ignition temperature of the graphite slabs. Graphite is carbon. Carbon burns.
But it couldn't burn without oxygen, and oxygen was carefully
excluded from the mix of gases in the surrounding jacket. If
the temperature of the reactor climbed too high or fell too low,
there would be a signal from the expensive imported Western
instruments that monitored it. Then the operator would engage
the motors that thrust a few rods farther in or took them a bit
less deep. If it climbed drastically high, the operator would not
be involved at all; automatic pumps would rush floods of new
cold water into the core to cool it down.

That could not happen this night, because the automatic
system had been turned off hours before, but then, no one ever
wanted to let things get so far that the automatics were tripped
anyway.

Another thing no operator wanted—at least, Kalychenko
certainly didn't want it!—was to try to lower the temperature
slowly. That was a sweaty business, because at low power levels
the RBMK was notoriously hard to control. The trouble was
that it was so big. The temperature sensors could not be
everywhere. One part of the core could be at exactly the
temperature desired, while another, an arm's length away, could
be soaring to dangerous levels without warning. So Kalychenko
did sweat, and swore under his breath, because the bitch was
obstinately rising and falling, down to ten percent power, then
up to thirty, slowly down again as they inched a few rods back
in—then almost dying on them, down to the range where
xenon began to form, until they had withdrawn all but six of
the rods entirely and were coaxing it back to life.

When Kalychenko took his eyes off the board long enough
to glance at a clock it was only one A.M.! He wasn't sleepy any
more. He was simply exhausted. Only one, and he had worked
harder than he usually did in a full shift. And everyone else was
on edge too.

Even the GehBeh, Khrenov, had lost his warm, hooded
look. Just behind where Kalychenko sat at his board, Khrenov
was quarreling softly with the Chief Engineer. "What is the
matter, Varazin?" he demanded. "Can't you control this thing?
Must I find Smin and bring him here?"

Varazin flushed, glancing at the observers. "I am Chief Engineer, not Smin," he whispered fiercely.

"And I am responsible for Personnel. Perhaps I have been deficient in my duties. It may be that I have not screened this plant's personnel with sufficient care."

Varazin flinched, but said sturdily enough, "If you have complaints in that respect, Comrade Khrenov, there will certainly be time to discuss the matter. This is not the time. May I remind you that I am in charge here?"

Khrenov looked at him thoughtfully for a moment, then gave a long sigh. He turned to the observers with the smile back on his face. "What a pity," he said genially, "that this operation should take so long. Since most of you are, after all, more interested in the turbines and the steam generation than in the nuclear aspects of the operation, perhaps we should take a look at some of the other systems?"

"Can we take a look at something to drink?" one of the visitors grinned.

"We can do our best. Let me see, it's one o'clock. If we come back, say, at two, I think things will be in order. Don't you think so, Comrade Varazin?"

"I hope so," said Varazin.

At least with Khrenov gone everyone breathed a little more freely, but the job didn't get easier. It got worse. With great difficulty they managed to stabilize the power output of Reactor No. 4 at 200 megawatts electric, a fifth of its normal capacity. Kalychenko called out the reading and reached for the switch that would maintain that level. "Shall I engage the automatic systems?" he asked, finger poised.

"Certainly not," snapped Varazin, looking frayed. "It is far too high. Cool the reactor a bit."

"There are six pumps already going," the shift chief reported.

"Engage a seventh!"

Kalychenko marked the time when the seventh pump was cut in, three minutes after one. And indeed the temperature of the core began to respond; it was not the cooling of the water that made it happen, but the added liquid water in the system absorbing a few more neutrons.

The atmosphere in the control room was excited now,

with the engineers and operators calling the numbers back and forth to each other, like spectators at a football game. Even old Varazin was shifting from one foot to another as he watched the readouts with them, and Kalychenko began to think about what all this meant. If this experiment succeeded, it could well be a model for every nuclear power plant in the Soviet Union. There would be commendations, perhaps cash awards—perhaps they would be written up in *Literaturna Ukraina*, even in *Pravda*! Well, no, he cautioned himself, that was not likely; this sort of thing one did not advertise in the open press, since the West had no business knowing what went on in critical Soviet industries. But it would be in the records! Even Khrenov would not fail to list all the people who had contributed to such a success somewhere in his file folders. . . .

"It is still too high," Varazin announced. "Add another pump!"

It was seven minutes after one. And all of a sudden, without transition, Kalychenko's bright mood vanished. He began to worry.

The first indications of trouble were the pressure readings in the water system. "Pressure is dropping in the drying drum," reported one of the engineers.

The shift chief glanced at Varazin, who said impatiently, "Yes, of course. Carry on." But he looked nervous too. With two extra pumps forcing water into the system, the steam generation had slowed; there was more water coming in than the core could boil into vapor at once, and so in the great drum, where the steam was extracted to feed into the turbines and the remaining water pumped back into the circulation system, pressure had begun to fall. Paradoxically, that meant more steam there, as the water that had been squeezed liquid found room to expand. Kalychenko listened and thought he could hear, in the distant throb of the pumps, a laboring sound as they tried to pump vapor instead of liquid water.

Then the state printout computer flashed a warning: *Reactor should be shut down at once.*

"Chief Engineer Varazin!" Kalychenko cried. The old man was looking strained now, but he said:

"Yes, of course. We are operating under unusual conditions, which the program is not designed for."

"Then shall I—"

"Certainly not!" said Varazin, biting his lip. "Comrade Khrenov and our guests will be back at two, and I don't want to have a dead reactor for them." He glanced at the clock. It was twenty minutes after one. "Close the stop control valve," he ordered.

Kalychenko looked at the shift chief for confirmation before he obeyed, but the man only nodded. His face was pale. Reluctantly Kalychenko switched the stop control valve off; it was the last of the automatic safety features. . . .

Then it all went sour.

"Temperature's rising!" screamed the shift chief. And everyone stared at the thermal readings—from seven percent of normal power, already at fifteen . . . twenty . . . in ten seconds it went to a full fifty percent of normal power. And in Kalychenko's mind, as he gazed awestruck at what was happening, there flashed a picture of the interior of the reactor core, with each of the 1,661 tubes filled with water . . . only the pressure was dropping . . . and the water turned prematurely into steam, steam that was not dense enough to soak up neutrons, that let the reaction pick up speed. . . .

There was a distant thud.

"What was that?" Varazin cried, and then in the same breath: "Insert rods! Fifty percent rods, immediately!"

But the rod operator was reporting that the control rod motors were not responding; the rods would not penetrate the core. "Emergency shutdown then! At once!" Varazin shouted, and held his breath.

But the rods would not go in. "Something is blocking them!" the rod controller shouted, his voice shaking. Kalychenko heard the words incredulously, for that was impossible! There was nothing to block the rods in their sockets—why, it would mean that the interior of the reactor itself had suddenly become warped, or shrunken, or broken—

The next explosion was much louder. The walls shook. Dust sprang out from the walls, hanging like a sudden shimmer of ice fog in the air. The lights went out—all of them, even the lighted meters and dials on the full-wall instrument board.

"Oh," moaned Varazin, "my God."

"Emergency circuits!" cried the shift chief, and the man next to Kalychenko, muttering oaths, reached for the switch.

At least then the instrument lights went on again, but what they said was insane. Temperature readings simply off the scale, radiation levels that could not be believed. And the noise did not stop with the explosion. There was a rumbling thunder of walls going down, a patter of something hard falling on the roof, a crackle that could only be flame.

"Go and see what has happened to the reactor," ordered Varazin.

It was at least an instruction to follow. Most of the men in the main control room jumped up to comply. Even Kalychenko rose from his useless board, but as he started through the door he caromed off one of the other hurrying men, who swore and thrust him out of the way. Kalychenko fell heavily. By the time he got up, most of the men had rushed out to peer down at the reactor chamber.

Kalychenko's arm hurt where he had fallen on it. He hesitated, rubbing the arm, then turned and went the other way. It was unquestionably a cowardly act. It also saved his life.

CHAPTER 6

There is a difference between the nuclear reactions in a power plant—even a plant with a "positive void coefficient"—and an atomic bomb. The difference lies mainly in the fuel. Power-plant uranium is slightly enriched with the touchy isotope, U-235. Bomb uranium is very much so. This governs the speed of the reaction in which one fissioning atom releases a neutron, which strikes another atom and causes it to fission, and so on in the familiar "chain reaction." The links of this chain happen very fast in either case. In a bomb, there can be a hundred million successive links in a single second. In a power plant, only about ten thousand. For a human operator the difference doesn't really matter much, because he can't react quickly enough to intervene in either case. But within the core it is the difference between a nuclear accident and a bomb blast. If the core of Reactor No. 4 had been of weapons-grade uranium, the nuclear reaction would have gone on to involve far more of the fissionable material before the force of the explosion had time to blow it away. Since it was not, the nuclear explosion "blew itself out." Its kinetic force scattered its own fuel elements, and in the process destroyed only part of one building instead of an entire city. The later consequences, however, were of course another story.

In that first moment the shift engineer, Bohdan Kalychenko, had saved his life by running away from the reactor. On the perimeter of the plant, the hydrologist-engineer, Leonid Sheranchuk, saved his by running toward it. When he saw the great fireworks display blossom terribly overhead, he stood transfixed. Flaming debris rained down on everything, on the ground, on the buildings, on the man with the bicycle, on the man on foot twenty meters away, even on the roof of the ambulance that was slowly turning around to return to the scene of the explosion. A huge chunk of something the size of a football fell only meters away; it blazed blue, and he could feel the heat of it. Graphite? Could it be *graphite*? From the core of the reactor itself? He couldn't tell; really, if that were the case, he didn't want to know. But none of the debris fell on Sheranchuk.

At first he was shielded by the guard's cabin. Then he ran for the nearest entry to the plant—not because he reasoned out that that was the right thing to do, but because the plant was in mortal peril and he could not do anything else—and it happened to be the door to the section of the building that contained the main control room for Reactor No. 4, on the far side from the blazing, spitting inferno that had been the reactor itself, with the whole turbine hall between.

Even as he entered he heard the clanging alarm that ordered evacuation. But that was wrong! Sheranchuk knew instantly that it was wrong; you didn't run away from a nuclear plant because there was an accident; you had to do whatever you could, whatever that might be, to keep the accident from becoming terribly worse.

"Stop!" he yelled, trying to bar the door with his body, but someone roughly pushed him aside and someone else stumbled past to the red-lit outside. "No, wait!" he cried. "What are you doing? Go back to your stations! You can't leave the plant untended!"

Some swore at him, some did not hear. Some he seized by the shoulders and turned around by brute force. There were too many for him—shift operators, maintenance workers, radiation monitors, two older men he thought were observers from another plant—he even caught a glimpse of two men, wrangling as they trotted away along another corridor, that looked like Khrenov and Chief Engineer Varazin.

Then the alarm bell stopped in mid-clang. From outside, almost drowned in the hideous crackle and crash of the burning reactor building, Sheranchuk could hear the lesser sirens of the plant's fire brigade racing to the disaster point. "Do you hear?" he yelled. "The firemen are coming! Help them, get back to your work, make sure the other reactors are safe!" And then, abandoning the effort, he pushed past the dazed ones and hurried through choking smoke and alarming sounds of crash and rumble to the stairs. He was hardly aware of the long climb, and when he reached the control room for Reactor No. 4, he could not believe his eyes. Below the window, the entire turbine room was in flames. The top of the reactor building was simply gone. He could not see the burning core itself— that saved his eyes, as well as his life—but there were fires everywhere, everywhere, and the world had without warning come to an end.

What went wrong at 1:23 A.M. on that Saturday morning in Chernobyl occurred in four separate stages, but they followed so closely on each other that they were only seconds from beginning to end.

First, there was the power surge in one little corner of the vast graphite and uranium core. Although the reactor had been throttled back almost to extinction, a small section went critical; that was the atomic explosion.

The second stage was steam. The nuclear blast blew the caps off the 1,661 steam tubes. All of them blew out at once, and the broken tubes of water were exposed to naked, violently hot fuel material. The water squeezed under sixty-five atmospheres of pressure was suddenly under no pressure at all. It flashed into steam, and the steam explosion shattered the containment vessel. At that point the disaster was completely out of control and everything that followed was inevitable.

The next explosion was chemical. The terrible heat and pressure caused the steam from the ruptured pipes to break down into its gaseous elements, hydrogen and oxygen; the zirconium in which the steel pipes were clad helped the process along as a catalyst. That produced a hydrogen-oxygen explosion, the powerful reaction that drives spacecraft into orbit. The wreckage of the immense steel and concrete containment box was hurled into the air. The refueling floor, just above the reactor, was tossed aside, along with the forty-ton crane that transported the fuel rods. Fiercely radioactive material was thrown in all directions. Anything nearby that could burn was ignited. Major fires began on the tarred roofs of the building complex, and that was the third stage.

All of those things happened in an instant, and then the fourth stage completed the holocaust.

The graphite that contained the core was now exposed to the open air, with its containment shattered. Graphite is carbon. Carbon burns, even (though with more difficulty) when it is in the dense, poreless form of graphite. Moreover, thick steam from ruptured water pipes now roiled over the hot graphite. This is a classical chemical reaction that is demonstrated every day in high school chemistry labs all over the world; it is called the "water gas" process. Chemistry teachers write the equation $C + H_2O = CO + H_2$ on the blackboard for their students, meaning that the carbon and the water combine to produce carbon monoxide and free hydrogen. The carbon monoxide is quite combustible when exposed to air. The hydrogen is explosively so.

At that point the basic event was complete. The edge of the graphite blocks had begun to burn. All the fires together produced a vertical hurricane of hot gases that carried along with it a soup of fragmentary particles and even ions of everything nearby ... including the radionuclides of the core. Lanthanum-140, ruthenium-103, cesium-137, iodine-131, tellurium-132, strontium-89, yttrium-91—they laced the soot of the smoke, mingled with the plutonium and uranium of the fuel elements, spread out in a cloud that ultimately would cover half a continent. The first three explosions wrecked Reactor No. 4 of the Chernobyl Power Station, but it was the fire that carried the calamity over a million square miles.

There was no longer anything that anyone could do in the main control room for Reactor No. 4. There was nothing left of Reactor No. 4 to control. The wall of meters showed readings that were reassuringly staid or wildly impossible, but they were no longer registering any reality. The only person left in the room was the shift chief, who said, "There's nothing to do here. Everybody else has gone; you might as well get out too."

"But then, why are you still here?" Sheranchuk asked.

The man did not look well at all; he was sweating and rubbing at his mouth.

"Because I haven't been relieved yet," he said.

Halfway down the stairs again it occurred to Sheranchuk that he could simply have said the words, *I relieve you, then,* and the man might have accepted the release. But, after all, he was as safe there as anywhere else, Sheranchuk reasoned. In any case, he would not go back.

At the ground level he could not resist another look outside. There were plenty of firemen present now, from the town of Pripyat as well as the plant's own brigade, and yellow militia cars were arriving with their green lights flashing. Searchlights paled the flames from burning debris and picked out the shapes of firemen on the roofs of some of the buildings. Beyond the milling firemen on the ground was the dark hulk of the plant's office block, looking curiously deserted—because, Sheranchuk saw, all of its windows had been blown out in the force of the explosion.

Somebody was shouting at him—a militiaman, face black with smoke and sweat. "Hi, you there! Are you all right? Give a hand with these people!"

Sheranchuk did not stop to think about whether that was what he should be doing, he simply obeyed. He was glad for the order, because an order to follow was better than helplessly trying to decide what to do. For what that was he simply could not guess.

He helped a fireman to stumble toward the waiting ambulance; the man limped and held one hand to his face. He was not the only casualty already. The doctor who had given him a lift was loading a bundle of charred rags into his ambulance that Sheranchuk would not have thought human if it hadn't been cursing steadily in a faint, high-pitched voice. Three other firemen were coughing as they sat on the cement roadway, waiting for someone to bring them oxygen, or, better still, new lungs to replace the ones filled with smoke. (Why weren't they wearing respirators? Sheranchuk asked himself. But, for that matter, why wasn't he?) Glazouva, the tough old woman who ran the plant's night coffee stand, had managed to stay together long enough to help two of her customers to safety, but when Sheranchuk saw her, she was collapsed under the plaque of Lenin at the plant entrance, sobbing helplessly, not responding to anyone's attempts to talk to her. A militiaman lay stunned on the ground, his hair scorched where a bit of flaming debris from the sky had knocked him out and, likely enough, cracked his skull.

There was room for only two in the ambulance, but the doctor promised to send more from the Pripyat hospital as he got in to drive away. "And hurry, please!" Sheranchuk shouted after him.

The next ambulance to arrive, though, didn't come from Pripyat. It was from the town of Chernobyl, thirty kilometers away, and with it came half a dozen new fire trucks. There were more than a hundred firemen on the scene already, the stentorian throbbing of pumps adding to the shouts and the ominous thuds and snaps and crackling sounds from the fires; and in the center of it all, stark and incredible, the splintered walls of what had once been Reactor No. 4.

Burns, bruises, cuts, contusions, smoke inhalation, heat fatigue, simple exhaustion—put them all together and there were forty or fifty people lined up to be taken away in the ambulances shuttling between the Chernobyl Nuclear Power Station and the hospital in Pripyat, just a few kilometers away. Sheranchuk thought it strange that when the ambulances left the plant they went without sirens or bells, and seemed to take a roundabout way that circled the town before heading directly for the hospital. Was it possible they were being considerate about waking the townspeople up? He stood amid a tangle of hose lines, his mind weary of questions, pondering that irrelevant one.

"Hi! You! Get back behind the lines, you're just in the way here!" A brigade commander was shouting at him as a new fire truck, from one of the farm villages, tried to inch its way through the congestion to take station with the others. Sheranchuk shook his head, trying to clear it. What was the thing someone had said? People still unaccounted for, somewhere inside the plant?

Well, that at least was something he could do. He retreated toward the gate, slowly, until the fire commander wasn't looking at him anymore, then hurried to the nearest entrance to the plant. Exactly why he did that Sheranchuk would have been unable to say. It was partly to see if there was anyone who needed help getting out, partly because he just couldn't stay away.

Inside the building the noise from outside dwindled, but there were new and worrisome sounds. He could hear the creaks and thuds from what was left of Reactor No. 4, and an irregular throbbing that bothered him. The building he was in was attached to the turbine hall shared by Reactors 3 and 4, and it had not been left untouched. The walls were seamed with huge cracks. In places whole sections of paneling had fallen out, and these he had to dodge around. The floor of the hall he trotted along bulged in places, and was littered with fluorescent light fixtures, fire extinguishers—fire extinguishers! —and odds and ends of unidentifiable things that had been shaken off the walls and ceilings by the blast. Most of the windows here, too, had been blown out, and broken glass crunched under his feet as he raced from door to door in the halls. A nasty, choking chemical-smoky smell was everywhere. It made him cough as he trotted along, stumbling in the gloom because only a few emergency lights were still going.

Most of the doors were tidily locked for the weekend. When he flung others open, he shouted inside to see if anyone were there, but there were no answers. He was on the fifth floor of the building when he began to think he was accomplishing nothing productive with his time.

He stopped and considered. It did not occur to him that he was being courageous, only that he might be doing something that had no purpose.

The irregular throbbing was still there. He listened, frowning, one hand against the vibrating beige wall of the corridor. It took a moment to recognize that what he heard was the sound of turbines still running in the hall that served both Reactors 3 and 4.

Its control room was only two stories away, and Sheranchuk took the stairs on a dead run, arriving breathless in the room. There were only three men there, the shift chief and two operators, and they turned to greet him with angry expressions as he burst in. He stared around the room incredulously. The immaculate control room was *dirty*. When he gripped the back of a chair to steady himself, sooty dust came away on his fingers. "What's going on here?" he demanded.

"The devil knows," the shift chief snarled, waving a hand

at the instrument wall. The lights were flickering, but Sheranchuk could read the indicators.

Startled, he shouted an obscenity. "Be careful! You'll have this one off too!"

The supervisor rasped furiously in return, "Screw God and your mother, *both*! What are we supposed to do? First that cow Number Four blows up, then we try to stabilize our own reactor, then we get the order to evacuate the whole plant at once! So we begin to shut this one down—then they countermand the order and it's keep the working units working, boys, we need the power."

"But Turbine Six—" Sheranchuk began, waving a hand at the hydraulic pressure meters.

"Turbine Six your mother's ass! They've all gone mad! Your pipes have sprung a leak, plumber!"

Instinctively Sheranchuk picked up a phone to call the pump control room, but, of course, there wasn't any sound from the instrument; its cables, too, like most of the others in that building, had been fried somewhere along the line. Sheranchuk didn't wait to argue. He went down the stairs faster than he had come up, nearly falling half a dozen times in the gloom. When he reached the pump control room, he almost expected it to be empty, but at least one of his people was there—the pipefitter they called "Spring," Arkady Ponomorenko. "You're not an operator!" Sheranchuk said accusingly.

"There's no operator here," the football player explained softly, shy and deferential even now. "I was told there was damage to the pumps, so I came to take a look. Look, Leonid, the pressure is dropping; I've tried to cut in another pump, but still it falls."

"We have to have pressure," Sheranchuk snapped. "Here, let me see." He shouldered the pipefitter roughly out of his way, glaring at the intractable pressure gauges before him. But Spring had been right; of the main pumps all were already engaged, though three of them did not seem to be operating at all, and the pressure in the system was slowly creeping downward.

Sheranchuk rubbed a fist across his eyes. Outside he heard someone shouting, but he paid no attention. "We'd better have a look," he said. "There's probably no power down below; is there a light here?"

"I've already got it out," said Spring eagerly, holding out a hand torch.

"Come on, then!" But just outside the door a fire brigade commander was hurrying toward them shouting.

"Is this the place where the plumbers are? Look, you two! We've got some kind of flame going that we can't put out, somebody said it's yours."

"Flame?" Sheranchuk repeated. Then, understanding, "Oh, the hydrogen flare! Yes, of course, it only needs to be turned off—"

"Then come along and do it!" yelled the fireman.

"I'll do it," the pipefitter volunteered. "It's only a matter of turning a valve, after all, and then I'll come back to help you."

He didn't wait for permission. He simply pressed the torch into Sheranchuk's hand and loped away with the brigade commander. Sheranchuk put the matter out of his mind. It was the hydraulic system that was his business, not a simple flame that only needed to be shut off like the stove in his wife's kitchen.

Five minutes later he was standing on the bottom step of the flight that led down to the basement, shining the light into a steamy gloom, appalled at what he saw.

The hydraulic shock of the explosion had gone completely through the return-water system. Every pipe on the floor had been neatly severed at the joints, the flanges that linked the units together opened like flowers. The water that should have flowed through them back into the systems of Reactors 3 and 4 was pulsing slowly out of the opened joints to add to the steaming, centimeters deep pond on the floor of the underground pipe hall.

Sheranchuk's first rational thought was that Reactor No. 3 had to be shut down. If the return-water system was breached, at some time not very far in the future, the pumps would have nothing to send through the core of No. 3 but air, and then No. 3 would join No. 4 in blowing up. His second thought was that the person with the authority to order the shutdown was Chief Engineer Varazin, wherever Varazin might be. He reached those conclusions slowly and painstakingly; but his body acted without waiting for a formal decision. Long before he had concluded that he must find Varazin he was already out of the building, running along in the dark night away from the hullabaloo at the fire, heading toward the door of Reactor No. 2.

The door was more than a hundred meters away and, even running, Sheranchuk had time to notice that there were bright stars in the sky and a scent of something green and flowery— lilacs, again?—in the air. At this end of the great joined structures the smoky smell was gone, sucked away by the strong wind. There was nothing, Sheranchuk thought detachedly, to keep him from going on running, straight ahead, over the fence if he had to, and away.

Of course, he did nothing of the kind. When he came to the door he grabbed for the knob.

The door was locked.

Sheranchuk shouted angrily, but once again his body acted without waiting for instructions from his rational mind. The door at the end of the block would be open, though with a guard to keep intruders away.

The door was indeed open, and with no guard in sight. Sheranchuk pounded up the stairs, pausing only at the fifth level to cross quickly over to the No. 1 turbine room (no, no one there, though the turbines were howling peacefully away) and to peer into the refueling chamber over the No. 1 reactor. It was empty, too, and quite normal in every way to the eye, with the great crane squatting silently in one corner. No one was in the crane's control room, either, but Sheranchuk had not really expected to find Varazin there.

He was breathing quite hard by the time he got back across the building and up to the main control room for No. 1 Reactor.

Varazin wasn't there either. The six people in the room were the normal nighttime crew. They looked pretty strained, not to say scared, but they were carrying out their duties in the business-as-usual way. "Varazin? No," said the shift supervisor. "Someone said that when last heard from he was heading for Pripyat, but I didn't see him myself."

"Could he be in Number Two?" Sheranchuk fretted. "I'd best run over there and see—"

The shift chief looked astonished. "As you wish, but wouldn't it be better simply to telephone?"

"Telephone?" Sheranchuk blinked at the strange idea,

then recollected himself. And indeed, the phone in Control Room No. 2 was picked up at the first ring, though Varazin was not there either. The shift chief for No. 2 volunteered that Khrenov had stopped by a little earlier to urge them to stay at their posts, but Khrenov was no use to Sheranchuk. On the chance, he tried to ring No. 3, but its lines were still out of order.

"I'll have to go to Number Three," he groaned, and was gone before anyone in the room responded.

At the stairs he realized there was an alternative to seven flights down and seven back up again. The alternative was to cross the roof of the building.

But that was not to be either. As soon as he opened the door to the roof a fireman shouted at him to go back. Indeed, there wasn't any choice. All across the broad expanse of roof joining the reactor buildings was a spattering of bonfires, some tiny, some huge. Firemen were limping about in the softened waterproofing of the roof, trying to get hoses on them all at once, but as soon as one fire was out another would start up. At the entrance of the stairs for No. 3 Sheranchuk saw a curious sight picked out in the searchlights of the firefighters: a sort of black fountain, half a meter high, dark droplets flung up and cascading back down to the source. Smoke was rising from it, and as he watched, it burst into flame when the chunk of white-hot graphite that had buried itself in the bitumen finally ignited the stuff.

It would have to be seven floors down and seven back up again, after all—only now, because he had made the extra climb to the roof, it was eight each way.

When at last, sobbing and coughing for breath, he got to the main control room for Reactor No. 3 he saw that the two operators had become six, as volunteers came in to replace the absent ones. But the shift chief was obstinate. No, Chief Engineer Varazin was not here, nor had he been since the explosion. Yes, granted, there was something wrong with the turbines and the water system. But no, positively no he would not shut his reactor down.

"Do your mother! You *must*!" Sheranchuk gasped. "Are you crazy? Do you know what will happen when the water runs out?" But the engineer, his face a frozen mask, was shaking his head.

"We have no orders!" he said.

"Orders! I order you!" Sheranchuk shouted.

"In writing, then, if you please," said the engineer, ludicrously firm, "for I will not take the responsibility of failing to fulfill our plan, with only four days to go until the end of the month." And incredibly, comically, Sheranchuk found himself scribbling a written order for which he had no authority at all—*I direct that Unit No. 3 be placed at once in standby mode*—before the man would stand aside and allow the operators to get on with their work. Only two operators now, Sheranchuk noted; the others had fled. The two remaining, cursing and swearing, labored over the boards until a series of thuds, almost lost in the constant noise of fire and firefighting, told them that all the boron rods were firmly socketed.

"What are you doing, Sheranchuk?" asked a gentle, sorrowing voice from behind him.

Sheranchuk knew before he turned that it was the Director of the First Department, Gorodot Khrenov. "I am helping shut down this reactor," he said.

"Yes, yes," Khrenov said absently. The liquid brown eyes seemed clouded, and the man's expression was detached. "You appear to have given orders in matters that don't concern you," he observed, gazing around the room. The operators stood watching the encounter.

"He only told us to do what we have orders to do anyway in such a case," one of them called.

Khrenov's eyes swept over the man, whose face stiffened. Sheranchuk spoke up to draw the fire to himself. "The Ministry must be notified at once," he said.

Khrenov's eyes widened, but the operator spoke again. "That's been done. I telephoned a report to Moscow myself."

"Ah," said Khrenov, nodding. "Someone else who takes responsibility onto himself. And what did you report, then?"

"That Reactor Number Four had exploded, of course. I know," the shift man added apologetically, "that that is the duty of the Chief Engineer, but I couldn't find him."

Khrenov said thoughtfully, "Chief Engineer Varazin felt that he had the obligation to make sure our guests were safe. I believe he is in Pripyat with them now. Well. Let us get on with controlling this—accident. And remember, at all costs, we must avoid panic."

*   *   *

Avoid panic? Yes, of course, Sheranchuk kept telling himself. That was absolutely essential.

But it was also impossible. A dozen times there flashed through Sheranchuk's mind a schooldays parody of an English poem—was it by Rudyard Kipling?—that went:

If you can keep your head when all about you
Are losing theirs,
Then you probably simply haven't understood what has
    been happening.

The difficulty for Sheranchuk was that he understood what was happening all too well. It terrified him in ways he had never expected to feel. It was not simply that he himself might have been in danger, it was the ending of an age. Helping once more with the endless task of aiding the casualties to the never-caught-up shifts of ambulances, he could hardly remember that peaceful time, not yet six hours ago, when he had in calm and leisurely fashion left his flat to look in on the Chernobyl Nuclear Power Station.

There was no calm at the Chernobyl station now, nor leisure either. Sheranchuk was astonished, as he passed by a cluster of fire-brigade commanders, to learn that they had declared the fire officially out an hour before. True, little blazes were springing up now and then, where hot bits from the core continued to try to ignite whatever they touched. Certainly the core itself was not out, looked as though it never would be out as its blue-white glare starkly illuminated the charred walls around it. And certainly nothing seemed to halt the steady trickle of wounded and sick men. There were still burns, still sprains and worse as the firemen slipped and fell on the sticky, slippery roofs, but more and more of the men were simply exhausted, pale, sweating, sometimes vomiting uncontrollably.

One of them was the man from his own department, the pipefitter called Spring. "Sorry," he apologized as Sheranchuk spoke to him. "I just feel sick—but I got the hydrogen flare out for them, Leonid."

"I was certain you would," said Sheranchuk, and gazed thoughtfully after him as he climbed by himself into an ambulance and was taken away. But there were others to claim his attention. A tall, slender man was moaning as he sat clutching at his burned feet; for a moment Sheranchuk thought it was the operator, Kalychenko, but it turned out to be a fireman named Vissgerdis. As Sheranchuk turned away, someone grabbed him and shook him roughly. He did not recognize the woman at first. "Fool," she was screaming at him. "Where is your protective clothing? Do you want to die for nothing?"

He had forgotten about radiation.

And it was not until he was pulling the hood over his head that he realized that the woman had been his wife.

Really, there was not much left for someone like Leonid Sheranchuk to do—the professionals had taken over—but he could not help trying to do something anyway. When there were enough trained medical personnel on the scene to do a better job helping the injured than he could, he went back inside the buildings, once more looking for any possible wounded or simply dazed people who might have crawled away into one of the storage areas or workshops. There weren't any, as far as he could tell. He was alone. It was hard and hot work, and not without danger—he searched the entire building of Reactor No. 3. Inside it was dark, and even with the flashlight he had managed to cling to all this time he was constantly stumbling over debris. Only a wall was between him and the fulminating ruin of No. 4, and No. 4 sounded at every moment as though it were trying to come to him right through the wall. Even the cracked walls radiated heat, soaked up on one side from the 4000-degree graphite and sent on to him from the other. He peered out at the roof, where there were no visible fires anymore, but still plenty of firemen, almost ankle deep in the syrupy bitumen, still playing hoses on the smoldering embers.

Sighing, he made his way back down to ground level. He wondered if anyone had told those firemen that it was not only heat and smoke and burns they faced, but the invisible, lethal storm of radiation that billowed up at them with the smoke.

In the four months Sheranchuk had been at Chernobyl he had diligently studied all the literature on nuclear power plants. He had understood the special dangers of a core meltdown, and the particular risk of a graphite fire in an RBMK—after all, there had been experience of it abroad. The British had had one of their own, at a place called Windscale, decades before. But nothing in his reading or imagination had prepared him for this. It occurred to him almost to wish that Smin had never telephoned him with the unexpected job offer; certainly nothing in the burning of peat could have produced this particular nightmare.

But he had no time for such thoughts. No one had time for anything in this endless night in which every second was filled with a new alarm or a new task. Yet Sheranchuk never forgot that he was Simyon Smin's Comrade Plumber. He kept an eye on his own special charges whenever he could spare a thought from the urgencies of his rescue work. His pumps and pipes and valves were still doing as much as possible of their job. Cooling water still flowed out of the pond; in the two working reactors, the circuits were still pumping through the cores.

Firefighting was, after all, a matter of plumbing. When he saw the huge hoses that were sucking water from the pond for the firemen, swearing men holding the intake ends of the hoses underwater, he almost wondered if they would pump the pond dry. But that was only a fantasy fear. The locks to the river were wide open, and they would not pump the Pripyat empty in a thousand years. There were firemen there now from, it seemed, scores of communities; even Kiev was not the farthest. There were militiamen to reinforce the plant's security forces from as many; ambulances from he could not guess where were screaming in with doctors and medical assistants, and roaring away again with the injured. Tank trucks of gasoline were refueling the firemen's pumpers as they worked. And the noise was endless and indescribable.

At some point someone thrust two tin cups into Sheranchuk's hands. One cup was of hot, concentrated tea, the other pure vodka. Sheranchuk slumped to the ground for a moment as he swallowed them both, turn and turn, gazing upward. He had not paused to see what the pyre looked like before. What it looked like was terrifying. A red-bellied smoke cloud was shooting straight up from the burning reactor, only bending away toward the north and east when it was so high that it was almost out of sight. The stars were gone; the smoke obscured them.

But Sheranchuk had no time to gaze; already someone was

shouting for him, waving him toward the perimeter fence, where the latest batch of injured firemen were groaning on the ground. These, he saw, had been fighting the fire from the top of the turbine building next to the shattered reactor, and they, too, had been grievously harmed by its smoldering tar surface. He helped carry two men with severe foot burns away, and as he deposited the second one at the foot of a thick, short man in enveloping hood and coveralls, the man said softly, "Well, Comrade Plumber Sheranchuk! We've made a mess of it this time, haven't we?" And he saw the man was Simyon Smin.

CHAPTER 7

Simyon Smin's wife, Selena, could not be said to be a bad woman. No one would deny, however, that she is a collector. A humbler Soviet woman would be the kind who never left home without her little string bag, the *avoska*, "just on the chance" that she might happen somewhere to find something worth the trouble of buying. Selena, as the wife of the Deputy Director of the Chernobyl Nuclear Power Station, does not have to do that. She gets what she wants, or nearly. More nearly than most. She has special stores to shop in, though she must go to Kiev or Moscow for the best of them. She even has the "distribution," that special perk of the high in rank that allows her to order food over the telephone—and not just what the local gastronom might carry, but high-quality food from the listed stores—and have it delivered to her flat or dacha. This is a source of great pleasure to Selena, who was a not quite successful dancer when she married Simyon Smin. There were no such luxuries in Selena's early life. She has eaten well since then, and if she no longer has a dancer's figure, Smin does not seem to mind. Selena has a job of her own, of course; she is in charge of cultural and physical fitness matters at the Chernobyl plant, and often, at eleven in the morning and one in the afternoon, when the handsome young couple in leotards do their daily exercises on the television to the accompaniment of a

pianist and the orders of a trainer, Selena joins the workers and leads their calisthenics. Her position technically
puts her in the First Department of the plant, under the
direction of Gorodot Khrenov, but Khrenov never inter-
feres with the wife of the Deputy Director. He only makes
sure that the Deputy Director knows that.

There was not much sleep on that Saturday morning for Selena
Smin. At six she got up and dressed slowly, wondering what
the urgent summons from the plant had meant. At seven, while
she was having a cup of tea with her mother-in-law, there was
another knock on the door, and this time it was a telegram:

REMAINING HERE. REQUEST YOU AND VASSILI STAY IN KIEV
FOR WEEKEND. SMIN.

"But I can't do that," complained Selena. "I have things
to do, and the boy should not miss his school."

"He has missed it already," said old Aftasia Smin practically.

That was true enough; Vassili was still curled on the
couch, blond head buried under the blankets as the women
talked softly. But still! Remain in Kiev to do what? Without a
car, without even a telephone? "I can't even call him to find
out what this is all about," she complained.

"You can do as I do," Aftasia said. "The Didchuks have a
telephone."

"The Didchuks have one! And we do not! I will certainly
speak to Simyon about this again." Selena thought for a moment. "And which apartment are they in, then?" she asked.

It was only one floor below. Two minutes later Selena had
descended the dark stairs and knocked politely at their door.
The Didchuks were at home—all of them, for it seemed that
there was a child and a couple of grandparents in the flat as
well as the teachers themselves. They were all awake. They
were not fully dressed—the woman had her hair in curlers, the
man was wearing a robe over his trousers—but they were, of
course, quite polite, even welcoming, and certainly she could
use their telephone.

But then it seemed she could not, really, because all of the
lines to the plant were engaged. They remained engaged, were
engaged on the first time she tried them and on the fifth. The

Didchuks politely went about their morning business, stepping around her when they had to come into the little living room with its small TV set and worn, brocaded couch and window that had thin, bright drapes. The old father greeted her in a mannerly way on his way to the bathroom. The old mother came out of the kitchen and offered her breakfast, which she declined graciously, but accepted a cup of tea, brought to her by the ten-year-old daughter of the teachers. Even the telephone in her own flat in the town of Pripyat did not answer; it was not engaged, but it rang uselessly until she put it down. So Smin, wherever he was, was at least not at home. "Well, what a nuisance," she declared, smiling at the young woman. "But what pretty drapes! You have done so much with this room!"

The woman said modestly, "It is difficult when we both work."

"For me too," Selena agreed, and chatted amiably with the young woman and her tiny, blonde mother-in-law while, in her mind, she tried fretfully to decide what to do with this day. A day in Kiev with the car, yes, that was always quite useful. In fact, it was a treat. There were places to go and stores to visit, and then one could count on finding a friend or two at the club for lunch. But without the car—

The thought of the club gave her an idea. "One more call, if you don't mind," she begged prettily, and dialed the Great Gate Hotel. But the operator could not find any Mr. and Mrs. Dean Garfield from America on the roster.

"You must have a room number," the operator explained. "One cannot complete a call without a room number, of course."

Selena exploded, "What nonsense! I am Selena Smin and I am making this call for S. M. Smin, the Director of the Chernobyl Nuclear Power Station."

The operator retreated. For quite a while, leaving Selena to hold the whispering, hissing phone while she thought wistfully how nice it would have been if she could have invited the Americans not merely to lunch at the club—pleasant though the club was—but to their own home in Pripyat, to see how a decent Soviet family lived in a decent home, not this Khrushchev tenement. (But, of course, that was only a fantasy, since one did not invite foreigners to Pripyat.) And then when the operator returned she said only, with some satisfaction, "The Americans you speak of are no longer in the hotel."

"But of course they are in the hotel! I saw them only last night!"

"They have departed," the operator said triumphantly. "Perhaps if you were to consult Intourist, they could inform you of their itinerary."

"Ah, well," sighed Selena to the young couple, who were beginning to glance surreptitiously at their watches—they would have to leave for their Saturday morning classes. "Simply one more call, if I may, just to call for a taxi."

But where was she to go in the taxi? To the club? And do what there, especially with Vassili? Who should, in any case, be on his way to school by now. And as she looked out the window, she heard distant thunder and saw that it was beginning to rain.

CHAPTER 8

SATURDAY, APRIL 26

A Saturday in the Soviet Union is not quite like a Saturday in London or New York. The Soviets do not work a five-day week. Schools are in session. The working force works. But a Saturday is still, after all, part of a weekend, even in the Soviet Union, and those who are in a position to get away for some relaxation generally do.

In Moscow this Saturday, for instance, the telephone rang from Chernobyl. The duty officer at the Ministry of Nuclear Energy heard the voice say, "This is Vitaly Varazin, Chief Engineer at the Chernobyl Power Station," and the officer exploded.

"At last! What has been going on? We had a call that there had been a serious accident, nothing more, and no one answers your telephones?"

"Yes," said Varazin, "Quite a nuisance that was. Communications have been interrupted because of a fire in a generating unit. But emergency crews responded at once."

What the duty officer responded was not quite audible. It was definitely obscene, for he had spent a nasty hour in the middle of the night trying to track down his superior. Unfortunately his superior had left the night before for his dacha at Peredelkino, and so the duty officer had been forced to act on his own. He groaned as he thought of what those actions had been. "The situation is under control, then?" he demanded.

"Quite under control, yes."

"Then tell me something," the duty officer snarled."What are you going to do with the planeload of experts in the special commission that is even now on its way to Kiev?"

There was a pause on the line. "A special commission?" Varazin asked.

"Twenty-four people," the duty officer said grimly. "All woken up in the middle of the night on the basis of the first report from Chernobyl. Their plane left Moscow at six."

"I see," Varazin said faintly. The duty officer waited him out, drumming his fingers on the desktop.

"Well," Varazin said at last, "it was quite a *serious* fire, to be sure. Certainly we can use guidance from the Ministry."

"Certainly you are going to get it," snapped the duty officer, "because the first echelons will be helicoptered to your plant in the next hour or so."

"Thank you," said Varazin softly, and hung up.

His voice sounded unhappy to the duty officer, which gave the officer some satisfaction. Actually he was feeling much better. His worst fears were allayed, responsibility for the twenty-four man commission was off his back, and now he lifted the phone again and called off the search for his chief. It would be time enough to disturb the highest authorities, he decided, when the full report was in. And with any luck, he'd be off by then, anyway.

In Novosibirsk, at the headquarters of the All-Union Ministry of Power Plant Structures, they took the call more seriously—until they found that the Yemeni visitors had left before it happened. At least, they reassured one another, there had not been the embarrassment of seeing one of their plants wreck itself in the presence of three potential foreign customers.

In Kiev it was another matter. The load dispatcher was shocked. "Yes, all right, two of your units are damaged. Naturally they can't generate power—but, really, why must you shut the other two down as well? A precaution? Precautions are very good, but do you have any idea what sort of trouble that makes for me?" And when he hung up he was swearing; Chernobyl was the plant he could always count on, and where on a Saturday morning was he going to find three or four thousand megawatts of electrical power to replace it?

*   *   *

When the phone rang in the headquarters of the International Atomic Energy Authority in Vienna it might have caused more action, except that this particular call was not to give information but to ask for some.

The engineer on duty put down his cup of tea to answer the telephone. His caller had an accent, quickly explained when he said he was calling from the Soviet Ukraine. "Do you have information on controlling graphite fires in reactors?" he asked politely.

The duty engineer that morning happened to be an Englishman; he had no difficulty in understanding the question. "Do you mean the Windscale sort of thing? Yes, I think so. That was a Wigner-effect event." He paused to see if he would be required to explain the Wigner effect. The Wigner effect is a change that takes place in the molecular structure of graphite after long exposure to ionizing radiation. The molecular structure stores energy from the radiation. This has potential dangers, and so once a year graphite moderators of that sort must be "annealed"—which is to say, heated up sufficiently that the molecular bonds slacken and relax when cooled. In England's Windscale in 1957 that heating got away from its operators, causing the graphite to burn and destroy the reactor.

"One moment," the Ukrainian said. There was a sound of muffled voices, and then the man came back on the line. "No, not in regard to the Wigner effect," he said. "I ask of control measures. Of ways for dealing with such an event if it should occur."

"You mean to ask how they put it out?" the Englishman said. "They simply kept drenching the thing with water. Diverted most of a river onto it, if I remember aright. Wait just a moment, I think we do have some documents in the file—shall I mail you a set?"

The voice on the phone disappeared again. When it returned it said politely, "No, thank you, we do not think that will be necessary."

The Englishman hung up, finished his tea, and examined the pot to see if there might be another blackened cup left. That, he thought, had been a curious call. He looked through his files to see what he could find about graphite-moderated reactors in the USSR. There were plenty of them, but nothing that seemed relevant to the call.

Still, he wanted to tell someone about it and so, after a moment's consideration, he picked up the telephone again and dialed a colleague in the United Kingdom. "What do you reckon they're up to?" he asked, after recounting the call.

The colleague yawned; he had been sleeping in on a rainy English weekend morning. "Russkies," he said, explaining everything. "You know what they like those graphite reactors for. The things are useful to make a little plutonium on the side. They don't want to know about controlling anything, in my opinion. They're simply hoping to find some better ways of increasing the yield."

"It could be that, I suppose," said the man in Vienna. "They've got a mass of those RBMKs going. I found a note from one of our masters, warning that the beasts were not entirely safe."

"That would be Marshall, I expect," said the one in London. That was Lord Walter Marshall, head of the United Kingdom's General Electricity Generating Board. "That was donkey's years ago, wasn't it?"

The engineer in Vienna said doubtfully, "You don't think I should report it to someone?"

"Report it to whom? And what is there to report? No," said the voice from England, "I'd forget it if I were you. It's what I'm going to do myself."

CHAPTER 9

If Vassili Smin lived in Moscow, he might easily be one of the westernized, pampered, English-speaking, *Playboy*-reading "Golden Youth" whose Wrangler jeans and Gucci loafers make the disco scene in the Blue Bird nightclub. Vassili has as much going for him as any of the spoiled Moscow darlings. His father is high in the Party, as well as being the Deputy Director of an immense industrial complex. Vassili himself had been a leader in the kids' patriotism-Communism-scouting organization, the Pioneers, had moved up to join the Komsomol as soon as he reached the tenth grade in school. He has spending money almost equal to the wages of the peasant girl who lovingly makes his bed every morning and unfailingly shines his shoes. Vassili, however, does not live in Moscow. He lives in a small town a hundred and thirty kilometers from Kiev, and even in the city of Kiev the most pampered youth are less spoiled than in the capital. The other thing that makes Vassili unlike Moscow's Golden Youth is that he has a lot of his father in him. He certainly wishes to succeed. But he knows that the way to do that is, first, to make sure of getting into a first-rate college, and, second, to join the Party as soon as he can. The Party meetings will surely be boring, but there is no other way to a high position. And, although his father has the influence to get him into almost any college in the USSR, he is far from powerful enough to plant his boy in a leadership post for life. Vassili knows that what happens after college will depend on his grades.

It would also, Vassili knew, be helped along a good deal by commendations from his Komsomol leaders, but that was not the only reason why, that Saturday morning, he left his grandmother's apartment and took a bus to the outskirts of Kiev. Then he stood on the edge of the Pripyat road, holding a five-ruble note in the air for passing vehicle drivers to see. He was not merely reluctant to miss a day's school, or the Saturday-afternoon meeting of the league for young Communists, the Komsomol, which would put the finishing touches on their May Day plans. He was also worried.

A five-ruble note was statistically certain to get a ride from at least half of any random selection of truck, ambulance, or private-car drivers, but this morning it wasn't working. There was traffic in plenty, but most of it was official and all of it in a hurry. Vassili saw a dozen fire trucks, military vehicles, and militia cars go by before, at last, a lumbering farm truck pulled up beside him. "What's going on?" the driver demanded, leaning out of the window without opening the door.

"I don't know," said Vassili, waving the bill at him. "But I have to get to Pripyat."

"Pripyat! I'm not going to Pripyat. But I can take you fifty kilometers."

"For one ruble, not five," Vassili bargained, and settled finally for two. Thrown into the bargain was nearly half an hour's conversation from the collective farmer, divided almost equally between complaints about the stinginess of customers at the free market in Kiev and invective against the other drivers on the road, who raced past him at a hundred and twenty kilometers an hour. Nor were they the normal assortment of trucks and buses. The bulk of the traffic still seemed to be emergency vehicles, all in a hurry, and Vassili was beginning to get seriously worried.

When at last the kolkhozist turned off onto a side road, Vassili was picked up almost at once by a soldier who was driving, of all things, a water cannon. "What, is there a riot in Pripyat?" Vassili begged, aghast at the notion, but the driver only shook his head. His orders were to go to a checkpoint thirty kilometers south of the town. He had no other information; it was all in a day's work to him, and he resented losing his Saturday to it.

Then they came to the checkpoint.

Vassili hopped down from the truck, frowning. There was a barricade across the road. Civilian vehicles had been turned back, and had already worn muddy ruts through the margins of a field of sunflowers as they turned around. There were soldiers there manning the barricades, and with them a rabble of young people—young people?—why, Vassili saw with shock, they were Komsomols! From his own troop! One of them his friend Boris Sheranchuk; and as soon as Boris saw him he waved him over. "Here, we've been called out to help the militiamen, so you're on duty too."

"Duty for what?"

"To make sure no one gets past, of course. There's been an awful accident at the power plant."

"An accident!" Vassili cried. "Have you—do you know where my father is?"

"I don't even know where my own father is. It's bad. People have been killed."

For all that long day Boris, Vassili, and the other young Communists were kept on duty. It was not their job to turn vehicles back, that was work for the militiamen. For the Komsomols the task was to make sure that none of the diverted vehicles got hopelessly stuck in the sunflower field, to try to keep them from doing more damage to the crop than was absolutely necessary, and, when trucks turned up with water and food for the guards, to help serve it. It was not glamorous work. And it was not enjoyable, for no one seemed to have any hard facts about what was happening at Chernobyl. The traffic was almost all one-way going in. The vehicles that came back were generally ambulances, and none of them stopped.

To be sure, the best source of news was the sky to the north, for there an occasional wavering dark pillar of smoke on the horizon told its own story. Vassili would not have believed there could be so much to burn. When a truck at last came from the city and stopped, Vassili was the first to reach its side. "Is the city burning?" one Komsomol demanded, but the people in the truck were only young Pioneers, twelve and thirteen years old, and they knew very little. No, certainly Pripyat itself was not on fire; what an idea! But yes, of course, the fire in the power plant was very severe, no one could say when it might be under control; and none of them had any knowledge at all of Vassili Smin's father. Or of Boris Sheranchuk's; or, indeed, of anything at all except that when their Pioneer troop had been called out to put up these signs, they had been frightened. The signs were placards with the ominous three-cornered radiation symbol in bright red, and a warning to keep out; the Pioneers toddled off in groups of three and four to hammer them into place in a perimeter that would completely surround Chernobyl.

Surround Chernobyl? In a perimeter thirty kilometers away? Vassili could not swallow the thought.

The sun was dropping toward the horizon, but inside his protective smock Vassili was sweating. When it got dark and another truck came up, with bread, tea and vegetable soup, he hung back until the militiamen had gotten theirs. Then he took his tin tray away to a corner under an old tree, and while he ate, he wept, staring at the ugly red glow that hung over the northern horizon.

He stayed at his post until after midnight, when a Soviet Army truck took the exhausted Komsomols back to Pripyat.

After the manner of boys and puppies, Vassili was ready to drop, but even so he had enough energy to be astonished at how peaceful the town was. Could it be possible that they didn't know? Of course, at midnight one did not expect much activity in the streets of Pripyat—but *nothing*? When he got out of the elevator and entered the sixteenth-floor apartment he shared with his parents, he thought of eating and dismissed it, thought of bathing and put that aside, too, but stood for a moment at the window that looked out toward the plant.

He could not see the smoke in the darkness, but there were still lights there.

He threw himself onto his bed, thoroughly shaken. His father's power station *could not* have blown up! It was the very latest triumph of Soviet technology, with all the safety features his father had been proud to display to him as they toured the giant plant. It was too big and too magnificent to explode! And, besides, it was his father's.

CHAPTER 10

At nine o'clock on this Saturday morning the Chernobyl Nuclear Power Station is no longer a part of the Ukrainian electrical grid. No energy flows out along the high-tension lines. Reactors 1, 2, and 3 have been tripped to zero output, and the terrible fires—the fires in the buildings, at least—have been declared out long since. It is only the hundreds of tons of graphite in the exposed core of Reactor No. 4 that continue to burn. So far only one edge of the graphite is ablaze, with a blue-white heat as painful to the eyes as looking at the sun itself, and the firemen can do nothing about it. Their hoses still play on the roofs of the nearby buildings, on the smoldering heaps of rubble, on the walls around the wreck of No. 4, but they have not been able to extinguish the graphite. It is simply too hot; the water flashes into instant steam. There is another problem with using the fire hoses. The water that does trickle away from the core and from each bit of radioactive matter, small or large, dissolves radioactive material as it flows; and then it carries that radioactivity with it wherever it happens to go.

On that morning Vassili Smin's father was sitting in a militia car ten meters outside the gate of the Chernobyl Nuclear Power Station, feverishly making notes. They had the windows rolled up tight in the car, and the militia colonel at the wheel was smoking a Bulgarian-tobacco cigarette, the kind that laborers bought for forty kopecks a pack. The car was filled with the heavy smoke. Smin didn't notice. He didn't even hear when, now and then, the militiaman picked up the microphone and issued commands on his radio, or when messages crackled in. Smin had pushed back the white hood of his garment because it made his face and neck itch—he was sweating, and the scar tissue could not sweat—and trying to get everything down while it was all fresh. It was a list of the things that had gone wrong because of deficiencies in training, equipment, and supplies. It was becoming quite a long list:

> Drs. not trained radiat. sickness
> Fire brigs. not trained radiat. proceds.
> No radiat. protect. garments for station
> No respirators.
> Need equip. for station + near towns, etc.
> Need reptd. drills emgcy proceds.

Smin paused, scratching the itchy scars just below his ear and gazing blankly out at the emergency vehicles that were standing around, engines running, while the few active firemen continued to play their cooling hoses on the endangered walls. None of the things he had written, he realized, attacked the real question: what in the name of God had gone wrong? He wondered if he would ever find out. The stories he had pieced together—that one by one the operators had systematically dismantled all the safety systems, just when the reactor was at its touchiest condition—were simply too fantastic. Smin refused to believe that anyone in the Chernobyl plant could have been that arrogantly stupid. It was almost easier to accept the possibility of that word that had not been much heard in the Soviet Union in recent decades: *sabotage.*

But that, too, was impossible to believe! Yes, certainly, the CIA or the Chinks, they were quite capable of blowing up a power plant simply to inconvenience the Soviets. But there was no way such a thing could have been possible without the concurrence of everyone in the main control room—and to believe that was as preposterous as to believe in simple, crass, spectacularly gross stupidity.

And the cost of it! Not simply the ruble cost, though that

was going to be heavy. Not even the cost to the Plan; it was the cost to human beings that weighed on Simyon Smin. So many casualties! Nearly one hundred of the worst already on their way to the airstrip in the town of Chernobyl, where a special plane was going to take them right up to Moscow for treatment. And two dead already! One man never found, but dead all right because he had been last seen in the reactor hall itself, minutes before the blast. The other dying early this morning in the Pripyat hospital, with burns over eighty percent of his body and terrible radiation damage as well . . . and there would be more—

He bent to the pad on his knee and wrote quickly:

Anti-flash cream?
Spl. burn facil. in hosp.?

"Comrade Smin?"

"Eh?" He looked up at the militiaman, who was replacing the microphone on the dashboard again.

"I said the helicopter from Kiev will be landing one kilometer away, by the river, in five minutes. With the team from the Ministry of Nuclear Energy."

"Oh, of course," said Smin, looking at his watch—nine o'clock! They'd made good time. "Would you mind driving me out to meet them?" And as the militia officer started to say of course, Smin said sharply, "'No, wait. Can you turn on that outside speaker of yours?" He was scowling out the window at the idle firemen in their white hoods and jumpsuits, clustered in knots as they watched their comrades playing water on the walls. "You there!" Smin cried into the microphone, and heard his amplified voice bounced back to him. "Get those men behind shelter! Have you forgotten everything you've just been taught about radiation?" As they turned to gaze at him, he snarled, "Do you want your balls fried?"

It was satisfying to see them jump—but how long had they been standing in the open like that before he noticed them?

As the militia car pulled away from the plant gate, Smin caught a glimpse through the trees of the bright towers of the town of Pripyat, prettily colored in the morning sun. He should, he thought, have put his message to his wife and son more strongly, so that they would keep away until things became more normal—

If things ever would. But Smin, at least, had a pretty clear idea of what the radionuclides that had erupted from Reactor No. 4 were going to do to the buildings, streets, and soil of Pripyat, once the wind changed—were already doing, no doubt, to the little farm villages in Byelorussia, just across the border to the north.

Smin recognized the little park by the river. It was where people swam in the summer, and the plant's football team practiced on its greensward. Now the goal cages had been torn away and the people there were not playing football. Some were on stretchers, waiting for the airlift to the larger hospital in Chernobyl.

Smin was surprised to see Chief Engineer Varazin bustling toward him. The man was neatly dressed, even freshly shaved, though the lines on his face suggested he had not slept. "Eh, Simyon," Varazin sighed gloomily. "What a night! Wouldn't you know, the minute the Director goes out of town!" Then he brightened. "You'll be glad to know that I've made sure all our observer guests are safe, and I've made arrangements for the new ones from the Ministry."

"Well, that's very good, anyway," Smin said wonderingly.

"Exactly! Put the past behind us. Get on with the work ahead, right, Simyon? But I'd better be doing it than talking about it," Varazin said, and trotted away, glancing up at the sky.

Smin shook his head. Was it possible the man thought that escorting the observers to Pripyat would do anything to ameliorate the miseries that lay ahead for him? Well, for both of them, to be sure, Smin thought resignedly; but there was no time to worry about that sort of thing now. He peered up into the sky. He could hear the helicopter approaching from the southeast, but it did not come directly to the pad. It veered away and slowly circled the Chernobyl plant. Sensible of them to take a good look at the ruin, Smin thought, and wished he could do the same.

"Deputy Director Smin?" It was one of the Ponomorenko brothers, the footballer they called Autumn.

Smin searched for his actual name and came up with it. "Hello, Vladimir. No game today, after all."

"No. Can you tell me, please, if you know anything of my cousin Vyacheslav? They say he is missing."

"Was he on duty?" Smin thought for a moment. "Yes, of course he was. On the night shift. Well, no, I haven't seen him. Probably he had the good sense to go home when the plant was evacuated."

"He isn't at home, Deputy Director Smin. Thank you, I'll go on looking." Ponomorenko hesitated. "My brother is in the hospital over there," he said, waving toward the distant towers of Pripyat. "He got some radio thing."

"He'll have the best of care," Smin promised, trying to sound more certain than he was. "We can't spare the Four Seasons, after all!" He glanced up. The helicopter from Kiev had completed its leisurely tour and was fluttering down toward them. "Well, here come the experts from the Ministry of Nuclear Energy, so we'll have everything straightened out quickly now."

It was a way of trying to reassure the football player, but it was not, Smin admitted to himself, a realistic statement. Even the experts from the Ministry had had no experience of anything like this, since nothing like it had ever happened before. Not even in America, Smin thought wryly, remembering how he had boasted to the Americans just the night before. It was a definite first in nuclear technology, and once again the Soviet Union had led the way.

There were four of the experts from the Ministry of Nuclear Energy jumping out of the helicopter, and Chief Engineer Varazin was ducking under the blades even before they had stopped revolving to greet them. Smin recognized a couple of the men, but Varazin introduced them all around anyway. "Comrades Istvili, Rasputin, Lestilyan," he said, and waited for them to introduce the fourth man. They didn't. Rasputin, the one Smin had not met before, shook Smin's hand heartily.

"No, I am not the mad monk," he said, smiling. "I'm simply from the section on biological effects of radiation. I'm not related to the writer, either."

"A pity," Varazin said chattily. "My wife is a great admirer of his thrillers." He hesitated. "I had thought perhaps our Director Zaglodin might have been with you."

Istvili shook his head. He was a tall, heavyset man, with

the dark, almost Mediterranean look of a Georgian. "We hoped that, too, but he had not been located when our special plane left Moscow—at six this morning," he added. "It's been a long trip."

"Of course," Varazin sympathized. "Well. I've prepared a command post just five kilometers away; it will all be ready when you require it. I think it will be suitable. But first I'm sure you would like to inspect the station—"

Smin was listening in amazement to the casual chatter; why, Varazin was talking to these men exactly as though they were visiting Yemenis, no more than a mild annoyance to a busy man. "Can I borrow your helicopter?" he asked brusquely.

Istvili understood at once. "Of course. It's worth a look from above. Then"—he glanced at his watch—"it's eighteen minutes after nine now. Can we meet at ten in this command post for a first conference? Good, then let's go."

Simyon Smin had seldom been in a helicopter before, but the rapid, efficient movements of the pilot didn't interest him on this occasion. His eyes were all for the plant. "Stay away from that plume of smoke," he ordered the pilot. "Not too low—not below two hundred meters. But get as close as you can."

"Of course," the pilot said, not even looking around—no doubt he had had the same orders from his last passengers. But Smin wasn't listening, either. He was staring out the window, scuttling over to the seat on the other side as the helicopter turned, keeping the plant always in view. As they approached from the undamaged side, over the cooling pond, the plant looked almost normal—at least, if you did not count the pall of dark smoke that was drifting slowly northward from the still-smoldering embers. Firemen were methodically removing their suction hoses from the pond. The roof was not yet in view.

Then it was, and Smin groaned. There were still firemen on the roof, and they were still playing hoses on patches that smoked. Idiots! Didn't they know the debris on the roof was radioactive—some of it right out of the core itself? Then, as the helicopter lurched upward, the ruin of Reactor No. 4 came into view, and Smin forgot about the endangered firemen.

From the ground he had not seen quite how terrible the destruction was. There was actually nothing at all left of the reactor building, no refueling hall, no roof. He saw twisted metal that might once have been the refueling crane. Most of all, he saw the naked core itself. He squinted between his fingers, instinctively protected his eyes, suddenly aware that even two hundred meters was not too far to be from that radioactive ember. An arc of brilliant blue-white light from one edge showed the burning graphite—not more than ten percent of the exposed surface burning now, Smin thought, and wondered if that was less than an hour ago—or more.

The helicopter veered away from the smoke plume. The pilot called, "Shall I duck under the smoke? Or would you like to go back around again?"

Smin sank back in his seat. "I've seen enough," he said.

Varazin's "command center" turned out to be nothing more or less than Varazin's own comfortable dacha, set a hundred meters off the road in the fir forest. Its large main room was twice the size of anything in Smin's flat, but it was crowded by the time the meeting began. Smin, Varazin, the four men from the Ministry, the general of fire brigades, the head doctor from the Pripyat hospital, Khrenov (looking worn but confident), two men from the Council of Ministers of the Ukrainian Republic (when had they arrived?), half a dozen from the Pripyat Party Committee, an Army general. Smin looked at the crowd in dismay. This was an emergency meeting, not a Party rally. It was his firm conviction that the effectiveness of any conference was in inverse ratio to the number of people sitting around the table, and over five you might as well sleep through the proceedings.

But Istvili, the Georgian from the Ministry of Nuclear Energy, took firm charge. For a man who'd been wakened at four in the morning and had been traveling ever since, he was surprisingly clear-eyed and collected. "We won't wait for the people coming from Kiev by car," he announced. "Our first order of business is a situation report. I understand the Chernobyl plant is now completely shut down."

"I gave the order for Reactors One and Two myself," nodded Varazin. "As a precaution. Of course, I consulted the load dispatchers in Kiev first."

"So that situation is stable," said Istvili. "Now we come to damage control."

"The fire was extinguished at eight minutes after three this morning," said the general of fire brigades.

Smin cut in. "Yes, but, excuse me, your firemen are still on the roof and the hoses are still going."

The general looked down his nose at him. "They are cooling the scene down and extinguishing small outbreaks."

"I don't think I am making myself clear. All that water from the hoses is contaminated with radioactivity. It must go somewhere, and wherever it goes it's dangerous."

"Radiation," said the general thoughtfully. "That's not our concern. Our business is fighting fires, and we put this one out in an hour and a half. Radiation is your business."

"It's the business of your firemen too! They're in great danger, out there without protective gear!"

Istvili raised a hand. "Please. Two issues have been raised now, contamination of water from the runoff from the fire and proper gear for the workers controlling the damage. When we have finished—What is it, Varazin?"

The Chief Engineer only wanted to announce, "There is some tea and mineral water coming in now. My wife is bringing it."

And his wife, with a young girl beside her, was hovering in the doorway, trays in their hands. "Thank you, Comrade Varazin," Istvili said dryly. "As I was about to say, when we have finished this preliminary conference, we will establish working groups to deal with each of these. First we have to deal with immediate problems. The graphite in the core is still burning."

Everyone turned to look at the fire commander. He looked annoyed. "That is a different question from the fire in the structure," he explained. "However, we are continuing to hose it. We have more pumpers coming, even a couple of water cannon; they should drown it, just as the British did at Windscale."

"No, no!" cried Smin, but the other man from the Ministry, Lestilyan, spoke ahead of him:

"That is unacceptable for the reasons Smin has given. Also, it probably will just fracture the graphite and expose more combustible surfaces to the air. We'll have to cover the core."

"What with?" the fireman demanded. "Foam's out of the question."

"Things much denser than foam. Sand, clay, even lead. Probably boron, too, because that swallows neutrons."

"And how are you going to get it on the core?" the fire commander asked sarcastically. "Do you want my men to carry it up there in hods, like bricklayers?"

Lestilyan said crisply, "Of course, we will need heavy earth-moving machinery. That, too, I think, should be referred to a working group?"

"Exactly," Istvili said promptly. "In fifteen minutes I will adjourn this meeting and we will start the work of the groups. Comrade Rasputin? Do you want to say anything about the casualties and risks?"

"All of the injured are being evacuated; the Pripyat hospital can't handle them all, so most of them are being sent elsewhere—"

The head of the hospital raised his hand. "The hospital itself should be evacuated, I think. And probably also the town itself."

"Of course," Smin put in. "As soon as possible."

One of the men from the Council of Ministers in Kiev stirred himself. "Why of course? The wind is blowing the smoke the other way, isn't it?"

"It could change at any moment."

"That's true," added Rasputin. "And rain would be a serious added problem; rain brings fallout. It was raining in Kiev earlier this morning."

"It isn't raining here. Evacuation would cause mass panic," the man from Kiev stated.

"Then at least the people should be informed," Smin said doggedly. The man frowned.

"That decision is not ours to take, Comrade Smin."

"But if we wait for Moscow to approve, it could be hours! At least, let us have an announcement on the Pripyat radio station," Smin urged.

Istvili took over command of the meeting. "We simply do not have enough information yet for public announcements to be made. When we have full facts to give them, yes. Then it will be authorized. For now that discussion is closed. Now let us turn to the cause of the accident."

There was one thing you could say for these high-powered people from the Ministry of Nuclear Energy, Smin thought to himself. At least they got things done. All three of the section chiefs had spoken quickly but unhurriedly; the meeting had been going less than seven minutes by Smin's watch. Against his will, Smin was beginning to respect, even almost to like them; it was hard for him to remember that these men were the "they" who had bombarded him every week with stern orders to hurry up, increase the proportion of working time, fulfill the Plan! Even the fourth man, the one no one had bothered to introduce, was appearing to be getting down to business. For the first part of the meeting he had been sitting quietly, smoking a cigarette and sipping his cup of tea as he gave each speaker polite but detached attention. But now that they had come to the question of the cause of the accident, he had taken out a pencil and was beginning to make notes.

"It appears," said Istvili, "that the accident occurred during the course of an unusual experiment, which involved shutting off some or all of the safety systems of Reactor Number Four. Is that correct?"

Chief Engineer Varazin set his cup down so hard he spilled some tea. "It was not an 'unusual' experiment. It was approved in advance in all particulars by the Ministry!"

"Not quite in all particulars, I think," said Istvili. "Not to take place at one o'clock in the morning. Not without a safety inspector present."

Varazin said obstinately, "There was no directive about the time or about safety inspectors."

"There was also no directive giving authority to dismantle the automatic systems, however," Istvili pointed out, and Smin sucked in a deep breath.

"Then it's true," he groaned. "Is it? The idiots turned everything off? My God, Varazin! How could you let them?"

Chief Engineer Varazin had never been a really close friend, but it was in that moment, Smin saw, that he had converted him into a irreconcilable enemy. The engineer kept his face straight, but muscles were jumping in his cheeks as he ground out, "At least I was there! And, if *you* are so wise, Deputy Director Smin, why weren't you yourself present?"

The whole meeting waited patiently for Smin's answer. Why? Because the Chief Engineer should have been responsible? Because at last word the experiments had been postponed indefinitely? Because he had not for one second imagined such stupidity?

Smin shook his head, more to himself than to the men from the commission. "I agree that I should have been present," he said clearly, and watched the silent man from Moscow carefully writing his words down.

CHAPTER 11

Dean Garfield is thirty-four years old and he really is a highly successful television producer in America. The reason for that, perhaps, is that his father's money from the jewelry-findings business had paid for four years and a subsequent master's degree from the University of Southern California at just the right time, in the early 1970s. Just then a lot of bright young college boys were getting ready to be the film and TV geniuses of the later 1970s, and they remembered their classmates when they got big. A consequence of that, perhaps, is his wife. Candace Garfield—her professional name is Candace Merlyn—was the star of Garfield's first sitcom. Unfortunately the show failed to get past the eight-week cutoff, and Candace had been looking for another series ever since. She is very happy about Garfield's present success with his all-black series, which has just been picked up for a third year, except that there are no ongoing parts in it for tall, beautiful blondes. She is confident, however, that she could play a tall, beautiful, blonde Soviet nuclear engineer —or Soviet almost anything—in a new series, and she has been developing this idea for Garfield since breakfast.

Actually, it started out as Dean Garfield's own idea. It came to him as he was peering out the window, slightly hung over and too restless to sleep, at the misty Ukrainian sunrise over the city of Kiev. When he saw that his wife's eyes were open and watching him from the bed, he grinned. "I guess I'm all charged up. How many Americans get to see the inside of a real Russian home—Ukrainian, anyway," he amended. "You know what? There ought to be a story here. All this local color! Let's go out and take a look at the city."

"We already saw the city," Candace yawned. "I haven't got the strength for one more museum of teeny-tiny paintings on human hairs."

"I don't mean the tourist stuff! I mean the way the people *live*. Ride in the subway. Walk around a tenement district. See a, I don't know, a whatever they have to eat in that's like a McDonald's."

"That Intourist guide is really not going to like that," his wife said absentmindedly, because actually she had begun to take an interest when he used the word *story*.

"So screw the Intourist guide," Garfield said happily. "We'll just tell the hall lady, hey, no speak Russian. Then we take off. What can they do?"

His wife was looking doubtful but persuadable. "Dean? Are we talking about a new television series?"

"I don't know what I'm talking about—yet. All I'm saying is what could it hurt to hang around and take a look?" And so they had, even though the hall lady had done a lot of head-shaking, even though it had begun to rain.

During the morning they had found their way into a grocery store and a dairy store, even a department store— Candace Garfield aghast at the people waiting in one line simply to see what was available to buy, then a second line to pay the cashier, then a third line at last to get whatever it was.

They never did find anything like a McDonald's, but they decided to treat themselves to the best meal they could find in Kiev. By the time they were ready for lunch, Dean Garfield was just about convinced that not only was there a possible show but his wife might well be the star of it. "Maybe you shouldn't be an engineer," he said thoughtfully as they waited for a table at the Dynamo restaurant. "How about if you were an Intourist guide? You get into all sorts of funny situations with the tourists. You know? Every week there's a new batch of tourists— American, Japanese, everything—so we have guest stars doing vignettes—"

"Like *Love Boat*?" She was frowning as the headwaiter led them up the stairs to a table on the balcony, but it was a frown of concentration, not anger. Garfield well knew the difference. He sat down with a groan of satisfaction.

"It's nice to get off my feet," he observed, glancing around. They had been walking around Kiev for four hours, and Candace had been talking the whole time. The hangover was gone, and he was getting really hungry. When the waitress arrived with the menu, he didn't even look at it; ten days of travel in the USSR had taught him that of the hundred dishes printed in any given menu, only the dozen or so with prices attached were ever available, and not necessarily all of those. "Do you speak English?" he asked. When she shook her head, he got up and looked around at the other tables. When he saw something that looked edible he pointed to it, then to himself and held up two fingers.

"Not steak, I hope?" Candace said absently; she had her glasses on and was already writing things in her notebook.

"I think it's kind of a veal stew," said Garfield. "Smelled good, anyway. And I ordered a bottle of that white wine over there."

He lit a cigarette and gazed down at the floor below. There seemed to be at least two wedding parties, one bride in traditional white, though without a veil or a train, the other in a pale green business suit. A four-piece orchestra was playing what Garfield recognized as "Raindrops Keep Falling on My Head," and two couples were on the tiny dance floor. "Even if we don't get a show out of it, I'm glad we decided to stay," he told his wife.

Candace looked up from her notes. "You do get some really neat ideas sometimes, hon," she acknowledged. "You know? I was a little worried that some KGB guy might grab us for running around without an escort or something."

Garfield accepted the complimentary tone with a modest shrug. "I was pretty sure they wouldn't bother us," he said, although, in fact, for the first hour or two he had felt an uneasy itch every time any Russian looked twice at them. "You know what I'd like to do? I'd like to see my relatives again, only how are we going to get in touch with them?"

Candace had already returned to her scribbling. "Call them up," she said absently.

"Call up who where? Simyon doesn't live in Kiev, and I don't know Aunt Aftasia's address." The old lady had phoned them at the hotel and then sent a car for them the day before, and it had not occurred to Garfield to ask for addresses or phone numbers.

"There has to be a telephone book," said Candace.

"In Russian? Besides, the old gal doesn't have a phone."

"So we wait until Monday and call up the power plant. Listen, I'm an Intourist guide, like you said. Maybe sometimes I'm a stew on Aeroflot. Each week we get a different bunch of tourists, and we go to different locations. Moscow, Leningrad, Kiev, I don't know, maybe Tashkent, Yalta—there's a million places in Russia. Like *Love Boat,* you know? We get in a lot of scenery, right?"

"How're we going to do all of those locations?"

She put the ball point pen down to look at him over the top of her glasses. "You don't think the Russians will cooperate with filming?"

"I'm thinking about production costs," he said, "not to mention trying to get along with Russian film labs and technicians."

"I'm thinking about a title role for me," said Candace decisively. "How about calling it *Comrade Tanya*? You can figure out the location stuff. Send a crew to go all over for background shots—hell, Dean, there's probably plenty of stock footage around. Cathedrals, rivers, airports. Then what do you need? A bus. A hotel lobby and some rooms. A beach—any beach will do, just put a lot of people on it in Russian bathing suits."

"It could happen," Garfield conceded; and then, when he saw the beginnings of that other kind of frown, "I mean, we'll certainly give it a shot. I'll get a writer in as soon as we get back. And here's our wine!"

The stew turned out to be pork rather than veal, and the white wine was warm, but it was still a good lunch. What made it a particularly good lunch was that Candace was bubbling over with her new idea, and Dean Garfield had begun to feel confident that even if no part of it ever got before a camera, the development would make their whole Soviet tour beautifully and unchallengeably tax deductible.

He used up their last roll of film shooting the bridal parties, the wood-beamed ceilings, the waiters in their dinner jackets, the funny little orchestra with three of the four players female. Even the terrible thick sweet coffee did not blight his mood. He leaned back and lit a cigarette, regarding his beautiful wife. Nearly everyone in the restaurant had stared at this tall, slim American woman in the pale blue suit. It was Garfield's opinion that the women were looking at the suit and the men were busy imagining what was under it. It wasn't a new thought for him; that was his general opinion every time they went out together, and he was certain it was right. He did the same kind of looking himself. He was doing it now as he contemplated his wife across the table, though in his case he was not imagining but remembering. Though not, unfortunately, from recent experience; it was not only on *The Love Boat* that couples went traveling to try to save their marriages.

He stubbed out his cigarette decisively. Since Candace had filled the ashtray with the carefully amputated fat from her pork stew, he had to use a saucer. "I think," he said, "we could use a little nap about now, don't you? So let's go back to the hotel."

His wife gave him a good-humored look. "So let's at least finish the wine while we're here. Then maybe I'll show you my scar, like the old lady."

"Yeah, tell me about it. She actually showed you a bullet wound? I'd like to see that."

Candace laughed. "Not a chance. It's right near her crotch. She had to take her underwear off to show me—and, honest, hon, you wouldn't believe the kind of bloomers she had on."

"She said she got it in the Revolution?"

"Well, the teacher said it was the Civil War—is that the same thing? The old lady said all kinds of stuff, but that lady schoolteacher only translated about a quarter of it. That's a pain. Even if we did get a chance to see them again, how are you going to talk to them?"

"We'll worry about that on Monday," Garfield said expansively. "Finish your wine. I'm real anxious for a little lie-down."

It was turning out, he thought, to be a pretty good day. They even found a taxi letting people out in front of the restaurant, and the driver was even willing to take them to their hotel. Only when they got out of the elevator and presented their hotel card to the concierge, or keeper, or whatever the old woman who kept an eye on everything was called, it began to go sour. The first thing was that Candace gave a faint scream as she saw all their luggage piled behind the woman's desk. The second was when the woman told them, in heavily accented English, that they were, after all, scheduled to leave for Tbilisi that morning with the rest of their Intourist group; their room was needed for new guests, who were in fact already occupying it, and would they please remove the bags at once? "But I left a note at the desk!" Garfield cried. "I told them we'd changed our plans."

The woman looked shocked, "No, that is impossible. Your group has already left. You must immediately go to Reception and clear your bill, then a porter will remove your luggage."

Reception was no kinder. No, there were no rooms available in the Great Gate Hotel. No, there would be no rooms in any other hotel in Kiev, either; after all, it was coming time for the May Day celebration in just a few days, and every hotel was naturally full.

Garfield turned his back on his wife because he did not want to see the look on her face. "Well," he said, his tone self-assured and relaxed in just the way that had seen him bluff his way through many a meeting with network executives, "I'm sure there's someplace we can stay. Not necessarily a hotel. A private home? You know, a kind of bed-and-breakfast place?"

"It is against the law for foreign nationals to stay at the home of any Soviet citizen," she said primly.

"But then what are we going to do?" he cried; but the best the reception clerk would do was to concede:

"We will store your luggage for you until you pick it up." She nodded graciously, turned her back, and disappeared into another room.

Garfield opened his mouth to call after her, but his wife was plucking urgently at his sleeve. "Let's go outside," she said. Her tone prevented Garfield from arguing.

Out in the street he complained, "But we can't sleep in the street, hon."

She said tightly, "There was a man standing right behind you, and he was listening to every word."

"What are you talking about? You mean like somebody with the secret police? But we haven't done anything."

"Come *on*," she said, pulling him down the street. Passing citizens were looking at them curiously. Candace was silent until they had rounded a corner. Then she turned on her husband: "You should have made sure about the room before we went out," she accused. "What are we going to do now?"

"Now, don't worry, honey," he said in his confident, network-meeting voice. "We've got plenty of traveler's checks. This is a big city; there's bound to be someplace."

"Why don't we get in touch with Intourist?"

He thought for a moment. "Nah," he said. "We'd just have to do the routine tourist things." Then he grinned. "This could be a real adventure, you know? And I bet we'll get some good stuff for *Comrade Tanya*." He could see her doubts wavering. "We'll just find a room—God knows it won't be the Beverly Wilshire, but we can stand it for a couple of days. Worse come to worst, there's Aunt Tasia's apartment; she's got an extra room, because the Smins were going to sleep in it last night."

She reminded him, "How are you going to find them? And anyway, an adventure's one thing, breaking some kind of Russian law is another. You heard what the woman said about renting rooms to foreigners."

Garfield thought for a moment. "We'll keep Aunt Tasia as a last resort," he conceded. "Well, what about Simyon? He's a big wheel. He can pull some strings for us."

"Dean," she said patiently, "he doesn't live in Kiev. Do you even know the name of the town where he lives? And—oh, God! Here comes that man again!"

Garfield spun around. It was true. The man coming toward them was, he recognized, the same one he had seen in the hotel lobby. He did not look like Dean Garfield's idea of a KGB operative. He was not much more than twenty years old. He looked quickly about and then said ingratiatingly, "Please, you excuse me? You want house room to sleep? I know nice place, right near bus to Metro, you have U.S.A. dollars to pay?"

CHAPTER 12

The home of Simyon Smin and his family is not a "flat." It is a handsome apartment on the sixteenth floor of one of Pripyat's best buildings, and it has five rooms. Five! It is, of course, also in keeping with Smin's high position, and besides they can quite properly claim space for Nikolai, their elder son. Nikolai Smin is now on duty with the Air Force, though Selena Smin does not like to think about where. It is a very comfortable home. The kitchen has a stand-up freezer as well as the fridge. The bath has a stall shower in addition to the tub; it also has a bidet, and Selena Smin has already engaged an engineer to make sure the floor is sturdy enough to bear the weight of the next fixture she hopes to acquire. She has almost succeeded in arranging for the importation of a Jacuzzi to replace the tub. The bed she shares with Smin is king-sized, with sheets from England and a white Irish lace counterpane, and there may not be another like it anywhere in the Ukraine.

There are coffee-table books in Russian, French, and German in the living room. The prize book is a wonderfully illustrated volume on the art treasures of Leningrad's Hermitage, printed originally for export only, and hence regarded as a rare book. But there are also handsome volumes of travel scenes from all over the world—and there is a glass-topped coffee table from East Germany to put them on. There is, of course, a television set in the living room, and it has a VCR attached. The Smins possess a library of nearly twenty video cassettes, mostly of ballets and operas for the parents, but with four or five American films that belong to Vassili. His special favorite is *Jesus Christ Superstar*. (There is a second small television in Vassili's room, which has posters of Soviet spacecraft and cosmonauts on the wall, and a signed portrait of the American astronaut, Edgar Mitchell.)

Selena would deny that they live "Brezhnev style," although she would point out that since her husband has had his job since Brezhnev's time they had every right to the more opulent display that was the acceptable. With all her activities Selena can't hope to keep such a large apartment in order, but there is a seventeen-year-old maid from the nearby kolkhoz who comes in every morning at seven and, if there are guests, sometimes remains until almost midnight.

When Selena came to her apartment that Sunday morning, the maid was absent. So was her husband, but her younger son, Vassili, was slumbering fully dressed across the checkered spread of his bed. His clothes were stained and muddy. He was snoring gently.

Selena let him sleep. There was nothing she specially wanted to say to him—now that she knew he was alive! There was not even anything she wanted to hear from him, for Selena Smin had heard too much, and seen and experienced and felt too much in the last twenty-four hours; what she wanted was for it all to go away so that she could get back to organizing a May Day party for a few selected friends and planning for the Jacuzzi.

As a practical matter, the first thing for her to do was to get clean. Selena had been wearing the same clothes for two days. She put the tea kettle on (running her finger along the edge of the gas range and resolving to have a word with the maid when the girl chose to show herself again) and got under the shower.

There was only a trickle of lukewarm water.

The kitchen tap had been slow too. Selena sighed and used the tepid flow as thriftily as she could, soaping herself thoroughly. She thought wistfully of the Jacuzzi, and glumly of the last two days in Kiev. The visit with the American cousins had been exciting and pleasurable, but it now seemed like something that had happened to her when she was a young girl, like the first solo part in a student production of *Swan Lake,* or the time when Simyon Smin had taken her out among the cherry trees to tell her he wished to make her his wife. The orderly part of her mind filed a reminder to speak to Smin again about that apartment in his mother's name: was it really worthwhile to have a pied-à-terre in the city when it was in a Khrushchev slum?

Selena Smin did not dislike her husband's mother. In fact, they got on rather well—but, really, what an odd fish her mother-in-law was! What was the use of a mother-in-law who knew everyone in high places—at least, knew everyone's father, or even grandfather—when she lived like a collective-farm pensioner? Yes, all right, Aftasia Smin preferred to live quietly and inconspicuously. Very well, nothing should prevent her. But couldn't her son get a nicer apartment? In a better neighborhood? With more space to store clothing and other things they might need and, for the love of heaven, at least a *telephone*? And preferably without the grandmother sharing it? And, while she was at it, a little car of her own, if only a Moskvich, perhaps, so that she would never again have to take a *bus* from Kiev to Pripyat—and then to be dumped unceremoniously at a checkpoint, with fifteen other passengers hoping to get somewhere in the perimeter, left to make their own way to their destinations if they possibly could! She had not been alone. Yvanna Khrenovna, the wife of the Director of Personnel and Security, had been caught in the same checkpoint—no car to meet her when she returned to the Kiev airport from her trip to visit relatives in Smolensk; her hired taxi turned back at the checkpoint by soldiers who did not care whose wife she was. Or who Selena was, for that matter. Even Yvanna had had to shout to get an ambulance to take her the mere two kilometers to her own home. But at least she had given Selena space in the ambulance.

Despite the meager supply of water the shower refreshed Selena. She began to think of what had to be done. There was food in the refrigerator, so the special distribution from the stores had arrived, and she didn't have to worry about shopping. Vassili should not be allowed to sleep all day, otherwise he would not get to sleep this night. Her husband would certainly be home, or call home, before long, and he would have to tell her whether this thing at the power plant was likely to cause any inconvenience to their plans for a May Day party to watch the fireworks.

Those were the things that crossed the orderly part of Selena Smin's brain; but as she was toweling herself and gazing out the window she saw the pall of smoke that had been visible from many kilometers away, and felt an uneasy lance of doubt pierce her comfortable sense of security.

She was trying one more time, without hope, to get through to the plant on the telephone, when she heard the elevator grind to her floor. Its door rattled and slammed; there was a key in her door, and her husband came in. "Ah, you're here, good," he said. "Is there anything to eat?"

Selena Smin had never seen her husband look as he now did. His tailored suit was filthy, the cuffs of his trousers soaked with mud, his shoes a wreck. His plump face seemed to have lost weight. There were ash-gray half moons under his eyes, and that terrible scar of shiny flesh almost seemed to gleam. "Oh, my dear," she said, helping him off with his coat. "Sit down! Wait, I'll find you something. You look terrible. What has happened?"

Simyon Smin looked at his wife with eyes that were reddened with broken veins. He waved an arm to the window, where the serpentine crawl of smoke bent toward the northern sky. "*That* has happened," he said.

The soup was more than two days old, but it seemed all right to Selena's sniff and she boiled it for an extra minute to make sure. The bread was quite fresh. By the time Smin had come out of the shower in his quilted brown robe she had the meal on the table.

"Did you have enough water in the shower?"

He said, "No more than enough, anyway. There is a temporary power restriction. I suppose it has affected the pumps for our building."

Selena poured tea. "You ought to rest," she scolded.

"When I have eaten," he said, "I will sleep for one hour. No more. Be sure to wake me."

"You really must go back to the plant?"

"Who else?" said Smin, his mouth full of bread. "The Director is still in Moscow. The Chief Engineer fell apart last night. Now he is attempting to run things from six kilometers away."

Selena put a spoon in her own bowl of soup, but just stirred it around. "It is really bad," she said, not as a question.

Smin said, "Of the three hundred technical workers forty are in the hospital and one hundred and three have reported for duty. The rest have simply run away and not come back."

"I don't blame them!" Selena cried, surprising herself. "I wish—"

"You wish," Smin filled in for her, "that you hadn't come back, either. So do I. It is not safe here, Selena."

"It might blow up?"

"It already has blown up," he corrected her. "It is not explosions you have to worry about. That smoke is full of poison. Every bit of it—oh, God, wait!" And he got up from the table, closing the windows. "Never leave a window open until I say you may!" he commanded. "While I am sleeping dust the sills! Dust everything that has dust on it, any kind of dust. Use newspapers, then throw them away and wash your hands very carefully!"

"But the maid—"

"We will see the maid again," Smin said heavily, "when pigs fly. Or when this situation is under control, whichever comes first. And the clothes I just took off are in a paper bag. Don't open it, just throw them away."

"Your good suit!"

Smin sighed and didn't answer. Then, mopping up the last of the soup: "When Vasya wakes up, don't let him go out. If anyone comes for him, say he has been vomiting; they will think it is radiation sickness and they will leave him alone."

"Radiation sickness!"

"Can't you do anything but repeat what I say?" Smin asked almost jocularly. "Please. Do it. And don't go out yourself. When I have an opportunity I will arrange to have both of you evacuated, perhaps back to Babushka in Kiev. Pack what you need, but no more than two suitcases."

"For how long must I pack?" Selena asked. She was not surprised when her husband didn't answer. He got up from the table and walked slowly into their bedroom, moving as though his back pained him, as it often did.

She cleared the table, bent to find some old newspapers, and began carrying out her husband's instructions about wiping up dust. When she dampened the wadded-up papers, the flow from the kitchen faucet was even weaker than before. She thought she would weep. Instead, she flung the papers to the floor and marched into the bedroom.

Smin was not in bed. He was standing at the window, looking at the pall of smoke. "Selena," he said without looking at her, "it is really very bad. It exploded. There was no chance to do anything. If we don't put it out there will be dead people all over the Soviet Union from the radiation in that smoke, and how we will put it out God alone knows. Nothing is working."

She said desperately, "You will find a way, Simya."

"I hope so. I do not have your confidence."

"But you will! I am sure of it! And then, when the inquiry is held, of course the Director will have to go, and then your turn—"

She stopped, because her husband had turned to stare at her. "My dear Selena," he said, "are you thinking that I will gain from this?"

"Everyone knows you do all his work! Certainly you are entitled to promotion."

"Promotion!"

"It is true," she insisted. "The Director—he wasn't ever here—And he is, after all, the man in charge. As everyone understands, you simply correct his mistakes and cover up his failings. Surely he is the one to blame!"

Smin studied his wife for a moment. "Can you really believe," he asked gently, "that there will not be blame enough for everyone?"

CHAPTER 13

The town of Pripyat, with its shops, its film theater, its library, its five schools, its hostels and apartments for nearly fifty thousand people, exists only to serve the Chernobyl Nuclear Power Station. Pripyat is a new town, enclosed by wide fir and pine forests. Few of the buildings are much more than ten years old. Neither is the Chernobyl Nuclear Power Station itself. During the Great Patriotic War, the ground where the town stands was a battlefield where Germans and Soviets slaughtered each other in thousands. When the foundations were dug for the pretty sixteen-story apartment towers, skeletons of men and machines came up with the backhoes.

The people who live in Pripyat think themselves lucky. They are affluent, because pay is good at the power plant, and even at the radio factory and the construction works that are the town's other chief industries. They are young—the average age is no more than thirty, even without counting all the children. Their town is architecturally "advanced." Town planners come from all over the USSR to study it. It was purpose-built, but it serves its purposes not only well but gracefully. Even with a human dimension; Pripyaters are proud to say that their main avenue was redirected so that three cherished old apple trees, that somehow survived the war, could be preserved. The apartment buildings are faced with ceramic tile, white and pink and blue, and they glow in the sun. The boulevards are wide. It was sensible to make them so. After all, the land was cheap, being nothing much but sand. The town is filled with greenery. No Pripyater would ever have considered being tempted away with another job—at least, until now.

Senior Operator Bohdan Kalychenko woke to a thunderous pounding at his door. Kalychenko crossed himself as he hurried to answer, but when he opened it, the person standing there was not from the First Department of the plant, come to demand to know why Kalychenko had run away from his post. It was only Zakharin, the man from the milk store around the corner. Without his white jacket and little white cap Zakharin looked quite different, and he was oddly hesitant after his violent banging. "Did I wake you, Comrade Kalychenko?" he asked. "I wasn't sure you were here. I thought you might be at the power plant."

"It is my day off," said Kalychenko, rubbing at his right arm, which was nestled in a sling made from a large red kerchief.

"Oh? Are they keeping to a regular schedule, even now? But I thought—" The man from the milk store took a closer look at Kalychenko's arm. "Oh, but I see you are injured."

Kalychenko cradled the arm in his other hand. "What do you want?" he demanded.

The man cleared his throat. He was much shorter than Kalychenko. Looking up, he began diffidently, "You understand these things, Kalychenko. I do not. I am only a storekeeper. You have technical training. You see, we are frightened. This explosion—this smoke—some of us think it is not safe to stay in Pripyat. Is it so serious, do you think?"

"The authorities will decide that," Kalychenko said gruffly.

Zakharin was insistent. "The authorities are completely overwhelmed, Kalychenko. There is hardly a militiaman on the street. There is not a fireman left in Pripyat, or a piece of equipment. Hot coals have fallen in the woods! My own sister's husband saw them. What if this building should catch on fire now, what would we do?"

"None of this is my concern," Kalychenko said angrily. He looked with hostility at the man from the milk store, quite strange in his Sunday morning suit and tie. Zakharin looked both older and less sure of himself than in his store, counting out eggs for a shopper or carefully stowing the plastic bags of milk in the cooling compartment. He also seemed quite frightened, though he was trying to conceal it. That touched a chord in Kalychenko's own heart. "I don't know what it is you want from me," he said unwillingly.

"Information, first of all, if you please! You are a scientific man. My son, who is fourteen, says that the smoke from the power plant contains atoms of radium and other substances which can cause our hair to fall out and our blood to dry up, and perhaps to kill us. Is this true?"

"No, not that," Kalychenko said. He hesitated, and then added, "But it is true that there can be danger from fallout."

"Fallout! Like from the Americans testing nuclear bombs! Then should we not be taken somewhere else until the danger is past? Please, Comrade. I have three children. Several of us have talked of these matters—I have hardly slept all night—I think we should go to the authorities and demand that the children, at least, should be taken to a place of safety. But we don't know how to explain this; none of us are scientists. So, please, come with us to the Party headquarters—"

"No! That is completely out of the question!"

Zakharin stepped back before the vehemence of Kalychenko's tone. His eyes blinked; without his cap, Kalychenko saw that the man was nearly bald. "I must report in to the plant now," Kalychenko added firmly. "This is, after all, an emergency. I'm sorry I can't help you."

"I will talk to the others again," the man said stubbornly as Kalychenko closed the door on him.

Kalychenko did not, as it developed, "report in." He did seriously intend to. He actually had his hand on the telephone, not once but four times, and each time there was some confounded interruption that prevented him from making the call.

First there was the need to go to the toilet. Then there was a sudden noise outside and he had to go to the window, to look out on the courtyard, where at least thirty people were standing together, talking, arguing, pointing in the direction of the plant; it was out of Kalychenko's sight, but he knew that it was the distant drift of smoke they were pointing at.

Then, with his hand on the telephone, he said to himself, "But they have this telephone number, if they simply take the trouble to look for it. They will call me if they need me. In any case, I should shave before I report for work." And he did shave, with meticulous care, twice over, using the tube of shaving cream that his fiancée had given him for his birthday just days before.

Kalychenko was a tall, pale man and his beard was so fair that shaving more than twice a week was no more than an affectation; but he told himself that if things were really as bad as they had seemed the day before, it might be a long time before he had an opportunity to shave again. Then he put the sling back on his right arm (which he had used quite freely while shaving), and marched firmly to the phone for the fourth time, and there was the door again.

This time is was Raia, his fiancée. She squeezed in hastily, closing the door behind her. "The man from the milk store," she began, and Kalychenko groaned.

"What, has he been after you too?"

"But, Bohdan, isn't he right? Please! How many times have you told me how dangerous these radioactive chemicals can be? I am not concerned for the man in the milk store, or for you and me. Have you forgotten what I am carrying for you?" She spread the fingers of her hand over her still quite flat belly.

"I have not forgotten for one second, Raia," he said sourly.

"Then listen to what Zakharin says! I really think you should help him. Make the authorities understand what must be done!"

"Raia," he said patiently, "it is not our responsibility to make such decisions. In any case, do you really want Pripyat evacuated? If they send everyone away, then what? Thousands of people must be moved in that case. There will be immense confusion. Suppose you are sent to Kiev and I to Kursk or some other place?"

"Surely we can find a way to stay together."

He said seriously, "Yes, perhaps, sooner or later. But it could take time, and what about our wedding? Can we make arrangements for a reception in a train station? Where will our friends be?"

"People get married everywhere, Bohdan! So we won't be able to have a reception in the Red Room at the plant; all right, we'll get married anyway and have the party another time, after we all come back to Pripyat—"

"Come back to Pripyat? With all this poison falling all over? And when would that be?" He started to say more, but checked himself as he saw her eyes widen at his words. "All right," he said reasonably. "Let's think this out, step by step. I agree, perhaps you should leave, for the sake of our baby. The next question is, can I leave too? I don't know; perhaps they will want every hand on duty at the plant. But let us say I can. Very well. You leave now; I will follow when I can. Your parents in Donetsk will put us up if we marry there. So you can take a bus—"

"A bus! There aren't any buses, Bohdan. Even the streets are covered with white foam!"

"White foam?" Kalychenko disliked the sound of that. Foam on the streets meant that someone had decided the danger of fallout was quite real.

"Yes, foam, and no buses. Haven't you been outside at all? I went to the highway to see what was happening, and that's where the buses are, carrying militiamen and troops and firefighters. The highway is full of emergency traffic. No, please. The whole town must go or none of us will."

"I do not think this is a good idea," Kalychenko groaned uneasily. Raia sighed in exasperation, then held out a hand.

"At least let me see your arm," she ordered. He assumed a stoic expression as she unwrapped the scarf and pulled up the sleeve of his tunic. "Is it tender?" she asked, poking.

"No. Yes—there, a little."

She worked the arm back and forth gently, and then sighed. "Do you know," she said, "I think I have a sore throat this morning."

"Because you smoke too much."

"No, I don't think this is from smoking, dear Bohdan. Also my face—I can't describe it exactly—it tingles a bit. As though someone were poking tiny pins at it. I don't mean that it's painful. Simply strange."

"Maybe all those cigarettes are cutting off your circulation."

"But to my face? Well, if you don't think it's serious—"

She put the bandaged arm down. "There's no bruise," she said doubtfully. "You should see a medic."

"What, when there may be many people very much worse hurt?" He rose and said abruptly, "Excuse me, I must go to the bathroom." With the door closed behind him he felt better. These silly symptoms of Raia's were, of course, imaginary. He had never read of sore throat or pins in the face indicating exposure to radiation ... but, of course, he told himself unhappily, he had never quite got around to reading all the stuff they threw at you when you came to work in a place like Chernobyl.

With Kalychenko out of the room Raia took out a Stewardess cigarette and inhaled the menthol smoke deeply. And at once she began to worry. Should she be smoking at all? Would it be bad for the baby? Her husband-to-be had informed her quite definitely that it was, but at the clinic they had only shrugged and talked about moderation.

She wished she had thought to ask at the clinic about radiation. But who could have imagined such questions were necessary? She touched her stomach hopefully, and worried. Until now the only questions seriously troubling had been whether her fiancé would actually go through with the ceremony, and whether the child would have his blue eyes.

Now—would it have any eyes at all?

By the time Kalychenko came out of the bathroom, Raia had frightened herself into stubbornness. "You must come to the Party headquarters," she said firmly.

"And leave the telephone? What if I'm needed at the plant?"

She said reasonably, "How would they find you here? As far as the plant knows, you're still at the hostel for single men, isn't that so?"

"I think I informed the plant that I would be staying here," he said, although it was a lie. Actually, he had not thought it anyone's business if he temporarily borrowed this apartment from the friend who had followed his wife to Odessa, hoping to talk her out of a divorce. In any case, judging from some of the remarks Khrenov had made, even this telephone number was almost certainly somewhere in the Personnel and Security files.

"And in all this confusion will anyone remember that? No, really, Bohdan, if you're worried that the plant needs you, call them. But first come to the Party headquarters. There's nothing else to do, is there?"

Perhaps there wasn't. Kalychenko could think of no way out. He could not simply go on hiding in his friend's apartment as he had done all the previous day. In the long run he sighed, threw up his hands at his fiancée's gentle nagging and went reluctantly out to tell the man from the milk store that after careful consideration, he had decided that he would go along to talk to the people at the Party committee building. It was not that he thought it was a good idea. He simply didn't have a better one.

There were a hundred people in the crowd that marched doggedly through the streets to the Party headquarters. The white foam had caked solid and was soiled, and there was an unpleasant smoky, chemical, almost ammonia-like smell in the air. It was true enough that there were no buses on the streets this day. There was little traffic of any kind, with nothing coming in from outside the town. They strode along the center of the roadway itself, with no militia around to fine them for jaywalking. Zakharin was in the lead, with Kalychenko looking stern enough and determined enough as he strode along just behind him.

It was still early morning, not as much as ten o'clock, but it was a sullen, coppery-colored sort of day. There weren't many clouds. The sun was bright enough, even hot. But overhead, covering half the sky, was a thin pall of smoke from Chernobyl. Citizens who would normally be sitting in their bathrobes, drinking tea in comfortable relaxation on their day off, were peering out the windows or standing on the sidewalks; they called back and forth to the clot of men moving down the center of the street, and some joined the march. Most merely looked worried.

Outside the Party headquarters the flag was stirring listlessly in the breeze. A couple of older, exhausted militiamen stood in front of the door. "What is the matter with you people?" one of them demanded. "Why are you making a disturbance at this critical time?"

"We want to speak to the Party secretary," Zakharin said boldly.

"On a Sunday morning? Are you out of your mind?"

"It is an emergency," Zakharin insisted.

The other militiaman said, "Of course it is an emergency, and the Party secretary is at his post of duty. Go back to your homes at once."

"No," said Zakharin. "We demand that something be done. The town must be evacuated! The danger is very great to all of us. Comrade Kalychenko here is an expert on such matters. He will explain it to you."

But Comrade Kalychenko did not, because when Zakharin looked around for backing from his technical expert, Bohdan Kalychenko was nowhere to be seen.

CHAPTER 14

There is no "core meltdown" at the Chernobyl Power Station. At least that particular disaster was impossible, for uranium dioxide does not melt until it reaches a temperature of 7,000 degrees Fahrenheit. Even burning graphite never gets much hotter than half that. When the graphite burned, it was, after all, only a simple chemical matter of carbon combusting in the presence of oxygen, not basically different from the blazing logs in the fireplace of a split-level ranch house. Although it was a real nuclear explosion that started the disaster, the nuclear reaction blew itself out in the first fraction of a second after the initial blast. So there is no longer any real danger of that famous nuclear nightmare, a core meltdown, but another danger is most ominously present. In a way it has become even worse.

As the carbon in the graphite reacts with the oxygen in the air in that fire, the smoke rises. It has no chimney, as the fireplace logs would, but it doesn't need one. At such temperatures the fire creates its own chimney, as the column of hot smoke and gases thrusts upward through the atmosphere. The column carries other gases and tiny bits of solid matter along with it. That is where the real, and most terrible danger lies. That smoke contains deadly poisons. It is not just the uranium in the core that is radioactively poisonous now. The reactor has created its

own new poisons, some of which are far more worrisome
than uranium. It is inevitable that it should. Even if a
nuclear reactor could start with pure, and nearly harmless
materials, its purity would not last. Its own radiation
corrupts it. Some atoms are broken into fragments, and
each fragment is a new chemical element. Nuclei gain
particles or lose them. Elements which do not exist in
nature—the "transuranic" ones—are created. Many of the
new elements are fiercely radioactive. This is the unique
danger of nuclear accidents.

Without exception, all radioactive elements are harmful to living things—every living thing, from fungi to
human beings. High doses of radiation kill quickly. Lower
doses take more time. At the lowest possible concentration—a single particle striking a single cell—there may be
no detectable damage at all, because the rest of the body
may be able to repair or replace the cell. Or it may not; in
which case the damage may not show up for decades,
appearing only late in life as cancer.

Say what you would about the men from the Ministry of
Nuclear Energy, Smin thought wearily, you at least had to
admit they got things done. He had lost count of the number
of experts—specialist doctors, engineers, construction people—
who had poured into Chernobyl in the last dozen hours. Of
course Chief Engineer Varazin's dacha was far too small to
hold all the meetings and individuals concerned in the effort to
control the damage to Reactor No. 4. Perhaps, Smin thought,
it was also a bit too close to the naked core for the comfort of
the experts; at any rate, a new command post had been established thirty kilometers away, in the regional Party headquarters of a collective farm village.

It was not just men the people from the Ministry had
conjured up, it was matériel. A steady flow of heavy machines
lumbered through the checkpoint on their way to the plant.
Trucks had arrived all through the night, bearing all sorts of
things that the Chernobyl Nuclear Power Station had never
had before. Everyone now carried a little aluminum pen-shaped
dosimeter. Everyone, even at the checkpoint, wore coveralls,
caps that came down over the neck and ears, even cloth masks
to put over the mouth and nose, though at the checkpoint all

of those hung loose around the wearers' throats. You could not tell a general from a laborer. In white or green, they were all covered from head to toe. It made them look like robots.

But if they had been robots, there would not now be the steady stream of casualties coming from the plant.

Almost all of the wounded now were firemen. Many suffered severe burns, but most of them also had worse than burns. Already a few of the victims had suppurating cold-sore blisters on their faces and mouths, and those were not just burns; those were the first signs of radiation sickness, and the fact that the black herpes blisters had popped up so rapidly was certain indication that the exposure had been very great.

But Rasputin, the specialist in the biological effects of radiation, had instituted tight procedures for dealing with them. Each man was carefully undressed by white-robed, white-gloved, white-hooded orderlies as he lay on his stretcher in the open air. His clothing, every scrap, went into a bin to be buried in the open field, where a bulldozer was excavating a deep trench. Then the doctors took over, first carefully washing every inch of exposed skin, checking with radiation monitors; then they redressed him in a hospital gown and poulticed the burns. A separate set of ambulances waited at the control point; when they were full, they roared away. Some ferried the patients with the worst radiation damage to the airstrip in Chernobyl town, for the plane that would take them to the special hospital in Moscow. The others were put into other ambulances to start the two-hour trip to Hospital No. 18 in Kiev.

The highway crossed a little stream at the collective farm village—it was why that spot had been chosen for the checkpoint. One fire truck was permanently posted there, its pumps constantly going to suck water from the stream. With that water each ambulance was hosed down before it went back to the plant for more of the endless supply of wounded. The ambulances from the Chernobyl Nuclear Power Station never passed beyond the checkpoint to the outside world. They never would.

Returning to the command post for another installment of the endless meetings, Simyon Smin saw a little two-man helicopter sitting on the ground just off the roadway. Its rotor was turning slowly, and the pilot was leaning back in his seat, gazing at the distant smoke plume from the power station. Smin ducked under the rotor and banged on the door. "Pilot! Who are you?"

The pilot blinked at him. "Lieutenant of Militia Kutsenko, at your service. Pilot to Major General Varansky."

"Of course," barked Smin, just as though he had known who General Varansky had been all along. "I have the general's orders. Take me up. I want to survey the site." And, as Lieutenant Kutsenko opened his mouth for a question, Smin snapped: "At once! Do you not understand that this accident endangers the entire country?"

Smin had never been in such a small helicopter. It bounced and swooped staggeringly, far worse than the one he had borrowed the day before, but his mind wasn't on the ride. It wasn't even on his fatigue, or the facts that his scars itched, his eyes ached, and the corners of his mouth were sore. What he was thinking about was what he had come to see.

When they were only five or six kilometers away, the plant began to come into view. The great drift of black smoke snaking into the sky seemed far thicker than the day before, even though most of the fires were long since out; it was, Smin knew, the smoldering embers that produced the pall. As they approached over the towers of Pripyat, Smin could see that the streets were full of people. Their white faces stood out sharply as they gazed up at the helicopter. "Fools," muttered Smin.

The pilot craned toward him. "What?" he yelled. "Did you speak?"

Smin shook his head; the people of Pripyat had to be gotten out of that area, there was no question about that, but there was nothing the pilot could do. "Up higher, if you can," he urged. "But stay out of the plume!"

The pilot nodded, and kicked and turned his controls. The machine spun and lifted, first away from the reactor, then swinging back to approach it from the windward side. They were no more than three hundred meters above the inferno. Smin could look almost directly down into it. As the pilot hovered, Smin opened his door and leaned out, staring down at the end of so many hopes and the death sentence passed on so many friends.

Even so high, the heat beat at his face. It was true that all the lesser fires were out, but he could see clearly that all the efforts of the firefighters had done nothing at all to stop, or even to slow, the terrible combustion that was going on in the graphite core of the destroyed reactor. If only ten percent of the graphite had been burning yesterday, now it was nearly a third that was aflame. The still-unburning surface of the graphite was a rubble of lumps and cracks and hillocks. The burning part was as bright and hot as the sun. Great rainbow-shaped streams of water came up from the hoses and down onto the furnace, but to no avail. Where the streams of water hit the fire, there were clouds of steam, but when the jet wavered away the fire was still burning as fiercely as ever.

On the ground Smin could see bulldozers grinding away as they heaped up berms of earth. Beside the bulldozers a pair of water cannon were blasting away at the lower reaches of the reactor shell; whether any of their water was getting through, or what good it was doing if it did, he could not tell.

The smoke billowed toward them. "Get away!" Smin shouted, pulling himself back inside and slamming the door. The pilot was already slanting away, but the vagrant gust of air was faster than he; for a moment there was smoke all around them, and a stink of burning chemicals that tore at Smin's throat. Then they were clear. Both men were coughing, and the helicopter lurched as the pilot spun it away. "Better get down," Smin managed to rasp out, and the pilot didn't even nod. He was already heading back to the perimeter post.

By the time they were on the ground the coughing fits were over. "Thank you," said Smin gravely, and got out to confront the man in the green coverall who was watching them impassively from the door of the headquarters building. Even without the insignia on his shoulderbars, Smin knew who he was. He said, "Thank you, also, General Varansky, for allowing me to borrow your aircraft."

The general didn't even smile. He only murmured, "Why should I refuse one helicopter, when you people have already borrowed half the moveable equipment in the Ukraine? But should we not go inside for the meeting?"

The general's remark was not much of an exaggeration at that. From the air Smin had seen literally scores of trucks, bulldozers, ambulances, fire vehicles, and examples of almost everything else that moved on the roads around the stricken plant.

Smin followed Major General Varansky into the meeting room. The only conference actively going on was with the special doctors from Moscow. At least these specialists knew exactly what they had to do and could get on with it. Their home base, Hospital No. 6, had been designated the center point for radiation injuries, and the first job of the task force that had flown in the night before was to screen every victim for radiation—more than a thousand so far, with nearly two hundred of them already on their way to Moscow for whatever treatment there was to give them. They were explaining this to some Party and town officials for Pripyat, who were looking glum.

Smin paused a moment at the door, where there was a rack of the pen-shaped dosimeters. He glanced around while the general went on ahead. No one was looking. Smin unclipped his old one and threw it into a basket and fixed a new one to his jacket before he went in.

"I do hope," the Pripyat Party secretary was saying cheerlessly, "that you are not proposing to test everyone in Pripyat."

"Of course they will test everyone in Pripyat," Smin snapped, aware that his tone was offending the man, aware that the secretary would be writing a report on what was happening—aware, most of all, that none of that mattered. Smin wrinkled his nose at the faint smell of animal manure that permeated the meeting hall; the cow barns were only a dozen meters away. "It is not all that has to be done," he said, "in the town of Pripyat. Those people's lives are all at risk. They must be evacuated."

Two of the Moscow doctors nodded, but the men from Pripyat looked thunderstruck. "Impossible!" cried the Party secretary. "What are you saying? We do not want panic!"

"It is better that they be frightened than dead," Smin said flatly.

"I refuse," the man said. "This very morning some panic-mongers in Pripyat came to the Party headquarters with the same ultimatum. It was almost a demonstration! We taught the ringleaders a lesson, I assure you."

"If you put them in jail in Pripyat," said Smin, "you will teach them a final lesson, because they will die there. Everyone in the city will die if they remain there long enough. They must be taken away at once."

"Taken to where?"

"To sleep in the fields if they must," Smin cried, "because that is better than dying in their flats! If you won't do it on your own authority, then call Moscow. I will talk to them myself. I insist—oh, what is it now?"

The biological-effects man, Rasputin, was standing in the doorway, next to a doctor who was holding a glass vial of water. Hydrologist-engineer Sheranchuk was beside her, looking as weary as Smin himself, but he spoke first. "It's the stream," he said. "The one where they get the water they are using for the wounded, and to wash the vehicles. It is showing radioactivity now."

Leonid Sheranchuk did not just look weary. He was sodden with fatigue. He had not slept at all—for, what? He had lost count. More than forty-eight hours, at least.

He could have gone home when the militia and fire brigades and emergency workers of all kinds began to show up in strength, because they no longer needed amateur rubble-shifters and stretcher-toters. But then he remembered that he was a highly trained expert in hydraulic flow, and hydraulic flows were the only things that were keeping all the rest of the Chernobyl Nuclear Power Station from joining the stricken reactor in flames. It was Sheranchuk who managed to get some of the station's primary pumps working to provide pressure for the hosemen and give a little relief to the straining fire trucks, Sheranchuk who directed the pumper intakes to the deepest and least sedimented parts of the cooling pond. . . .

And Sheranchuk who, watching the streams of water running down the sides of the building and spreading across the sodden ground, thought to wonder where that water was going.

When he found Rasputin and expressed his fears, the man from the Ministry responded at once. He commandeered one of the doctors and set out. The radiation detectors gave the answers. The clear, purling waters of the brook by the command post were registering radioactivity.

It wasn't an immediate problem. The brook water was still good enough to wash down the trucks. That was not important, anyway. In any case there were the wells of the collective farm ready to supply the need for drinking water and to clean the wounds of the injured.

The problem was that the brook did not stop flowing at the highway.

That brook came from near the Chernobyl Power Station. It wasn't just picking up radiation from the fallout of soot from the fire. It was the conduit—one of the conduits—for the wastewater from the firefighting. Millions of gallons of water were being pumped out of the Pripyat River and the plant's cooling pond to pour onto the fire. What did not turn into steam ran away into the ground and across it, into that brook and every other nearby—into the Pripyat River itself, sooner or later.

"And," said Sheranchuk grimly, "the Pripyat River flows into the reservoirs that supply the city of Kiev."

He looked directly at the Party secretary, who frowned back. After a moment he said, "Yes?" And then, raising a hand to keep Sheranchuk from answering, "I see what you are implying, but surely that is not important—the hose water from a few fire engines, against a reservoir?"

"That hose water," said Smin wearily, "is full of radioactive material. What do we do, Comrade Plumber?"

"We must dam up the overflow," Sheranchuk said at once. "We must dike every stream, every little river that flows near Chernobyl. The cooling pond, it must be diked off from the Pripyat. Sewers, drains—they must be diverted or simply stopped up."

The Party secretary stared at him. "Stop up the sewers?"

"Exactly," said Rasputin. "Just as Sheranchuk here says. We don't have a choice."

"Or else we will poison the people of Kiev," said Sheranchuk.

Smin sighed, and stood up and said, "Let's go, Comrade Plumber. Show me where you want to build these dikes."

But in the long run, of course, it wasn't Sheranchuk who decided where the dikes should go. It wasn't Smin, either. It was the men from Moscow. By the time Smin and Sheranchuk got back to the command post, someone had produced a hydrological map of the area—Sheranchuk's eyes were bulging;

he had not even known that such a map existed—and the dikes and trenches and diversions were already being marked.

Smin knew that it was all out of his hands now. Higher authority had taken over. Higher authority listened, spoke, looked at some plans, then picked up a phone and issued instructions. Higher authority did not have to bribe or wheedle to get what it wanted. It simply gave an order, and somewhere in the Ukraine or Moscow or Byelorussia someone began calling workers in to load a truck with whatever was required and send it speeding to Chernobyl.

They did not send Smin away, though he was reeling with fatigue. They did not object when he appeared at one of the endless meetings to plan for the implacable future while, simultaneously, dealing with the catastrophic present. They even listened courteously when he spoke. But that was not often, for higher authority knew its resources better than he did. He listened and marveled.

To Rasputin, explaining to the head of the Pripyat hospital that the reason his clinic had been evacuated was not only that it was better for the patients to be farther away, but that his staff was simply not adequate to the problems. "Your doctors are diagnosing burns, shock, heat exhaustion, even heart attacks—but where is one diagnosis of radiation sickness?"

To Lestilyan, patiently reasoning with the general commanding the fire brigades. "We must use other methods." The fire in the core was not out. It had not even slowed down; the supply of burnable graphite was endless, and every atom of it hungered to unite with the oxygen in the air. The terribly hot core was a massive reserve of heat. Even if they cooled the surface a bit, the vast interior store reheated it and kept the temperature of the graphite blocks well above the ignition temperature.

"Exactly. So water is no good," the fire chief complained. "It boils right off."

"Of course. So we must smother it. Cover it with sand, maybe. Something that will keep the air out."

"Sand through hoses?" said the fire commander. "What nonsense! I have never heard of such a thing."

"Not through hoses," Lestilyan said patiently. "In some other way, and quickly. What is it now, six hundred microroentgens an hour in Pripyat? And more all the time!"

"I know nothing of micro what-you-said," the fire commander said stubbornly. "I know only what to do with fires." He meditated for a moment. Then he said, "Well, then. Can we get helicopters to drop it in? Or do you want my men to carry the sand there in their helmets?"

"Of course," said Lestilyan, nodding. "Helicopters." And picked up the phone to call the Air Force.

To everyone. Smin listened carefully to all of them, and spoke little. And that was the day, one emergency falling on top of another, no time to solve one problem before the next arose. At least the Air Force promised helicopters would be on the scene by nightfall. At least a crane was brought from Pripyat to the burning reactor and an operator found brave enough to try dumping dirt, broken rocks, slabs of cement onto the blazing reactor even before the heavy helicopters got there. At least the medical problems were now being dealt with by experts. At least—

At least, Smin thought grimly, his wife and younger son were out of it. He had passed them through the checkpoint himself, in their own car, not twenty minutes before the order had come to let no more vehicles through.

But nearly fifty thousand other people were still in the town of Pripyat.

When someone thrust a plate of bread and Army soup in front of him, Smin realized that it was well past noon and he had eaten nothing since he arrived at the control point, well before daybreak. He wished he could put his head down, just for a minute, close his eyes—

But it would not be a minute. The aching weariness in every bone, the sullen throbbing that was beginning between his temples—no ten-minute nap would heal those. So Smin did not put his head down. Instead, he got up from his meal he had picked at and walked out the door, because he had heard the sound of a helicopter approaching.

Could it be the Air Force, arriving so quickly?

It wasn't. It was a little two-man craft, like that of the major general of militia, and the man getting out of it was the Director of the Chernobyl Nuclear Power Station, T. M. Zaglodin. He spoke deferentially to Istvili, the man from the Ministry, before he turned to Smin. "Well, Simyon Mikhailovitch," he said angrily. "I am called away on business for a few days, and a fine mess you make!"

What the Director had to say meant nothing to Smin. In any decision-making sense, he no longer mattered. He had not been present when the first decisions had to be taken, and now that the men from Moscow were on the scene, nothing he, or Smin, decided would be final without ratification by them. Smin ignored him. "Comrade Istvili," he said, "I request a decision on the question of the urgent evacuation of all unnecessary personnel from Pripyat."

Istvili raised his hand. "The buses are already on the way," he said, but he didn't seem interested in the subject. He was peering curiously at Smin's face. He said soberly, "Comrade Deputy Director, I think you will have to leave these matters to us now."

Smin scowled, and the sudden, sharp crack of pain at the corner of his mouth informed him what Istvili meant better than any words. He touched the spot. When he brought his finger away he was not surprised to find it damp with the fluid from a broken blister.

Istvili had already turned away to order an ambulance for Deputy Director Smin. "Ambulance?" Smin protested. "There is work that I must do here! Why do I need an ambulance for a blister?"

"Not for the blister," Istvili said gently. "For what caused it. What you will do now is what the doctors will tell you to do, in Hospital Number Six. You're relieved of your duties, Deputy Director Smin." He turned to Zaglodin, his face hardening. Then he paused, looked back at Smin and added, "Good luck."

CHAPTER 15

Although the Soviet Army soldier Sergei Konov was born in Tashkent, he is both Russian and Muscovite by ancestry and upbringing. He does not remember anything about Tashkent. He doesn't even remember coming to Moscow with his parents when he was two years old. He remembers very well leaving it when he was ordered up for his military service in June of 1984, when he was twenty, because he did not at all want to go. Konov has not been a good soldier. He did not want to be a soldier at all, since he didn't like any of the possibilities that suggested. You could be sent to Afghanistan and die there, you could go to Poland and have the Solidarity girls shun you; you could, at the very best, have to spend all your time doing dull and arduous things for a couple of years, with no chance to put on the beautiful Wrangler jeans and join friends in the Blue Bird nightclub off Pushkin Street, or listen to Beatles and Abba tapes in someone's flat until daylight.

But what Konov wanted had not mattered. There was no way to get out of it, though he had tried. The entire jar of American coffee powder he had forced himself to brew and drink just before his examination by the military doctor had certainly made his heart pound, but the doctor had not been impressed. All he had said was,

"Less coffee, please, Konov; you will serve your country better if you sleep at night."

Konov has a reputation in his unit as a sloppy soldier. He has deserved it. He doesn't get along very well with most of his comrades, few of whom are Slavs like himself (and none, of course, Byelorussians, since the Byelorussian Republic is where his 461st Guards Rifle Division is based.) He avoids all the details he can—pretty successfully now that he is a fourth class soldier, with his discharge not far away and thus in a position to make the juniors do his work for him.

He has one ambition, and that is to avoid being sent to a punishment battalion before his time is up. Since Konov was in the summer 1984 intake, his term of service will expire exactly two years later, on June 12, 1986. He knows that date well. He has been looking forward to his demobilization date for exactly 684 days so far, and as he bumps along in the Army truck to his new assignment, he calculates that that date is (he looks at his watch) now just 66,240 minutes away.

Konov didn't know that Chernobyl was the name of the place they were going to on that Sunday afternoon in April, the one day in the week that should have been their precious own. Konov didn't know anything at all about where they were going or what they were supposed to do. Neither did any of the other twenty-odd soldiers in his truck, bouncing along a country road at a hundred and thirty kilometers an hour, until they stopped at a crossroads and were ordered out of the trucks.

They straggled down from the truck to relieve themselves, lined up along the edge of a field of winter wheat, exchanging with the soldiers from the other trucks the same guesses and denials they had been exchanging with their truckmates for the past two hours. No one had any facts. None of the units was even complete. The 461st Guards Rifle Division had been put on alert at two o'clock that afternoon and the units that were in camp ordered to be on board the trucks with full gear at fifteen minutes before three. "It can't be the Americans attacking," said one, "because we'd be going east, not south."

And another said, "Americans your asshole. It's the fucking Ukrainians. They've found another Cossack bandit to lead them, so they're trying a revolt." And another still was certain it was the Chinese, sneaking over the border from Iran—or the Afghans, bored with shooting down Soviet troops in their own country and now invading—or the Martians; and it wasn't until the sergeant came trotting up to shout at them that they got any information at all. Then it wasn't immediately helpful.

"Assholes," he yelled. "You should all piss on the east side of the road—the west is where you're sleeping tonight!"

"Sleeping here, Sergeant?" called one. "You mean we're going to be staying in this place? What are we here for?"

And the sergeant waved a hand to the distant pillar of smoke on the southern horizon. "You see that? That is what we're here for, and you'll all be damned lucky if you ever live to see anything else."

It was just his way of talking, Konov's comrades reassured one another.

But an hour later, when they were in the town of Pripyat, Konov was no longer so sure. Some of the militiamen guarding the approaches had called to the soldiers, and the words they used were scary. *Atomic explosion. Out of control.* Worst of all, *People are dying here!* And no one seemed to think that was an exaggeration. And then they were all issued light little aluminum things that looked like fountain pens. The men turned them over curiously, and when they were told that these objects were called dosimeters and their purpose was to measure how much dangerous radiation each of them might receive, the mood of the soldiers became quite thoughtful.

Their job turned out to be getting the people out of the town of Pripyat. An endless creeping caterpillar of buses—city buses, highway buses, military buses; Konov had never seen so many buses in one place, eleven hundred of them someone said!—were snaking along the highway toward the town. The first task of the soldiers was to get the people out of their houses and onto the transport. *Immediately.* In pairs they were assigned blocks and buildings. And Konov found himself running up and down stairs, bawling to the occupants that the town of Pripyat was to be evacuated—simply temporarily, as a precaution—and everyone was to be ready to leave in half an hour. Meanwhile, were there any sick? Pregnant women? Old people, or people with a heart condition who would need special help?

It surprised Konov that the Pripyaters took his shouted orders so lightly. Of course, they had had ample warning that something was up. If somehow they had missed seeing that worrisome distant smoke cloud, then certainly the militia cars cruising every block with their loudspeakers blaring were letting them know. And yet there were people who didn't want to go, there were people who couldn't make up their minds to go and people—many, many people—who definitely wanted to be taken out of the threatened town as fast as possible, but first wanted to be given time to make decisions, help to pack up their food, their clothes, their pets, their children.

There was no time. "In thirty minutes," shouted Konov, "you will be out of this building, or we will be back to drag you out! You must take food and necessities for three days, do you understand? And in thirty minutes there will be a bus at your door to take you!"

When he first saw Pripyat, Konov felt almost jealous. The eight-story concrete buildings of flats on the outskirts were quite like those that had swallowed all the green fields around Moscow—like, in fact, the ones Konov's parents still lived in just off the Leningradskaya Prospekt. But the ones farther into the town were something quite different. They were, in a word, beautiful. They were well kept, too, and surrounded by trees and parks. It was not just that someone with a bulldozer had sculptured a greensward here, a circular flower bed there; Pripyat's trees were native firs as well as chestnuts and fruit trees, and some of them were already in blossom. How fine it would be to live in a place like this, Konov thought. The only things that reminded him of home were cars drawn up on the sidewalk, some of them on blocks, nearly half of them still covered with the canvas shrouds that had protected them through the Ukrainian winter. And inside the buildings it was even more like home, for, new as they were, the hallways held that omnipresent Russian aroma of old cabbage.

For the first time in his Army career Konov felt he was doing a job that was worth his while.

It was frightening, at first—a nuclear accident! But it was obvious that the important thing was to get all these people to safety. Konov moved faster than he had moved in the last year and ten and a half months, and yet it didn't seem to him that it was fast enough. By the time they had made their first pass through the two buildings assigned to them, Konov was itching to get on with the job. Pripyat was a town of young, healthy people, it seemed. Hardly any had needed special attention because of age or illness. The men of Konov's platoon hunkered down and smoked, waiting for the orders to finish the job.

"Miklas," Konov said to his partner, a dark-complected Armenian. "We can do this faster if we split up."

"Why do we want to do it faster?"

Konov hesitated. "To help these people?" It had turned into a question as he said the words.

Miklas looked at him with curiosity. "Seryozha," he said reasonably, "if we finish fast, they'll just find something else for us to do."

"Even so."

Miklas shook his head. "Well, why not? All right. You take the tall building, I'll take the other one."

Well, that served him right, Konov thought as he entered the second apartment house in the block. He had already figured out a new skill to meet the needs of the situation. It was better to start from the bottom of the building and to work his way up than to begin at the top. In his new system, he reasoned, you could double-check every flat on the way down because when the people were out of the top floor the ones lower down were already informed of what they had to do. Even, if you were lucky, many of them might already be in the street, trudging toward the loading zones on the sidewalks with their belongings in their arms and perhaps one child on their backs. He had to use threats at one of the first-floor apartments, but on the second floor he got unexpected help.

A tall, pale man with his arm in a sling was standing at the stairs, waiting for him.

Surprisingly, although the weather was warm in this late afternoon, the man was wearing a turtleneck sweater and a woolen cap. "Let me help you," he said, his tone oddly supplicatory. "My name is Kalychenko. I am an engineer. I worked at Chernobyl."

Konov frowned at him. "And how can you help now?" he demanded.

The man said apologetically, "At least I can explain to the people what they are facing! Many of them simply do not understand the danger of radiation."

"But you are hurt," Konov objected, eyeing the man's arm. It was not in a proper sling but a woman's shawl. "If you go down now, there may still be some ambulances for the sick people."

"I don't need an ambulance. I'll have it looked at later."

"Come on then," said Konov, turning away. He paused as the man tossed his own suitcase inside his apartment door. But he left the door open. "Aren't you afraid that will be stolen?" he asked.

The man laughed. "But that is impossible," he said. "There is not one person leaving Pripyat who can carry one more thing than he already has. Come on! The sooner we get these people moving, the sooner we all will be gone!"

Konov would not have believed it possible, but in less than ninety minutes from the time they entered Pripyat, a town of nearly fifty thousand people had become a wasteland.

The street Konov had been assigned to was almost the last to be evacuated. He patrolled the sidewalk with Miklas, always watching to see that none of the complaining citizens obeyed that impulse to go back for one more thing while they waited. "It would have been better," Miklas told him, observing the scene with a critic's eye, "to assemble everyone in the main squares and load from there."

"Nonsense," Konov said, equally critical. "They keep them at their houses because they don't want them to panic. Only they should have assigned each bus to a specific address at once, of course, so there would not be this long waiting."

"Nonsense to you too," said Miklas amiably, "and up your asshole. What would the Soviet Union be without long waiting? That is why you are not an officer, Sergei. You do not understand Soviet life."

"I will understand it perfectly when I am back in it," Konov said, and then, calling sharply, "You! Stay by the curb! Your bus will be here directly."

It wasn't, though. Konov could hear buses grinding their gears in the next block, but so far their own had not been reached. Only soldiers were moving on foot in any of the streets. Militia cars were all that roamed the avenues. Konov watched the knots of people on their block carefully for those who might change their minds, or remember something irreplaceable that they must certainly go back at once to retrieve. Some tried. None got through.

Now they could see the next block loading almost the last of Pripyat's people, as they were herded into the hundredth, or perhaps it was the thousandth, of the buses that patiently crawled through the emptying streets, loaded, and rolled away. The buses were of all kinds. Some had been making their runs in Pripyat itself, most seemed to be from the distant city of Kiev, others perhaps came from other communities nearby. There were even a few trucks with Army markings, perhaps the ones Konov and his comrades had come down in not two hours before. "So we walk back to our campground," grumbled Miklas, and Konov clapped him on the shoulder.

"You may be luckier than that," he said. "Look, they are putting one soldier on each bus; maybe you'll spend the night on the Black Sea!"

If that was where the buses were going, some of the people waiting to be evacuated had made bad guesses. Many wore sheepskin coats, even boots; one man even had a pair of skis. Another had a tennis racket; well, since they had been told the evacuation would be for only three days, no doubt they planned to have a little vacation to make up for the pains. (But where did the man with the skis think they were going?) And the things they carried! A live chicken, even; Konov saw it with his own eyes, under one old woman's arm. There were bird cages and rolled-up blankets, there were suitcases and duffel bags, paper sacks, cardboard cartons, table lamps with rosy pink shades, television sets, a stereo or two—there was nothing in any Soviet home small enough to carry, Konov thought, that he did not see on the backs or in the arms of some of the thousands. What possessions could there be that had been left behind? And yet, Konov knew, the answer was *everything*. Even the poorest owned much more than he alone could carry away, and the officers had been adamant: what a person could not lift aboard a bus in one trip stayed on the ground when the bus pulled away. There was already a mound of discarded, wept-over belongings stacked helter-skelter just inside the building door—to add to everything left in the flats, or at people's places of work—and the washing on the lines; and the food on the tables—

It must, Konov thought, have been like this nearly half a century ago, when the Germans finished their sweep around the Pripyat Marshes and overran all this land. But this was not Germans. This was not the work of any external enemy; it was, Konov thought uneasily, simply the result of what they had done to themselves.

He did not like that thought.

Konov pulled the unfamiliar dosimeter instrument off his cape and held it up to the light. When he peered through it he could see cryptic numbers and symbols, black on a white background; but what the symbols meant no one had told Konov.

At the end of the block the sergeant was in an altercation with a man who was shouting and pointing to a car, while the sergeant uninterestedly shook his head. "Look," said Miklas, "the poor man only wants to evacuate himself in his Zhiguli. Why won't the sergeant let him?"

"Because they don't want traffic jams, of course," said Konov, but there was something he wanted to ask the sergeant for himself. He was beginning to be very hungry. He got up and walked toward the sergeant, almost bumping into the pale man with an arm in a sling who had helped him evacuate one of the buildings—the one with the Ukrainian name, Kaly-something-or-other—but Konov had more important things on his mind. He barely returned the man's greeting, though he noticed the young woman beside him in the line was good-looking. Konov approached the sergeant, who was standing by himself and sipping something that came out of a Fanta orange-drink bottle but looked and smelled like beer. "Sergeant," Konov said politely, "it is past time for us to eat, I think."

"You will eat when you are told to. There will be food at the bivouac area, probably."

"Yes, sergeant," said Konov, "but that, too, is a question: if our trucks are being used to take these people out of danger, how will we get to the bivouac area? It is at least ten kilometers from here."

The sergeant said thoughtfully, "It is nearer twenty." He looked at Konov, and then added cheerfully, "But you won't have to walk. I was about to select a man to board that bus to keep the refugees in order. You'll do. Get on it."

"Get on it to where?" Konov demanded, recoiling a step.

"To wherever it goes," said the sergeant, reaching to pluck the dosimeter from Konov's blouse pocket. "But first give me that; we will need it for the patrols that remain on duty here."

"But, Sergeant!" Konov yelped. "I don't know what it says! If it turns out I have already been exposed to too much radiation, how will we know?"

"Of course we will know," said the sergeant, jerking a thumb toward the bus, "because we will get a report from wherever you are going to tell us that you are dead."

The mood in the bus was cheerful enough at first; someone had an accordion, and a few people in the front were singing as though they were teenagers off to their Komsomol camp for the summer. Then the bus rolled out onto the highway. It had to squeeze past a long line of Army vehicles, ambulances and heavy machines rolling toward the plant.

Everyone in the bus craned to look at the convoy. The holiday mood evaporated at once.

The bus was filled with people and their belongings. There was no seat for Konov, only the stairwell by the bus door; but at least he was on what seemed to be an intercity bus, not one of those urban ones where even the stairwell was so cramped no one could sleep in it. Konov did sleep, leaning back, his head almost under the driver's seat.

So, after a while, did most of those on the bus, even Kalychenko. He and his fiancée, too, had been lucky. They had managed to get two seats together. They had even managed to get into the very back of the bus, where there was a little more room on the floor to set down Raia's straw suitcase, her cooking pots, her sack of flour, and already-melting half kilo of lard; and every ten minutes for the first fifty kilometers she would jerk up straight in her seat with something else she had forgotten; "The wine, Bohdan! The champagne for our wedding, it's still in the kitchen cabinet, they gave me no time to think!"

And Kalychenko would hush her, his arm twitching with pins-and-needles as it rested around her shoulder where she had been leaning against him: "Shush, Raia, it's all right. We're not leaving forever, you know?"

But was that true? Kalychenko knew quite well that "three days" might indeed stretch to forever. The fact that the town had been evacuated so hurriedly and utterly was certain proof that the radiation level had been not only above warning levels but definitely very dangerous indeed. (And how much radiation had each of them received already? Not as much for Kalychenko himself as he would have if he had remained at his post of duty, of course—but that line of thought led him to worries almost worse than future leukemia.)

He performed calculations in his mind, trying to remember the half-lives of all the deadly radionuclides that were likely to be in the smoke from the explosion and fire. Suppose (he thought) the firefighters and the engineers managed (somehow) to put out the flames and control the fission reactions. Suppose they sealed it all off. Very well. There would still remain all the tiny radioactive particles that had already fallen from the sky. The soot from the fire, the morning dew, the air itself had already left invisible films of radioactive cesium, iodine, strontium, and a dozen others. And all of them were still there in Pripyat, emitting radiation. Well, but some of them had short half-lives, he reminded himself. In just a few days half of the iodine would have radiated itself into some other element, a harmless one; in a few months the same would be true of the cesium, the strontium. In just a year or less the radiation would be only a fraction of its current levels. . . .

A year or less! He did not even think of the long-lived transuranics, like plutonium, with a half-life of a quarter of a million years. A year was already an eternity.

And anyway, it all depended on how much there was to begin with. A quarter of a little bit was perhaps no more than the normal background, while a quarter of very much might still be enough to kill. And, worst of all, when could they start the patient clock that would tell them when they might return? For as the bus pulled out of Pripyat, Kalychenko had craned his neck to stare back. He could still see, in the waning light of that April day, the distant, uneven column of smoke. There seemed to be helicopters fluttering around it—sight-seers? Foolish ones, if they were, because if they flew through that plume, they would learn caution very thoroughly, if too late to do them any good.

The plume had been not one whit smaller or less frightening than it had been the day before.

So it could easily be a year before any of them saw Pripyat again. Kalychenko told himself. It could be much longer. It could be never. And what then of his precious stereo from East Germany, his *magnetizdat* tapes of Okudjava and the Beatles, his hopes for a car, his career? What of Raia's ten thousand forgotten treasures? What of their wedding? When she started up again—"My raincoat from Czechoslovakia! What if it rains where we're going?"—he patted her silently. It would rain, all right. It would rain many, many times before she saw that smart, new, black trench coat again.

When he woke from an uneasy sleep an hour later, it was because Raia was leaning across him. She was trying to help the woman in the seat ahead of them with her wailing baby. The infant had soiled itself, and the mother was trying to make a flat space on the clutter of bundles, bags, and personal possessions of all kinds that were piled in the aisle so she could change it. Under the circumstances, it was a major undertaking. The mother had not failed to bring everything she needed with her, especially including the rolls of gauze bandages that were used for diapers. Unfortunately, the child was in her lap and the bandages were in a bag buried somewhere along the aisle of the bus.

Kalychenko suffered his fiancée to climb over him, changing seats so that she could be more use to the woman ahead. Raia held the crying infant's shoulders securely while the mother dabbed him clean, then grumpily wound a head scarf around the baby boy's bottom.

Kalychenko averted his eyes. He could not avert his nose, and when the woman carefully rolled up the soiled diaper-bandages and deposited them at her feet, he complained to his fiancée, "She should throw them out the window! It's not fair, making us stand all that stink!"

Then it was Raia's turn to shush him. "And then what would she use when we got where we are going? It's all right, Bohdan. Here, let me make it smell better—" From her pocketbook she pulled out a little flask of cologne and patted it on

Bohdan's cheek. "You don't mind about the scarf, do you?" she added shyly.

"The scarf? You mean you gave that woman my sling?" Kalychenko was suddenly outraged.

"But you don't seem to need it anymore, Bohdan dear. You lifted the bags with both hands. And, think, in just a few months, when we have our own little one—"

"I suppose it is all right," he grumbled. "Let us go back to sleep." Obediently Raia put her head on his shoulder again and presently closed her eyes.

But for Kalychenko it was not so easy. Raia's last remark had reminded him of another problem of radiation. What about the baby she was carrying? Just how much radiation had Raia absorbed? He didn't know but had an uneasy feeling that pregnant women, or their babies anyway, were especially subject to radiation damage. In any case, he told himself, there was nothing he could do about it right now. But he remained wide awake, trying not to think.

He squirmed carefully in his seat, not wanting to disturb Raia. The woman ahead had politely opened her window a crack to try to dissipate the odor pervading her immediate area, but as a result a blast of damp, cold night air was striking Kalychenko just on the side of his head. His bladder was full. His future was murky. His mood was dour.

There was no doubt in Kalychenko's mind—well, no *real* doubt—that he wanted to go through with marrying Raia, even less that he wanted the child she was carrying. Of course, one should have a son! But his stomach churned with fear. Perhaps there was a way to have Raia checked for radiation. As for himself, the little bruises on his elbow, got when he fell as he fled the exploding reactor, no longer seemed very convincing even to him. Especially since Raia had given his sling away! The sling, of course, was no more than camouflage, simply circumstantial evidence to add credibility to the story he was planning to tell; but Kalychenko was aware he would need all the help he could get when questions were asked.

And, sooner or later, questions surely would be asked.

Kalychenko groaned—stifling it, so Raia would not hear— and tried to settle himself again for sleep. But the bus seemed to be slowing down, even stopping. It came to a dead halt, then lurched slowly forward again.

Kalychenko tried to raise himself to see ahead. There were lights in the road. Someone was shouting directions; the bus crept forward, then turned into a space on the side of the highway and came to a complete stop. The passengers began to stir.

The overhead lights on the bus came on and the door opened. Up ahead there was a muttered colloquy between the driver, the soldier who had gotten on with them, and someone from outside; then the soldier stood up: "Everybody is to get out here," he cried, his voice hoarse with sleep and fatigue. "Leave your belongings on the bus. Now, please, hurry up!"

It had not, after all, been altogether a good idea to sit at the back of the bus, for it took them forever to get out.

Emptying the bus was a complicated logistical problem. First the people in the front seats had to stand up and lift some of the things from the aisles onto the seats they had vacated before those in the next row could move into the aisle. The process had to be repeated, row by row, the whole length of the bus before it came to Kalychenko's and Raia's turn. There was no way to speed the process. All they could do was peer out the windows. They could see that they were in what seemed to be an agricultural station of some kind. There were other buses there, a dozen of them or more, and people milling around under bright lights. As they limped forward and stiffly disembarked, the soldier was calling, "Please, everybody! Listen. Remember your bus number, bus number eight two eight. Eight two eight, remember! When the bus number is called, follow instructions—and especially when it's time to go, make sure you get back on bus eight two eight, for it is my ass if you aren't!"

An old woman chided him: "Is that a way to speak, a Soviet Army soldier? Would your mother like to hear such talk?"

"I'm sorry," Konov said, abashed. "But please—bus eight two eight, don't forget!"

Men were drifting to the right, back down the road they had traveled, women to the left. Kalychenko went far enough to avoid the messes those before him had made and then relieved his bladder at the side of the road, stretching and shivering in the cold night air. One by one the buses were pulling up to a gasoline truck for refueling, then returning to their parking spaces while the drivers hurried to take care of their own needs. They closed the doors behind them. Soldiers—other soldiers, with the green flashes of the internal army—were keeping everyone but the drivers away. Still other soldiers were clustered around a pair of wooden tables, with people lined up before them, and from the back of a truck dirty, tired Komsomols were serving some kind of food.

Well, at least that was something. Kalychenko looked around for Raia, and when she returned from her own necessities along the southward stretch of the road, they lined up to get what was offered. The Komsomols looked both exhausted and keyed up as they dished out bread, sausages, and strong tea.

"I wonder where we are?" said Kalychenko as they found a low wall to sit on while they ate.

"A woman said it is a place called Sodolets," Raia told him, raising her voice to be heard. It was a noisy place to be, with bus motors grumbling and racing as new ones arrived and old ones left. "South of Kiev. We've come a long way." She was gazing at the mother from the bus who, her back modestly turned, was nursing her baby. "I hope we're nearly there," Raia fretted. "It's not good for the child, being up so late in this night air."

"It's not too good for me, either," Kalychenko grumbled, but softly. And then their bus number was called and they lined up one more time, under the bright lights, before the tables where an Army colonel was standing, scowling, smoking a cigarette while two lieutenants were, wonder of wonders! Giving away money! When he reached the head of the line, Kalychenko displayed his passport. The lieutenant painstakingly copied his name onto a long list and then carefully counted out twenty new ten-ruble notes into Kalychenko's hand. "For what?" Kalychenko asked, astonished.

"For you," said the lieutenant. "To help you get settled in your new home. A gift from the peoples of the Soviet Union. Now move along quickly, there are others behind you!"

Kalychenko counted over the notes, frowning. He followed Raia to where the passengers from bus number 828 were now ordered to assemble. The soldier from Pripyat was standing there at the closed bus door, a mug of tea in his hand. He looked more cheerful than before, and he nodded to Kalychenko. "Now all of you listen," he ordered. "When you get back on the bus, be sensible. The ones in the last rows go first. Take the same seats you had before. Otherwise it will simply be a disorderly mess, and—"

Then he fell silent as an Army captain came up with a clipboard. "Reboard now," he ordered in a weary voice, punching at the door until it opened. "Just a few more hours, Comrades, then you'll be in your new homes. Where?" He looked at the clipboard. "This is bus number eight two eight? Well, you've got a trip still ahead of you. It's a place called Yuzhevin."

CHAPTER 16

Radiation kills the cells of living things by spoiling the way the cells grow, and so it is the fastest-growing parts of the human body that suffer the most. The lining of the mouth and the digestive tract are quickly damaged, but it is the bone marrow that is most at risk. The marrow of the bones is where the blood's cells are manufactured, thousands at a time, to replace those that are always being lost in the body's normal wear and tear. When the bone marrow is damaged by radiation, blood counts drop. The blood loses its ability to fight off infection, to carry oxygen from the lungs, even to clot. It does not much matter whether the harmful radiation comes from nuclear war, from a natural source, or from something like Chernobyl. What matters is how much radiation is received.

There are many ways of measuring the damage caused by radiation, but the handiest unit is called the "rad," which is short for "radiation absorbed dose." (In technical terms, one rad is defined as that amount of ionizing radiation that deposits 100 ergs of energy in each gram of exposed biological tissue.) The number of rads tells the story. A person who has received no more than 150 rads is likely to recover completely. Around 300 rads his life is in balance, but blood transfusions, antibiotics, and the best of nursing care should pull him through.

Five hundred rads and over means that the bone

marrow is destroyed, and without bone marrow no one can live for long.

In the swaying, jolting ambulance en route to Hospital No. 18 in Kiev, Tamara Sheranchuk wished she had ironed fewer of her husband's shirts and taken more time to look at his books. Perhaps there would have been something in them about these "rads" and "roentgens." She knew very well that such dose numbers were very important. The experts from Moscow's Hospital No. 6 had explained that to all of the Pripyat and Chernobyl doctors, in that quick, twenty-minute briefing that was all anyone had time for that weekend. Unfortunately, she didn't really know what they meant. Even more unfortunately, the casualties who came to her medicpoint didn't wear numbers. Some of them didn't wear much of anything at all. Before they got to the medics they went through radiometric screening. As often as not, the counters squealed the alarm as they sniffed the garments, and then their contaminated outer clothing was taken away from them and added to the heap of condemned goods. They were lucky if they got a smock or a bathrobe from the dwindling stores to cover their underwear. They were luckier still if it was only their clothes that made the detectors squeal.

And even the ones who had swallowed or inhaled radioactive material were not as frustrating as those who had merely been exposed to intense radiation. They were the hardest ones to diagnose. There wasn't any visible wound. They were weak, they felt nauseated, they vomited unpredictably; yes, very well, those were precisely the early symptoms of radiation sickness. They were also the symptoms of shock or overexertion or a hundred other things, even simple fatigue, and certainly every human being working to control the damage from the accident had every right to a great deal of fatigue. Including Tamara Sheranchuk herself.

So what Tamara had been doing, before she was ordered onto an ambulance to accompany four of the seriously wounded to Hospital Number 18 in Kiev, were the simple medical things she had always done for injured people: poultice and debride, sew and dress. It was not enough.

There wasn't really room for four patients in the ambulance, much less for Tamara herself and the stands that held the plasma and antibiotics that trickled into the bloodstream of two of the patients. There were not enough clamps for so many stands, and so, as the ambulance swayed, Tamara had to have one hand to steady a glucose drip and another to catch a stand of saline solution that was about to topple, and none at all to keep herself from bouncing about.

These particular patients had—at least, were thought to have had—only light doses of radiation, if any at all. Three of them were seriously burned. Unfortunately, only one of the three was unconscious. The other two could not help moaning and crying out as the ambulance lurched and Tamara fought to stay awake and steady the IV stands. There was a nasty smell in the ambulance, part vomit and part smoke and part what really smelled most of all like burned meat.

The fourth patient was a woman, with chest pains, perhaps the beginning of a heart attack. She was elderly and conscious; she lay there without speaking, watching Tamara as she tried to deal with the others. When Tamara sat back for a moment, brushing hair out of her eyes and wishing she dared close them for a moment, the woman spoke. "I've seen you before," she said, and when Tamara identified herself nodded. "Yes, to be sure. Don't you remember me? I'm Paraska Kandyba. Deputy Director Smin's secretary."

"Of course," said Tamara, letting go of the saline stand to reach for her chart. "Yes, and they've given you heparin and nitroglycerine. How are you feeling?"

"A headache. Nothing more now."

"Yes, that is from the nitroglycerine. It is unpleasant, but it's better if I don't give you anything for it until you reach the hospital."

"I don't want anything." The woman added apologetically, "I know it was very foolish of me to try to help out, at my age. But in such a terrible thing—"

Tamara saw that the secretary was weeping. Yes, certainly it had been very foolish; Paraska Kandyba had been near the plant all day, begging for the chance to get into the administration block to rescue her boss's papers, and what was the importance of that? But all Tamara said was, "It was very brave of you."

Paraska raised her head to stare at the doctor. "Brave? But not sensible. And Deputy Director Smin is also not sensible! He is not a young man. And yet I saw him in and out of the plant, right with the firemen, until they sent him off to the hospital in Moscow. Oh, he didn't want to go, I can tell you!"

"No, of course not," Tamara soothed, letting go of the chart to rescue the toppling saline stand again. "Tell me, Paraska," she ventured. "Did you by any chance see my husband today?"

But Paraska Kandyba only shook her head and continued weeping. It was obvious that her tears and her concern were all for Deputy Director Simyon Smin.

When they reached Hospital No. 18 in the city of Kiev, Tamara Sheranchuk dragged herself out of the ambulance for the transfer of the patients. She wasn't needed. She stood aside while the hospital's own orderlies took over, efficiently unloading the patients and wheeling them into the receiving room. She was looking forward to the ride back. It would be nearly two hours! Two hours in which she could stretch out in the ambulance and sleep. She leaned against the door of the ambulance, dreaming of that wonderful two-hour trip, when she realized the driver had poked her and said, "Look at them."

Tamara blinked. "Look at what?"

"Those people! Look, they are acting as if nothing had happened!"

It was true. She gazed around the streets of Kiev wonderingly. Here in Kiev, at least, it was, after all, a peaceful Sunday afternoon! People were strolling the wide streets, children were laughing as they played, a few early blossoms were on the chestnut trees, the bright posters were everywhere for the May Day celebration. How incredible, Tamara marveled, that all these people could be going about their normal lives, unaware of the hell that was raging less than a hundred and fifty kilometers away.

"They're lucky," grumbled the ambulance driver, and Tamara shook her head.

"Not really," she said. "No one is very lucky today. They simply have not yet found it out. Are we through here? Then let's go back to Chernobyl."

As the ambulance driver, who had had no more sleep than Tamara, wearily started to turn the vehicle around, a man came running out begging for a lift. He explained that he was a doctor trained in radiation sickness, called in from his weekend for the emergency. Tamara made herself stay awake; here was a chance to learn something useful! She asked him about the numbers. "Yes, exactly," he said, "above 500 rads the only hope is to somehow give them living bone marrow."

"And how is that done?"

"Fetal liver transplants," he said. "In some places they actually transplant bone marrow—this is done in America sometimes—but there are great problems. First of all, the patient's own bone marrow must be destroyed, otherwise the transplant will be rejected. Then there must be an exact typing match, and it is not easy to type bone marrow—and if that is wrong, the transplant will still be rejected. Of course, that itself is serious; a patient who might otherwise recover could be killed by the rejection process."

"And what is the fetal liver procedure?"

"In the embryo," he said, "it is the liver cells that perform the functions of the adult bone marrow in manufacturing blood cells. So from aborted fetuses we extract the liver, purify the cells, and inject them into the patient." He hesitated. "That, too, has a poor success rate," he admitted, "but for patients with more than 500 rads there is, after all, no choice."

"Ah, yes," said Tamara, "but how do you know what the exposure has been, since not all the victims are thoughtful enough to carry dosimeters?"

The young specialist said enthusiastically, "That is the key, of course. The doctor in Hospital Number Six in Moscow, where I trained, has developed a procedure. We take blood counts at two-hour intervals and compare them with a standard profile. We can see how rapidly the cells deteriorate, and from that we can determine what the exposure has been. . . ."

But by then Tamara was asleep beside him.

Tamara had almost allowed herself to hope that by the time she got back the fire would be under control, the emergency over. But it seemed it was worse than ever. Pripyat had been evacuated. (And where had her son, Boris, gone?) The ambulance was sent on to Chernobyl town, thirty kilometers away from the reactor. It was, it seemed, as near as was really safe, and so now there was talk that everyone, *everyone*, within that thirty kilometer radius of the plant was to be ordered away. And where would they find places for all these people to stay? There were a dozen villages and nearly thirty collective farms in the area; where would they all go?

It was not just the people now. Half the farms in the area raised livestock, cattle mostly, but any number of sheep, pigs, goats, even a few horses. Many of the animals came from the kolkhozists' private ventures, which made their owners doubly desperate to save them.

As they circled around the town of Pripyat and the stricken plant, Tamara looked longingly out of the back of the ambulance. Sheranchuk was there. Doing, Tamara was sure, something doggedly heroic and certainly dangerous. If only she could take him and Boris and run away!

It did not occur to her that this was almost the first time she had been separated from her husband when her principal worry had not been that he might be with another woman.

When they reached the town of Chernobyl they were directed to the bus station.

There Tamara Sheranchuk set up shop, but she had no more than entered the room set aside for the medics than her boss, the chief of surgery from the Pripyat clinic, wrinkled her nose and scowled. "When did you change your clothes last?" she barked. "Go at once. Shower. Eat something. Get cleaned up. Don't come back for one hour."

"But there are so many patients—"

"There are plenty of doctors now, too," said the elder woman. "Go now."

And indeed when Tamara came back in a clean white gown, her hair still damp but pulled neatly to the back of her head, there were four strange doctors taking their turns with the influx. Two were from Kursk, one from Kiev, the dark, small, Oriental-looking woman all the way from Volgograd.

"But they must have emptied out every hospital in the Soviet Union," said Tamara.

The woman from Volgograd said, "No, the hospitals are all fully staffed. It is people like us who were off duty, now we give up our Sunday to come here to help."

"And are the people in Volgograd so concerned about an explosion in the Ukraine?"

"The people in Volgograd know nothing about an explosion in the Ukraine. Neither did I. I was simply told to report to the airport at nine this morning, Sunday or no, and here I am. What is holding up the line? Send in the next patient!''

Even the patients were easier to deal with here. Triage had already been done—again, by teams of fresh doctors brought in from everywhere, taking their turns at the medicpoint in the Chernobyl town bus station. The seriously injured ones had already been sorted out and sent off to hospitals elsewhere. The ones that were coming through were lightly injured, or not injured at all. For most of them all Tamara had to do was a quick physical check—the eyes, the pulse, the blood pressure, the inside of the mouth; a quick questioning about symptoms and a few cc's of blood drawn for a lab somewhere to make a count. Then she passed them on. Most of them went directly onto buses or trains, for those who were able to travel were counted at once as evacuees.

"Mother," said a voice from the next queue, and when she looked up from her patient she saw that it was a young boy. His face was filthy and he wore an outsized Army blouse, not his own; it took a moment for her to realize that it was her son.

"Boris! Are you all right?"

"I think so. Only they are sending all the Komsomols away now."

"And quite time for it, too! But where are you going?" she demanded.

"Oh, to a summer camp, Mother! A good one! Maybe Artek, down on the Black Sea—and, oh, Mother," he said joyfully, "it isn't going to cost us a kopeck!"

CHAPTER 17

Smoke does not last very long in the air. What makes a column of smoke visible are the tiny particles of soot and other things that it contains, and they are transitory. The larger particles fall fairly quickly to the ground; the others fall more slowly, or are washed out of the air by rain, and in any case, diluted by the air they float in, quite soon, they can no longer be seen. The gases that go with the smoke, however, remain. In the gases from the nuclear accident are many which are invisible but not undetectable. Chemical analysis will spot them readily, but if it took a laboratory to detect them, they would not cause much concern. Unfortunately they announce themselves in a different, and much more alarming, way. That is by the radiation they give off.

The first person to observe anything amiss in the air about him was a Finnish soldier. There was no smoke left by the time the Chernobyl cloud reached the Finnish border, so he saw nothing. His instruments told the story. The soldier's duty was to supervise a radiation-detection station on the border between Finland and the USSR, and what his instruments noticed was a small but unexplained increase in the normal background radiation. The soldier reported it at once to his superiors, of course.

They puzzled worriedly over the information, but, for the

time being, they decided to keep it to themselves. There was a political problem they had to take into account. Finland is not part of the Warsaw Pact, but all the same, Finnish leaders have learned a good deal of discretion. It was possible, they thought, that the radiation came from an unannounced Soviet nuclear bomb test. Disturbing reports about nuclear events in their Soviet neighbor are not broadcast indiscriminately in Finland.

Finland, however, was not the only foreign country to discover that there was something wrong with the air on that otherwise peaceful Sunday in April. It was only the first of them. At two o'clock that afternoon, in the Swedish nuclear power plant at Forsmark, a worker coming off shift went through a radiation scan. The test was pure routine, but the results were not.

The man's shoes were radioactive.

Sweden does not take the discovery of unexplained radioactivity lightly. There is a powerful antinuclear movement among the Swedish people. Everything that happens at an atomic power plant is scrutinized at every step with great care. So this information was reported on the nationwide alert network at once. It caused immediate concern, multiplied when other stations reported that their air, too, was unexpectedly as radioactive as after a nearby bomb test. Or even after a real bomb.

The first thought (after they decided that the Swedish plants themselves were innocent) was a terrifying one. Most of Scandinavia's air comes from the west and south. (It is for that reason that the smoke from England's factories kills Swedish lakes; the British got rid of their pea-soup fogs with huge stacks that export the pollution to Scandinavia.) So their first thought was that the source of the radiation was in the United Kingdom. Was it possible that England had suffered a nuclear attack? But the English radio stations were still prattling away. Alternatively, could the English, the Germans, or the Dutch have—totally unexpectedly—set off a nuclear bomb test? Then meteorologists traced the recent movements of the air masses over Sweden, and informed the nuclear authorities that the patterns were a bit unusual. It was not from the west that the radioactive cloud came; untypically, the most recent incoming air had originated to the south and east.

It had come from the Soviet Union.

The Swedes are as conscious of their Soviet neighbor as

the Finns, but less careful about Soviet sensibilities. They saw no reason to keep the matter secret. The news services were informed. The report made instant headlines. In an hour most of the world knew that something big and nuclear had happened in the USSR . . . almost all of the world, in fact, except for the USSR itself.

CHAPTER 18

The Embassy of the United States of America in Moscow is on the ring boulevard, in the section of the boulevard named after the composer Tchaikovsky. The Embassy isn't a single building. It is a collection of several structures, linked together in a ramshackle red-brick compound. At every entrance to the compound a couple of uniformed KGB guards loiter, smoking cigarettes and chatting to each other, until someone approaches: then they interpose themselves in front of the door and request U.S. passports or hotel cards. When the documents are found to be in order, the KGB guards then say, or the more polite ones say, *"puzhalsta,"* which means "please," and perhaps they even touch the visors of their caps as they step out of the way. (There have been times when they have been less polite and a very great deal more energetic, especially when, as has now and then happened, some desperate Soviet citizen has tried to hurl himself past them to sanctuary.)

Really, the American Embassy in Moscow is a slum. It should have been abandoned at least a dozen years ago, but the chilly state of U.S.–Soviet relations has caused endless bickering and delays over every detail, and so plans for the splendid, modern new embassy building have remained incomplete. Its best feature is its cafeteria. There the American staff can get the only authentic hamburgers, French fries, and milk shakes to be found anywhere in Moscow. Its worst feature may well be that of its scores of drivers, telephone operators, translators, kitchen workers, and cleaners, almost all are locally employed Soviet nationals and nearly every one of those is known to have a second career—or, really, a first one—as an officer in the KGB.

Warner Borden, the assistant Science Attaché at the Embassy, was yelling at Emmaline Branford, the Press and Cultural Affairs officer, about the fact that the astonishing news was coming in over the open teletypes. "Keep the nationals out," he said angrily, meaning the translator and the cleaning man.

Emmaline Branford looked at him in astonishment. "But all we've got here is the open news services, Warner. There isn't anything secret about it."

Lowering his voice, Borden hissed, "Sometimes we *talk* in here, don't we? Keep 'em out till I come back!"

"Are you going to check the code room?" Emmaline asked, and Borden gave her a mock frown.

"See what I mean?" he asked, and then, "I'm gone." Emmaline sighed as he dashed off toward the secure teletypes in another part of the Embassy, with their Marine guard always at the door. At least, she reflected, he hadn't patted her bottom this time.

Across the narrow hall her translator, Rima, was bent over her morning *Pravda,* meticulously putting a story about fisheries production goals in the Baltic Sea into her careful English. Rima had a last name—it was Solovjova—but for most of the American Embassy staff most of the Russians had only one name, like plantation hands in old Dixie. For Emmaline, a black woman, some of whose ancestors had been named Cuffee, Napoleon, or Jezebel, the practice was unpleasing. But the Russians themselves seemed to prefer it that way. Perhaps that was because they didn't enjoy American attempts to pronounce names like "Solovjova." Emmaline stopped beside her and said, "Look, Rima, we'd better do what he says."

Rima said, looking down at her desk, "It is no problem, Emmaline."

If the Russian woman had any interest in this nuclear radiation flap that was burning up the teletypes, she was keeping it to herself. Emmaline tarried for a moment, thinking. She wanted to ask Rima Solovjova if there were anything at all in *Pravda* about unexplained radioactive emissions, but she already knew there was not. Emmaline herself had already scanned the paper. Although her command of Russian was still a long way from easy, she would not have missed a story like that—not even in, or actually especially not in, the short paragraphs on an inside page where any kind of bad news was usually to be found.

Of course, Rima could not have missed hearing something about what was going on. There had been plenty of talk in the teletype room, just as Borden had said. The simplest thing would be to come out and ask her what she'd heard and what she thought, but nothing was that simple in the relations with Soviet nationals. The relations between Emmaline and her translator were friendly enough. Certainly they did friendly things. Emmaline saw no harm in an occasional gift to Rima of a box of American tampons or a shopping bag advertising Macy's or Marshall Field's. And Rima was helpful beyond the call of duty in locating off-the-books painters, plumbers, and carpenters, and supplying Emmaline with homemakable recipes to replace the things that even the hard-currency stores always seemed to be out of—roach spray, for instance. Still, Emmaline had not been stationed in Moscow long enough for them to become anything like close enough to bring up politically embarrassing subjects. While she was debating whether or not to try it anyway, Rima Solovjova looked up, her face drawn.

"Is it possible that I could be excused for an hour?" she asked. "I do not feel well."

"Oh? Is there anything I can do?"

"Simply that I could lie down for a bit," the translator said apologetically. "One hour at the most, then I will be all right."

"Of course," said Emmaline, and watched the woman put a paperweight on her translation, pick up her imitation-leather pocketbook, and depart. Rima didn't look back. Emmaline listened to her modish heels clatter down the narrow staircase until the bang of the outside door informed her that Rima hadn't gone to the little ladies' room on the ground floor, but outside the building.

It had been Emmaline's assumption that the Russian woman was having the onset of her period. Now she revised it. More likely she was going somewhere outside to make a telephone call, perhaps to ask for instructions on what to do in the light of the unexpected news. Emmaline sighed, and remembered the cleaning man. Practicing her Russian, she said, "Andrei, can you finish this later on, please? After lunch would be good." And went back to the teletype room to see what else was coming in.

What else was coming in was scores on yesterday's National League baseball games, the Cubs at Montreal, the Mets at St. Louis. Emmaline waited a moment to see what the Atlanta Braves had done, but it seemed they'd been rained out.

She went back to her own desk and opened the folder on the American jazz pianist who was being brought in to tour Moscow, Leningrad, and Volgograd, and the novelist who had a special invitation from the Union of Soviet Writers to follow. Her heart wasn't in it. Clouds of radioactive material coming from the USSR was big news.

Emmaline's first thought, of course, had been the same as everybody else's, namely that the Russians were sneaking in a nuclear test in spite of their self-imposed moratorium. But that made so little sense! The United States was going on with testing whenever it chose. There was nothing to prevent the Soviets from doing the same—except if they were stupid enough to lie about it, in which case whatever propaganda benefits they had gained from their moratorium would be more than wiped out by the deceit.

Then there was the possibility of an accident of some kind. Warner Borden had told her all about the mysterious Kyshtym event, more than twenty-five years earlier. It seemed that the Soviets had been storing radioactive wastes in Siberia, near the town of Kyshtym, and somehow carelessness had allowed some of them to flow together, reaching critical mass.

It had never occurred to Emmaline Branford that waste could turn itself into a little atomic bomb, but Borden assured her that that was the best explanation for the—the whatever it was—that had poisoned hundreds of square kilometers of the Siberian landscape, caused the abandonment of a dozen villages and any number of collective farms, poisoned lakes and rivers and even changed the Soviet maps.

Of course, the Soviets had staunchly denied that anything of the sort had happened. But, of course, they would.

So when Warner Borden called for her to join him again at the teletypes and said, "I talked to one of the Swedes. They've fingerprinted the cloud, and it definitely was not a nuclear test," her first response was, "Something like Kyshtym again?"

"No, no, nothing like that. Not a nuclear weapons plant, either, although for a minute I thought that might be it. But the wrong elements were in the gases, according to the Swedes. It's"—he looked around and closed the door—"it's got to be an accident in a nuclear power plant. It could even be a meltdown."

"Oh, my God," said Emmaline, thinking of the movie *The China Syndrome*. "But if there were that kind of an explosion—"

"It wouldn't have to be a big explosion. Anyway, that's what the Swedes are saying—they've tested the cloud, and the proportions of radioactive materials match what the Russians would have if a power plant blew up." He was studying the teletypes eagerly, but all they were producing now were weather reports. "I've checked the maps," he said. "There are two nuclear power plants up on the Baltic. It has to be one of them. Maybe both of them."

"*Two* power plants blowing up at once?"

He grinned at her. He seemed almost happy. "What are you, one of those no-nuke nuts? These are *Russian* plants. You have to expect they'll blow up now and then."

He leaned cozily over the teletype next to Emmaline, one hand negligently resting on her hip. She moved patiently away, not willing for a fight just then. (Why were white Georgia boys so often turned on by a black skin?)

"I'd better get back to work," she said, and returned to her office. Rima was back, diligently working away on letters in her own room. She didn't look up. Emmaline paused at the window by her desk, looking out on the broad, traffic-filled Tchaikovsky Boulevard. Didn't those people know that their power plants were blowing up? Shouldn't someone tell them? She sighed and sat down.

And there on her desk was an opened copy of a magazine.

She had not left it there. She picked it up and discovered it was something called *Literaturna Ukraina*. Emmaline's Russian was more or less adequate, or at least as good as anyone else's after taking the crash foreign-service course, but this magazine was not published in the Russian language. It was in Ukrainian.

Most of the words were nearly the same, but with distinctively Ukrainian twists. Emmaline frowned. The article seemed to be about deficiencies in a nuclear power plant, but it wasn't about a plant located on the Baltic. She looked across the hall at Rima Solovjova, but the translator did not look up. Emmaline thought of asking Rima if she had put the magazine there, but if she intended to say so, she would have done it already. But why was Rima—or someone—giving her an article about a place called Chernobyl?

CHAPTER 19

Vremya, the nine o'clock television news broadcast, is a Soviet institution. It is watched by tens of millions of people every night, but not very attentively. Generally it is what would be called in America a "talking head" show; the real news is read by a man at a desk, briefly and unemotionally, and there is not a great deal of it. The only film clips are generally of collective farmers bringing in a record harvest, or shipyards launching a new icebreaker. Russians joke that one can always tell when the news comes on, because one hears through the thin apartment walls the sounds of neighbors walking about and flushing their toilets as they leave the television set after the night's film or sports event or concert.

In just that way, when the news came on that Monday night, Igor Didchuk got up to go to the kitchen for a cold drink of mineral water from the refrigerator, and Oksana would no doubt have done the same if she had not been occupied in finishing the last row of her knitting. The ballet on television that night had been the Bolshoi company itself, in a production called *The Streets of Paris*—nothing like *La Bohème* or *Gaîté Parisienne,* but a sober, stirring dance drama about the French Commune of two centuries before. "But the dancing was beautiful," Oksana said to her husband as he returned.

"Of course," he said with pride. The Bolshoi was a Russian company, not Ukrainian, but Didchuk considered himself a truly internationalist Soviet man. In his view, the Bolshoi troupe was *Soviet*—and one day, just possibly, their own daughter, Lia, already getting solo parts in the dance academy where she attended school for two days of each week, might well be the Plisetskaya of the year 2000. Lia was nine, and already sound asleep in her "room"—actually, just an extension of the flat's central hall. Oksana's parents were rustling around the living-dining area which was also their bedroom, and it was, after all, time to go to sleep.

Didchuk paused to glance at the news broadcast when his wife said, "Yora? Did I tell you? That Bornets boy came in today with a temperature of thirty-eight, can you imagine?"

"No, you didn't mention it," he said.

"And when I made him go to the clinic, he came back with a note saying that the doctor was not in today. Called away on some emergency."

"I suppose," said Didchuk amiably, "that she is getting ready for May Day, like everyone else. What did you do?"

"What could I do? I couldn't send him home. His parents would both be at work. So I made him lie down in the teachers' lounge but, really, Yora, that isn't fair to the other teachers. And suppose I brought home some virus to our own family?"

"You look healthy enough to me," he said. "Well, let's go to bed." And he was reaching out for the knob on the television set when the announcer put down one sheet of paper, picked up another, and read, without change of expression: "There has been an accident at the Chernobyl power plant in the Ukraine. People have been injured, and steps are being taken to restore the situation to normal."

There is a conversion table that Soviet people apply to government announcements of bad news. If the news is never broadcast but only a subject of rumor, then it is bad but bearable. If the event is publicly described as "minor," then it is serious. And if there is no measure assigned to it at all, then it calls for resorting to "the voices."

The only radio the Didchuks owned was not in the kitchen with the television set; it was in the other room, where the grandparents were preparing for bed. Didchuk knocked on the door and excused himself. "The radio," he said. "I think we should listen for a moment."

"At this hour?" his mother-in-law demanded, but when she heard about the news announcement, she said, "Yes, I understand now. That Mrs. Smin Saturday morning, it was clear that she was concealing something. But please, not too loud for the voices."

Didchuk didn't need to be told that. He turned on their Rekord 314 radio, the size of a baby's coffin, and waited patiently for the tubes to warm up. The volume he set only to a whisper. It is not exactly illegal to listen to the Voice of America and the other foreign broadcasts beamed into the USSR, but it is not something most citizens want to advertise.

There did not seem to be anything coming in from abroad in Russian, and most of the other foreign stations, of course, were jammed. All they could find was the broadcast from France. That, for reasons no one had ever explained, was almost never jammed; but it was also in French, and none of the Didchuks spoke that language.

But even they were able to pick a few phrases out of the rapid-fire announcements, and those included "*deux milles de morts*" and "*un catastrophe totale.*"

"But the Chernobyl power plant is more than a hundred kilometers away," Oksana protested, her face pale.

"Yes, that's true," her husband agreed somberly. "We are very fortunate to be so far. They say that radiation can be very dangerous, not only at once but over a period of many years. Cancers. Birth defects. In children, leukemia . . ."

And they looked at each other, and then into the hall, where Lia lay peacefully asleep, with her head on her fist and her lips gently smiling.

CHAPTER 20

The control point for fighting the disaster at the Chernobyl Nuclear Power Station is no longer at the collective farm. There are far too many people now to be held in a farm village, and so it has been moved to the town of Chernobyl itself, thirty kilometers away. The evacuation of the town of Pripyat has been expanded to include every community within that thirty-kilometer ring. Where more than a hundred thousand people lived seventy-two hours earlier, there is now no living person except firefighters, emergency workers, and medics. Two squadrons of heavy-lift Soviet Air Force helicopters have joined the damage-control forces, and day and night they load up sandbags and nets filled with bars of metal, take them on the five-minute flight to the reactor, dump them into the white-hot glow, and return for another load. The helicopter cabins have been lined with sheets of lead, which seriously cuts down the loads they can carry, and their pilots are working twelve-hour days. The crews battling the accident on the ground are allowed only three two-hour shifts out of the twenty-four. Even so, each man is stuck twice a day to yield a blood sample so his white corpuscles can be counted, and when the count is down, he is out of business entirely.

Sheranchuk understood the reason for the two-hour shifts perfectly, but no one told him what to do in the six-hour stretches when he was forbidden entry to the zone. What he did, mostly, was try to sleep. When that failed, he ate, and smoked feverishly, and made a nuisance of himself.

He knew that he was being a nuisance, because he had been told so when he visited the Chernobyl town hospital to see how his wife was getting along ("Well enough, my dear," she told him, "but really, we're very busy here."), and when he tried to call the hospital in far-off Moscow to check on Deputy Director Smin. ("His condition is being carefully monitored; he is conscious; and, please, don't tie up our telephone lines at this time!") He couldn't help it. He missed Smin. All these new experts and volunteers from all over the USSR were well enough, but after all, the graphite core was still burning, was it not?

He was pacing back and forth, scowling at the distant smoke on the horizon, when the armored personnel carrier pulled up outside the Chernobyl town bus station. He jumped in to join the fourteen others ready to take their turns.

It was a half-hour ride to the plant, and none of them spoke much. On the way they all pulled on their radiation coveralls, checked one another's dosimeters, made sure the hoods were fastened. As soon as the personnel carrier came to a stop, Sheranchuk trotted right to the closed-circuit water system to check the Bourdon-gauge pressure readings.

Overhead he heard the choppers flutter in and swoop away. One came in just overhead. It looked like an airborne whale, with a rotor on top and the revolving flukes of the tail assembly. He could see someone kicking a bag of something— sand, no doubt—out of the door.

Then he was at the pipes, and he didn't look up at the helicopters again, not even when he felt a rustly patter of dust on his helmet and knew that one of the bags had come apart as it was dropped. It was only loose sand, after all. If he had been hit by one of the bags, or by one of the falling sacks of lead shot, he would not need to look up. He would be dead—as had happened already to at least one of the firemen whose work kept them closer to the drop point.

That was the good part of Sheranchuk's immediate task, which was to free the great water valves to the steam system. They were in a sheltered location that kept him out of the direct range of the helicopter dumps. The bad part of the job was that the valves didn't want to be freed. The electric motors that were meant to drive them had shorted and burned themselves out when applied, because something inside the valves was jammed. The control wheels outside failed to move the giant leaves within. When Sheranchuk reached the scene, he saw that his relief crews had tried a different tack. They had drained the system of cooling water from the pond in order to attack the valves with crowbars; but that hadn't worked, either, because the steam system had run so hot that there was little liquid water in the pipes. It was now nearly steam all the way through; no one could work in that heat, and so they had to open the dikes and let the cooling water in again. By the time Sheranchuk got back with the new crew, the action had shifted to the external valve wheels again.

Sheranchuk saw that the previous shift chief had rigged up a system of crowbars interlocked in the wheels, and the crew was trying doggedly to move the valves with the added leverage.

Sheranchuk saw at once that it was risky. The great danger was not only that it probably wouldn't work, but that if too much force were applied, it might merely snap the shaft, sturdy forged steel though it was. So when Sheranchuk took over, he urged the crew to be gentle: "No battering-ram stuff, now! A steady push—go! Keep it going! All your weight—" And when that effort accomplished nothing, he tried backing the wheel off a little for another attempt. It almost worked. The wheel moved, grudgingly, a few centimeters of a revolution; and back and forth, back and forth, they kept up the hard work, sweating inside their coveralls, in the noise of the helicopters overhead and the rattle of dropped sand and metal bars, and the rumble of fire pumps and the hoarse cries of the men.

Sheranchuk was astonished when someone laid a hand on his shoulder. He blinked up at his relief. Had two hours gone by already? And what had been accomplished?

He knew the answer to that one, anyway.

At least now they were no longer alone. It wasn't just the forces of the Chernobyl Power Station that were fighting the accident, not even just those of the region or of the whole Ukraine. Help came in from everywhere, by every means possible. By road, convoys of trucks pounded toward Chernobyl from every quarter of the compass. By air, there were planes to the little field outside the town of Chernobyl and helicopters besides. Barges came into the port at Chernobyl town, trains chugged into the Yanov railroad station—and these were not just ordinary goods trains, with a packet or two for the firefighters; they were dedicated trains, their cargoes reloaded into expendable flatcars at the edge of the evacuated zone and pulled back to the plant itself by locomotives that would never leave. Doctors, firemen, engineers, militiamen, soldiers—half the Soviet Union seemed to be descending on the Chernobyl Power Station in its agony.

It was a truly impressive effort. The only question in Sheranchuk's mind was whether it was going to be enough.

They were ordered to shower without fail every time they came in off duty, and as often as possible in between times, just to make sure. As soon as Sheranchuk was out of his protective clothing and had allowed another few drops of his blood to be siphoned out, he headed for the showers, rubbing the inside of his elbow. The medics were finding it harder and harder to pick a spot on his arm not already sore from taking the blood samples. They looked tired too. So was Sheranchuk. He pushed his way through the other tired, naked men waiting their turn and let the cold water pour over him. He soaped well, wondering what load of radioactive poison was in the water itself. But that was a useless worry. They had to shower, anyway. And besides, those moments under the shower were the only ones he had to relax and think about his wife and his son. The last word from Tamara was that Boris was already on his way to a Komsomol camp on the Black Sea with twenty other young people from Pripyat. Sheranchuk took consolation in those good thoughts. At least his family was out of danger. . . .

If—thinking of the cloud of gases that blew helter-skelter across the face of the earth—anyone in Europe were out of danger. Or anyone in the world.

The pleasant moment had turned sour.

Sheranchuk got out of the shower and dried himself on a pair of his own undershorts—towels were among the niceties no one had yet thought to truck in to the control post. He pulled on a cotton shirt and a pair of work pants and felt slippers. As dressed as he needed to be, he shuffled down the length of the improvised dormitory, past the rows of bunks, some of them with men snoring away, and the tables where other men were talking or playing cards, to his six o'clock conference.

That was the bad side of the good fact that so many Soviet citizens had hurried to help. Meetings. With more than two thousand men and women deployed to fight the explosion and its consequences, the people in charge had to keep in almost constant conference to coordinate their efforts.

In the meeting room there was a table with an unshaded light hanging over it, and half a dozen men were waiting for his report. He gave it quickly: "The valves won't open. They're trying to force them now, but I think they'll just break."

Looking around the table, Sheranchuk realized that he was now nearly the highest-ranking person left on the scene from the peacetime—he corrected himself, the pre-explosion time—of the Chernobyl Power Station. Smin was in his hospital in Moscow, fighting for his life. After the Director had arrived, he had insisted on taking charge of the emergency effort just long enough to be removed from it. Where he was now was easy to guess, and the Chief Engineer along with him. Others were in Hospital No. 18 in Kiev, or evacuated with their families, or simply run away. The people around this table now were all from outside the district, from Moscow and Kiev and Novosibirsk and Kursk. Most of them wore military uniforms under their coveralls.

The person chairing the meeting, however, was the civilian from the Ministry of Nuclear Energy, Istvili. He was no longer as dapper as when he first arrived, but he was still energetic as he received Sheranchuk's bad news. He did not seem surprised. He only said, "The plenum has to be drained." The plenum was the reserve of water under the reactor itself, built there so that in the event of a rupture of a single tube the steam would bubble through the plenum and cool back down to water instead of bursting the containment shell. Of course, against what had actually happened at the plant it was useless—worse than useless, a danger.

The general of fire brigades stirred restlessly. "I don't see why we can't just leave it alone," he said.

"Because, Comrade General, we don't want water down there, we want concrete. We need to isolate that entire core from the world outside, top, bottom, and sides."

"You're talking about work that will take months!"

"I hope we can do it just in months. In any case, we don't know how much strength there is in the structures that hold the core; if it should fall into the plenum, it would be serious."

Serious! It was already serious enough for Sheranchuk, who put in obstinately, "Nevertheless, I don't think those valves will open."

Istvili nodded. "Then what do you propose?"

"Attack it from another direction," Sheranchuk said, throwing his cigarette on the floor to free his hands. "Here, let me show you." He quickly sketched the outlines of the ruined reactor and the water-filled chamber below it. "If we cut into the tank from another side, we can pump it dry. Here. Where it approaches the plenum for Reactor Number Three. Pump that one out, then people can get in to cut through."

Istvili studied the sketch, unsurprised. "I approve. Also, I think, we should try digging another shaft from—here. It will be longer, but easier to cut through, perhaps."

"My men aren't moles," the fire general barked.

"We won't need your men for that, Comrade General. A team of miners from the Donetsk coalfields is already on its way. Now. As to the fire in the graphite itself?"

The fire brigade commander said, "The helicopter drops are helping. Another fifty tons of sand are needed, though, at least."

"Comrade Colonel?"

The Air Force officer rapped out, "Of course. We have requested another squadron of men and machines; they should be here in the morning. With them, we will continue the drops on schedule."

Istvili looked at the fire brigade commander, who shrugged. "If that is so, then perhaps we ought to have more volunteers to fill the sandbags. Also my men can't get through the rubble near the reactor building."

"Have it bulldozed away!"

"To be sure, Comrade Istvili," the fireman said mildly, "but to where? Some has already been dumped into the pond—"

"Good God, man," Sheranchuk cried. "Not the cooling pond! We've poisoned enough water already."

"So I have said, but then, where?"

Since no one else spoke, Sheranchuk said, "There's a

foundation dug for another reactor on the other side of the station. I doubt it will ever be built now; can't you shove everything in there?"

"Do it," said Istvili, turning to gaze at Sheranchuk again. He asked the meeting at large, "Is there anything else we need our hydrologist-engineer for at this time?"

Sheranchuk said quickly, "There is something I need the meeting for, at least."

"And what is that?"

"It is simply impossible to accomplish anything in a two-hour shift a couple of times a day. I request permission to work for longer periods."

"How long?"

"As long as I have to! Four hours at a time, at least."

Istvili drummed his fingers on the table, looking around. "How are your white-blood corpuscle readings, Comrade Sheranchuk?"

"Who can tell? They simply take it and go away somewhere. At least they have not told me I am in danger."

Istvili nodded. Then he sighed. "Permission granted," he said. "Now let us see how we stand for matériel. . . ."

CHAPTER 21

Except perhaps for the anniversary of the October Revolution (which occurs in November, because of the changed calendar), the paramount public holiday of the Soviet Union is on the first day of May. It is called International Labor Day, or more frequently simply "May Day." There is no village in the USSR so small that it does not have at least a celebration on May Day, and in the largest cities the event is an immense production.

"But we can't watch it on the TV," Candace Garfield told her husband reasonably, "because we don't have one in this delightful little toilet you found for us, and they'll just charge us extra if we want to use the one in the living room, and it's in black and white anyway."

"Well, hell, hon," said her husband, also reasonably—it was only eight in the morning, and they were both still being reasonable—"who wants to watch it on TV? We might as well be home in Beverly Hills if that's all we want to do. We'll go on into town, and—"

"And walk to the subway, right? Because those buses don't ever run?"

"They were running all right yesterday, honey. It was only like on Sunday and Monday that we couldn't find one."

"And today's a holiday, right? So they probably won't be running at all."

Garfield opened his mouth to respond a touch less reasonably, because his own temper was beginning to run short after four days on their own in Kiev. They were saved by a knock on the door. "Oh, poop," said Candace, "that's Abdul for the rent. Wait a minute till I get something on."

Abdul was who it was, although his name was surely not Abdul. He was some sort of Arab in some sort of diplomatic post at some Arab consulate—for four straight days he had managed to avoid telling them which nation paid his salary.

He was a constantly smiling slim young man, no more than thirty. This time, as always, he greeted them with a cheery "Good morning to the both of you!" and an outstretched hand. As always, he took Garfield's hundred-dollar traveler's check, and returned the change in rubles. He had every reason to smile, Garfield thought. The agreed-on bed-and-breakfast rate was sixty-five dollars American each day. The thirty-five dollars' worth of rubles Garfield got back in change were always calculated at the official rate, and Garfield was quite certain the man got his own rubles from one of the furtive young men who hung around the tourist hotels, at no more than twenty-five cents apiece instead of the official rate of over a dollar and a half.

Of course, they hadn't had much choice. It was not really that bad a room—in fact, it was reasonably nice, especially by Soviet standards—even though they didn't have a bath of their own. It was in a new and attractive building. They were in a sort of diplomatic ghetto; you got into it through a gate, and when you arrived in a taxi a militiaman peered in to make sure no locals were sneaking into the place reserved for foreign residents of Kiev. There did not, unfortunately, seem to be any Americans or even English or Canadians in the compound, and their host had urged them (still smiling, but very emphatically) to avoid contact with the neighbors as much as possible. "Is not against Soviet law exactly, no, but still is a matter for discreetness, please."

That May Day morning, though, when he had carefully paid out Garfield's twenty rubles and some odd kopecks in change, he lost the smile. Looking at them seriously, he said, "I am very sorry to bear ill tidings, but all things must end. Tomorrow must be last day of you to be here. Due to the changed circumstances, I am required to leave and must close down my flat."

"What changed circumstances?" Garfield demanded. The man only shrugged.

"Now, come off it," barked Candace from the table. "Where are we supposed to go? You've got to let us stay here just for a couple of nights, anyway!"

"But it is impossible," he explained, once more smiling broadly. "Your luggage? Yes, if you like, you may leave it here until you call for it—no later than six tomorrow evening. And now I must leave at once to prepare for our May Day reception, and then we must pack for departure. My good wife will now have your breakfast ready. It has been very great pleasure to know you, really. And, oh, yes, for the extra hours in your room due to leaving the luggage, that will be additionally twenty-five dollars American."

Breakfast was like each of the other three mornings they had spent in the diplomatic flat, with the silent, pregnant wife serving them the same soft-boiled eggs, thick slices of bread, and strong tea, except that this time while they were still at table a swarthy man knocked at the door. He and the diplomat's wife talked in low voices for a while—it was not an Arabic language, Garfield thought, but almost certainly not Russian, either. Then the man handed her a thick wad of currency. The woman counted it all over twice, then fished a set of car keys out of her apron pocket and gave them to the man. A moment later the Garfields heard the sound of a car starting in the courtyard below. Through the window Garfield saw the man driving away in Abdul's huge old canary-yellow Mustang convertible.

As they walked out of the compound, nodding familiarly to the cop at the gate, Garfield said, "Abdul's not going to come back here at all. He sold his car."

"So?" asked his wife, peering toward the avenue where there might have been, but was not, a bus.

"So nothing," said Garfield cheerfully, deciding on the spot not to press the question of what "changed circumstances" caused Abdul to flee with his wife. "Look, there's no use trying to get a bus, and it's only about a twenty-minute walk to the Metro."

"Next time I go anywhere with you," Candace said grimly, "I pack my Adidas. Dean? This little adventure is beginning to get bor-*ing*. I think it's time to go home."

"Honey, you know what they said at Aeroflot. No space available to Moscow until the seventh."

"So are we going to sleep in the airport for the next week?"

Garfield winced. But when they got out of the Metro station on the far side of the river, even Candace began to show signs of excitement.

For one thing, it was a meltingly beautiful spring day. The city was full of roses and chestnut blossoms, and it was in a holiday mood. The streets around the Kreshchatik were full of people getting ready to parade past the dignitaries on the stands. Trade unions, schools, Army detachments, government workers—every group seemed to have a detachment of its own to strut past the great billboard of Lenin, six stories high, with his chin thrust resolutely forward to challenge the hostile, encircling world.

There seemed to be thousands of people crushing toward the route of the parade along with the Garfields—not just marchers, but no doubt the families of people in the line of march as well. There were children carrying little flags, mothers with string bags—not on this day in the hope of finding something wonderful to buy, but only to hold picnic lunches for the children. There was a barricade at the entrance to the streets nearest the reviewing stands. The Garfields could not hope to enter the square, or even get very close to it, but they could see that it and all the surrounding streets were gay with banners and posters. The face that dominated the event belonged to V. I. Lenin, but Marx and Engels had their huge portraits too.

Candace gazed uneasily at the scores of uniformed militiamen keeping the throngs in order. "I keep thinking one of them's going to ask us what we're doing here," she fretted.

Garfield grinned. "We're doing what everybody else is doing, right? We're watching the parade. Listen, if they were going to give us a hard time, they would've done it long ago."

"Yes, but I'm getting real itchy. What are we going to do tomorrow?"

"Well," said Garfield slowly, "I've been thinking about

that. See, today's the holiday, right? So I bet that along about checkout time tomorrow the hotels're going to empty out pretty fast, and probably we'll be able to get anything we want."

"Probably," his wife repeated flatly.

"What do you want from me?" he demanded. "All right, as soon as the parade's over we'll go around the hotels and see if they're going to have a room. How's that?"

His wife only sighed. "I wish we could sit down somewhere and watch this," she said.

Garfield took her hand. "Aw, but honey," he pleaded. "How many Americans get to do anything like this? Think about the stories we're going to tell. Think about *Comrade Tanya*. Why, when we get back— Hey!" he cried, pointing to a group of children surrounding their teacher on the far side of the barrier, girls in cocoa dresses with sparkling white pinafores, boys in navy blue jackets and caps, every third child with a banner to pass to the next child in rotation as small arms grew weary. "Isn't that what's-her-name? The teacher that speaks English, from Smin's party?"

Oksana Didchuk didn't see the Americans, didn't even hear them calling to her or notice the little argument they had with the militiaman when they tried to cross the barricade. Oksana was busy with her class, rehearsing them in the slogans they should chant, reminding them to march in step, cajoling, warning, telling them stories to keep them quiet until their turn to march. "Look," she said, pointing at the contingent of tall young men in gold-braided black uniforms, swords at their sides as they swung past, "those are cadets from the Kiev Naval Academy. Someday some of you may go there!"

But the girls were looking at the folk dancers twirling in their bright traditional Ukrainian costumes, and most of the boys were gazing popeyed at the huge T-60 tank that was shuffling up the avenue toward them, a trail of smart Soviet Army soldiers goose-stepping along behind. Oksana sighed, peering around to see if she could get a glimpse of her own daughter, but there were too many groups of schoolchildren, too many floats and bands and military vehicles, too many people entirely.

Oksana Didchuk wondered if it could possibly be true

that this thing at the Chernobyl Power Station could be dangerous even to people here in Kiev. What was one to believe? The voices had been more strident than ever that morning. The Didchuks had even managed to catch a few minutes of Radio Free Europe before the jammers discovered the wavelength they had switched to and the warbling *tweeweeweeweep* had drowned it out. But what was one to do? At school the authorities had been quite firm: "There is certainly no cause for panic. If any extraordinary measures are required, of course we will be informed at once!"

And yet the rumors grew—twenty-five thousand dead and buried in a mass grave on the banks of the Pripyat River, one colleague had whispered, or so he had heard one of the voices say. Almost certainly that was untrue, Oksana thought staunchly. Especially considering the source. No one believed Radio Free Europe ... but what a pity that they could not get the calm, trustworthy voice of the BBC.

And then the signal came for their unit to begin the march. Oksana gathered up her group and they took their places in line. What angels they were being this day! Every one of them, little as they were, unruly as sometimes they could be, marched along bravely; and as they passed the reviewing stand, each did a perfect eyes-right and shouted together: "We will defend the motherland of Socialism!"

Her eyes were moist as they passed under the great posters of Marx (the size of the head demonstrating the immense power of the great brain that lay inside it) and of Lenin (sharp gaze ever alert to seek out those who sought refuge in the twin enemies of the working class, God and vodka). And then, at the very edge of the square, was a tiny poster of Khrushchev. Oksana stole a quick look around as they passed it to see if any of her class had noticed that a new face had been added this year. None of the children seemed to. So there would be no difficult questions—although, Oksana told herself, it was, after all, quite proper that the man who had held the city of Kiev together in those terrible days of 1941 while the Germans hammered past it on both sides should be recognized on Kiev's May Day.

One must always remember that it was Khrushchev who, years later, had insisted on adding Kiev to the short but illustrious list of the USSR's "Hero Cities" for that desperate resistance ... though, of course, at the time of that resistance a good many Kievans, listening to the traitorous words of defeatists and saboteurs, had not been nearly as eager for their tasks as the people of Moscow and Stalingrad. Nevertheless! The delay at Kiev had cost many thousands of lives, but it served a purpose. It had slowed the Hitlerite drive toward Moscow just long enough to make it fail. And of course—

One of the little girls was tugging at her sleeve. They were out of the square now, stopped, waiting for the signal to be dismissed. Oksana said sharply, "What is it, Lidia?"

"Those people," the girl whispered. "They're calling to you." And when Oksana turned, she saw the American couple, waving urgently at her from behind a pair of scowling militiamen. "Mrs. Didchuk!" the woman cried. "Help us! Please!"

It was nearly dark by the time Oksana Didchuk had finished with her responsibilities and could take the Americans to the apartment house. They found Mrs. Smin and her son with Smin's old mother on the roof, waiting for the fireworks to begin.

"Are we ever glad to see you," grinned Dean Garfield. "We got thrown out of our hotel, and we've been staying at some Arab's apartment ever since, and we're about to get thrown out of *that*." But he was surprised to see that Selena Smin did not seem really delighted to see them again. The expression on her face as she listened to Oksana Didchuk's translation of their adventures was hooded—no, worse than that, worried; she was not at all the same gracious hostess who had pressed them to eat just a little more just a few days before.

Selena Smin thought for a moment before she spoke, then she watched the Garfields gravely as Oksana translated. "You have heard nothing of the accident at Chernobyl?" And when Garfield shook his head, she began to speak rapidly, so rapidly that Oksana could hardly keep up. It was not just that, either; Garfield saw that Oksana Didchuk was hearing some of this for the first time herself, as Selena Smin told of the explosion, the radioactive gases that were reported from many parts of Europe, the injuries, the evacuation of the town of Pripyat, the dead. "And my own husband," she finished, "is now in hospital in Moscow, perhaps gravely ill—they cannot be sure yet.

Our son, Vassili, is to be sent to a Komsomol camp for the summer, but first—first I suppose he will accompany me. I will go to Moscow tomorrow, to be with my husband."

"Oh, my God," whispered Candace, gripping her husband's arm.

Garfield said thickly, "I bet that's the 'changed circumstances' that Arab son of a bitch was talking about. But he wouldn't tell us a word!"

Candace wasn't listening to him, but to a quick soft-voiced exchange between Selena and the translator that made Oksana look suddenly pale. "What's she saying now?" Candace demanded.

Oksana hesitated. "I only asked her what I should do about my own little girl," she said. "She said she didn't know." Selena Smin spoke sharply again. "But as for you and your husband," Oksana translated, "there is only one thing to do. You must go home quickly. Mrs. Smin or her mother-in-law will arrange everything; you will fly out to Moscow or Warsaw or Bucharest in a few days, and then home. Many foreigners have already left."

Vassili Smin had been listening to every word, but now he turned away. "Look now, please," he said in English. "The—ah—the pyrotechnicals is begun."

Off toward the skyline of the city, rockets were blossoming over the Dnieper River, red and gold and white. Below, hidden by the buildings between, was a huger, steadier glow. "That is a Soyuz spacecraft in pyrotechnicals," said Vassili, carefully rehearsing each word. "We cannot view it properly because—because"—he fumbled for the words, helped himself out with gestures—

"Because it's turned to face the city instead of us?"

"Exactly," he said, beaming. "It is turned face to the city instead of to us. I think it will be quite beautiful."

Candace said gently, "And what are going to do now, Vassili?"

He said proudly, "Tomorrow I fly to Moscow!" Then he swallowed and added, "It is that my father, he has—a failure of the blood? And they think that out of my—bones—they can get something which will make him better."

"I'm sure it will!" Candace said, pumping confidence into her voice. And then, "Ah, Vassili—?"

"Yes, Mrs. Garfield?"

"My husband was so distressed at your news that he forgot to mention it, but we don't have a place to live after tomorrow. So if we could live with you—"

"One moment, if you please." The boy talked quickly with his mother and grandmother, and then turned to the Americans, smiling happily at being able to oblige them. "You will have a hotel room, of course."

"But there aren't any hotel rooms!"

"What nonsense!" the boy scoffed. "Believe me, a room will be found. After all, my grandmother is still Aftasia Smin."

CHAPTER 22

What is wrong with a state so centralized that everything has to be decided in the capital is obvious. It suppresses initiative, it slows decision-making, it leads to waste and mismanagement and corruption. But there are advantages too. Nothing happens until some high-up authority decides it shall; but then it happens with blinding speed. That's how it is with the evacuation of the entire zone within the thirty-kilometer perimeter centered on the Chernobyl Nuclear Power Station. Moscow says, "Evacuate!" and a hundred towns, villages, and collective farms outside the perimeter make room for the occupants of the towns, villages, and farms within. Buses appear for the people. Trucks arrive for the farm machinery and livestock. Of course, everything is checked for radioactivity before it moves a meter away from its origins, but most of what fails the first test needs only to be hosed down. Then the specks of sooty fallout are rinsed away and it is safe. When the caravans arrive at their destinations, farmers go to farms, townspeople to towns, children to schools that are ready to receive them.

The place Sheranchuk found himself in was the collective farm of Kopelovo, a hundred kilometers outside the evacuated zone but by no means peaceful. Eighty evacuated families from Pripyat and smaller communities had been settled there, forty others, like Sheranchuk and his wife, were sent there on holiday. Holiday! It was no holiday for Sheranchuk, it was thirty-six hours of enforced exile. "I should be at the plant," he fretted as soon as they arrived.

Tamara said, "It is exactly because you were too much at the plant already that you are here, dear Leonid. Content yourself. Rest. Go to bed, but, first, let me take your temperature again."

They had arrived together in the early morning of May Day, taken at once to a soft feather bed in the home of the Party Secretary of the kolkhoz. In spite of everything, the Kopelovo farm had gone ahead with its May Day festivities, for the enjoyment of their unexpected guests and for their own morale. The celebration was wasted on Sheranchuk. He slept through the whole day, leaden, unmoving, and neither the blare of the band nor the amplified speeches penetrated his stupor. He woke up at dusk, long enough to go to the bathroom (flush toilets! Some collective farms did very well for the kolkhozists!) and eat with the Party Secretary's family, and then back to bed with Tamara.

By this time he had recovered enough to take advantage of the opportunity. They made love with the speed and success of practice, and they lay awake whispering to each other for hours until he dropped off again and slept through the night.

On the morning after May Day there was farm work to be done, legal holiday or not, and it started at sunrise. Tamara Sheranchuk got up quietly as soon as it was light. The village was already astir with farmers going out to their fields. The two sons of the Party Secretary, ousted from their room so that the Sheranchuks could have it, came back from their neighbor's, where they had spent the night, in order to have breakfast at home. Tamara joined them, talking quietly. In twenty minutes they had eaten and were gone with their father, and the woman of the house was glad enough to accept Tamara's offer to tidy up the kitchen so that she could get on with her own work.

It took very little time, even in an unfamiliar kitchen. Then Tamara made herself another cup of tea and peeped in on her sleeping husband.

Sheranchuk was curled on his side, snoring gently. Very good, that was exactly what he was supposed to be doing. She wished she had taken his temperature one more time before they'd gone to sleep but, of course, they had not been thinking like doctor and patient, only like wife and husband. (It did not occur to her to take her own, although the reason they had been sent away was that both were near collapse from exhaustion, and already close to perilous levels of exposure to radiation as well.)

Tamara left her husband asleep and investigated the shower cubicle. Yes, there was hot water; yes, there was soap and quite nice towels, probably from abroad. She bathed and dressed, feeling quite luxurious.

The inferno at the Chernobyl Power Plant was far from her mind.

It was not that she was not aware of its terrifying meaning. Partly it was that she had been so close to it for what seemed so long that her senses were numbed in that area; she had closed her mind to it for the thirty-six hours of their enforced leisure. However, there was something else on her mind. They had taken no precautions in the feather bed of the Party Secretary. As a doctor, Tamara knew well that she was at the most fertile point in her cycle. It was by no means unlikely that she was in the process of becoming pregnant.

She wondered what Leonid would think of having a new baby in the family.

She didn't wonder at all about herself. Although Tamara Sheranchuk was nearly forty, she knew that she was in as good physical shape as she ever had been. Yes, older mothers had sometimes more difficult pregnancies and deliveries than the twenty-year olds (but sometimes not). Yes, older mothers were at slightly greater risk of having a child with a birth defect (but by far the greatest number were perfectly normal!) . . . yes, she told herself soberly, there was one other factor to be considered. Although the radiation she had received was very unlikely to affect her own health significantly, the damage to an embryo might be much greater.

But what did that mean, after all? Should women stop having children?

And besides, her husband *deserved* a new baby. Even though he didn't know how much he deserved it. She put down her empty cup, turned from the window on the now-quiet street, and went back to look in on her sleeping husband.

Who was not, after all, asleep. He opened his eyes and gazed at her. "Have you heard anything from the plant?" he asked at once.

"There is nothing to hear," she said. "You are supposed to put it out of your mind while we're here."

He snorted angrily, but then smiled. "Is it possible to have some breakfast?" he asked, glancing at his watch. "After all, the bus will pick us up at ten o'clock, and now it is nearly eight."

By the time the bus came with its load of new "holiday" people from the emergency workers, Sheranchuk was pacing back and forth on the farm village street. As soon as they were inside he was questioning the driver. Facts? The driver had very few facts. Rumors? Oh, yes, there were rumors. It was said that of the first three hundred firemen to report, at least a hundred and eighty were already dead or dying. Another three hundred militiamen, put on close perimeter guard for a six-hour shift, had been forgotten and left there for twelve—half of them were in the hospital too. And the town of Chernobyl itself was to be evacuated.

"But that is impossible," Sheranchuk protested. "The town is thirty kilometers from the plant, well out of the danger zone!"

The driver shrugged. "I am telling you what I have heard," he said. "It is all I know. Perhaps it is only temporary, because the wind has shifted."

Sheranchuk returned to his place next to Tamara, holding on to the backs of the seats as the bus bounced along the narrow road. They were in the middle of farm country, flax and wheat and orchards of cherry and apple trees. He took out a cigarette.

"You shouldn't smoke," Tamara said automatically.

He shrugged, lighting it.

"You are being very foolish," his wife said. "You've already received nobody knows how much radiation. Do you want to die of cancer before you are fifty?"

"If I die of the radiation, I won't have time to die of lung cancer, my dear," he said. He looked at her curiously, struck by her tone. After eighteen years he knew all her tones. When she advised him to give up smoking, it was with the doctor voice; in most of the communications of their daily lives it was the voice of a team worker dealing with their joint problems. This time she sounded younger, less sure of herself, more vulnerable—no, the right word was the first one he had thought of. Younger. She sounded like the girl he had met in the forest and married. "Tamara? Are you worried about me?"

"I want you around for the next twenty years," she told him seriously.

"Only for twenty years? After that I may be excused to die if I like?" he joked.

She ignored the joke. "Did you like the farm?" she asked.

"It was quite pleasant, I suppose," he conceded. "That house was really quite up-to-date."

"It was peaceful," she said, "and the air was clean. A person could live happily there, I think, without worrying about nuclear reactors blowing up." She looked directly at him. "And, in your case," she added, "without worrying about adding to the already considerable load of radiation you have been exposed to. It may be, Leonid, that you are never going to work in a nuclear power plant again."

He scowled at the thought. "And what would I do on a kolkhoz?"

"We could live there quite well. We would be safe. It is worthwhile, just to live, and to raise a family in clean air."

"Really, Tamara," he said, surprised at her tone. "I'm a trained hydrologist-engineer. Do you think they need me to turn the valves on the irrigation pipes, or fix the flush toilets that they seem to have so many of?" She didn't answer. "No," he said, "if I can't work at Chernobyl, I'll work at some other power plant—there are big new coal plants going up, and gas and oil. Perhaps a water power plant; that would be perhaps out in the open air, if it is getting away from cities that you want. But— "

"But you haven't given up on Chernobyl," she finished for him.

He said rebelliously, "The Chernobyl Nuclear Power Station is a valuable asset to the country, Tamara. It isn't going to be thrown away just because one reactor caught fire. It will be back in operation in a year, I'm sure of it."

"Let's see," said his wife. "You want to stay at Chernobyl

because you admire Smin; very well, I admire him too, but do you really believe he will keep his job after this?"

"He is not the one at fault!"

"He may not even live, Leonid. And as to yourself, your white corpuscle count is down; you've taken at least twenty rads already—it could be a hundred, because you weren't wearing a dosimeter at first. You certainly can't afford to be exposed to more."

He shrugged, looking out the window. They were entering the town of Chernobyl. If the town was about to be evacuated, it displayed no signs of it. The streets were full, the townspeople themselves trying to go about their normal lives while thousands of emergency workers milled about, most of them waiting their turns to be ferried to the turmoil at the plant.

"Are you listening?" his wife asked. "You've done your part, Leonid. You can let others take over from you now."

"I suppose I'll have to," he said somberly.

But in that he was quite wrong, because when he reported to the control plant, the news was bad. Radiation had surged up again, to almost seventy-five percent of the level of its first day. The attempt to get to the plenum from No. 3's pool had failed; too much steel and concrete.

An hour later he was back at the station.

A forward control point had been established in an underground bunker, once the dormitory for the plant's fire brigade, now the command post for the disaster-control operation. It was thick with stale cigarette smoke and not much ventilation; the same air was recirculated over and over because, however it might stink, it was better than what was outside.

It was hardly forty-eight hours that Sheranchuk had been gone, but so much had changed! The helicopter drops were nearing their objective. Almost *five thousand* tons of boron, lead, sand, and marble chips had already been dumped on the still-burning graphite of the reactor core, but the burning graphite was no longer the immediate problem.

The immediate problem was the plenum under the ruined reactor. It contained water, and it was therefore in Leonid Sheranchuk's department.

Of course, the purpose of the plenum was to act as a safety feature, to quench the steam if one or two pipes burst.

But that safety feature was now the greatest danger the core of Reactor No. 4 still faced.

Hanging over it was a mass of one hundred and eighty tons of uranium dioxide, whatever was left of eighteen hundred tons of graphite, the fragments of the 200-ton refueling machine and associated materials, the rubble of the collapsed walls—and the five thousand tons that had been dumped over it all to stop the deadly emissions. The structure had never been designed to support such a load. Worse, the structure itself had been shocked and damaged by the violence of the explosion. It was weakened in unpredictable ways. The whole thing might come down at any moment ... and if it collapsed those two thousand tons of uranium and graphite would plunge into the plenum. And ... and then that water would flash into steam, and the explosion that followed would be perhaps even worse than the first.

With the whole thing to do over again—not to mention killing a good many of the people frantically working to contain the accident.

It was a major general of engineers who was now in command of the operation, and he had a plan of the underground reservoir spread before him. Sheranchuk hunched over the drawing as the general explained: "Our miners from Donetsk pushed this tunnel through, here. Then we had a team of eight volunteers—nine originally, but one of them just fell apart—and they've worked steadily for a day and a half to break through—"

"You've broken through to the plenum?" Sheranchuk demanded. "Then what is the problem? Simply drain it and pour in your concrete."

"It won't drain," the general said.

"Won't drain? Why not? Ah, of course," Sheranchuk said, placing his finger on the plans. "Those valves need to be opened first."

"But those valves," the general said gloomily, "are now under water. All those passages are filled with runoff. Someone must go down in a diving suit and open the valves. We have two volunteers ... but neither of them knows where the valves are."

"I do," Sheranchuk cried.

The general studied him for a moment. "Yes," he said, "that is what I thought."

What Sheranchuk expected from the words "diving suit" was the kind of thing you saw in films, the big man-from-Mars helmets and trailing air hoses. It wasn't like that. What the volunteers got to breathe with were simply scuba masks, with tanks on their backs for air. What they wore on their bodies were wet suits, rubbery things that were stiff and cold and nasty to put on and chokingly tight where they were not chafingly loose to wear—of course, they had not had time to be very scrupulous about sizes. They did not have portable under-water lights. What they had was a floodlamp on a long cable—the electrician swore he had done his very best to make it watertight—and one of the two volunteers to carry it. They didn't have phones, either. Once they were in the water, there was no one to talk to, and nothing to hear.

Nothing, that was, except the ominous creaks and thuds and settling sounds from the six or seven thousand tons of material that was waiting to fall on them from overhead.

They couldn't help hearing those sounds. If their ears had been plugged, they still would have felt them as shudders and shakes in the water all around.

At least they weren't cold. At first Sheranchuk thought that was a blessing, because the wet suit had been horribly clammy to put on. Then it was not so much of a blessing, because the water was distinctly warm—hotter than blood temperature, with the furious heat of the core raging just over it. Sheranchuk found himself sweating in a suit that gave the sweat no place to go.

That was not the worst of it, either. Sheranchuk was angrily aware that the water was hot in other and even more unpleasant ways, for most of it had run down through mazes of radioactive rubble to fill the concrete passages they were swimming and pushing their way along. None of them had taken a dosimeter along. There was no point. The water was only mildly contaminated with radioactivity—as far as anyone could tell from outside—and anyway the job had to be done. It was essential.

The only question was whether or not it was also impossible.

The concrete-walled passages Sheranchuk had once walked along without a thought were now mazes. The floodlight showed the walls, the floor, the ceiling, the useless light fixtures, the inoperative instruments—but how different they all looked when they were underwater! It took twenty minutes of struggle, more swimming than walking, to reach the passage where the plenum valves were located.

When Sheranchuk was sure of what he was looking at, he splashed around to face his companions. Squinting into the watery glow of the thousand-watt lamp, he beckoned them to come to him.

Just then, without flash or warning, the light went out.

"God and your mother!" Sheranchuk shouted into the darkness. All he got for response was a mouthful of water as he dislodged the scuba mask, and a strangling coughing fit once he got it back in place. No one heard. No one spoke, either, or if they did, he could not tell.

Hanging, almost floating, in that total underwater blackness, Sheranchuk could not tell up from down, could not guess where the walls were, much less where his comrades had gotten to. He thrashed about in panic until he caught one wall a bruising blow with his knuckles. Then he reached out for it and felt along it until he encountered a railing, pulling himself back along the rail until something caught him a violent kick in the side. He reached out and caught the foot of one of the other men.

Which one? There was no way to tell until he felt the third man brush against him and, feeling his arms, found the useless floodlight with its cable.

Sheranchuk thought for a moment. They could go back for another light. But would it work any better? And how much longer could he spend in this place without beginning to glow in the dark?

He found the lamp bearer's shoulder and slapped it twice to get his attention, then thrust him gently back down the corridor: there was no further need for him. The other man he pulled toward the wall, found his hand, put it on the railing. Then he tugged the man forward as he himself turned and pulled himself farther down the flooded corridor.

With thanks to the God he had never believed in,

Sheranchuk felt the plenum pipe under his feet at the end of the corridor.

From there it was, if not easy, at least simple. The two of them felt their way along the pipe until they came to the first valve. Sheranchuk put the other man's hand on it and there in the dark, with the contracting sounds of the core shaking them, they put their weight on it.

It turned.

A moment later they had found the second valve. It, too, turned; and through the water that surrounded them they felt the gurgling suck of the plenum emptying itself.

In the open air Sheranchuk blinked at the light, fending off the workers who were trying to hug him as he was doing his best to strip off the wet suit. He was triumphant, but most of all he was very tired. He tripped on the duckboards at the floor of the miners' tunnel, but a half-dozen hands were quick to grab him.

By the time he was back in the bunker he was ready for a cigarette, but when he saw a doctor coming toward him with a clipboard, he knew what she was going to say. He stood up to greet her.

Funnily, he could see her mouth moving as though she were speaking to him, but he couldn't hear the words.

As he was opening his mouth to tell her this interesting fact, the world began to spin around him and the lights, Sheranchuk's personal lights, went out. He could feel himself falling heavily forward into the doctor's arms, and then he could not feel anything at all.

CHAPTER 23

The Committee for State Security, or *Komitet Gosudarst-vennoy Bezopasnosti,* is usually referred to by its Russian-language initials as the "KGB." It has been a constant presence in the life of every Soviet citizen as long as there has been a Soviet state. Its name has changed from time to time. So has its image—somewhat.

At the present time its image is still feared, but perhaps mostly as a looming presence offstage, somewhat as lung cancer is feared by a heavy smoker who won't quit anyway. It is no longer feared in quite the same way as in Stalin times—it was called the OGPU then, and later the NKVD—when it was feared as plague is feared during an epidemic, when death and destruction strike often, ruthlessly and seemingly at random.

The founder of the organization (which was then called by still a different name, the Cheka) was Felix Dzerzhinsky, the "divine Felix." (The great square in the center of Moscow that contains both the Lubyanka Prison and the city's most popular toy store is named after him.) It was said that Dzerzhinsky, if nothing else, was at least humanly fond of children. There is a story Russians tell about him. Once Dzerzhinsky was greeted at a railroad station by a pretty young girl who ran up to hand him a bunch of flowers. Dzerzhinsky hesitated for an awful moment. Then he smiled and patted the child on the head.

"So he can be kind, after all," one Muscovite breathed to another. "So it seems," said the other. "After all, he could have had her shot."

The first indication Smin had that the GehBehs were coming to visit him was when the nurse came hurriedly in to surround his bed with the heavy screens that were usually put around a patient who was terminally ill. "So I have company?" Smin asked, and was not surprised when the woman did not answer.

He sighed and propped himself up as best he could. He was quite sure he knew what was coming. The screens could not be to shield him from the gaze of his roommate, because his roommate had been taken away to surgery the night before and had not returned. But it was a nuisance to have the interrogators come to question him now. The doctor taking his blood samples just an hour before had told him that his Comrade Plumber, Sheranchuk, had just been admitted to Hospital No. 6. Smin had been planning to put on his slippers and go out to plead with the head nurse to allow Sheranchuk to occupy the now vacant bed. Smin had been quite looking forward to having his Comrade Plumber in the room to talk to, especially because he was feeling, really, quite good. Those confounded blisters were still there, and his arms were sore from the dozens of needles that had been thrust into them for samples of blood and to pour other things into his veins; but he was in no particular pain.

Of course, that was only a temporary state, the result of the first transfusions of blood. The doctor had warned that his condition was critical. Smin didn't need to be told that. Although he had tried to refuse hospitalization, he knew quite well that those early blisters indicated something very wrong inside him. He was aware that this period of well-being might quite probably be the last such feeling he would ever have. He was determined to enjoy it while he had it.

And what a nuisance that the Chekists should turn up to spoil it!

There were two of them, of course. Smin saw immediately that these were the variety of GehBeh that advertised what it was. They could not wear the traditional slouch hats and trench coats in the hospital. They looked far less worrying in the white hospital gowns and caps all visitors were made to wear. "So, Simyon Mikhailovitch," said the younger of the two agreeably, "they tell us you are feeling much better today."

"Temporarily," nodded Smin. Indeed, apart from the sores in his mouth and the weak dizziness and the diarrhea, he had been feeling fairly fit.

"Oh, I hope more than temporarily," beamed the other. "But those scars? Surely they are not from this disaster?"

Smin's sheet had fallen away, and the full extent of the wartime burn scars was visible. "Only an old memory," he said. "This, however"—he touched the little bandage where the doctors had pulled bone marrow out of his chest—"this is new, but unimportant. Surely you did not come here to discuss my health."

"In general, no," conceded the younger one. "But we are, of course, concerned. We don't want to distress you with questions if you aren't feeling well."

"Questions," Smin repeated. "I see. Please feel free to ask what you like."

And they did. Politely at first. Even almost deferentially. Then less so. "You are of course aware, Simyon Mikhailovitch, that the decisions of the Twenty-seventh Party Congress projected that nuclear electrical power generation is to double by 1990 to three hundred ninety billion kilowatt hours?" ("Of course," said Smin.) "And you are familiar with the assurance given by Chairman Andronik Petrosants of the USSR State Committee for the Use of Atomic Energy to the Central Committee, just three years ago, that the odds were a million to one against a disaster such as yours?"

"As *mine*?" Smin asked. "Are you calling it *my* disaster? Is that the same as accusing me of causing the explosion?"

"You were the senior administrator present, Comrade Smin. The Director was absent. That counts against him, and, in fact, he has already been removed from his post and expelled from the Party, as you are perhaps aware. But you were in charge while he was away."

"Actually," Smin remarked, "I wasn't present either. I was off duty when the explosion occurred."

"Indeed you were," said the other one severely. "And where were you?" And then more unpleasant parts of the interrogation got started. Smin had left his post of duty to attend a religious service, had he not? Was he in fact a nonregistered believer? ("Not at all," Smin protested. "My mother—") But they were not interested in hearing about his mother. They put aside the question of religion and moved along. He had utilized the automobile furnished him by the state for this private expedition—diverting state property to his personal use—even dismissing the driver and driving it himself more than one hundred kilometers. And to what purpose? To consort with foreigners at a religious ceremony in the apartment in Kiev.

As to that apartment, how had he obtained it? Was it not the case that, although it was nominally his mother's, he was actually, and quite illegally, the proprietor of the flat—in addition to his own home in Pripyat, and to the dacha he was proposing to build out in the countryside—Comrade, the older man said sorrowfully, addressing the younger, what sort of man have we here, who can live in three homes at once?

Smin listened attentively to all these charges but spoke little. For one thing, the sores at the corners of his mouth hurt when he spoke. For another, these were of no importance. The GehBehs were simply building up a case. In his heart Smin had been quite certain that sooner or later one would be made against him. Only when they turned to the specific details of the construction of the power plant did he sit up. "No," he said strongly, "I reject the assertion that any construction work that was being done was unauthorized. The plans were approved at the Ministry. Then in the day-to-day work the Director gave exact instructions. I followed his program completely in this respect."

"Ah, I see," the older man nodded. "In this respect. But in others? Did the Director instruct you to use substandard materials?"

And with a flourish he produced that copy of *Literaturna Ukraina*, with the article calling attention to the disastrous conditions of Chernobyl's projected fifth reactor—defective materials, poor maintenance, slipshod management. It seemed clear, the Chekist said sorrowfully, that it was not the suppliers who had tricked Smin with substandard cement and flawed piping, it was Smin who had conspired to cheat the State, heedless of danger to the property of the people.

"But that was about Reactor Number Five. And it was not

defective material that caused the accident," Smin burst out. "In any case, none of that material was used in essential construction—it was all discarded, and only satisfactory materials were employed." But that only led to the succeeding charge, that under Smin's management three thousand bags of expensive cement (substandard or not, what was the point of trying to defend himself in that way?) had been allowed to stay in the open until rains soaked them and turned them into blocks of crumbly stone, while scarce and costly steel piping (oh, that, too, was defective, Comrade Smin? But how much defective material did you accept, after all?) was allowed to rust. And then there was the question of the baths. "Why such lavish ones, Comrade Smin? Did you think your workers were ancient Romans?"

"Workers dealing with radioactive materials must be allowed to shower when necessary," Smin pointed out.

"So magnificently?"

"After all, we had plenty of hot water," Smin snapped.

"And plenty of high-grade tiles?"

"No," Smin said strongly. "Of that, none in surplus; all the good tiles went into the turbine room. But the rejects were good enough for the bath."

"I see," said the investigator. "But why, please, did you endanger the plant by making the reactor more explosive."

Smin sat up in bed at that one. He blinked at the man. "What did you say?"

The KGB man peered at his notes. "You are stated to have authorized an increase in the uranium-two-thirty-five content of the core by eleven percent. That is, from one point eight to two percent of the total uranium."

"*I* authorized that?" asked Smin, astonished. "But that was the Chief Engineer's decision. I merely initialed his order. And that did not make the core more explosive. It went the other way, in fact. It was to reduce feedback between steam generation and the nuclear activity of the core."

The KGB man looked at him without expression. "You admit, then, that you approved this change. And at the same time you took out some graphite, is that right?"

"We reduced the density, yes, if that's what you mean. It was part of the same procedure. But in that case I believe it was Director Zaglodin, not I, who initialed the order. In any case, really, that was more than two years ago!"

The older Chekist sighed and glanced at his slim, obviously foreign wristwatch. "We promised we would not stay more than twenty minutes," he reminded his colleague.

"Oh, but I feel quite able to answer questions, Comrades," Smin said. "Of course, you're very busy. I suppose you've already questioned Comrade Khrenov?"

There was a change in the temperature of the room. The younger man said curiously, "For what purpose do you suppose we would be questioning Personnel Director Khrenov?"

"Perhaps because he was there, as I was not?"

Now the man was careful. "Are you suggesting that Comrade Khrenov was in any way involved in the accident?"

Smin thought that over. Then he said justly, "No. I'm not. At worst, I am only saying that he was on the scene because he thought the experiment would succeed, and then he could claim some credit for it. But I have no reason to think he blew the reactor up; that was left to the operating technicians themselves."

"We will take note that you see no wrongdoing on Comrade Khrenov's part. After all, how could there be? It wasn't a matter of personnel that caused the accident."

"Wasn't it? But I think it was, Comrades. It was actually utter stupidity on the part of the entire control room crew that caused the explosion. One by one they turned off every safety device, and then they were surprised that the reactor wasn't safe any more."

The elder man said mildly, "Are you trying to shift the blame for your failings of leadership onto someone else?"

"Not at all! But what kind of leadership can there be when the First Department takes on the kind of people who drink, and stay home when they should be on duty, and even run away? . . . Still," he added thoughtfully, "in a sense, I suppose you are right. The decisions of the Party congress to bar drunkenness and absenteeism were not merely Khrenov's responsibility to follow. I could have been more ingenious, I suppose. I managed to find uses for substandard tiles by putting them where they could do no harm. I suppose I could have done a better job of finding unimportant jobs for useless people."

The men from the organs looked at each other. "Well," said the elder, standing up, "we must not tire you in your condition, Simyon Mikhailovitch. Perhaps on another day you will be feeling more cooperative."

Smin closed his eyes and leaned back against the pillow. All he said, without looking at them, was, "I wouldn't count on it."

What Smin needed more than anything else at that moment was a bedpan. Fortunately the nurse came at once. When he had relieved himself she began taking the screens away, Smin watching her.

"I don't suppose you are a drunk," he told her gravely.

Although nurses are used to hearing all sorts of things from their patients, she gave him a quick, puzzled look. "Me a drunk? What an idea!"

"But it is strange, isn't it, that our Soviet women drink very little, while the men pour it down. Why is that, do you think?"

"Drunkenness is a great social evil," she told him severely. "The decisions of the Twenty-seventh Party Congress—"

"Yes, yes, the decisions," Smin said. "But why do our men drink? Because they have jobs they don't like, for which they are not paid enough, and the money they are paid can't buy them the things they want. Isn't that true? But if it is true for men, how much more true it must be for women! Wouldn't you like to have an electric dishwasher? A blow dryer for your hair?"

"I will have those things soon enough," she said properly. "The production in consumer goods is increasing all the time."

Smin smiled up at her with real fondness. He said, "You are a very good girl."

When she had gone away, looking puzzled, he lay back and closed his eyes. The interview with the GehBehs had tired him more than he had expected. He really should go out to speak to the head nurse about Sheranchuk, he thought. He was determined to do that, very soon . . . but first he allowed himself to close his eyes for just a moment.

When he opened them, one of the doctors was standing over him, a smile on her cool face. "And how are you feeling now, Deputy Director Smin?"

"I will feel better," he said at once, "if you put Leonid Sheranchuk in that other bed. It's lonesome here."

The doctor nodded thoughtfully. "I believe Comrade Sheranchuk has requested the same thing. Perhaps it can be arranged. You should properly have a room of your own—"

"I don't want a room of my own! I want Sheranchuk here."

She said, "What you want, Comrade Smin, is to get better, and that's what we want too. It is up to the hospital director to decide if having him as a roommate will be good for you. Now, I asked how you are feeling."

"Very tired of being in hospital," he said. "Otherwise not bad."

"But that is only a temporary remission, you know." She hesitated, then asked him in an accusing tone: "Did you do something to your dosimeter?"

"I? To my dosimeter? Why would I do that?" Smin asked, determined not to tell her of the switch.

"Because you wished to be a hero? I don't know, I only know that your physical condition does not match the dose record. According to the state of your white blood corpuscles, you must have received well over two hundred rads. It may have been as many as five hundred rads."

"That sounds like a great many rads," said Smin.

"If you remained untreated it is enough to kill you, without question, in approximately thirty days after exposure." She counted on her fingers. "Without treatment you would not be likely to die before the twenty-first of May, perhaps you might survive even until the beginning of June, but no longer. However," she went on, smiling her icy smile, "in this hospital we have the best treatment for radiation disease. Even perhaps when the patient is not cooperating as he should. Also, we now have a wonderful American doctor who has just arrived yesterday, a gift from our American friend Dr. Armand Hammer."

"Who is Dr. Hammer?"

"He is one of the good Americans, Deputy Director Smin. He has always been a friend to the Soviet Union, since the days of Lenin, and now he has brought us help in this unpleasant business. This Dr. Gale from America has developed special methods of treating people like yourself. We will get rid of the dying marrow in your bones and replace it with healthy new marrow—as soon as we can find a satisfactory donor."

"All right," Smin said. "Now just leave me alone until it's time for the operation."

The doctor said triumphantly, "Unfortunately, it is not that easy. First we will have to make you ready for the transplant. And that, I'm afraid, is not a very enjoyable process."

When the doctor had finished telling him how unenjoyable the process was going to be, Smin lay with his eyes closed, thinking the matter out. He was not in pain. From time to time he found himself nauseated, or sweltering even under the light sheet. But there was no real pain now, and his head was clear.

He might have preferred a little less clarity, he thought.

It had all been explained to him and, yes, he agreed, there was nothing that one would enjoy in his immediate future. The real question was how much of a future he had.

The doctor had been quite clear about what was ahead. There were classically four stages in cases of radiation sickness— first, the "prodromal syndrome"—the onset of the illness— when there was vomiting and faintness. That, the doctor told him, was not serious; it was probably only the impact of the radiation on the nervous system that produced the symptoms, and they passed.

As they had, in only an hour or so.

Now he was in the "latent period." The patient felt better at this point—as Smin indeed did, not counting the badness of the feelings resulting from the things they were doing to him to try to save his life. Not counting that his hair seemed to be falling out. Not counting, especially, that the latent period would not last more than a couple of weeks, and then it would be time for the "febrile period."

It was in the febrile period that he would probably die, because the stage after that held only two possibilities: either he would slowly begin to recover. Or he would be dead.

He opened his eyes as he heard a sound at the door. His son Vassili came in, looking scared and very young in his cap and white robe and bootees. "They took a sample of my bone marrow," he said proudly. "Do you know what they did? They pushed a kind of a knife right into my chest! Right into the bone!" He gently touched his clavicle to show where the knife had gone.

"That must have been very painful," Smin said, wishing he could put his arms around the boy—if it were not so painful to move—if he did not know that Vassili was afraid, as everyone who came into the hospital seemed to be afraid, that somehow some of the radioactive materials would leap from his skin to theirs if they got too close.

Vassili bit his lips, pondering a response to make to that which would not be either teenage bragging or inadmissible sentimentality. "I was glad to do it," he said awkwardly, and changed the subject. "What will they do now?"

"Well," Smin said, changing position on the bed uncomfortably, "you see, because I am sick it is necessary to make me much sicker. Because the marrow of my bones has been damaged, they must now finish the job and destroy it completely, so that when they put your good marrow into me, it will find an empty place waiting for it."

Vassili swallowed, his eyes large. "Ah, but there is a bright side," Smin said quickly. "I've received so much radiation already that that, at least, they don't need to give me again. Only chemicals. All the medicines do is make me vomit, but I was doing that anyway."

But the boy was frowning. It was apparent that he had already been told what lay in store for his father. He said, "They took bone marrow from you too?"

"What little there was to take, yes," his father smiled, touching his breastbone. "Help me into the wheelchair—no, wait," he corrected himself, remembering that visitors should not touch the patients. "I'll get the nurse to do it later. I want to find out about my friend, the hydrologist-engineer, Sheranchuk."

"Yes," said the boy absently. "He is here, also with too much exposure to radiation." Then Vassili came back to the main subject on his mind. "Father? If my bone marrow isn't good for you, what will happen?"

"Then we will ask someone else to give me a bit," Smin said cheerfully. "It does not have to come from a relative. Simply that is usually the best place to find a match, but it could be taken from some total stranger who simply happens to match my type."

"And if there isn't such a stranger?"

"Then they will do a fetal liver injection, of course. Do you know what that is? Before they are born, children manufacture their white blood corpuscles in the liver; and when a supply of fetal liver is obtained, it is injected into people like me. Just like the bone marrow. Three people in this hospital have already received such injections." He did not add that all three had died. He changed the subject: "And have you been assigned to a school while you are here in Moscow?"

"Oh, yes," the boy said, his eyes gleaming. "Such a school, Father! There is a computer in the math class, and my teacher of English herself studied in America!" That reminded him: "And there are American doctors here, did you know? Two of them now, and more, they say, coming—with all sorts of medicines and machines and things; they will have you well in no time, I am sure!"

"Of course they will." The effort of reassuring his son was beginning to tell on Smin. He could feel himself sweating, and it was obvious that the boy still had something on his mind. Smin sighed and took the plunge. "What else is worrying you, Vassili?" he asked.

The boy bit his lip, and then forced out: "What did those men want?"

Smin sank back. Of course! "Ah, I see," he said. "The organs. They had simply questions to ask, of course. Naturally something like this must be investigated with complete thoroughness."

Vassili nodded doubtfully. "But you did nothing wrong," he protested, unable to keep it from sounding like a question.

Smin said gently, "The accident did not happen by itself, Vass. When everything has been studied, we will know who is at fault, that's all." He threw the sheet back, revealing himself in his red and white striped pajama bottoms, with no top. Even in front of his children Smin had always been shy about exposing the vast shiny burn scars on his torso, but right now, he thought, he would have welcomed Vassili's questions on the subject. What could be better for the boy to hear at this time than the tale of his father's ancient heroism in the tank battle before Kursk?

Almost as good, there was an interruption. Smin looked

up gratefully as the doctor came in, but under the white head scarf her face was grave.

"I am sorry," she began, looking at Vassili rather than at Smin, and Smin knew at once who she was apologizing to.

"Ah, Vass," he said, smiling even though it hurt the corners of his mouth terribly, "it is your good fortune that you took after your mother, but this time, I'm afraid, it isn't mine. The doctor is trying to tell us that your bone marrow doesn't match."

CHAPTER 24

The village of Yuzhevin has an unfortunate label that was affixed to it by the ministry in Moscow. The label is "unpromising." The easiest way for a village to become unpromising is for it to lose most of its young people to better jobs in the cities, the factory complexes, or (in the case of Yuzhevin) the mines of the Don basin. There is no development capital for an unpromising village. As it dwindles, it is likely to lose its electricity and (if it ever had them) its telephones. The village is lucky if it keeps its store, its clinic, its school. Yuzhevin has not been that lucky, but, like many unpromising villages, it does have a surplus of one useful commodity that is very scarce indeed in most of the USSR. There is plenty of unused housing in Yuzhevin. To be sure, the available housing is not in any sense luxurious. Hardly any of the houses in Yuzhevin have more than one room. They have no indoor plumbing, and no one in the village has seen any reason to do any repairs or cleaning on the houses that have been abandoned. Yuzhevin, however, is definitely not radioactive, and in that way, at least, it is far better to be there in Yuzhevin than to remain in Pripyat.

Since Yuzhevin was not even on the highway, Bohdan Kalychenko had to walk a kilometer and a half, picking his way around the muddiest parts of the road, to meet Raia's bus.

Then he had to wait an hour for it, because the bus was late, and then Raia was not even on the bus. By the time he was back in the village he was not only hot and thirsty, he was beginning to be very hungry.

Although Kalychenko was a nuclear-power engineer—well, an operator, at least, which in his view was almost the same thing—he was defeated by the kerosene stove in the cottage he shared with another male evacuee. After a good deal of swearing he managed to get one of the burners alight to make tea, hacked off a few chunks of bread from what the truck had brought the day before, and, chewing slowly, sat on his doorsill to look out at the village street. In the village square thirty meters away a group of his fellow evacuees were playing cards around a table in the hot sunshine. They waved invitingly, but Kalychenko was not in a mood to join them.

At least his roommate, the postman Petya Barisov, was not there to bother him. When the villagers had offered farm labor to any of the evacuees willing to work the fields, Barisov had been quick to accept—not so much for the money as to get away from the ancient mother who had been evacuated to the same village and never stopped complaining about the treasures she had been forced to abandon in Pripyat. Now Barisov was off in the cattle pastures, repairing fences. So Kalychenko had a moment of privacy.

Unfortunately, Raia was not on hand to make some use of it. Not that there was ever any real privacy in Yuzhevin anyway, with the villagers always obsessively curious about their new neighbors, and the walls of the cottages made of cracked boards. He was certain that he had heard the sounds of people breathing just outside his window at night. The people of Yuzhevin were certainly friendly to the rich city people. It was not only that the evacuees were so much more sophisticated than the kolkhozists. The city people were a great boon to Yuzhevin, because they had brought with them the every-other-day trucks with food and even, sometimes, such things as toilet paper and occasional articles of clothing. It was not like having the village's own store again, but it was more than they had had for half a dozen years.

Kalychenko contemplated the options available to him. At home he would have had no problem. He would have turned to his East German radio, or his well-loved stereo from Czechoslovakia, but, of course, those were still in Pripyat, along with his television and all the other treasures, and even if he had had them, there was no electricity to make them work.

He could, he thought, write a letter to the plant at Chernobyl, asking to be returned so he could go back to work now that his arm was healed. Surely one day soon at least Reactors No. 1 or 2 would be back in service, now that (one heard) the fire was out in No. 4. But that would entail explaining the not very explicable reasons why he had never been treated for injury or evacuated with other wounded.

Well, then. There were other alternatives. He could have done some of the things he had promised Raia he would do. Sweep the floor of the cottage. Wash again some of the windows that Raia had already washed once—but the coal dust in the air dirtied them in no time. He could have tried, as he had promised, to repair the door to the privy in the back yard, which had warped so that it would not close properly and a decent person had to hold it closed with one hand while going about his business inside, in the dark.

Those were all useful and productive things Kalychenko could have done, but none of them appealed. Besides, he remembered that he had a more interesting project.

He had managed to buy half a kilo of early raspberries from one of the villagers that morning—at a shocking price, almost half of what he would have had to pay in the private markets at Pripyat. He took the raspberries out of the cupboard, along with the two bottles of vodka, which had cost him four hours of standing on line to get. He unscrewed the tops of the bottles and set them on the table. Patiently he plucked the stems from the raspberries and, one by one, dropped them in to flavor the vodka. As the bottles began to fill, he soon had to stop. He was equal to that challenge. He wiped out a cup and poured off enough of the liquor to get the remaining berries in.

As there was no sense leaving the vodka in an open cup, he sipped at it as he added the berries. By the time he replaced the caps on the bottles and put them away, he had swallowed the warm surplus. He was therefore in an agreeable mood when one of the villagers appeared in the doorway. "You Kalychenko?" he asked.

"That's my name," Kalychenko agreed, polite to this shitkicker in the dirty shirt. "Would you like a drink?"

The man grinned. He was a big old fellow, nearly bald, and although he wore rough clothes and shitkicker boots, there was an impressively expensive-looking watch on his thick wrist. "Never say no to gorulka," he said. "What, it's not gorulka? The Russian stuff? Well, by all means, anyway."

His name, he said, sitting down, was Yakovlev—"Call me Kolka"—and he had heard that Kalychenko was some kind of engineer. When they had each tossed down a glass of the vodka, barely flavored yet with the berries, Yakovlev asked, "Does that mean you know anything about machines?"

"I know *everything* about machines," Kalychenko boasted.

"Yes, well, no offense," Yakovlev persisted, "but what I mean is, do you know how to drive a tractor?"

"Dear Kolka," said Kalychenko, refilling their glasses, "I did not come to this metropolis of Yuzhevin in order to help you out with your agricultural pursuits. I shouldn't even be here, do you understand? Our bus was the only one sent to a place like this."

"I only asked if you could handle a tractor," the man persisted.

"A tractor? I am a nuclear engineer, do you understand what that means? It means that I am an expert who has trained for many years with the highest of high-tech machinery. I will be recalled to duty very soon, because there are not very many of us in the Soviet Union, and we are not only scarce, we are very well paid."

"Uh-huh," said Yakovlev agreeably. "More than nine hundred rubles a month, I suppose."

Kalychenko's eyes bulged as he was swallowing the new shot. He almost exploded, but managed to gasp, "How many rubles?"

"It is what I would be paying my son to help me drive the tractors, only the boy has decided he would rather be poor in Odessa than rich in Yuzhevin. Does that sort of salary interest you? Yes? Then, dear Bohdan, I think we've had enough of this duck piss. Come to my place and we will drink some good French brandy while I find out if you know enough to take an eighteen-year-old's place."

When Kalychenko's fiancée, Raia, trudged back to the village, she went to the hut Kalychenko shared instead of the one where the three single women had been assigned. She was not surprised that he wasn't there. She wasn't surprised, either, at the fact that none of the repairs had been done, and nothing had been cleaned, although the empty vodka bottles on the table did raise her eyebrows.

Still, she told herself, setting about trying to restore order, you could not expect a man like Bohdan Kalychenko to turn into a housewife.

Raia did not have very many illusions about the man she intended to marry. It was his pale skin and his blue eyes that had made her willing to go to bed with him, not his character. True, his job at the Chernobyl Nuclear Power Station was socially well above her own status—Raia worked as a conductor on the town buses—but in Pripyat there were plenty of young men with good jobs. Only they didn't look like Bohdan Kalychenko.

She knew quite well that Kalychenko was scared. She saw no reason to mention it to him. There was no way she could reassure him, because he had every reason to be afraid. There was inevitably going to be an *enormous* investigation of the disaster at Chernobyl, and her fiancé had nominated himself for the position of major scapegoat by running away from his post of duty.

Raia didn't excuse him for that. She didn't bother blaming him, either. Certainly it must have been terrifying to be right on the scene when Reactor No. 4 blew itself up. She simply accepted as a fact of life that there was a real chance that when her child was born, its father might be five thousand kilometers away, chopping logs to lay across some Siberian permafrost. This did not make Raia reluctant to marry him. It made her want to get the ceremony performed—soon—right away, in case one night the organs appeared and the next morning he was on his way to Lefortovo Prison. As to the possibility that her son might suffer any effect from radioactivity, after her first horrid vision of a child with no eyes, Raia had simply dismissed any such idea. After all, she was healthy. It could not happen to her. . . .

Raia paused and lighted a cigarette, frowning at the stove that would not give up its coat of grease.

It was necessary, she thought, to make alternative plans in case the worst happened.

Raia's capacity for reasoning was excellent. She perceived that she had four alternatives. First, she could marry Kalychenko and bear his child; that was the best thing, if it could be made to happen. Second, she could bear the child unmarried. A poor second choice; a single woman with a child would never marry, and Raia definitely wanted, if at all possible, to have a home and a husband. Third, she could have an abortion—but that she simply ruled out, not by logic but only because she could never do such a thing.

There remained a fourth possibility.

There was Volya Kokoulin, her fellow bus conductor, who had let her know very clearly that nothing would give him more delight than to steal off into the woods with her and make love.

If Kalychenko were taken away before they married, it would not be hard, Raia thought, to discover where Kokoulin had been evacuated to. She could find him. Having found him, it would be quite easy to sleep with him, to inform him a few weeks later that he had made her pregnant, and to marry him. There might be some unpleasantness about dates when the child was born, but by then what would it matter? And if Kokoulin were as hungry for her flesh as he indicated, he should be easy enough to convince that premature babies ran in her family.

She was smiling to herself, perched on the edge of the table, when Kalychenko came unevenly in the door. She threw her arms around him in real pleasure. There was nothing feigned about it; this was the man she intended to marry—if at all possible—because really, when you came right down to it, all of Kokoulin's virtues did not outweigh the fact that Kalychenko was tall, blue-eyed, and graceful, and Kokoulin was *ugly*.

When Kalychenko stumbled back to his cottage to find Raia entering just before him, he was glowing all over with his news. "Really, my dear," he said at once, "this Yuzhevin is not such a bad place after all."

His fiancée was flushed and sweaty, with two filled string bags still on the table. Kalychenko peered into them even as he greeted her with a cheerful kiss. "Ah, my darling," he said fondly. "You've had a long walk, I'm afraid. But I have good news! I've been offered a job driving a tractor here! No, no, don't look so disapproving. Wait till you hear what they pay tractor drivers! Why, this head driver, Kolka Yakovlev, he has that big house just outside the village, you know? With fruit trees all around it? And the Volga parked in the backyard? Sixteen thousand rubles he paid for that car, that's what kind of money a tractor driver earns in Yuzhevin, because everyone with skills runs off to the city!"

"That's very nice," Raia said, gazing out the cottage door with sudden intensity.

"And if you're not too tired tonight, he has invited us to come to his house to watch some American films! He has television tapes of all sorts of things—*The Wizard of Oz*, and motion pictures with Clark Gable and even Mickey Mouse! Oh," he said apologetically, "but, of course, you're worn out carrying those things. It's my fault. I went to meet the bus, but—"

"I did not come on the bus; I missed it. I came in a car, Bohdan. Two men gave me a ride almost to Yuzhevin."

"Well, that was lucky," he beamed.

"No, Bohdan," she sighed. "It wasn't really lucky, I think. The men didn't say much to me, but I didn't think they were coming quite to the village. Only there is their car, just across the square. Do you know what I think, Bohdan? I think those men came here to interview evacuees like us. I think they are from the organs."

CHAPTER 25

Within large continents, air generally moves across the surface of the Earth from west to east, with a slight curve toward the poles. For that reason, the weather in Chicago usually comes from somewhere in California, and Moscow gets a large part of its weather from Spain or France. At any particular place or time, however, the winds can be quite fickle. If the Soviet air masses had been moving in the prevailing direction in April and May of 1986, the gases from the Chernobyl explosion would have been carried out over Siberia and the Pacific. They weren't. First they moved north. Then east. Then everywhere.

The first stops for the wandering witches' brew from Chernobyl were Poland and eastern Scandinavia. The invisible cloud was greeted with confusion and panic. In Poland, the official press was reassuring. The underground press, which was what the Polish people read to find out what is going on, was not. So Polish pharmacies were sold out of potassium iodide overnight, for the scariest ingredient in the cloud was its radioactive iodine-131. The trouble with the radioactive iodine was that every human being has a thyroid gland, and every thyroid gland has an insatiable appetite for iodine. If the iodine happens to be the radioactive isotope, the gland swallows it anyway. There the iodine stays, ceaselessly bombarding the victim from within with its radiation. Cancer of the thyroid is one of the commonest consequences of exposure to radioactive leaks.

Before long the winds took Chernobyl's gases south and east, to blanket most of the European continent, but by then iodine-131 was no longer the greatest fear. Radio-iodine has at least one virtue. It is short-lived. In only eight days half of it decays into something else. Two other isotopes were by then more worrisome, and they were xenon-133, a gas, and cesium-137, normally a solid. (But, like the iodine, volatile enough so that large amounts went up with Chernobyl's smoke and remained in its cloud as finely divided particles.) The xenon, being a gas, is particularly troublesome. Rain won't wash it out of the air; it is there to be breathed until it, too, decays. The cesium is even worse. It takes thirty years for half of it to decay. When it finally falls to the ground, it remains in the soil and water for a long, long time.

Of course, even after the thirty years of xenon's half-life have passed, not all of it will be gone. Half will still be there; that's what "half-life" means. If one were to follow the history of one small patch of someone's backyard onto which one million atoms of radioactive cesium from Chernobyl had fallen, by the year 2016 five hundred thousand atoms would still be there. There would still be over sixty thousand radioactive atoms of the stuff by the beginning of the twenty-second century. Sooner or later, of course, it would all be gone from that little patch, and the last of those million atoms would have turned into something else. That should happen somewhere around six centuries from now.

When the little particles of radioactive cesium finally settle out from the sky, they cling to whatever they land on. Some of them have landed on farms of lettuce and spinach (which people eat), or on grassy pastures (which cows eat, and turn into cesium-bearing milk for people).

So all over Europe governments ordered, or people simply decided on their own, that fresh milk and leafy vegetables should be removed from the daily diet. That was nasty for parents of small children. It was even worse for farmers. Exports of any of those things from Eastern Europe were refused at the borders. When the cloud reached as far south as Italy, the authorities banned the sale of even locally grown leafy vegetables and Italian farmers, broken-hearted, saw their crops dumped into fields to rot.

CHAPTER 26

TUESDAY, MAY 6

Moscow's Hospital No. 6 takes up most of a large city block. The hospital is not entirely devoted to patients who suffer from radiation sickness. If that were so it would be nearly empty nearly all the time; Chernobyls are rare. But when a Chernobyl happens, Hospital No. 6 is ready, for it is there that the USSR has concentrated the best doctors specializing in that ailment. It is a very good hospital. The wing devoted to radiation disease is built to an old-fashioned plan, with high ceilings and large rooms, and in this warm May the sun floods in. The wing has a total of 299 patients flown in from the Chernobyl explosion. These are the worst cases, the ones who have taken the most radiation. They are getting the best care possible, but for many of them it is not enough.

When Leonid Sheranchuk got there, however, he was protesting that it was more care than he needed, and more than he really wanted by far. The admitting doctors paid his arguments no attention. Since he was there, he would stay until released; but they did allow him one boon. Most of the patients were in private rooms, but they granted his plea to share the room of Deputy Director Leonid Smin, and that kindness made him stop protesting.

Sheranchuk was not at all sure, however, that it was a kindness to Smin. The Deputy Director had certainly welcomed his company. But the Deputy Director had been fading rapidly ever since then. On the first day Smin had been alert, if very sick; he had even greeted his Comrade Plumber and joked about his own internal plumbing. But now, as Sheranchuk could hear, Smin's internal plumbing was giving him trouble again. After the bone marrow, the next targets that radiation destroyed were the soft tissues of the mouth and the intestinal tract, and one of the most unpleasant effects of an overdose was the terrible bloody diarrhea that resulted.

When the nurse came out, carrying the covered bedpan with respect because what came out of Smin's body was not only unpleasant but contaminated with radioactivity, Sheranchuk asked, "How is he?"

She said, "I think he will sleep for a while. How about yourself? How are you feeling?"

"I am feeling quite well," said Sheranchuk automatically. It was almost true, not counting the aches and twinges where needles had been stuck into him. He was even thinking of getting up for a visit to some of the other patients, although he felt, as always, a bit fatigued.

She nodded, not even listening—after all, she knew his condition better than he did. "Do you need anything?"

"Only to get out of here." He grinned. "Preferably alive."

"You have a very good chance," she said strongly. "And in any case, you have a new doctor. Four or five of them, if you count the Americans, but one doctor in particular I am sure you will be glad to see."

"And who is that?" asked Sheranchuk, but she only smiled and left him.

Sheranchuk picked up a magazine, shifting uncomfortably in his bed. A voice from behind the curtain said softly, "She did not tell you the truth, you know."

"Deputy Director Smin?" Sheranchuk cried. "But I thought you were asleep."

"Exactly, yes. You thought that because that nurse told you I would be, but, as you see, I am not."

"Let me pull the curtain back," said Sheranchuk eagerly, swinging his legs over the side of the bed.

"No, please! Don't exert yourself. I am not at my most handsome just now, as you may suppose, and I prefer not to exhibit my wretchedness. We can talk perfectly well this way."

"Of course," said Sheranchuk.

There was a silence for a moment. Then Smin's voice said gravely, "I am told you behaved with great courage, Comrade Plumber."

Sheranchuk flushed. "They needed to get concrete under the reactor. Someone had to do it. I hope only that they have succeeded."

"At least it is well begun," Smin said, and paused to cough for a moment. Then he said, "I spoke to the plant on the telephone last night. It is going well. They decided they needed to drill a tunnel under the core to get the concrete in, but the mud was too soft. Then they found an engineer from the Leningrad Metro to show them how. They froze the mud with liquid nitrogen, and now the concrete is in place."

"So everything is safe now."

There was a long silence from Smin. "I hope so, Comrade Plumber," he said at last. "Isn't it almost time for the doctors' morning rounds? I think I will sleep a little until then, after all."

When the doctors came through, they kept Smin's curtains closed, and Sheranchuk sat on the edge of his bed, kicking his heels irritably against the metal legs, listening. There was not much to hear. All the resources of Hospital No. 6 were not making Smin better. He was weaker today than he had been when Sheranchuk was admitted. As the doctors moved about and the curtains parted a bit, Sheranchuk could see how bad the old man was. His skin looked like—like—like a leper's, Sheranchuk decided, though he had never seen a leper. It was blotchy. Under the dressings were sores that ran. The part of his chest that was not covered with the great old burn scar now was dotted with the little pink blossoms of burst blood vessels the doctors called "petechiae." Reminded, Sheranchuk examined his own chest and arms, but there were none of the things there.

He really was not, he told himself again, sick enough to be in this place.

When it was Sheranchuk's own turn, the doctors were more relaxed. It was only, "Open your mouth, please" and "Please, if you will just remove your pajama bottoms"—so they could poke around his balls—and then they peered at his charts for just a moment.

"I should be sent away from here," he told them. "I'm taking up space others need more."

"We have plenty of space, Leonid," the head doctor smiled. "We also have plenty of doctors—even some new ones coming from America, soon."

But actually Sheranchuk thought they already had all too many doctors, especially the radiation hematologist, Dr. Akhsmentova. He did not care for the woman, and was not pleased when she stayed on after the other doctors had left. "Just a few more drops of your blood, if you please, Comrade Sheranchuk," she requested. She didn't wait for permission. She had already pushed him back on the bed and seized his arm.

"The nurses are gentler than you," Sheranchuk complained as she stabbed once more into the heart of the bruises left from other needles.

"The nurses have more time. Stop wriggling, please." He glared silently at her. Glancing at his bright steel teeth as she withdrew the needle, she said, "And one other thing. When the American doctors see you, try not to smile. We do not want them to think so poorly of Soviet dentistry."

When she had gone, Smin said from behind the curtains, "I hope the Americans don't see Dr. Akhsmentova at all, because we don't want them to have a poor opinion of Soviet hematologists."

His words were cheerful enough, but his tone so faint that it alarmed Sheranchuk. "Please, Simyon. Don't tire yourself talking."

"I am not tired," Smin protested. "Weak, a little, yes." He stirred fretfully; through the gap in the curtains Sheranchuk could see him trying to adjust the sheet more comfortably over his body. "Although perhaps you are right and I should rest again. I am told that I am to have distinguished visitors today, and I should try to be alert and witty for them."

The GehBehs again! Couldn't they leave the poor man alone? Sheranchuk begged, "Then do it, please. And try to eat your lunch when they bring it." But he heard the anger in his voice, and to account for the bitterness in his tone he added, "But it is true that I should not be here."

"Leonid," Smin said patiently, "you are here because you are a hero. Do you think everyone has forgotten what you did under the reactor? You are a precious person, and everyone wants to make sure you don't die on us because you foolishly did one heroic thing too many. Now go and eat your lunch."

The patients' dining room was half the floor away, and as he walked down the hall toward it, Sheranchuk peered into each room he passed. To have the Deputy Director call him a hero! But everyone in this place was a hero—the firemen, the operators who had stayed steadfast, the doctor who had come back and back to help the victims until he became a victim himself—not least among the heroes was Deputy Director Simyon Smin himself, if it came to that! And almost all of them were far worse off than Leonid Sheranchuk, who had merely been weak enough to faint from exhaustion.

The patients' dining room proved that. There were hardly more than a dozen patients at the tables that could have seated dozens more. It was not that there was any shortage of patients to fill the room. It was simply because so many of them were too sick or too weak, or merely too encumbered with pipettes and catheters and tubes of trickling medicines to get up and walk to their meals.

Sheranchuk paused in the doorway to sniff at what was offered. Fish soup at least, he thought approvingly; say what you will, the food was better here than in any other hospital he had ever heard of. He looked toward one of the tables by a window and was surprised to hear his name called.

The man who got up was hard to recognize at first, in the hospital whites, and then Sheranchuk saw that it was Vladimir Ponomorenko, one of the Four Seasons of the football team. "Autumn!" Sheranchuk cried in shock. "Not you, too!"

"Oh, no, Comrade Sheranchuk," the football player said apologetically, and Sheranchuk recognized that he was in the whites of a visitor, not the red-striped pajamas of the patients. "The nurses said it was all right for me to eat here, but I'm only here to see my cousins, in case they can use my bone marrow."

"Your cousins? Both of them?" Sheranchuk repeated blankly. "But, Autumn, I had no idea. Both Spring and Summer, here in this hospital? Here, let me sit down with you, tell me what's happened to them."

But none of the news was good. The two who were

Vladimir's cousins, the fireman, Vassili, who was called "Summer," and the pipefitter, Arkady, who was called "Spring," had both taken serious amounts of radiation. The prognosis for both of them was not good. The fireman did not merely have radiation sickness. He had been badly burned; one foot, at least, was so destroyed that he was almost sure to lose it, and he was so full of morphine that he had not even recognized Autumn beside his bed. And the pipefitter Arkady—when he went back to turn off the hydrogen flare he paid for it. "But he's in my own section," Sheranchuk said, stricken. "I let him go there! And I didn't even know he was here!"

"He was on another floor," Autumn explained. "They only moved him up here yesterday, when a room became vacant." Sheranchuk winced. He knew how rooms became vacant in this wing of Hospital No. 6. Although he ate all of the good meal—the fish soup, and the shashlik and the cucumber salad and the heavy, dark bread—he hardly tasted any of it. "Volya," he said, "are you finished? Then let's go see Arkady, please. I want to apologize for not coming to him before."

But when they entered the pipefitter's room, Spring would have none of it. "Apologize for not visiting me? But, Comrade Sheranchuk, I at least knew you were here, so it is I who am at fault for not coming to you." And he grinned, because the plastic pouch of blood that was trickling into his arm was evidence for all that he was not in a position to pay social calls.

"When you're feeling better we will visit back and forth like grandmothers," Sheranchuk promised.

But he knew it was not a promise they would be able to keep. The pipefitter was not likely to walk very far. Radiation sickness took different people in different ways, and what it had done to Spring was stop his digestive system. Big, tough, muscular Spring had suddenly become gaunt. He was no longer the flame that licked down the football field. He wasn't the shy, hesitant, preoccupied pipefitter Sheranchuk had worked with all these months, either. As his body grew weak, his spirit had become almost boisterous. He joked and laughed, and winked at the nurses.

"So you like it here," Sheranchuk offered, feeling like a visitor instead of a fellow patient.

"Why not? The food is good, the nurses are pretty, and photographers come every day to take my picture. Next they will want me to autograph the photos for them. I may stay right here in Moscow. The Dynamo team can use a few good players!"

But the nurses would not let them stay very long, and when Sheranchuk walked out with Autumn, the other member of the Ponomorenko family was solicitous. Of Sheranchuk! He said seriously, "You should not be tiring yourself, should you? Let me walk you back to your room."

"I would like to see your other cousin," Sheranchuk said obstinately.

"But he is on the first floor. The stairs—"

"I can manage a flight of stairs," Sheranchuk growled. "In any case, my roommate is having important visitors. It is probably better if I stay away for a while."

Autumn shrugged. "Imagine," Sheranchuk went on, thinking about the disaster. "Both your cousins in the hospital at once. What a terrible thing! But at least your brother Vyacheslav is not here—" He broke off as he saw the way the football player was looking at him. "What is it? Has Winter been injured too?"

Autumn said apologetically, "I thought you knew. My brother was in the Number Four reactor room itself. They say he was the first to die, but they haven't been able to find his body. It's still there, they think."

Smin was dozing lightly when he became aware he had company again. "We didn't wake you, I hope?" said the taller of the two men who had parted his curtains.

"It's a pleasure to know that I can still wake up," Smin said, nodding to them. "Fedor Vassilievitch Mishko. Andrei Pavlovich Milaktiev. I am honored to be visited by two members of the leadership."

"By two old friends, Simyon Mikhailovitch," Mishko corrected. "If not friends, at least men with whom you have worked in the past. Are you feeling well?"

"I am feeling very poorly," said Smin, his smile now an uncomfortable grimace. "I would feel a little better if I knew whether you were here to inquire after my health or to tell me I am in disgrace."

"Unfortunately, both," Milaktiev said heavily. He was a slim old man except for a pot belly that his expensive, Western-cut clothes nearly succeeded in concealing. His hair was still dark and so was his thick, bristly mustache—almost a Stalin mustache, Smin thought.

"Nevertheless," Mishko added, "also as friends. I hope you believe that, Simyon Mikhailovitch."

Smin thought that over carefully. The men had pulled the curtains behind them, but they had taken chairs in with them. They had seated themselves, waiting patiently for his answer. "I believe," he said at last, "that my mother had the very highest regard for your father, Fedor Vassilievtch."

Mishko grinned. He was taller than his partner, and dapper in a pale tan sports jacket and paisley tie. "In fact," he said, "if my father had not been purged in the Stalin years, you and I might now be stepbrothers."

"So my mother has told me," Smin said. "She has spoken often of the Stalin years."

"Which, I am sure, she never wants to see return."

They had been speaking softly in any case, but Mishko both lowered his voice still more and glanced at the gap in the curtains as he spoke. So even a member of the Central Committee wondered who might be listening at times! "I do not suppose," Smin said, "that you came here to discuss the cult of personality with me. Would you mind telling me what you want?"

Mishko sighed. "Actually we have two purposes. The official one is to ask you some questions about the accident."

"The GehBehs have already asked me."

"And no doubt they will ask you more." Mishko nodded. "The organs are still thorough. But it is, after all, a serious matter, Simyon Mikhailovitch. I suppose you know that every RBMK generator in the Soviet Union has been shut down?"

Smin was shaken. "I didn't know that."

"The economic consequences are serious. We've lost export sales of food because the foreigners think our tomatoes will make them glow in the dark. Production is down in the factories requiring electrical power. Tourism, of course—there is no tourism now. And I do not even speak of the loss of life."

"Am I charged with sabotage?"

"Simyon," the other man said gently, "you aren't being charged with anything. Do you mind if I smoke?"

There were *Ne kurit* signs all over the room, but Smin shrugged. "I wish I could join you."

Milaktiev lighted up before he spoke. He considered for a moment. Then: "When the Party entrusted you with a very high position, it expected you to live up to its responsibilities. Have you given your people good leadership?"

"I gave them good food, good housing, good pay, fair treatment—as much as I could, with the First Department breathing down my neck. I don't know how to measure leadership."

"One way to measure it," said Milaktiev, "is by the number of shift chiefs, engineers, and others who deserted their jobs. There were one hundred fifty-eight of them at the Chernobyl Power Plant."

"And nearly three thousand others remained for duty," Smin replied.

"What about defective materials?"

"There were some, yes. I have reported this in full. They were not in essential places. After the article in *Literaturna Ukraina* appeared—I believe you are familiar with it—"

"Oh, yes," Mishko smiled, answering for both of them.

"—I instituted a complete inspection of all essential systems. Where there were faults, I replaced them. In any case, if anything failed and so helped to cause the accident, it probably was the instrumentation."

"The instrumentation?"

"Which was imported from France and Germany," Smin pointed out. "Go sue the French."

The man from the Central Committee said, "We are not speaking of lawsuits, Simyon Mikhailovitch. We are speaking of faults in the management of the plant. If you say to me, 'I did everything correctly,' then I say to you, 'But still it happened.'"

Smin shrugged. "I was only Deputy Director."

Mishko sighed. "The Director will face prosecution," he said.

"And will I?"

"I hope not, Simyon Mikhailovitch. Of course, you are likely to be dismissed from your post. You may also, of course, be expelled from the Party."

"Of course," said Smin bitterly. "Now, if you will excuse me, I would like to vomit."

The two men looked at each other. Then Milaktiev, stubbing out his cigarette, leaned forward and spoke more softly still. "If you must vomit, do it. But now we're finished with the official part of our visit, and there is another matter to discuss."

"And what is that?" asked Smin, fighting against fatigue; there was something going on here, and he had to know what it was.

"Would you, Simyon Mikhailovitch, make a complete statement for us of what happened at Chernobyl? I don't mean the accident. I mean before the accident. We are asking you to describe everything that made it difficult for you to run the plant properly. Directives which could not be complied with, or which did actual harm. Political pressures. The appointment of a Director who was incompetent. The corruption. The drunkenness and absenteeism. The interference from the First Department. Everything. Do you understand what I mean by 'everything'? I mean *everything*."

Smin was feeling really faint now. The sober old face grew fuzzy before him. "I don't follow you," he said faintly. "I've already given all this to the organs."

"Who may or may not pass it all on to us. We want it all."

"Do you mean that you want me to put on paper everything that is kept secret?"

"Exactly that, yes."

"And—" Smin licked his sore lips. "And if I do, what use will you make of it?"

They looked at each other again. Then, "I cannot say. I don't know," said Milaktiev. "Yet."

When Leonid Sheranchuk finally came back to his room, he saw that the curtains around Smin's bed were still drawn. Someone was there, because Sheranchuk could hear an almost inaudible mutter of voices. And when he bumped against his bed, a head popped out of the curtains to stare at him. It withdrew in a moment, and he heard one of the voices say to another, "Smin is almost asleep, anyway. We'll come back another time." But Sheranchuk thought that that head had looked familiar, and when its owner came out with another man, nodding politely to him as they left, he thought the face on the other man looked familiar too. Not as friends. Not even as someone he had run across in a casual meeting; as a face he had seen in a newspaper or on television. He lay down on his bed, pondering the question. Then he got up. Tired as he was, he hobbled to the open window and peered out at the courtyard.

Sure enough, a few moments later, there they were, tan sports coat and conservative gray, appearing on the steps below. From the other side of the little grove of trees in the courtyard a car purred forward from its parking niche to meet them.

The car was a Zil.

Sheranchuk stared at it as it spun away, traffic miraculously opening before it. He had never been in the presence of two members of the Central Committee before.

CHAPTER 27

WEDNESDAY, MAY 7

Smin's mother, Aftasia Smin, is four feet ten inches tall and weighs less than ninety pounds. At one time she was taller, though not much. Then old hunger and later osteoporosis knocked a few inches off her height.

She is eighty-six years old—the same age as the century, she says. Aftasia celebrates her birthday on the first of the year. That is really only a guess, since it was not the custom in the shtetl at the turn of the century to pay much attention to recording the birth of Jewish female babies.

Although she was never very big, she carried a rifle in the Civil War from 1918 until, seven months pregnant with Simyon, she left her husband to pursue the last of the White forces in the Ukraine. Aftasia returned to the shtetl to give birth. She still has a puckered scar, very high on the inside of her right thigh, where a bullet from the Czech legion put her out of action for two cold, painful, hungry months. The fiery young revolutionary husband she had left the shtetl to marry was later captured by Kolchak's forces. He was executed, after some barbaric questioning, the week after Simyon was born. Simyon was a year old before Aftasia learned that her husband was dead. She never found out where his body was buried.

*   *   *

What Aftasia Smin represented to her downstairs neighbor, Oksana Didchuk, was hard to define. To Oksana, the frail old woman was a bit of a conundrum, and a rather worrying one sometimes. There were some very good and neighborly things about Aftasia Smin. She was a generous acquaintance who always had something for the Didchuks' little girl on New Year's Day, and not just a chocolate bar or a kerchief but even things like a pretty, flaxen-haired doll from the Children's World store in Moscow, or even wonderful sugared almonds that had come all the way from Paris. Nor was it only the daughter who benefited from Aftasia's largesse. Let Oksana happen to mention that she had been unable to find plastic hair curlers in the store, say, and old Aftasia was likely to turn up the next day with a box of them, saying that her son had brought them back from a trip to the West, like the sugared almonds, and after all what did an old woman like herself want with such things?

On the other hand, there were things about Aftasia Smin that were troubling to her neighbors from the floor below. It was not simply that Aftasia appeared to be, in some sense, Jewish. There was nothing really wrong with being Jewish, provided you didn't actually become religious about it. Aftasia had never shown any signs of observing the Saturday Sabbath or of creeping off to Kiev's only functioning synagogue. (Though it was true that the Didchuks had been quite shocked to find that the meal she had invited them to on April 25th had been taken by the Americans to have some ritual significance in the yid faith.)

It was certainly not disturbing that Aftasia was an Old Bolshevik. Actually, it was quite an honor to know such a person. She had personally known some of the great heroes of the Revolution! She still knew some of their sons and grandsons, it seemed. But really, the Didchuks had often asked each other, if she is what she is, why does she live as she does?

To that the Didchuks had no answer. But when she asked them for any sort of favor, to use their telephone (but why didn't the woman have one of her own?), or to translate for those fascinating American cousins, the Didchuks were happy to oblige. And when she knocked on their door this worrying May morning, with all of Kiev in an uproar, they were downcast to be unable to agree at once. "But, you see," Oksana

Didchuk said sadly, "today they are sending all the children away from Kiev for a bit—purely as a precaution, of course. We would certainly be glad to help you get your American cousins to the airport, but we must get our own daughter to the train station. Also I must go to the market to buy some food for her to take on the train. Also there is some mixup with her papers for the trip, so really my husband and I should go to the station now to straighten it out."

But Aftasia Smin said crisply, "Leave that to me, please. My cousins don't leave until this afternoon. There's plenty of time to get to the station. To buy food first? Why not? If you will let me use your telephone, I'll simply have the car come a bit early and we'll go to the Rye Market together."

And so Oksana Didchuk found herself in the backseat of a handsome new Volga, with Aftasia Smin perched in front, next to the driver, ordering him to take them to the market and wait while they made their purchases. It was certainly a great improvement over standing in line for a bus, especially on this particular Wednesday, when everybody in Kiev seemed to be trying to get somewhere else. The radio and television broadcasts had been very specific. The city was *not* being evacuated; only foolish people and rumormongers would say such things. It was only that on the very remote chance that the levels of radiation might rise, it would be better for the young children, who were most at risk from such things, to be somewhere else. So there was no reason for anyone to be afraid.

It was astonishing, however, to see how many of the people on the street looked that way anyway.

Even the old Rye Market looked strange that morning. Ordinarily the vendors would not only fill the hall but overflow into the streets outside, on so beautiful a spring day, with all the fruits and vegetables coming in from all the private plots around Kiev. Not today.

Looking down on the trading floor from the balcony, Oksana Didchuk saw gaps in the usually shoulder-to-shoulder line of white-capped farm women standing before their wares. In the aisles were plenty of shoppers, but they didn't seem to be buying much. More than once Oksana saw a customer pick up a couple of tomatoes or a clump of beets, peer closely at them, even sniff them and then reluctantly put them back.

"Well, then," said Aftasia Smin. "What is it you wish to

buy?" She listened courteously while the mother explained what she wanted, and then corrected her plans. "Cheese, yes, but an old one—from milk taken before the accident. And, all right, a sausage, and bread, of course. And a herring, I think. There is nothing wrong with the oceans yet, at least!"

And when Oksana tarried before the slabs of snow-white pork fat and the naked-looking skinned rabbits, thinking of the supper she would have to make for her husband and parents that night, Aftasia vetoed those too. "Sausage again, if you please—and again an old one. Inspected? Yes, of course they are inspected— " For they could not have missed the long lines of vendors waiting their turns to put their strawberries and fresh hams under the radiation detectors so they could get a permit to sell them if they passed. "But if I were to stay in Kiev, I would not buy fresh meat just yet. Let the situation settle down a little."

"Then you're leaving Kiev?" Oksana ventured.

The old lady smiled at her. "Wouldn't you? I don't think that anyone named Smin will be popular in Kiev just now."

But, popular or not, Aftasia Smin still had friends. As she demonstrated to the Didchuks. They set off for the railroad station in good time, Aftasia Smin up front with the driver to give orders, the elder Didchuks in back with their daughter, and their daughter's boxes, bags, and paper-wrapped food parcels, squeezed between them.

The last hundred meters were the slowest, because the militiamen had roped off the square in front of the train station. The approaches were jammed. Oksana Didchuk made a faint worried sound as she saw the red numbers on the digital clock above the station. "But the train is to leave in an hour," she said.

Aftasia turned to her; she was so tiny she had to lift herself to peer over the back of the seat. "It won't leave in an hour," she said. "Look, the trains are just coming in now." So they were; the Didchuks could see the long trains snaking slowly in to the platforms beside the station.

Oksana made another worried sound, but she muffled it. The regular night trains between Kiev and Moscow were stream-lined, modern cars built in East Germany, proudly lettered with the names of the cities they connected. The ones now creeping in were something quite different. These extra trains to Moscow were made up in a hurry, of cars taken from repair shops and sidings, hard class and soft, dilapidated and spanking new, and for every space on the trains there were two people who wanted to board them.

The special trains were meant to carry children under ten away from the radioactive cloud that threatened Kiev, but every ten-year-old child had parents, older siblings, grandparents, uncles, aunts. Nearly every one of them wished they, too, could get on that train for Moscow and air that did not threaten lingering death. Some tried.

Some, on that Wednesday in Kiev, were trying all sorts of strange things. It was said that potassium iodide capsules saturate the thyroid gland with the element, and so would prevent the radioactive iodine from entering into the body and breeding a cancer in the throat. It was said that Georgian wine immunized one against radiation, or that vodka did; or that a cocktail of equal parts of vodka and turpentine did, or the white of egg, or even more repulsive substances. The first of those rumors happened to be quite true, and, as in Poland, potassium iodide vanished from the apothecaries overnight. The others were not, but that didn't keep people from trying them.

Many of the people in the terminal were all but reeling drunk, there were even one or two glassy-eyed children, and a few wound up in hospitals with assorted poisonings. Everyone was wearing a hat. Many of the children were sweating in winter clothes on this hot May morning, because everyone had been advised to stay bundled up whenever they were out in the open. Those near the doors of the station were constantly shouting at the people milling in and out to close them, shut them tight, keep them closed, to keep the outside air with its secret burden of sickness from poisoning the hot, sweaty, unwell air of the terminal.

When the driver had found a place to put the car, Aftasia ordered the Didchuks: "Wait here." She was gone nearly an hour, but when she came back she was triumphantly waving a boarding pass that let the Didchuk child into one of the newest cars on the train. Such passes were not for everyone. But not everyone had a Party card originally issued in 1916, and even an old woman had friends of friends who could do a favor. Even now.

When the child was settled, surrounded by her boxes and neat little traveling bag and sausage and bread for the long ride, the Didchuks thanked Aftasia. Businesslike, she brushed their thanks aside. "You can do me a favor in return if you will," she said. "I must take my American relatives to the airport. If you will come with me to translate, Didchuk, I am sure your wife can stay here with the child until the train leaves."

"To translate?" Didchuk asked. "But surely at the airport people will speak English—"

"I want to show my cousins something first," said Aftasia harshly. "If it is not too much of a bother?"

Of course it was not too much of a bother, though it was certainly not no bother at all, either; Didchuk would really have preferred to stay with his wife on the platform, waving and smiling at their daughter as needed until at last the train pulled out. Aftasia would not be denied. So the two of them got back in the car, its windows shut tight (as all windows were ordered to be) against the outside air, and the driver took them through the crowded streets to the hotel.

The Garfields were waiting just inside the door, guarding their pretty pale blue matched luggage from California. "A moment," said Aftasia, and got out to explain to the hotel porter that (if he would not mind) he should send the Garfields' luggage to the airport on the Intourist bus, since there was no room in the car for all of it. He, too, agreed not to mind, or not to mind much, and Aftasia ordered the Americans politely to hurry into the car. "But can't we have the windows open, at least?" Candace Garfield asked, and when Didchuk translated the driver exploded:

"Of course not! We have been told to keep out the air as much as possible and it is, after all, only May! We will be quite comfortable in here if no one smokes. If," he added, glancing at Aftasia Smin, "it is really necessary to make this side trip instead of going directly to the airport."

"It is necessary," Aftasia said flatly. When the driver had surrendered, the old woman began to engage her American cousins in a polite conversation through the teacher. It was wonderful, she said, that they had had a chance to meet, after all. She hoped that they had not been too frightened with this difficulty of her son's power plant. They would be all right, she was sure, because they had been exposed to whatever it was for no more than a few days. It was perhaps more dangerous for those who must remain in the Ukraine, but in just a few hours they would be in Moscow, and then the next day on their way to—where were they going first? Paris? Ah, how wonderful! She had always dreamed of seeing Paris—and, oh yes, especially of California, which (she said) she had always thought of as a sort of combination of Yalta, Kiev, and heaven.

With the snail pace of polite conversation relayed through an interpreter, it took half an hour for all these pleasantries to be exchanged, while the car crossed the Dnieper bridge, snaked through the traffic, and drove along the streets of the suburbs.

Aftasia fell silent, watching the streets they passed, and Didchuk took up the burden of conversation for himself. "This part of Kiev," he said proudly, "was only open countryside as recently as the war—did you manage to see our Museum of the Great Patriotic War while you were in Kiev? Yes? Then you know that there was much fighting around here. Now it is all very nice homes, as you see. The people who live here have the bus or the Metro, and in the morning it's twenty minutes and they're at work." He glanced ahead, and frowned slightly. "This particular area," he mentioned diffidently, "was in fact quite famous, in a way. . . . Excuse me," he said abruptly, and leaned forward to talk to Aftasia.

Candace Garfield looked around. They were passing a tall television tower, surrounded by nine-story apartment buildings. "I don't see anything that looks famous," she told her husband. "Unless it's that little park up there on the right."

Her husband was dabbing sweat off his brow. "What I'd like to see," he said, "is an airplane."

"Think of Paris," his wife said good-naturedly. "Paris in the springtime? The sidewalk cafés?"

"Those long, romantic evenings," Garfield said, perking up. "Dinner in our room, with plenty of wine—"

"Down, boy," his wife commanded, as Didchuk sank back and smiled nervously at them.

"This is the place," he said. "Mrs. Smin asks me to ask you if you have ever heard of Babi Yar?"

"Well, of course we've heard of Babi Yar," said Garfield,

and his wife, concentrating, added, "I think so. During the war, wasn't it?"

"Yes, exactly. During the war. Yevgeny Yevtushenko wrote a very famous poem about it, and there has been music, books, all sorts of things about Babi Yar," Didchuk confirmed. He seemed ill-at-ease, but waved toward the park. "Do you see the monument there? It is quite beautiful, don't you think? Many people come here to pay their respects, even leaving flowers—but," he added sadly, "Mrs. Smin does not wish to stop here. Still, you can get quite a good look at it as we go by."

By craning their necks, the Garfields could see a statuary group on a heroic scale. From directly in front it was only a crowd of stone figures, packed tightly together like subway riders, with a mother holding her child despairingly aloft. Then, as the car moved slowly along, Candace said, "What are they doing? It looks like the ones in back are falling into the valley there."

"That's it," Didchuk agreed. "They are falling into that ravine. I thought we would stop there, by the scientific institute, so that we, too, could pay our respects. But Mrs. Smin wants to go just a little farther—ah, yes, we are stopping here. She says this is the real Babi Yar. She says she does not care much for the monument," he finished unhappily.

The car stopped. The teacher looked at Aftasia Smin for instructions, then shrugged and opened the door. "Mrs. Smin would like us to get out and look around here."

"I thought she was afraid of radiation or something," Garfield said doubtfully.

"*She* is not," the teacher said, and trailed the old woman meekly up a grassy slope. Candace Garfield followed with her husband, perplexed. "I don't have much film left," Candace fretted, taking her camera off her shoulder.

"Please," said Didchuk hastily, glancing back. "It would be better not to take any pictures. Because of the television tower. A transmission tower, after all, is a legitimate military objective in case of war, and such things may not be photographed."

"Well, I'll just take a picture of the apartments, then."

"*Please,*" he said abjectly, looking at the cars whizzing by along the road as though he expected a troop of soldiers to leap out and arrest them.

Aftasia stopped at the crest, looking out over the little valley. Then she turned and spoke rapidly to Didchuk, who translated. "In September of 1941," he said, "Hitler decided to put off taking Moscow for a few weeks while he conquered the Ukraine. He ordered his troops to take the city of Kiev. Stalin ordered the Red Army to hold it. Hitler won. His armies passed to the north and the south of the city, then they joined together. Four Soviet armies were surrounded, more than half a million men. Most of them were killed or captured, and the Germans entered Kiev."

Aftasia was listening patiently to the English translation. When Didchuk paused and looked inquiringly at her, she thrust a hand out toward the city and spoke in rapid Russian. The teacher flinched and said something, but she shook her head firmly, gesturing him to go on.

"Mrs. Smin says to tell you that when the Nazis occupied Kiev, many ill-informed Ukrainians welcomed them. They even—" He hesitated, then said miserably, "They said things like, well, like, forgive me, 'Thank God we are free of the Bolsheviks' and 'Now we can worship God again!' Well, it is true, though perhaps there were not as many people like that as Mrs. Smin suggests." Aftasia rattled on. Didchuk nodded and relayed the message: "So when the German officers arrived, some Kiev people, even leaders, even Party members, came out to greet them with the traditional gifts of bread and salt, to show they were welcome. The Germans only laughed. Then they got serious. They stole everything, Mrs. Garfield, even the pots and pans from the people's kitchens."

He paused for the next installment. "Some Ukrainians even went to work for the Germans. Not simply as farmers or that sort of thing, you understand. As their allies against the Soviet Union. There were even Ukrainians who acted as police for the Germans. There were some—there was a man named Stepan Bandera, another named Melnik, others—some who led bands of guerrillas even before the Germans occupied the city, attacking the rear of the Red Army even while they were fighting against the invaders. They even wanted to join with the Germans to form a Vlasovite Army—"

"A what?" Garfield asked, frowning.

Didchuk seemed reluctant to answer. "Well, it was not only Ukrainians who became traitors; there was a Russian named Vlasov, a famous general; he was captured, and then he formed an army of Soviet soldiers who actually fought on the German side. But Mrs. Smin asks me to tell you about the Ukrainians. *Some* Ukrainians. When the Red Army liberated Kiev in 1944 they found posters—I'm sorry to say, Ukrainian posters—pictures of people tearing down the hammer and sickle, with slogans like 'Down with the Bolsheviks' and even, excuse me, 'None will cease to fight while our Ukraine is enslaved by the Communists.' " He was sweating now. He gave Aftasia an imploring glance, but she rattled on and doggedly he translated.

"The Ukrainians, of course, were fools. The Germans starved them and enslaved them and shot them. But some of them still tried to lick the boots of the Nazis. Especially about the Jews, because—please, I am just saying what she tells me, it is not true. Altogether. Because the Ukrainians hated the Jews as much as Hitler did. (But only a few of them, believe me!) The Ukrainian Nazi-lovers helped the Germans round up the Jews in the Ukraine. They robbed them, they stripped them, they put them into the death cars that went to the concentration camps.

"But that was not fast enough for them. So then, on September twenty-eighth, the Germans posted orders all around Kiev to say that all Yids—excuse me, Mr. and Mrs. Garfield, that is the word Mrs. Smin says was in the orders—must report the next day with warm clothing and all their valuables." There was a single sentence from Aftasia. "She says, 'I did not report.' "

"Well, of course she didn't," Garfield put in, scowling. "By then everybody knew that when the Jews were ordered to report, it meant the concentration camps."

Didchuk translated, then listened as Aftasia Smin, shaking her head vigorously, spoke in angry tones. "She says," he said uncertainly, "that they did *not* know what that meant. She says"—he glanced about apprehensively—"that because of the, ah, the—what can one call it?—because, that is, of the special relationship that existed at that time between the Soviet Union and the German nation—just before the invasion, that is—"

"Ah," said Garfield, understanding. "The Hitler-Stalin pact."

Didchuk flinched. "Yes, exactly," he said weakly. "The, ah, pact of nonaggression. At any rate, she says that for that reason nothing was known in the Soviet Union of German anti-Semitism. It had not been reported."

"For Christ's sake! How could they not know?"

Didchuk said obstinately, "I was not born then, Mr. Garfield. It is Mrs. Smin who says that even the Jews didn't know, and I suppose she is right. So all the Jews reported as they were told, almost all, and the Ukrainian Nazi police and the SS troops rounded them up and marched them out here. To this place. Babi Yar."

Garfield glanced around with a puzzled expression. "I heard of Babi Yar, sure, who hasn't? But I thought it was, like, a valley, way out in the country."

"At one time it was a valley, Mr. Garfield. It has been filled in so this road could be built, and then the city grew to take it in. But this is Babi Yar, yes, and they were all taken here. Men and women. Grandmothers. Little children. Even babies in arms. And they were made to strip naked, a few dozen at a time. And then the Germans shot them, and buried them, right here in this valley. You are looking, Mrs. Smin says, at one hundred thousand dead Jews." He stole a quick glance at Aftasia, and added, almost in a whisper, "I do not think it is quite that many, perhaps."

"My God," said Candace, clutching her husband's arm. "That's unbelievable."

"Yes, exactly," Didchuk said quickly. "It could not have been a hundred thousand of just Jews. Everyone knows there were also Party members, hostages, gypsies—oh, the gypsies were hunted quite as much as the Jews, though, of course, there weren't as many of them. And, as Mrs. Smin asks me to tell you, the Jews who failed to report were hunted down. Not just by the Germans. They were chased by Russians and Ukrainians as well because, you see, if someone reported a hidden Jew, he was granted the right to take what he liked from the Jew's belongings."

He glanced at Aftasia Smin almost hopefully, as though he thought his work over. His face fell as she went on.

"Well," he sighed, "there is more she wants me to say to

you. Later, when the heroic Soviet armies counterattacked and were in the process of driving the Hitlerites out of our land, the Germans got scared. They did not want all those bodies found. So they captured some more prisoners, and forced them to dig up as many of the bodies as they could." He wrinkled his nose unhappily. "They had been buried for several years, you understand. They were quite decayed, of course. Often, they fell apart. Then the Germans made their prisoners take down the headstones from a Jewish cemetery that was here—it was where the television station is now, Mrs. Smin says—and put the stones together to make big ovens. And in those ovens they burned the bodies. With wood they cut from the forests that were around here then. A layer of logs, a layer of Jews, and they burned them all."

As he paused, Aftasia said something in a somber tone. "Yes, yes," Didchuk said impatiently. "She wants me to be sure to tell you this part, although it is not a pleasant subject. She says to tell you that after the burning, the Germans took the ashes and the bones. They crushed them, and spread them on the farms. She says that this made the cabbages grow very well. She says that since then she does not care to eat cabbage."

They were all silent for a moment, even Aftasia. The Garfields peered down the length of the green park toward the distant monument, but there was nothing for them to say. The cars humming by on the roadway, the handsome apartment buildings, the tall television tower on the horizon, seemed to contradict the horror of the story of Babi Yar.

Finally Candace ventured, "I don't see why she didn't want us to stop at the monument."

"One moment," Didchuk said politely, and exchanged a few words with Aftasia. "She says the monument is all very well, but it comes a bit late. It was erected only eight years ago, and the plaque does not even mention Jews. That is what she says," he finished, his voice reedy with strain. "May I tell Mrs. Smin that you have understood what I have been telling you?"

"Damn right we have," said Garfield, shaking his head.

Aftasia rattled another sentence, and Didchuk translated. "In that way, Mrs. Smin says, we Soviet people learned not to trust foreigners. We discovered that the Germans were not interested in—she says, in 'liberating' us. They did not come to do us good. They were thieves, brigands, rapists; they were murderers."

Aftasia nodded and added a sentence more. Didchuk hung his head as he translated. "And we Jews, she says—I am speaking as Mrs. Smin says, you understand; I am not myself Jewish—we Jews learned not to trust even our neighbors."

CHAPTER 28

THURSDAY, MAY 8

Giving bone marrow is not an enjoyable process. A sort of hypodermic the length of a pencil is stabbed into one of the donor's largest bones—the hipbone is usually the easiest to reach. Marrow, which looks like blood, is sucked out, a teaspoonful at a time, until a pint or so has been accumulated. This is actually about a tenth of all the bone marrow an adult human has, but if he is reasonably healthy, he will regenerate it in a few weeks. The process of extraction takes an hour or more. Then the extracted marrow is centrifuged—whirled at high speed—to separate the lighter cells from the larger, older, useless ones. The light ones are then transfused into the patient from a bag hanging beside his bed, through a needle taped into the veins of his arm.

This procedure is not new. The first researches into curing radiation disease through bone-marrow transplants began in the United States in 1945, when the American nuclear bombs dropped on Japan caused some researchers to wonder what would happen if someone dropped similar bombs on America.

Thirteen years later the procedure was tried for the first time on human beings, when five Yugoslavs, exposed to radiation in a nuclear accident, were given marrow from the bones of relatives. Four of them survived, in spite of the fact that the odds against a successful transplant of unmatched marrow are around ten thousand to one, and at that time no one knew how to perform the special typing (it is called "HLA matching") necessary. There are really only two possibilities to account for the survival of the four Yugoslavs. Either they were not really all that sick to begin with and would have recovered anyway. Or they were miraculously, unbelievably lucky.

Whether Leonid Sheranchuk was going to have to test his luck or not was a very open question. Although his blood count was low, it was not critical. His estimated radiation intake was only marginal, so it was not certain that he was going to need a bone-marrow transplant. It was a lot less certain, even, that he would be able to get one if he did. His only near blood relative was his son and Boris's cells did not match.

The fact of the matter was that Sheranchuk did not think much about his own survival. If it happened, it happened. There were others a lot closer to death than he. Some had died already. A second Ponomorenko, the fireman Vassili, the one known as Summer—they had had to take off that leg after all, and he had been too weak to survive the operation. The third of the Four Seasons, his own pipefitter, Arkady Ponomorenko, seemed to be sinking fast. The doctors hadn't been able to find any bone marrow that was good for him, not even his cousin's, and so they had given him a fetal liver transplant. Whether that would save Spring's life was very doubtful. What was certain was that it had put him into a state of half-waking delirium, so that he raged at his cousin, Autumn, for ten minutes at a time with Sheranchuk sitting wordless beside them; and then, collecting himself, cracked jokes and chided poor Autumn for looking so depressed.

What worried Sheranchuk most was that he had been the one who had ordered—at least, permitted—Arkady Ponomorenko to expose himself to the radiation that was killing him. Sheranchuk could not forgive himself for that. It would have been just as effective for him to have sent the pipefitter safely to explore the ruptured pipes under the turbine room while he himself took on the more dangerous task of shutting off the hydrogen flare. He was older. He was more experienced. He could have done the job faster, he had no doubt of that, and got away with only a little radiation. . . .

Or he, too, could have been dying now.

But, Sheranchuk asked himself, what did that matter? If you did your job, you took the risks involved. If the dice fell against you, you had no right to complain.

What mattered most of all to Sheranchuk was Deputy Director Simyon Smin, and it seemed very clear to him that Smin was dying.

For Sheranchuk this was an acute and always present pain, far worse than the bruises where the bitch Akhsmentova insisted on stabbing him for more blood six times a day. He did not want the old man to die. Sheranchuk didn't think of Simyon Smin as a father—he was not so presumptuous as that—but no filial feeling could have been stronger. He owed Smin for giving him the chance at the Chernobyl plant. He admired Smin for the way in which he got his job done, no matter what obstacles were put in his way. His throat closed up with pity and respect as he saw how courageously Smin accepted his own responsibility and the nastiness of his physical state. It did not occur to Sheranchuk to add all these feelings together, but if he had, he would have been forced to give them a name: what he felt for the old man was simply love.

And every day Smin grew weaker.

When Sheranchuk ate his lunch that day he barely noticed what it was—borscht, the good Ukrainian kind, with garlic, specially made because so many of the patients were Ukrainian, with lamb to follow. He ate quickly, talking to no one. There were in truth not very many fellow patients left to talk to, since a few had been released and a good many were now too sick to come to the dining room. Then he skipped the fruit compote that was meant to be their dessert and hurried back to the room he shared with Smin, hoping to tempt the old man to eat, spoonful by spoonful.

Trying to make the Deputy Director eat was really the only service he could still offer to Smin. Even that was seldom successful. The old man would swallow a few mouthfuls as a courtesy, then he would shake his head. "But I have always been too fat, Leonid," he would say seriously. "To lose a few kilos is no bad thing." And then he would ask Sheranchuk, very considerately and politely, to draw the curtains again, please.

Smin spent most of his time now behind the curtains. Sometimes he was being sick, and then the nurses would come to help. Sometimes he was sleeping—Sheranchuk was glad for those times, though always with the fear that the sleep was, finally, something worse than mere sleeping. Often Sheranchuk could see through the gaps in the curtain that Smin was writing, writing, writing—writing something on a lined schoolboy's pad that he never showed to Sheranchuk, and shoved under the pillow when someone came near. His memoirs? A confession for the GehBehs? A letter to someone? But when Sheranchuk ventured to ask, Smin said only, "It's nothing, simply some things I want to put on paper—my memory may not be so good anymore."

But it was not simply his memory that Smin was in the process of losing.

This time there had been no need for Sheranchuk to cut his meal short to help Smin eat, for when he got to the door of their room, he saw that Smin's wife and younger son were there. The boy was standing by his father's bed, a plate in one hand and a spoon in the other, looking unsure of himself. "It's all right, Vassili," Serena Smin whispered to her son. "He did eat quite a bit, and now he needs to sleep." Then she saw Sheranchuk hovering in the doorway and smiled a welcome.

To Leonid Sheranchuk, Smin's wife had always been above criticism, simply because she was Smin's wife. To himself, at least, he might have admitted that he found her rather self-centered and perhaps just a bit proud. He did not think that now. She was quite an exceptionally handsome woman—hadn't she been a dancer once? And so much younger than her husband—but what he saw as he looked at her now was a wife and mother whose love for her family was written achingly all over her face.

He stepped courteously aside as she and her son came out of the room, but she paused to talk to him. "Vassili got him to eat nearly all of his lamb." She reported the small triumph with unreasoning hope shining through the desperation in her eyes. "I minced it up for him first. I tasted it myself; it was really quite good."

"They feed us well here," Sheranchuk agreed. Then he said, "Mrs. Smin? I've been wondering if having me here in the room isn't really a bit too much for him."

"No, no, Leonid! He is grateful for your company. Don't think he hasn't told us how much you do for him."

"I wish I could do more!"

"You do everything anyone ever could," Selena Smin said firmly. "I think he will sleep now, and so we will leave him for a bit in your good hands."

"Thank you," Sheranchuk said, awkward as he wondered whether to shake her hand or not, but she settled the matter by leaning forward and kissing him on the cheek. He gazed after her admiringly and hardly noticed when a doctor came up to him, hooded, booted, and robed in white. When the physician addressed him by name, Sheranchuk was astonished to find that she was his wife.

Tamara Sheranchuk reached up to kiss her husband, a feathery, distant kiss on his cheekbone—as much as was advisable, he knew, since even the tiny salt flakes from his sweat might also be radioactive, not to mention his saliva if they had kissed on the lips. "Isn't this great luck?" she cried in delight. "How am I here? Well, partly because my own count is a bit low, and partly because I am to learn how they test blood to determine the extent of radioactivity—just for forty-eight hours, I'm afraid. But most of all, I am here because you are here, my dear, and I asked for permission."

Sheranchuk looked at her in distress. "Your count is low?"

"Oh, quite marginal," she assured him. "No, my dear, it is you who are the patient here, not I. I have had a look at your charts with the other doctors. They're a bit puzzling."

"So they have told me. I am not as sick as I ought to be."

"Did they explain to you about Dr. Guskova's system? Since we don't know how much radiation you received, she has worked out a method of deducing it from the way your blood count falls off— "

"I have heard everything there is to hear about Dr. Guskova's system. But she did not tell me how much of a dose that was, and neither did anyone else."

Tamara hesitated. "Perhaps one hundred rads," she said reluctantly. "It is possible that it is more."

"And that means?" he demanded.

"In your case, my dear," she said, "it is difficult to say."

"I see," he said, thinking. Then, remembering how she had appeared from nowhere and made him put on coveralls, "It would have been more if it hadn't been for you."

"So I am good for something as a wife," she said. It was a light remark, but her tone was not light. He opened his mouth to ask if anything was wrong, but she was going right on: "Deputy Director Smin may not have had much more, but as you see, he is very ill and you are—not?"

"I feel all right," he said, stretching the truth. In fact, he felt tired much of the time and sometimes a bit feverish. But nothing like Smin, of course.

His wife sat down next to him on the bed, prepared to lecture. "The etiology of radiation sickness," she said, "is quite well known. Simyon Mikhailovitch doesn't fit the curve. He is getting worse faster than he should. He—"

Suddenly remembering, she glanced apprehensively at the closed curtains. "He's asleep," Sheranchuk assured her. "I heard him snoring a minute ago."

"Well," she said, lowering her voice, "your blood count is not dropping off as fast as his, or many of the others."

"Doctor talk again," he complained. "Which means what?"

"Which means we don't know what," she said. "Perhaps it means that all of your exposure was from external sources—dust and smoke on your skin, that was washed off. Smin, on the other hand, may actually have swallowed some, or breathed it. The radioisotopes are still in his body."

Sheranchuk was puzzled. "But I was exposed as much as he! I was in the area longer, even; he was away when the explosion occurred. We breathed the same air, ate the same food—"

"But such a little difference can make such a big effect, Leonid. You were within buildings much of the time. He may have been outside. It could be as small a thing as a stack of bread that was left too long on a table. Perhaps he had the top slice, and you only one from lower down."

Sheranchuk said, making his tone calm, "Does that mean that I will—"

He didn't finish the sentence. "It means that your chances are better," she said; and then, strongly, "Leonid! I think you will recover completely!"

Sheranchuk turned and raised himself on an elbow to

study his wife. He had never been her patient before, except now and then for a headache or a sore wrist. Was this how she always talked to those under her care? It was not at all the same free and easy way they spoke in their kitchen, or their bed.

"You do go on talking like a doctor," he complained.

"But, Leonid, I am a doctor. And, oh," she went on, "I'm sure of it! Especially with those American doctors here! You would not believe how good they are! Just this morning the hospital centrifuge broke down, and in just a few hours they had packed everything up and moved it to another facility. And their own instruments! They have a machine, you put into it a sample of blood, whisk, click, and in just a few seconds you have a blood cell count printed out, with every number! While for us it is necessary to put each blood sample under a microscope and someone must count every individual cell—half an hour at least, and after a technician has counted a dozen samples his eyes are weary and his attention flags, and how likely it is to make mistakes!"

"That sounds wonderful," said Sheranchuk.

She pursed her lips, preparing to announce some surprising news. "And did you know, Leonka, that one of them is not an American at all, but from Israel?"

That was astonishing; Israel and the USSR had no diplomatic relations at all. Therefore no Israeli citizen could possibly get a visa to enter the Soviet Union—unless, of course, someone very high up ordered that the laws be forgotten for this case. "That is even more surprising than a machine," he conceded. "Still, we've given the Israelis plenty of people, they can lend us one in return."

"The American doctor even said that in his country a hospital like this would be air-conditioned!"

"The Americans," Smin grinned, "will be air-conditioning their cars next." His arm was getting tired. He sank back on his bed, curled facing his wife as she went on describing the technological wonders that had flown in from California. Her manner was, after all, a bit puzzling. He welcomed the conversation because he didn't have many visitors and it was tiring to hold a book to read, but were these the subjects a wife would normally discuss under these circumstances? Was it possible she was keeping something from him? What could it be? "What about Boris?" he asked suddenly.

She broke off. "Boris?" she said, as though trying to recall who he was talking about. "Well, yes. It is a pity, but his cells do not match yours. Still, you may not need a transfusion at all—"

"I already know that," he grumbled. "I was asking if you had heard from him since he left."

"Oh, but of course I have," she said penitently. "He has been evacuated to the Artek camp—on the Black Sea—the very best Komsomol camp in the whole country, and it's all free for him."

"I have been told that too. I asked if you had heard from the boy himself."

"Certainly! Oh! I was forgetting—he even sent some photographs—look," she said, fumbling some out of her bag, "these were taken on a trip to Yalta." While Tamara was proudly telling him how Boris was actually learning to ride a horse, Sheranchuk gazed at the color prints. There was Boris on a beach, his arm on the shoulder of another teenage boy Sheranchuk had never seen before. Both were in swim trunks, grinning into the camera. Behind them was a gaggle of stout, middle-aged women in bikinis, industriously tossing a volley-ball. One had a huge caesarean scar across her belly.

"Can you trust him around such bathing beauties as these?" Sheranchuk smiled.

She took the pictures back, studying them for a moment before putting them away. "In a summer camp one can be tempted," she sighed.

Sheranchuk smiled a real smile. That at least was more like the old Tamara. "Or in a hospital, perhaps? So you think I am misbehaving with Dr. Guskova? She is a bit old for me, as well as a trifle heavyset for my taste. But there is a nurse on the night duty—"

But Tamara only pouted instead of railing back at him. "I saw that Serena Smin was here," she said.

"She has been very good with her husband," Sheranchuk said. "I admire her a great deal."

"Yes, and I saw that she admires you as well," his wife said flatly.

"Oh," said Sheranchuk, understanding at last. He grinned

at his wife. "You saw her kiss me. Yes, of course; she and I have been doing all sorts of things here, with her husband asleep in the next bed and her son standing guard in the corridor."

"I do not like to joke about these matters," Tamara said.

Sheranchuk groaned faintly. Was it possible that she was being seriously jealous again? He opened his mouth to reassure her, and then he caught a flicker of motion.

He turned to the door. A sunburned young man in Air Force blue was standing there. "I am Senior Lieutenant Nikolai Smin," he announced. "Is my father here?"

"Yes," Tamara Sheranchuk began, "but you must wear a robe if you want to—" And she was interrupted by a voice from behind the screens.

"Is that my son? Put the nightshirt on him, please, and let him come in!"

Nikolai Smin took the visitor's chair from beside Sheranchuk's bed, now politely empty as Sheranchuk let his wife escort him out of the way of the reunion, and put it next to his father's. He started to pull the screens away, but his father stopped him. "Leave them," he ordered. "You don't want to see me too well."

That statement was distressingly validated. Nikolai could not helping the freezing of the expression on his face as he got a good look at his father. Suddenly Smin was an old man, and one apparently close to a repulsive death. What were those awful pus-filled black blobs on his face? What were the red sores on his neck and shoulders that wept colorless fluid? And that unpleasant smell?

"Don't touch me, Kolya," Smin said. "Kiss the air for me and I will kiss it back."

Nikolai did as he was ordered, but protested, "I'm not afraid of catching something from you."

"But I am afraid for you. Also, it hurts if you touch me."

"At least you are, well—" Nikolai fumbled, looking for something positive to say.

"Conscious? Lucid? Yes, Kolya, for sometimes half an hour at a time, so please let's not waste it with pretending. I am wonderfully pleased to see you, my son. Was it bad where you were?"

Nikolai hesitated, choosing his words. "It is not that dangerous to be flying an MI-24 gunship in Afghanistan, Father. But it is dirty and boring, and no one but a lunatic loves shooting at civilians from the air. It is true that some of those civilians shoot back, but none have come close to me."

"And when you are done here you will go back to Afghanistan?"

Nikolai looked rebellious. "Of course," he said.

"I see. Still, your mother said something about volunteering to fly in the helicopters that are dropping things over the reactor—"

"It was an idle thought. They have no further need for pilots to drop dirt on your reactor, Father, so they have discontinued the drops."

"Oh?" said Smin, interested. "Then the core is completely safe now?"

"I think," Nikolai said, "that it is at least safer to continue to deal with it by other means than to have pilots dodging that stack. I have seen the photos, Father; it is not what a helicopter pilot likes to find in his path. Anyway, they've stopped. Then I asked if there were any other flying jobs in the area. They said not. Or almost none; the only flying missions related to what happened to your plant are now Yaks dropping iodine crystals into the clouds before they get to Chernobyl, so they won't rain on the plant. But unfortunately they don't need me for that."

"Unfortunately," Smin repeated. "Why unfortunately?"

Nikolai shrugged morosely. "No, really," his father insisted. "I would like to understand what you feel. Are you determined to retrieve the family honor? Do you think the accident was my fault and you must do something heroic to make up for it?"

Nikolai pondered for a moment. "I don't know what I think about that," he said at last. "Does it matter? At least I am here now."

"And I am grateful," said his father, willing to let the subject be changed. "I appreciate that you are here to try to save my life."

"If I can. I am to be tested this afternoon." The young man swallowed involuntarily, and Smin noticed.

"It isn't pleasant, what they want you to do," he said gently. "I am sorry to have to ask you to do it. And even sorrier that it is necessary. Kolya? Are you ashamed of your father?"

"Ashamed? But, Father! You did your best!"

"I thought that was what I was doing, yes," Smin agreed.

"No, really! My mother and Vassili have told me all about it. In the past three years you have made everything work so much better—"

"In three years, yes. And in another five years, perhaps, I would have finished the task and Chernobyl would have been fully up to standards in every respect. It is a pity, but I didn't have those five years."

"No," said Nikolai loyally. "So it is not your fault. Still—"

Smin waited. "What, then, Kolya?" he asked.

"I should be going for my test, not worrying you with silly things when you aren't feeling very well."

Smin actually laughed—not "feeling very well!" But it hurt him to laugh, and all he said, with great patience, was: "Tell me what you were about to say, Kolya. Fathers and sons should speak honestly to one another."

"Well— Only— The thing is," Nikolai went on, picking up speed, "there are such terrible stories! Concrete that crumbles into sand, walls that fall down!"

"Those are true stories, Kolya. I accepted many substandard products."

"But *why*, Father?"

Smin sighed. "Do they teach you nothing in the Air Force of what the world is like? Let us pretend, Kolya, that you are the director of a cement factory. Each month you have a plan to fulfill. Perhaps your plan calls for the production of ten thousand tons of cement and, look, it is the twenty-fifth of the month and you have only produced four thousand. But if you don't fulfill your plan, there are no bonuses for the workers, no commendations for you; you may even be reprimanded. Or worse than reprimanded. So what do you do, Kolya? You do what every other factory manager does. You put all your workers on overtime, with orders to storm six thousand tons of cement in five days. Can they do it? Certainly—if they slop the work through any old way; and on the last day of the month you have fulfilled your plan. . . . Of course, those six thousand tons are useless."

"But then you don't have to accept them, Father!"

"Yes, exactly," his father agreed. "One should reject them at once. But then what? Chernobyl did need cement. The cement maker needed not only to complete his plan, but to sell the production. So he says to me, 'You want some good cement, very well, I will give you all you need. But you must also take this other batch.' And I have no choice, Kolya. I take the bad, because if I don't, someone else will, and then he will get the good cement I need desperately. And with steel: the plan for the steel mill calls for another ten thousand tons, let us say; that is easy enough to make, if you make only mild, low-grade steel. But I need better! So to get the steel I need for my reactors I must persuade the steel man to make it, and to do that I must also buy a few thousand tons that are useless. Or I must bribe someone with money or even a car. Or I must send out expediters—expediters! They are gangsters, really. Flatterers. Toadies. Even pimps. And I send these slimy individuals out to wine and dine the suppliers and coax them to send me the things I really need instead of the trash they want to get rid of . . . and, even so, usually they will send me both."

"That is *shameful,*" his son said harshly. Then he added quickly, "Excuse me, I don't mean you, I mean—"

"Mean me, Kolya," Smin said gently. "I could have done things properly, after all. It is only that I do not think Chernobyl would have been producing four thousand megawatts of electricity for the network if I had."

Nikolai muttered something under his breath. "What was that?" Smin asked sharply.

"Nothing, Father. I must go now for my appointment. I will come back later." And this time he did, carefully but firmly, rest his hand on his father's for a moment before he left; but Smin did not respond. He was too busy wondering if he had been right in what he thought he heard.

To have a few minutes to himself when his head was clear—that was a precious thing for Simyon Smin. He did not waste it. He pulled out the pad on which he had been writing the letter to Mishko and Milaktiev, but after only a line or two his arms wearied and his vision blurred. There was the question, too, of how he was going to get it to the people who had asked for it. Would they come back? Probably yes, he told himself, but would it be while he was still in a position to hand it over? And he would not consider giving it to either his wife or his younger son to pass on; what if they were caught with it?

Kolya, yes. Perhaps. It was at least a possibility; Kolya was a grown man and by now, after eleven months of shooting Moslem tribesmen in Afghanistan, a reasonably tough and resourceful one. But there was the worrisome thing Kolya had said. Would he, after all, be the right one to trust with such a letter?

Which left only Smin's mother.

Smin lay back, slipping the pad under his pillow, thinking about his mother. At this very moment, he knew, she was somewhere in the hospital, doing what Kolya was doing, namely having her breastbone pierced with a great sharp knife to take a sample of marrow. For him. Always for him. Since the first days he could remember, for him. He remembered his mother in the village, when he was in school, when he was a Young Pioneer, when he went off at twenty to do his military duty (an annoyance at most, really; who would dare attack the Soviet Union in 1940, when the only other powerful state in Europe had sworn an unbreakable treaty of non-aggression?)—and had the good sense, or good fortune, to choose to serve in tanks. So when Adolf Hitler broke the unbreakable treaty and shoved his irresistible armies across the border a year later, young Junior Lieutenant Simyon Smin was not poured with two million other green recruits into the first terrible meatgrinder, because he was studying advanced armored tactics four thousand kilometers away.

He shook himself awake, sweating and almost ready to scream aloud; he had been dreaming; flames had been licking over him and his T-34 had been hit.

He took a deep breath to calm himself. Perhaps he was dying now, but at least he had not died then. As so many others had. He had been given forty extra years of life, and so he was owed nothing at all.

He hadn't wasted those years. Out of them he had married two good women, and had two good sons to show for it. It was a pity that it should end badly, but it was still more than he could have hoped for as he tried to claw his way out of the burning tank.

It was then, in the hospital, that his mother had asked him if he would really mind if she were to marry again.

Such a possibility had never occurred to young Simyon Smin. He was aware that his mother was quite a good-looking woman still, though a bit over forty. But to *marry*? And to marry so high a Party official? For Vassilievitch Mishko was second only to Nikita Khrushchev in the Party organization of the Ukraine, now just being won back from the Fascists.

He had given his approval at once, however. He hadn't been selfish. He had even been pleased to think of his mother having a life of her own again, without him to raise or a war or a purge to make everyone's life a misery; and it would have happened if F. V. Mishko had not happened to displease J. V. Stalin and wound up shoveling gold ore in Siberia. It did not surprise Smin that his mother had elected to live very quietly for the rest of her life. She had seen what happened when a person became too public.

"Are you awake, then?" a voice called softly from the gap in the curtains.

Smin shook himself. "Of course, Comrade Plumber," he said, working to create another smile. "What's the news outside?"

He was really glad to see Sheranchuk. He tried to listen while Sheranchuk told him his stories—the good news, his wife appearing unexpectedly at the hospital; the bad news, one of the Four Seasons dying, and another in delirium and pain. "I'm surprised you didn't hear him," Sheranchuk said. "He was shouting quite loudly a little while ago, but now he is quieter."

"Yes, yes," Smin said absently.

"And your older son came to see you. That's good news, of course."

"I suppose it is," said Smin, and his tone made Sheranchuk look more closely at him.

"Is something wrong?" he asked worriedly.

"What should be wrong?—No, Leonid, it is a bit of a worry. Kolya said something. We were talking about what was wrong at the plant—I don't mean the accident, I mean the difficulties with materials and personnel. He became quite indignant. Then he said—I think he said—'It would be better to have Stalin back.'"

"I see," said Sheranchuk.

Smin looked up at him. "Do you?"

"Well, yes, I think so," Sheranchuk said uncomfortably.

"He is a military man, after all. There are many who think the leadership has wasted too much time in Afghanistan."

Smin said in sorrow, "Are you saying that you, too, think Mikhail Gorbachev is too liberal?"

"No, no! Nothing like that. What do I know of such things, after all? I am merely saying that I have heard people say that sort of remark. There is, really, a great deal of waste and corruption."

"But under Stalin we had the same kind of inefficiency, Leonid, only then it was called 'sabotage.' And also we had the purges."

"I don't remember Stalin times very well," Sheranchuk apologized.

"Unfortunately, my son Kolya doesn't either. He has never had to worry about a knock on the door at two A.M. Now they are much more considerate, the GehBehs. They come only during business hours. Leonid? Have you been questioned yet?"

"Well, yes, a little. I simply told them that I was not on duty at the time of the explosion and that, as far as I know, it was Chief Engineer Varazin who insisted on pushing the experiment through without safeguards. With the encouragement of Gorodot Khrenov, of course." Sheranchuk paused, looking at Smin's face. "What's the matter?"

"Leonid! What did you say about Khrenov?"

"Only that. I simply told the truth."

"You told what you *think* is the truth. You told it about Khrenov," Smin said patiently. "Khrenov is with the organs. Do you think the organs wish to report that one of their own was involved, even only to encourage?"

"They did seem quite concerned about that," Sheranchuk admitted.

"Leonid, are you insane? Are you even right? How do you know what Khrenov did?"

"I know he hung around the Chief Engineer like a shadow," Sheranchuk said doggedly.

"That is what he is paid to do, Leonid. Why do you say 'encourage'? Were you present when Khrenov 'encouraged' Varazin to go ahead?"

"No, but he did!"

"How do you *know* that? You were not present," Smin

insisted. "Believe me, the organs know well what Khrenov did and Khrenov will answer for it to them. But not in public. So if there is a hearing, as there will be, and if you testify, as you must, you will simply speak the truth about what you saw and what you did. Not about what you think you know from some other person's reports." He hesitated, and then said softly, "All of these things are on the record."

"And the record will remain forever in the files of the GehBehs," Sheranchuk said bitterly, because suddenly he was afraid.

Smin paused. After a moment he said slowly, "Not necessarily. Remember Khrushchev's speech on the excesses of the Stalin regime. It is possible that everything will come out in some way." Then he shook his head and grinned, a woeful sight in that damaged face. "In any case—wait, what's that?"

Sheranchuk heard it too. He said worriedly, "I'm afraid Arkady Ponomorenko is shouting again. But what is it you were going to say?"

"Only that, in any case, perhaps we will all be lucky enough to die here in Hospital Number Six. But go to your friend; he sounds as though he needs someone."

At the door of the pipefitter's room a nurse stopped Sheranchuk. "Where are you going?" she scolded. "Can't you see he's in no shape to have visitors?"

"But I am not a visitor but a fellow patient. In any case he needs someone."

"And what good do you think you can do him now?" she asked bitterly. Behind her, "Spring" had stopped screaming at least, but was now addressing sober, thoughtful remarks to the air above his bed. "Well," she said, softening, "I suppose it can do no harm, at least until his cousin comes back."

But if Volya Ponomorenko didn't come back soon, Sheranchuk was sure, he would not see his cousin alive. The pipefitter was gasping for breath as he spoke. He was telling the air that the Chernobyl Nuclear Power Station had no right to be where it was. "It is the Russians, you see," he said dreamily, gazing at the ceiling. "They're the ones who need it, not us. We have farms in the Ukraine! We grow food, the best in the world; we don't need their factories or their power plants. If we want electrical power, we have the Dnieper River!

Already there are two dozen great dams on the Dnieper, so why bring in these atomic contraptions?"

"Shhh," said Sheranchuk nervously. "You should rest, please, Arkady."

The pipefitter gave no sign of hearing him. He addressed the ceiling reasonably. "So why do we have this nuclear power station at all? Because the Russians want it, you see. It is not a thing for Ukrainians at all. It is so the Russians can turn on the lights in Moscow and sell electricity to the people in Poland and Bulgaria. Let them make their own!"

"Please rest," Sheranchuk begged, glancing toward the door. Where were the doctors when you wanted them?

"But no!" cried Ponomorenko, suddenly loud again. "The Russians insist, and what can we do? Can we say no to them? Can we ask them please to make their filthy atomic messes somewhere else? Can we live freely in our own dear Ukraine, that Bogdan Khelmnitski freed from the Poles? Can we even speak the truth when we want to? No, we cannot, and do you know why? I'll tell you why!" he shouted.

"*Please!*" cried Sheranchuk, and then to the door, "Nurse!"

"This is why!" Ponomorenko cried, raising himself on his elbows. "Because we are *prisoners*! The Russians have taken us captive, and now we can't get free. My only wish—"

He burst out in a fit of coughing and fell back. And what his only wish was no one would ever know, because the way his head hit the pillow, the way one eye was half open and the other shut, the way his jaw hung slack, they all told the story: the brave pipefitter and daring football player, the "Spring" of the Four Seasons, Arkady Ponomorenko, was dead.

CHAPTER 29

Emmaline Branford is a conspicuous figure on the streets of Moscow, not only because she is a woman who wears fashionable American slacks and sometimes listens to her Walkman as she strolls, but because she is black. That is not the color of her skin, which is a pleasing caramel; it is her ethnic description. She knows that it is also the reason she has the career-building Moscow posting, since the U.S. State Department, like any other American employer, needs to burnish its equal-opportunity image. Her gender helped in this, too, of course; as Cultural Attaché, she is the second-highest ranking woman in the Moscow Embassy. Emmaline is a pretty woman, with a master's degree in sociology and a minor in Slavic languages. Her mother did not want her to go to Moscow. What Emmaline's mother wants is for her to take a teaching job in Waycross, Georgia, get married and get on with producing a grandchild. Emmaline's boyfriend wants pretty much the same thing; but, at twenty-seven, Emmaline is not yet ready to settle down.

The first thing on Emmaline's agenda as she dragged herself out of bed each morning was to start the brewer for that indispensable first cup of hot, black, kick-your-mammy coffee. The second was harder. That was the nasty task of taking out the brush and dustpan (actually that was the lid of a cardboard box, but it worked well enough) to sweep up the morning's accumulation of dead cockroaches. There were only a dozen or so this time, not much for a bright May morning, so Emmaline was into the shower and out of it again by the time the coffee was ready.

Dressed and ready to go, Emmaline looked out the window of her flat in the foreign ghetto as she finished her grapefruit—the last grapefruit she was going to have, until someone from the Embassy took another courier flight to Helsinki. She was waiting for Warner Borden, the Embassy's Science Attaché, to knock on her door. She had not made up her mind what to tell him—whether she would accept a ride to the Embassy in his little red Nissan hotrod or walk it on her own for the sake of the exercise. (At 124 pounds, Emmaline was convinced she'd grown hog-fat over the Russian winter.)

Then, she hadn't really made up her mind about Warner Borden at all. It was spring. It had been a long winter. It had been a lonely one for Emmaline, and along about March even Borden had begun to seem interesting; there were very few unattached American males in Moscow; and no black ones at all, unless you counted the nineteen-year-old Marine guards at the Embassy. Emmaline was not formally engaged to the guy back in Waycross, and she wasn't constitutionally opposed to a little experimenting around. She wasn't even, really, opposed to Warner Borden. But it took a lot of the fun out of fornication when you knew that the telephone headset, a microphone in the wall, and another in the bathroom were very likely to be faithfully transmitting every moan, gasp, grunt, and babble to someone with a headset and a tape recorder a block away. And the ears under the headset were not necessarily always Russian.

So (Emmaline being by nature a fair person) the decision to make about Warner was whether to encourage him or not. It was a decision that needed to be made. She thought about it as she was tidying up the remains of her breakfast, everything tightly wrapped to discourage the bugs, and was still thinking about it as she peered at herself in the bathroom mirror. As she gave her teeth a final brushing, she found three more roaches stirring feebly by the toilet. She went back for the brush and cardboard and, of course, that was just when Warner Borden knocked at her door.

She stood inside the doorway to greet him. "Thanks, anyway," she said, "but I think I'd better walk."

He did not seem disappointed. "You've got a nice day for it. Can I have a cup of coffee anyway?"

It was absolutely foolish to be embarrassed about the roaches, which were everyone's cross to carry. "Help yourself," she said, turning away. As she was capturing the last sick bug, cowering behind the toilet but unable to move fast enough to get away, Borden appeared in the bathroom door, holding his cup, to watch her flush them down.

He said with scientific interest, "You'll be lucky if you don't plug up the pipes with those buggers. What'd you knock them out with?"

"Rima's grandmother's recipe. You mix boric acid into cold mashed potatoes and roll up little balls. Rima says it makes them thirsty but it keeps them from being able to drink. So they die. Sometimes they do, anyway. I guess that's why they're always around the toilet and the sink."

Borden grinned. "Hanging around what they can't get. I do the same thing myself."

Emmaline slammed the toilet lid down to change the subject. "What do you hear from Chernobyl?"

He said sourly, "Still nothing. They've been having press conferences at the Ministry of Nuclear Energy, but only for the commie countries and Ted Turner. So much for *glasnost*." He glanced at his watch and swallowed the rest of his coffee. "I've got a meeting in half an hour. Maybe I'll find something out then. Anyway, the cloud's still heading east, so I guess we're okay here."

Emmaline made an effort to look at the bright side. "If it did come, it might at least kill the damn roaches."

"Oh, hon, no *way*. Roaches don't mind radiation. They eat it up. If you went to Chernobyl this morning you'd probably find a bunch of dead people—and about a million happy roaches sitting down to dinner."

"That many?" she asked, dampened.

"The million roaches? Oh, you mean the dead people. Well, how are you supposed to know? The Russians've only admitted to two. Everybody in Washington is saying it's a lot more, maybe hundreds—there was a story in New York that said there were fifteen thousand dead already."

"Which one do you believe, Warner?"

"Hon," he sighed, turning to rinse out his cup before leaving, "when you're in this place as long as I am you'll learn not to believe *anybody*."

On this pleasant May morning, the air, as Emmaline walked from the foreign compound past the walled Sovkino motion-picture studios to the Kiev railroad station, was just cool enough to be comfortable. The sun was bright. Still, she was glad she'd taken a sweater. There were traces of dirty snow at the bases of the tallest north-facing walls. Some of it had been there since October and was not yet melted away, but the trees were in leaf and green things were popping out of the ground.

Her mind was full of Warner Borden and Chernobyl. It was a little annoying that he hadn't seemed crushed when she refused his ride. Well, she told herself, the man was *busy*. His first appointment that day was to make another offer of American technical assistance to the Soviet authorities at the Ministry of Nuclear Energy, and his thoughts were obviously more on his appointment than her bod.

All the same, he hadn't even tried to grope her. She was piqued. It was certainly her privilege to make him leave her alone, but she hadn't counted on his giving up so easily.

And then she saw she was approaching the Metro station by the Kiev railroad terminal, and she forgot about Warner Borden, because she remembered what was happening there this day.

As she was heading toward the terminal, staring, she was stopped by a woman in slacks as well cut as her own, with a camera slung around her neck. "Excuse me," the woman said, "but you're an American, aren't you? What's going on?"

Emmaline had already seen the reason for the question. The Kiev railroad station was noisier and more crowded than ever, and the number of police, in uniform or not, at least ten times the normal quota. "They're bringing in children from Kiev," she said. "They've been evacuated."

"Oh, my Lord," breathed the woman, moving aside to get out of the way of a little procession of young evacuees. They seemed to be eight or ten years old, twenty or thirty of them in disciplined lines supervised by a pair of schoolteachery women. The children were obviously overtired, and not as clean as they might have been, but they were orderly and quiet as they walked toward a waiting bus. Each one of them clutched a bag of possessions and most were holding an apple that they had just been given by their surrogate parents. "We were just going to our hotel," the American woman said absently, her face worried. "That's the Hotel Ukraine, you know? And we took the subway to this station, and— Listen, is it safe here? We keep hearing all kinds of stories."

"As far as I know," Emmaline said carefully, "you're perfectly safe here in Moscow. The city shouldn't be affected at all. Your hotel is over that way, across the big boulevard they call Kutozovsky." She pointed, excused herself, and turned to see what was going on for herself. A Reuter's newsman, looking sweaty and harassed, hailed her. "Do you know anything I don't know?" he demanded.

"I don't know that much. Have you been talking to the children?"

"Talk to them! I can't even get *near* them without some KGB yobbo telling me I'm in the way of the evacuation. You're a dip, love. Walk right in there to the trains and take me along, there's a dear."

"Not a chance," Emmaline said firmly. "Tell me what's happening, though."

"Ah," the man said in disgust, "they've rounded up every little kid in Kiev and shipped them up here. They're supposed to be going to Young Pioneer summer camps outside of Moscow somewhere, but what I really want to know is what it's like in Kiev now and they won't let me talk to any of them. Listen, your Russian's better than mine. See that bunch of kids waiting to get into the W.C.? Let's see if we can just idle by and strike up a chat."

But Emmaline was shaking her head. "Another time, okay? I've got to get to work."

By eleven o'clock Emmaline had her desk clean, her telegrams dispatched, her day's program confirmed, and a car and driver ordered for the Rossiya Hotel at one. Warner Borden looked in. "Stonewall," he reported. "They thanked us for our kind interest but did not care to accept any offers of aid. What do they need the Embassy for, anyway, when they've got Armand Hammer's Occidental Oil?"

"Have you talked to the doctors they sent over?"

"Nobody has. They've been kept busy—I'd really love to get a word with one of them, just to find out how the Russians are doing with their radiation medicine. But even the Occidental Oil office hasn't seen them; it was all handled directly between Armand Hammer and, I guess, Gorbachev himself. The thing is," he said, sliding into the chair next to her desk, "I was wondering if you had any information on this man Smin."

"Who's Smin?"

"He's one of the patients in the radiation hospital, in bad shape; they say he was one of the biggies at the Chernobyl plant. Only I can't get a handle on him. Take a look at these."

He dropped a couple of photographs on Emmaline's desk. Three had been copied from newspapers and were very poor; the fourth showed several men at the Moscow airport, welcoming the IAEA man from Vienna, Blix. "We think Smin's one of these," he said.

"So? How would I know?"

"Maybe the same way you tipped us off on Chernobyl," said Borden. "Your credit's sky-high right now, you know. You were the first one to point out that the station in the Ukraine might be where the stuff came from, when we were all looking toward the Baltic. If your sources could help out here—"

"I'll see what I can do," Emmaline said. The truth, however, was that she didn't know what she could do, and didn't know if she wanted to ask her "sources"—there was really only one source, sitting concentratedly over her copy of *Trud* at her desk—to involve herself further. Had there been any risk to getting that copy of *Literaturna Ukraina* for her? For that matter, was it really Rima who had put it there? Rima had never said ... the other side of that coin, though, was that Emmaline had never come right out and asked her.

Emmaline sighed and got ready to leave for her one o'clock appointment. She went as far as she was willing to go. That is, as she left she stopped at the translator's desk. "I'm off to meet Pembroke Williamson," she said. And, "Oh, by the way, there are some pictures on my desk you might want to look at."

*   *   *

Emmaline walked over to the Metro and took the train to Marksiya, one of the complex of underground stations at the heart of Moscow. Why did Borden want to know about Smin? If the man was in the hospital he ought to be left alone. As she listened to the train conductor announce their arrival at her destination, she wished that not only Smin could be left alone, but maybe everyone in the Soviet Union could be left alone with this terrible and strictly internal disaster. They deserved a chance to try to heal themselves, didn't they?

But it was not merely an internal disaster anymore. Not with the cloud of radioactive gases wandering over half of Europe.

The quickest way to her meeting with the novelist at the Rossiya Hotel was to take the bus that circled around Red Square, but her watch told her she was early. On impulse, she walked through the crowded GUM department store and out onto Red Square, her heels catching in the cobblestones, eavesdropping on the Soviet tourists strolling by.

It was as normal as any May morning in Moscow ever had been. If Chernobyl was on anyone's mind, they were not discussing it where Emmaline could hear. A father with two young girls at his side was pointing at the spot over the Lenin Mausoleum where the great ones of the Party leadership had stood, just one week earlier, to watch the May Day parade roll through.

A family from one of the Eastern republics was gawking at the Spassky gate as a long, black Zil sedan came roaring out of the walled Kremlin, its curtains drawn and who could know who inside? Three separate queues of schoolchildren waited their turn to enter the candy-topped St. Basil's Cathedral, and two newly married couples were having their pictures taken at the mausoleum. The brides, elegant in white gauze and braided flowers in their hair, were placing their cellophane-wrapped bridal bouquets on the low wall before the tomb, under the expressionless eyes of the uniformed KGB guard. Emmaline tarried to study the bridal couples. In her experience, all brides looked rapturous and all grooms shared the same three-martini unfocused beam of tentative happiness. These two looked a little different. Both the grooms had identical slyly eager looks.

Emmaline understood at once. It was spring for them too. Whatever private encounters that particular he and that particular she had managed for the past six months, they had been severely circumscribed by shared flats, by parents who were always present and, most of all, by snow. There were no romantic trysts in the woods around Moscow in January. Or in April, for that matter.

So there were floods of pent-up hormones begging to be released, and what each of those men was dreaming of was the night ahead, with the parents for once bundled off to stay with relatives or even—oh, what luxury!—perhaps a round-trip ticket on the Red Arrow night train to Leningrad. That meant a whole day to see the great art gallery, the antireligion museum in what used to be St. Isaac's Cathedral, and the cruiser *Aurora* in front of the Winter Palace, but most of all it meant two whole nights in a private compartment with a lock on the door and no one to knock!

Emmaline was astonished at the quick rush of feeling in her own belly; it had, indeed, been a long winter.

The Rossiya Hotel is advertised as the second largest in the world (the first largest is also in the Soviet Union), but Emmaline had learned her way around it by now. She flashed her card, unnecessarily, to the factotum at the door and headed for the elevators.

The novelist's name was Pembroke Williamson, and he wasn't in his hotel room. Tipped off by the ever-vigilant concierge, Emmaline walked down to the end of the long corridor and, peering over the stair rail, saw him nursing a cup of tea and curiously counting over his change in the hotel's corner buffet.

"You've got American newspapers," she said at once, catching sight of the pages sticking out of his shoulder bag. "May I?"

While Pembroke tried to total up the English ten-penny pieces, the German marks, and the Swedish kroner he had been given in change for his American five-dollar bill, Emmaline happily scanned the headlines. Their little story had taken over the front pages; Chernobyl was in every paper. And what headlines! The *New York Post* had the craziest—

MASS GRAVE
15,000 REPORTED BURIED
IN NUKE DISPOSAL SITE

—but the UPI stories claimed at least 2,000 dead, and nearly every paper discounted the Soviet numbers.

"So what's the truth?" Pembroke asked. "Who's lying?"

"Maybe everybody," said Emmaline, wistfully trying to get a quick look at *Doonesbury* and *Andy Capp*. "The Russians still say that there are two dead; they were killed in the explosion, and that's all. Of course, they admit there are a couple of hundred in the hospital here in Moscow, and God knows how many others in other places."

"Do you believe that?"

She said primly, "I work for the State Department. Mr. Schultz said he'd bet ten dollars the Soviets are lying."

"How about one pound ten in sterling and about another two dollars in odds and ends?" Pembroke grinned.

"That's what the Secretary of State wants to bet. I don't bet, personally. Pembroke? You know what it's like here; we don't get much hard information, and what we do get is mostly classified. I was hoping you could tell me what happened."

The novelist leaned back, looking at her seriously. "Don't we have to get to the publishing company?" His book on Lincoln had just been published in the USSR, and the editors at the Mir Publishing Company wanted to make a ceremony of handing over to him a royalty check in good, spendable U.S. dollars.

"The car will pick us up downstairs in half an hour. Mir's only ten minutes away."

He said, "Want some coffee?"

And when he came back with two cups he tasted it, made a face, and said: "Do you remember what happened in Florida on January twenty-eighth?"

"I guess you mean the shuttle blowing up?"

"That's right. The space shuttle *Challenger*. It seems there's a defect in the rings that hold the external solid-fuel rocket together; NASA knew about the defect for some time, but didn't do anything until seven people got killed."

Emmaline looked at him in perplexity. "What's that got to do with Chernobyl?"

"I think it's the same thing, Emmaline. On the way here I

stopped off in London to interview an Englishman named Grahame Leman. He describes things like Chernobyl and the *Challenger* as the results of what he calls 'TBP'—means the Technical-Bureaucratic-Political system of decision-making. You see, what Leman's saying is that technological decisions aren't made just on the basis of the technological considerations. The technical experts didn't want the *Challenger* to go off that day. The forces in favor of it were bureaucratic and political. The bureaucrats are the bosses, so they can overrule the technicians' decisions, just because the guy higher up can always overrule the guy lower down. The political pressures are something else. NASA wanted to brighten up its image; it didn't want another delay."

"You're not saying they sent that ship up knowing it was dangerous?"

"Not a bit of it, Emmaline. I'm only saying they didn't *let* themselves know it was dangerous. There isn't any flag that goes up to say *Danger*! There's just a probabilistic assessment of risk. Same thing happened in England, God, I don't know, sixty or seventy years ago, when the R-101 airship smashed up. The engineers knew the R-101 wasn't ready, just as the Morton Thiokol engineers knew the *Challenger* wasn't ready—but they're only one leg of the triad, and the bureaucrats and the politicians outvote them. See," he said, glancing at his watch, "I don't want you to get the wrong idea. It's not exactly individual bureaucrats and politicians I'm talking about. It's the bureaucratic and political *pressures* that make the TBP syndrome dangerous. The worst railroad accident the English ever had was when an engineer on the Great Western Railroad wanted to make up time—that's the bureaucratic and political part—and overrode the automatic braking systems that would have stopped him after he went through a red light. They didn't. He smashed into another train. I'd say Three Mile Island was the same kind of thing too. And so was Chernobyl. The technology's not so bad on all these things, you know. It's the people who make the decisions, and the reasons they have for making them. . . . Oh, hell," he said, grinning. "I didn't mean to get wound up like this." Then, in a different tone, "Listen, there was something I wanted to talk to you about. Do we have time for another cup of coffee?"

"If we drink it fast enough, we do," Emmaline said, puzzled.

"Well, the hell with the coffee. The thing is, I got a call from Johnny Stark."

Emmaline almost choked on her last sip of coffee. "You got a call from Johnny *Stark*?" she repeated.

"I see you know who he is," Pembroke said, pleased at the impression he had made.

She glanced around quickly. There were plenty of other people rattling cups and dishes in the buffet, but the only ones near them were three businessmen carrying on a loud conversation in German. "He's the mystery man," she said softly.

"That one. The one with the American wife. The one that commutes to Paris and New York and drives the only Cadillac convertible in Moscow. What do you know about him?"

Emmaline thought for a second. "His real name is supposed to be Ivan something. He just uses 'Johnny Stark' for those guidebooks he writes, like *The Story of the Kremlin* and *English Speaker's Guide to Moscow*."

"I've seen the books."

"Well, he gets a lot of hard currency somewhere, and I don't think it's all from the books. He's *connected,* you know what I'm saying? He's way out of my league, Pembroke."

Pembroke studied her face. "Are you telling me to stay away from him?"

Emmaline thought for a moment. "No, not really," she said reluctantly. "He talks pretty openly when he wants to. The thing is, Stark has got to be very high up but nobody knows his official position, if any. So everyone is very careful around him. They say he invented *glasnost* before Gorbachev—what? Oh, *glasnost*. That's what they call the official policy now. It means something like 'frankness' or 'candor.' The funny thing is, lately they seem to actually be opening up—on occasion, at least."

"Like about Chernobyl?"

"Aw, no. Not even Johnny Stark's going to go that far." She hesitated, then decided to indulge her curiosity. "Mind if I ask what he called you about?"

Now Pembroke looked a little hesitant himself. "Well, that's the whole thing, Emmaline. I've got some friends, and they mentioned some kind of a manifesto that's going around."

Emmaline frowned. "What kind of manifesto do you mean?"

"They say it's all about what the USSR has to do to straighten itself out. Clean up the economy, get out of Afghanistan, have free elections with more than one candidate for each job—"

"Pembroke!" Emmaline said earnestly. "If you get yourself mixed up with dissidents—"

"No, no! They're not dissidents. I mean, I think they aren't. I mean, maybe some of them are, because the first person to mention it was—" He stopped in the middle of a sentence when he saw Emmaline's face.

"For heaven's sake, don't mention any sources. They could get into a load of trouble, you know." She spoke very quietly.

"Oh, yeah," Pembroke said, abashed. "I'm sorry. I mean—well, anyway, the document itself is supposed to come from real high-up people. They say it's got a lot of secret stuff in it that nobody else would know. And it's seventeen pages long, and that's about all I know. You've never heard of it?"

"You bet I haven't. What surprises me is that you did." Emmaline thought for a moment. "I could ask someone," she said, thinking of Rima—and rejecting the thought at once. There were limits beyond which you should not push any Soviet national, even a friendly one. She could also ask her local CIA spook, she thought, but that was an even worse idea. Emmaline did her best to stay away from the CIA man. Plus, he was always more interested in getting information than in giving any out. "But," she finished, "if I did find anything out, I probably couldn't tell you. What does Johnny Stark have to do with it?"

"I don't have a clue. Only that he called this morning and introduced himself, and said he'd heard I was interested in the government's future plans. I thought he was talking about the document."

"Pembroke," Emmaline said fervently, "you're full of surprises."

"So he said he'd call me again in a few days and maybe we could have lunch or something."

"My God. Just like an American businessman. Well, my friend, you're way beyond where I have anything to say, but if I were you I'd probably do it. Only I'd watch what I said to him."

"No names, no pack drill, right?" Pembroke grinned. "You think he's got something in mind?"

"The thing I know for sure about Johnny Stark," Emmaline said definitely, "is that he's always got two purposes for everything he does, and you're never going to find out what the second one is." She actually dropped her voice to a whisper. "He's mungo KGB, they say."

"Should be interesting, then."

She looked at him mistrustfully, then said, "Don't let it get exciting, please. I'd give a quarter to be a fly on the wall when you talk to him, though."

"Want me to try to get you invited?"

"No thanks," she said, rising, "there's no way he's going to agree to that. But if you hear anything juicy, just drop around to the Embassy and I'll buy you a hamburger with real fries."

CHAPTER 30

SATURDAY, MAY 10

What a Soviet Army soldier looks like is easy to see, for there are posters of him all over the USSR. He is blond and young. His face peers eagerly into the future, with his chin thrust forward just like Lenin's. His forage cap is cocked precisely over his left ear; his blouse is neatly buttoned, and, although you cannot see his boots in the picture, you know that they are brilliantly shined. That is the ideal Soviet Army soldier.

There is also Private Sergei Konov. Konov does not look that way at all, especially after returning from a day of shoveling clay to close a culvert or squatting in a muddy ditch on perimeter guard ... and yet there is something about Konov that is not like the Konov of only one week before. He has surprised his comrades. Most of all, he has surprised his lieutenant, who had never considered the possibility that Private Konov would ever volunteer for anything.

"You understand," the lieutenant said warily, "that this duty is a bit dangerous."

"I do, Senior Lieutenant Osipev."

"Of course, if you follow orders exactly, you'll be all right. Only you must be quick."

"I will, Senior Lieutenant Osipev."

"And then you get the rest of the day off. Well," the

lieutenant sighed, "you have my permission to volunteer, so get on with you then, Konov. The armored car is waiting to take the cleanup squad to the plant."

Konov wasn't the only volunteer. There were fifty others standing uneasily about in the top floor of the plant, just under the roof. It was the first time most of them had been inside the actual buildings of the Chernobyl Nuclear Power Station itself, and they were wary about touching anything, even about being there at all. When they were all gathered, the sergeant looked them over dispassionately. "We don't have any use for loafers," he told them. "You've got to move quick, do your job, jump back inside, and that's it. Otherwise you'll be as dead as the lad that's still inside there. And we don't have suits to fit freaks. If you're over a hundred kilos or under sixty-five, drop out now."

Six or seven of the soldiers fell out, most of them scowling—though some of them, Konov thought, were frowning more with relief than disappointment. The promise of a whole day off had sounded attractive, especially after a week of shoveling rubble, but up here it all began to sound a lot more serious.

The training was as simple as the requirements. When they had made their way to the last stairway to the roof—walking briskly all the time, sometimes running as the sergeant warned them past points of high radioactivity—a major looked them over, shook his head, and turned them over to a different sergeant. "Line up!" the noncom commanded. "Count off by fours! All right, you first four! Find a suit that fits you, put it on, make sure it's tightly closed or you'll never do your mothers again."

The suits were clammy, like rubber diving suits, and heavy with the lead they contained. "Don't fart in your suits, lads, think of the next man who'll wear it," the sergeant cautioned the first group. "Now the boots—lace 'em up all the way! The helmets. . . . The respirators—sure, a hundred other soldiers have been sucking the same masks, but just think of it as kissing your girl!" And then, before he had time to think, it was the turn of Konov's four.

Up the stairs to the roof on the double—"Go!" the major shouted—burst out the door, grab a lump of graphite the size of a woman's ass (hot, too! Thank God for the lead-lined gloves)—heave it over the side of the roof—another—another—another—and all the time the major yelling off the seconds, forty, fifty, sixty—

When Konov's four were inside again the major grinned. "Sixty-one seconds for the last man. You've done well. Now, off with you, and the brave ones can come back tomorrow and do it again."

And actually Konov thought he might. His dosimeter said that he'd picked up less than half a roentgen, and it was certainly more interesting than shoveling the dirt the bulldozers had missed.

It was also more useful. When the armored car had taken Konov's group back to the abandoned collective farm that was their headquarters, Konov wheedled a cup of tea from the cook sergeant and wondered what to do with this day off he did not particularly want.

To throw lumps of hot radioactive graphite off the roof of the plant so the bulldozers could scoop them up and cart them safely away—that was useful. Exciting, even, for those lumps had once been part of the very core that had exploded and caused the whole disaster. Frightening, a little, too, but it was as the lieutenant had said: if you were quick and followed orders, you would be all right—unless, of course, you stumbled and fell, or unless you left a seam open in your rubber-lead suit, or unless something else went wrong.

But nothing had gone wrong, and the day, really, had just begun. Struck by a thought, Konov counted on his fingers and realized that it was a Saturday. That was the Soviet soldier's day of freedom—when you weren't called out for a surprise inspection, or a twenty-kilometer forced march, which you were once or twice every month, anyway. It was the day when the soldier could sleep, or play football on the parade ground, or even go into town and see what the local girls were up to—but what could you do with a day off here, anyway? You couldn't even leave the old cow barn that was their barracks without putting on the radiation garments, and who could play football in a breathing mask? Even if there had been anyone else to get up a game with!

Konov knocked on the door of his lieutenant's quarters.

"Private Konov reporting for duty, Senior Lieutenant Osipev," he said, standing at attention.

The lieutenant looked startled. "Didn't you understand me? You have the rest of the day off."

"Yes, Senior Lieutenant Osipev. I wish to return to duty."

"What, are you suddenly addicted to shoveling dirt? Most of the men are raising dikes today."

"As the lieutenant wishes," Konov said agreeably.

Osipev peered at him curiously for a moment, then shrugged. "Oh, well," he said, "There's a truck going to Pripyat with more oil for the sprayers. You can go there, but be quick about it. The truck's ready to leave."

"Thank you, Senior Lieutenant Osipev," Konov said. As he marched away, he could feel the lieutenant's wondering eyes on his back.

Actually, that was the detail Konov liked best, to go in among the high-rises of the ghost town of Pripyat. That was a task of trust and importance. The vanished inhabitants couldn't protect their belongings from looters or weather or radiation; it was Konov's duty, and Konov's pleasure, to do it for them.

Today's job was a little different. The orders were to take a spray tank into Pripyat, to oil down all the patches of exposed earth that the trucks might have missed. He didn't go alone; there was a buddy system enforced, so they could watch each other—after all, the temptation to pick up some abandoned treasure might be too much for even a soldier to resist.

His partner was Miklas the Armenian, short, dark, angry at the world and especially at the Army that had taken two years of his agreeable young life—the second worst soldier in the detachment until Konov had vacated the bottom spot for him. But as soon as they were by themselves, they flipped a three-kopeck coin to see who would carry the radiation counter—Miklas got it—and then, to get the job done with faster, walked in opposite directions.

It was hard work. Konov was sweating at once inside his coverall and hood, but he was meticulous. He sought out and poked his long-handled spray into every corner of the garden plots (dead tomato vines and grape) and floral plantings (wilted stalks with buds that would never blossom through their thick coating of oil).

Looked at in one way, what Konov was doing was destruction. Where he saw green life, he killed it with his spray. Where a missed corner of black earth showed through the greasy film, he covered it at once with deadly oil. He didn't look at it in that way. He was wielding the surgeon's knife, he reasoned. He killed here to prevent a worse death somewhere else, and so he was painstaking at poking his spray behind dead shrubs, under wooden steps, into every corner that might have been overlooked.

It took him an hour or more to finish the grounds around a single building, and there were half a hundred high-rise apartments in Pripyat, not to count the parks and school yards and open squares and offices and stores. No matter. Not one centimeter was going to get by Sergei Konov. Nor did he neglect his collateral duties. All the time he was spraying he was alert for the sounds or sights of unauthorized others in the town.

There were, of course, some who had a right to be there, for he and his partner were not alone. Two other teams were spraying in other areas, and there were the big orange trucks that rumbled through now and then to water down the roadways one more time. But when he turned a corner of a building and saw a smaller truck standing there with its motor running and its back flaps up and no one in sight, he had one sudden thought: *Looters.*

He had to investigate. He shrugged the tank off his shoulders and set it down, and cautiously approached the truck. It was full of things! Things taken from the empty apartments! So perhaps there really were looters at work, because Konov could see radio sets and tape machines stacked inside the truck.

Yet each one was tagged with the number of the apartment it had come from, and surely looters would not care about such a thing. And just inside the tailgate were things that a looter would hardly bother with: books, magazines, papers, also all carefully tagged: 115 Victory Drive, Flat 22; 112 Marx Prospekt, Flat 18.

Konov's curiosity made him pick some of the printed materials up. Some of the papers were bound into volumes of their own, with blue cardboard covers on which someone had typed a title and a name. They were not real books, with illustrations on the jacket and printed pages. They were mimeographed, some of them hardly legible, carefully stitched together with cotton thread. When he read a few of the titles they were quite unfamiliar—authors with names like Vladimir Voinovich (who was Vladimir Voinovich? Konov often read books, but he had never heard of this author before), and Oksana Mechko (Mechko? another puzzle) and—what was this?—oh, Boris Pasternak, Andrei Amalryk—of course! All this was samizdat! Konov had seen samizdat before, but never so much, or so carefully collected.

It was not all samizdat, however. There were separate piles of brightly colored magazines, all foreign. These were not tagged at all but simply stacked in heaps, and when Konov got a look at the covers his eyes popped ... though not as much as they did when he turned the pages and saw—women! Beautiful women! *Naked* women! And not merely naked, but displaying all of their most private of parts in brazenly alluring ways!

Konov had never seen such pictures. He had never dreamed they existed—and here were twelve or fourteen magazines, all filled with them! True, the writing was in English and German and what looked to Konov like Italian, and incomprehensible therefore; but who needed writing to say what these photographs represented?

A harsh voice from behind him snarled: "And what do you think you're doing, pig's scum?"

Konov turned guiltily to confront two men, gloved hands filled with more papers and books. Their insignia was hidden by the white coveralls, but he didn't need to see their flashes to know what branch of service they represented. "I am on duty here," he said doggedly. "Are you on official business?"

"We are always on official business," the other one said, his voice light and pleasant. The eyes behind the gauze mask, however, were bleak. "We were gathering evidence. What, do you want to take one of these filthy magazines? Why not?" And he took one from the top of the stack in his arms.

"Not that one," growled the other man, pointing to the magazine with the English title *Hustler*.

"Then this one. And this. And take them away quickly, little soldier, because we are very busy."

*   *   *

Konov did. It was always better to do what the organs wanted you to do. And then, for half an hour, he sat just inside the doorway of one of the tall apartment buildings, so that he could see outside, carefully turning over every page. He could feel himself harden as he turned back to gaze again at one of his favorites, this one of the little blonde in her underwear, standing with her back turned and her head cocked coyly toward him, one thumb beginning to lower the panties; or this other of the slim, almost boyish brunette, lying on her back and looking impassively at him through her spread knees.

"And what have you stolen now?" asked his partner, Miklas, coming up to the door.

Konov jumped. Then he handed one of the magazines to Miklas and watched the man's eyes pop as he leafed through the pages. "And there are more of them in the truck?" he asked.

"Dozens more. Also samizdat, all kinds."

"Konov," said Miklas sorrowfully, "do you know what those magazines are worth? We could get ten rubles each for them."

"We could get arrested as looters, you fool."

"Only if we are foolish enough to be caught. We aren't looters; the GehBehs have done that for us. Also, what do you think they are going to do with that samizdat, but make some poor man's life miserable? It is our duty," Miklas said virtuously, "to protect the interests of the people who were thrown out of their homes without notice. We should do what we can to save them from harm!"

When the GehBehs came back, their arms full of more papers and a shortwave radio, they saw Konov and Miklas at the tailgate of the truck, running the radiation detector over the stacks of papers. "Hey!" shouted one of them. "Assholes! Get away from there at once!"

Miklas turned to them apologetically, running the prod over the magazines. "With all regret, your honors," he said obsequiously, "just listen!" The detector was screaming.

"What is this?" the GehBeh demanded. "Is this material contaminated?"

"All of it, I'm afraid," said Miklas sorrowfully. "Was it near open windows? Perhaps exposed to dust? Radioactivity is so tricky, your honors, one can never tell what is safe and what may be deadly—but simply listen! The count is going right off the scale!"

Cursing, the GehBehs kicked the papers out of the back of the truck and drove away. As soon as they were out of sight, Miklas knocked the bit of radioactive mud off the end of his detector and Konov sprayed it lavishly with the oil. "Now," grinned Miklas, "our only problem is figuring out how to get the magazines back to the barracks."

They could not simply be carried. "Perhaps one or two at a time?" Konov offered. "We can hide them somewhere and just take a couple on each trip, tuck them inside our pants?"

But Miklas's expression had changed. He was idly running the now-clean detector over the magazines. "Not next to my balls, curse it," he groaned, for the instrument was squealing its warning of contamination as loud as ever.

CHAPTER 31

Afghanistan has been called the Vietnam of the USSR. This is not just because it has gone on so long and drained off so many young lives. It resembles the American experience in Vietnam in another way. The Soviet soldiers in Afghanistan, for the first time in their lives, are exposed to an easy and cheap supply of narcotics. Drugs had never before been a major Soviet problem. The penalties were too harsh, the surveillance too complete. Small boats did not sneak into Soviet harbors by night or light planes steal across its borders with cargoes of heroin, cocaine, and pot. They would have been sunk, or shot out of the sky. Anyway, the Soviet people, like the Russians of the czarist times before them, took to drunkenness rather than dope as a favorite vice. But Afghanistan is changing all that.

Just before Simyon Smin heard that his elder son was under arrest for drug possession, he woke from a troubled dream. In the dream it seemed that he had been captured by fiends—Nazis, camp guards, the Spanish Inquisition—he could not tell who they were, but they had stabbed him in a hundred places and bound him to a bed while infernal machines clicked and hummed and gurgled all around him.

What a pity, he thought, that the dream was no dream. All those things were true. At least the people who had done all this to him were not enemies; they were trying to save his life, not to kill him in agony, but all the same he had needles in his arms and wrists and collarbone; his side was a mass of bruises where it was not blisters or running sores.

His first waking thought was to reach under his pillow to make sure that the schoolboy's pad was still there. His second was his body. With some effort he lifted the edge of the sheet and peered down at himself. His naked body was not merely naked. It was *bare*. The hairlessness of his chest did not stop at the edge of the great old wartime burn scar. There was no hair on him at all. None on his body, none any longer on his head. Even his limp organ lay exposed and as bald as a six-year-old's— and, he thought, about as useful, too.

He did not need to be told that the transplant of bone marrow from his elder son had not gone well. His body told him that with its pain and feverish heat. "Comrade Plumber," he called weakly. "Can you find a nurse? I need a bedpan very badly."

From the other bed Sheranchuk called back in a troubled voice, "At once! But your son Vassili is here to see you."

"Then let him get the nurse," said Smin, "and he may come in afterward."

Sheranchuk tried a reassuring smile at the boy waiting just outside the door. "You heard," he said, wondering what new worry it was that made Vassili Smin look so much as though he were going to cry. "The nurses' station is at the end of the hall, please."

"Of course," Vassili said, casting one more horrified glance toward his father's bed. Although the screens were in place, they did not conceal everything. Vassili saw the clamps that looked like long, ugly scissors hanging from tube connections to keep them tight, the orange and white hoses that dangled from plastic bottles on stands—worst of all, the blue-paneled box that clicked and blinked with red lights. When he had found a nurse and returned to the room, Vassili sat resolutely by Sheranchuk's bed, not looking toward his father. Certainly not listening to those ugly, intimate sounds that came from him.

Sheranchuk tried to help. "Look," he said, talking to cover the sounds, "see what the American doctors have brought us." He displayed a little flashlight, a pocket calculator, and best of all a wonderful small flat box, tiny enough to fit in the palm of his hand, that was an electronic alarm clock. "Your father has received them too. Perhaps he will give you the calculator."

But Vassili was not to be diverted from his misery. Alarmed, Sheranchuk said, "What is it, Vassili? Have you had some bad news that worries you?"

The boy looked at him through tears. "Yes, I have had bad news, and what worries me is that I must tell it to my father."

And when Smin heard the news a few minutes later, he sat up straight in his bed, regardless of all the tubes and wires and catheters, and cried, "Nikolai? Arrested on a narcotics charge? But that is completely out of the question!"

"It's true, Father," sobbed his younger son, casting an imploring glance at the other bed, where Sheranchuk was scowling blackly as he pretended to devote all his attention to reading a newspaper.

"It cannot be true," Smin whispered. But as he fell back against his pillow, he knew that it must be. He closed his eyes, cursing silently. This terrible weakness! It was worse than the pain. Yes, to be truthful, the pain was almost unbearable, in spite of everything the doctors could do. His whole body was a mass of stinking, running sores. He could hardly swallow, he could not piss or move his bowels without agony, and yet he must do those things every few minutes anyway. But the pain could be borne, if only he had the strength to act—to get out of this bed, at least. And go to see his son! Or to plead with his son's captors. Or to go to anyone, to do anything, to try to get this matter somehow set aside.

It was at least a mercy that he was having one of the less and less frequent periods of not only wakefulness but even lucidity. "Tell me exactly what happened, Vassa," he begged, and listened in misery as the boy explained how the organs had come for his brother. Yes, of course it was the organs; it was a matter of smuggling, after all, and thus under the jurisdiction of the KGB. They had simply appeared and taken Senior Lieutenant Nikolai Smin away. Why had they accused him? Because someone in the hospital had run certain tests on Nikolai's blood or urine or bone marrow—they had endless samples of all of his fluids, of course, to make sure the transplant might work. And that someone had found chemical traces of hashish in Nikolai's sample . . . and had reported it at once. "You must not blame the doctors," Vassili said sorrowfully. "It was their duty, of course."

"Of course," Smin croaked sourly. "And how is your mother taking this?"

"She has gone to see what she can do. Grandmother too. She insisted on going along. I don't know where."

Smin sighed despondently. He roused himself to turn on his side and call to his roommate. "Comrade Plumber? I must apologize for intruding this unpleasant family matter on you—"

"It is I who must apologize," Sheranchuk said soberly. "Forgive me. You are having a private conversation with your son and I should not be here. With your permission I will go out to visit friends for a while."

"Thank you," said Smin. He watched Sheranchuk silently as the man got out of bed, pulled a red-striped pajama top over his bare chest, and hurried away.

"He is the lucky one," Smin said somberly to his son. "I think he will be released soon, while I—"

"Yes, Father?"

Smin did not finish the thought. It was no longer important that he was sure he would never leave Hospital No. 6 alive. "Ah, my poor Kolya," he whispered in anguish. "If only he had confided in me!"

There was a pause. Then Vassili said, "What would you have done if he had, Father?"

Smin blinked at the boy. "Why, I would have tried to help him, of course. No matter what!" Smin studied his son, struck by something in his tone. "Do you think that would be wrong, Vassili?"

The boy said quickly, "Oh, no. Of course not, Father. A father should help his son."

There was still that false note, though. Smin scowled, trying to force himself to be more alert, more intelligent; something was troubling the boy. "What is it, Vassa? Have I done something wrong?"

"Of course not, Father!"

"Then"—struck by a sudden and unpleasant thought—"is

it—that is, have you—I mean, is there something you should tell me?"

"No, Father."

"Yes, Father," Smin insisted. "You have some trouble I don't know about, don't you?"

"Really not," his son said. "I give you my word as a Komsomol."

"Then what is it? I don't have the patience for guessing games, son. Is there something you want to ask me, perhaps about the accident, or something I have done?"

"No."

"Yes!" shouted Smin. "I have not raised you for sixteen years without knowing when something is troubling you. Tell me what it is!"

Vassili opened his mouth. Then he closed it, shaking his head, and abruptly burst out, "Why did you have me circumcised, Father?"

Smin gazed at his son in astonishment. The boy went on rebelliously. "Yes, it was done for health reasons, I know—but wasn't it performed on the eighth day after I was born, according to a Jewish religious custom?"

"How did you know it was on the eighth day?" Smin demanded, startled.

"I didn't know. *They* knew."

"You were *questioned*?" Smin whispered, in shock.

"Yes, by the organs, for two hours! But I knew nothing to tell them, only— Well, there was that dinner at grandmother's flat; they said it was a religious rite too. They called it a 'seder.' Was it? And then they asked me about a ceremony on my thirteenth birthday."

Smin waved a shaking hand. "What did they do to you?"

Vassili tried to be reassuring. "Nothing at all, Father. Really. They were only asking about these things and the difficulty was that I could not answer. But is it true? Did I have what they called a 'bar mitzvah' on my thirteenth birthday?"

Smin closed his eyes again. It was a mistake. He felt himself drifting off and he could not afford that. He forced himself to rouse and speak to his son. "On your thirteenth birthday you had a birthday party, of course. Thirteen is a significant age, worth special attention. What you had was the best party your mother and I could give you, but it was certainly not a bar mitzvah. You know that. Do you remember any religious services connected with it?"

"No, Father, but—"

"But you couldn't possibly remember anything like that, because there were none. Not even in secret. Tell me, son. Have you ever been given any religious instruction? Of any kind? By me, or by your mother, or by anyone?"

Vassili hesitated. "Grandmother sometimes tells me when it is Yom Kippur."

"Your grandmother," Smin sighed, "eats pork and crabmeat and other things that would be forbidden if she were a religious Jew. She has never been in a synagogue since she was fourteen years old. She is not religious. But she has some old-fashioned ways; there is no secret about that." He hesitated. "To be sure," he went on, "she is defined as a Jew because she was born of a Jewish mother. As I was, Vassili. But not you. She did not decide to think of herself as a Jew, even, until she was fifty years old, when it became quite unfashionable."

"Why unfashionable?"

"Why? Haven't you ever heard of the Doctors' Plot? No? Well, it was a bad time for Jews, when Stalin decided there was a Jewish conspiracy to destroy him."

"Do you mean Grandmother was not serious about being a Jew?"

"Your grandmother is always serious," Smin said heavily. The pain was coming back again. "Still, you are not Jewish. Look at your passport. It says 'Russian.' "

Vassili looked sullen. "Still, after they had questioned me," he said, "the GehBeh called me 'zhid.' "

"Then report the man!" cried Smin. "He had no right! You have done nothing wrong. You have nothing to fear."

Vassili gazed at him with the eyes of someone older than sixteen. "And do you have something to fear, Father?"

Smin considered that for a moment, then painfully shook his head. The proper answer would be "not anymore," because all of the scores he might have to face were obliterated by one central fact. He was beyond retribution. He was going to die and he did not fear that. He said, "Are you asking if I will go to prison? No. I am sure I won't."

The boy thought that over for a time, his face opaque.

Smin watched him, and then said gently, "Vassa, there's more. What is it?"

"What is what, Father?" the boy asked politely.

Smin begged, "Please. You still have something on your mind. Tell me what it is."

"Father, you are very tired," the boy explained. "It isn't fair to you to worry you." Then he took another look at his father's face and shrugged. "Before Nikolai was—arrested—we were, well, talking."

"About what?"

And then it all came out, the boy lecturing as though he were making a report to his Komsomol unit: the failings of leadership, the toleration of irregularities, the need for discipline. "Ah," said Smin, nodding, "I see. Your brother said that he wished we had a Stalin again. Is that what you mean?"

"But what he said makes sense, Father. With Josef Vissarionovich we had strong leadership! He was a great force for discipline."

"He was a murderer, Vassili!"

"Father!"

They were glaring at each other. Vassili looked away first. "You should be resting," he said penitently. "Yes, I know what you mean, Comrade Stalin had some people shot."

"*Some* people? Vassili, do you know how many?"

The boy shrugged. "A few hundred, I suppose."

"A few hundred? But there were millions, Vassili! Not Trotskyites and wreckers—half of the leadership of the Communist Party! Most of the high officers of the Army! I don't even speak of the peasants who starved in the forced collectivization of the land, or of the millions upon millions who were sent off to the camps to die there, or, maybe, a few, to come back with their health destroyed and their lives ruined!"

Vassili said, shocked, "But you make him sound like a tyrant, and that is impossible."

"Is it *true*. Don't you know anything? Have you never heard of Khrushchev's speech to the Party Congress in 1963?"

"In 1963 I wasn't born."

"But you should have known! You should have made it your business to know these things!"

"How could I know?" Vassili demanded. "If they are true, you should have told me!"

*   *   *

At ten o'clock Hospital No. 6 had quieted down for the night. Most of the patients were asleep. The vaulted corridors were empty. The nurses and the duty doctors spoke only in whispers as they made their rounds, checking temperatures, giving an injection of cyclosporine here and an antibiotic there, changing the dressing on a burn, providing a bedpan when needed, replacing the plastic sacks of plasma and whole blood and saline solution and glucose that trickled into the veins of the casualties. Even the dining room, where relatives were permitted to wait, was almost empty as Vassili curled up under a table and tried to sleep.

It wasn't easy. The boy berated himself for arguing with his father, just when his father needed all his strength and all the help he could get just to stay alive.

Vassili was also very hungry. The kitchen was long closed. The pale young woman with the Lithuanian name who was now asleep in a blanket on the floor had given him two slices of bread and half an apple out of her own store, hours before. But that was before she learned that he was merely a patient's son (proudly: "But I'm a sister, and so it is more likely my bone marrow will match"), and, even worse, that he was only sixteen years old.

It began to seem probable to Vassili that his father was not going to come out of this hospital alive.

It was a hard thought to face. Vassili had never considered the possibility that his father would die. It did not match anything in his experience. For the whole of Vassili's life Simyon Smin had always been there, and very much alive. The boy could not imagine a world that did not have his father alive in it somewhere. Thirteen days ago the thought of his father's death would have been ignored as a ridiculous idea. Now it was no longer ridiculous, but still he could not accept it.

On the other hand, Vassili was not at all stupid. When the doctor had paused in the hallway to talk to Vassili, he had carefully marked her words and tone and the look on her face. "His condition is very grave," she had said, "but we are doing everything we can." One could interpret that as hopeful, could one not?

But then, a moment later, he had listened while the doctor was talking to the Lithuanian girl, and the doctor's tone was the same, expression was the same, even the words were almost exactly the same; but Vassili knew for certain that what the doctor was doing was preparing the young woman for the fact that her brother, the fireman, was dying.

There was a geometric theorem that could be used to show that the cases were the same, and therefore the hope Vassili had drawn from the doctor's words was without basis in reality.

Vassili Smin untangled himself from the table and got up. There were too many worries. Even a sixteen-year-old couldn't sleep with his brother in prison and his father dying a few meters away. He peered into his father's room. The engineer Sheranchuk was snoring lustily, one hand thrown over his face. Behind the screens Vassili could see his father, also asleep. The boy thought of quietly taking a chair there, next to his father's bed. He rejected the thought—because he might wake his father; more than that, he was beginning to feel stifled in the hospital atmosphere. It was not merely that people were sick—well, what were hospitals for but to hold sick people? It was not even that his father was among them. What was hard to bear was how young these dying people were—boys, some of them, younger than his brother, but bald and bright-eyed, almost like babies. They didn't even have eyebrows anymore!

He slipped down the stairs, nodded to the sleepy guard at the door and stepped out into the mild spring night. Why, cars were driving along the streets! There were even people standing at the corner, shouting to try to stop a taxicab, just as though the price for the Chernobyl disaster were not being paid by so many, so horribly, only a building-wall away! Yet it was almost comforting to be on a street with people who were not involved in the tragedy; Vassili could almost feel himself free and safe among them. He walked easily down the block, toward the old church with its white and gold towers, turned left, kept going around the corners. It was a good long walk. It should have tired him out. It didn't. The sudden wave of weariness didn't hit him until he was back at the entrance, climbing the stairs again to his father's floor.

When Vassili peered into his father's room, Smin's eyes were open. He put a finger to his lips and beckoned Vassili inside.

*   *   *

When Aftasia Smin came to the dining room, angry and triumphant, pushing the limping and sullen Senior Lieutenant Nikolai Smin before her, she woke everyone up. Vassili rubbed his eyes, staring at his brother, as Aftasia demanded: "Your father, how is he? Why won't they let us in his room?"

The two wives of patients sitting side by side at one table whispered to each other, and the sister of the fireman with the Lithuanian name looked up at the man in the Air Force uniform with some interest. Vassili said, "They sent me away too, Grandmother. They said he must sleep."

Aftasia lowered her voice. "Then we will stay until he wakes so that he can see that this criminal son of his has been spared the penalty for his crimes."

She glanced around the room with eyes that told the other women to mind their business as the lieutenant sat himself carefully down next to his brother, wincing at the hard wood of the chair.

"But what happened?" Vassili asked plaintively.

His grandmother's expression was grim. "I got him out," she said. She didn't detail what old Party comrades she had called, or what luck it was that the prosecutor was the son of someone who had served under her dead husband. She only said, "At least they did not find any of his disgusting filth, which he says he did not have."

Nikolai said stubbornly, "My ass hurt where they stuck that sewer pipe into me. I merely took some pain relievers."

"Ah, yes," Aftasia nodded, "so you told the organs, and of course they laughed in your face. Dr. Akhsmentova is so foolish that she mistook aspirin for hashish—not to mention that the blood test was taken before you donated bone marrow." Nikolai shrugged. "At any rate," she went on, "if you will be intelligent enough to go to the place where you have hidden that stuff which you do not have, and throw it down a sewer before you are caught with it, then perhaps all of this will be forgotten. Otherwise, it will not be the flimsy evidence of a blood test that they arrest you on."

Nikolai ignored her and turned to his brother. "And our father, is he any better?"

Vassili hesitated, then said unwillingly, "A little worse, I think. They've put plastic drapes all around him now, and it is hard even to see him. We talked for a while, though."

"About what?" Aftasia Smin demanded.

Vassili puffed out his cheeks for a second, then made a clean breast of it. "We talked about political things, Grandmother. I—I'm afraid he got quite excited, and it wasn't good for him. And it was all my fault."

"Little idiot!" his brother scolded.

Vassili hung his head. "I know I was wrong," he apologized. "You are right. I was an idiot for troubling him when he was so sick, but at least—" He swallowed the rest of the sentence. It would have ended, *but at least I did not get arrested for smuggling dope,* and he didn't want to say that. "At least," he said instead, "he went to sleep then for a while. I saw him again later."

"And?"

"And he asked me to do something for him, but at first I could not understand what it was he wanted. It was to mail a letter."

"A letter?" his grandmother demanded. "What kind of a letter?"

"How should I know? It was quite thick. And it was addressed to himself, at your house, Grandmother. And then when I came back—" He hesitated. "Well, he talked quite a lot, but I think he was delirious. He looked at me, but he addressed me as 'Comrade Central Committee member.'"

Aftasia Smin frowned and looked around. When she spoke her voice was much lower. "Oh? And what did your father have to say to a member of the Central Committee?"

Vassili was near to tears. "He was saying really strange things, Grandmother. I couldn't really understand him. But he was telling me—or telling this member of the Central Committee that he thought I was—that he approved the suggestion of free elections to the Supreme Soviet. He said he agreed it would be excellent to have more than one candidate for each office, even perhaps running under the designation of another political party or two!"

"Ah," said Aftasia sadly, "I see. You are right, then. He was quite delirious."

CHAPTER 32

It is eighteen days after the explosion at the Chernobyl power plant. Every television set in the Soviet Union is turned on for an important address, and Mikhail Gorbachev appears on the screen. His face is grave but his bearing assured. He begins to speak.

"Good evening, comrades," he said. "As you all know, a misfortune has befallen us—the accident at the Chernobyl nuclear power plant. It has painfully affected Soviet people and caused anxiety in the international public. For the first time ever we have had to deal in reality with a force as sinister as nuclear energy that has escaped control.

"So what did happen?

"As specialists report, the reactor's capacity suddenly increased during a scheduled shutdown of the fourth unit. The considerable emission of steam and subsequent reaction resulted in the formation of hydrogen, its explosion, damage to the reactor, and the resulting radioactive discharge.

"It is still too early to pass final judgment on the causes of the accident. All aspects of the problem—design, construction, operational, and technical—are under the close scrutiny of the Government Commission.

"It goes without saying that when the investigation of the accident is completed, all the necessary conclusions will be drawn and measures will be taken to rule out a repetition of anything of this sort."

Thirty kilometers from the reactor, Private Konov was bent over his meal, but his eyes were fixed on the little television screen. He hardly knew what he was eating. A pity; it was a chicken, bought from a local farmer, and pronounced fit by the technicians after they had run their detectors over its feathers and even up into its opened belly. "He sounds like we'll be here a long time," the soldier beside him grumbled.

"We'll be here until the job is done, Miklas," Konov snapped. "Please be still! I want to hear this." And Gorbachev's voice went on.

"The seriousness of the situation was obvious. It was necessary to evaluate it urgently and competently. And as soon as we received reliable initial information, it was made available to the Soviet people and sent through diplomatic channels to the governments of foreign countries.

"In the situation that had taken shape, we considered it our top priority duty, a duty of special importance, to insure the safety of the population and provide effective assistance to those who had been affected by the accident.

"The inhabitants of the settlement near the station were evacuated within a matter of hours and then, when it had become clear that there was a potential threat to the health of people in the adjoining zone, they also were moved to safe areas.

"Nevertheless, the measures that were taken failed to protect many people. Two of them died at the time of the accident—an adjuster of automatic systems and an operator at the nuclear power plant.

"As of today two hundred and ninety-nine people have been hospitalized, diagnosed as having radiation disease of varying degrees of gravity. Seven of them have died. Every possible treatment is being given to the rest."

In their flat in Kiev, the Didchuks and the old parents were clustered around their set. "He has not mentioned the children who were evacuated," Mrs. Didchuk fretted.

"But none of those are suffering from radiation disease,"

her husband said soothingly. "After all, you spoke to our daughter on the telephone just yesterday."

"I do not want to speak to her on the telephone! I want to hold her in my arms!"

"Soon, my dear. And now, look! Comrade Gorbachev is angry!"

He was at least scowling as he said harshly, "I cannot fail to mention one more aspect of that affair. I mean the reaction abroad to what happened at Chernobyl." He paused for a moment. His expression softened as he went on. "In the world on the whole, and this should be emphasized, the misfortune that befell us and our actions in that complicated situation were treated with understanding.

"We are profoundly grateful to our friends in socialist countries who have shown solidarity with the Soviet people at a difficult moment. We are grateful to the political and public figures in other states for their sincere sympathy and support.

"We express our kind feelings to those foreign scientists and specialists who showed their readiness to assist us in overcoming the consequences of the accident. I would like to note the participation of American medics Robert Gale and Paul Terasaki in the treatment of affected persons and to express gratitude to the business circles of those countries which promptly reacted to our request for the purchase of certain types of equipment, materials, and medicines.

"But—" and now he was scowling—"it is impossible to ignore and not to assess politically the way the event at Chernobyl was met by the governments, political figures, and the mass media in certain NATO countries, especially the U.S.A.

"They launched an unrestrained anti-Soviet campaign.

"It is difficult to imagine what was said and written these days—'thousands of casualties,' 'mass graves of the dead,' 'desolate Kiev,' that 'the entire land of the Ukraine has been poisoned.' And so on and so forth.

"Generally speaking, we faced a veritable mountain of lies—most brazen and malicious lies. It is unpleasant to recall all this, but it should be done. The international public should know what we had to face. This should be done to find the answer to the question: What, in actual fact, was behind that highly immoral campaign?

"Its organizers, to be sure, were not interested in either

true information about the accident or the fate of the people at Chernobyl, in the Ukraine, in Byelorussia, in any other place, in any other country.

"They were looking for a pretext to exploit in order to try to defame the Soviet Union and its foreign policy, to lessen the impact of Soviet proposals on the termination of nuclear tests and on the elimination of nuclear weapons, and, at the same time, to dampen the growing criticism of U.S. conduct on the international scene and of its militaristic course.

"Bluntly speaking, certain Western politicians were after very definite aims—to blast the possibilities for balancing international relations, to sow new seeds of distrust and suspicion toward the socialist countries. . . ."

In Warner Borden's flat he rose to refill Emmaline's glass, but she put her hand over it. "No more, please," she said. "I've got to get back to my own place, but thanks for letting me watch your TV."

"Don't thank me," he smiled, holding the wine bottle ready in case she changed her mind. "Thank old Gorbachev. He's sure putting on a show."

Emmaline hesitated. "Actually, I think he's got a point—"

"About what? About what the papers said in America? Well, hell, honey, if the Russians had just come out with some real facts, all that speculation wouldn't have happened."

"I suppose so," Emmaline said thoughtfully. "Anyway, he did mention the American doctors."

"Sure. One line. And now—listen, he's getting started on disarmament. You don't want to miss this—and, look, there's just another drop in the bottle; we might as well finish it off."

"The accident at Chernobyl," Gorbachev was saying, "showed again what an abyss will open if nuclear war befalls mankind. For inherent in the stockpiled nuclear arsenals are thousands upon thousands of disasters far more horrible than the Chernobyl one. . . .

"The nuclear age forcefully demands a new approach to international relations, the pooling of efforts of states with different social systems for the sake of putting an end to the disastrous arms race, and of a radical improvement of the world political climate. . . ."

*   *   *

But in Simyon Smin's room at Moscow's Hospital No. 6, no one heard the last words of the whispered voice from the television set, though Vassili Smin was gazing at it, his eyes brimming with tears. His brother Nikolai was leaning against the window with his forehead pressed against the glass, his eyes closed. His mother was looking into space with an expression that was neither angry nor sad; it was the baffled look of a woman who would not have believed things could have gone so badly for her.

On the other side of the room his grandmother was closing his father's eyes. The plastic drapes had been pushed back. The blood-exchange machine sat silent, its lights dark. Simyon Smin looked as though he were sleeping, his mouth open, the broad, friendly face a mask.

"What did he say before, that nine persons were already dead from Chernobyl?" Aftasia asked. "Now it is ten."

CHAPTER 33

In the town of Mtino, not far from Moscow, there is a quiet cemetery. Two hundred yards from its gate a special plot has been set aside. It has only a few graves in it now, though there is space for a good many more. It is called the "Heroes' Plot." All the people buried there have one thing in common. They died in the same place—Hospital No. 6—and they came from the same place—the Chernobyl Nuclear Power Station.

There weren't many mourners at the funeral of Simyon Mikhailovitch Smin; altogether there were ten. His two sons, his wife, his mother. Two doctors from Hospital No. 6. His faithful "Comrade Plumber." The Second Secretary of the Communist Party of Pripyat, glad to take a day off from the other reasons he was in Moscow to pronounce the obsequies for Smin. And two others. It was the two others who astonished the doctors and probably the Second Secretary as well, because they arrived in a Zil and a whisper went around the group with their names: Comrades F. V. Mishko and A. P. Milaktiev. Members of the Central Committee. Only old Aftasia Smin had the temerity to walk up to them and greet them by name, though after that they spoke or at least nodded to everyone else, affably enough.

Said Aftasia to the older of the two, "Thank you for coming, Fedor Vassilievitch."

"Ah, but why not?" protested the minister. "Your son was a good man. He died a hero. There is no doubt in my mind that when the investigative commission finishes its work he will be found to have performed in an exemplary way. Also," he added, "there are not so many Old Bolsheviks left that I would not pay honor when a member of one's family dies."

Aftasia disregarded that. "Are you so sure about the results of the commission?" she demanded.

Milaktiev answered for him. "No one can predict the findings until all the evidence is in. Human error is always possible. But I myself have seen most of the depositions. Your son cut corners, Aftasia Israelovna, but always for the good of his plant, never for private gain."

"I agree," Mishko added, nodding. "And you see for yourself: he is being given an honorable funeral."

"But a small one," said Aftasia shrewdly. Then she relented. "It was good of you both to come, in any case. Let me introduce you to his widow and his sons."

Milaktiev cleared his throat, glancing around. They were out of earshot of the others, but he seemed hesitant to speak. "Aftasia Israelovna, may I say that you look extremely well? And yet we have heard so very little of you for many years. One had assumed you must be quite ill, or retired to a home for the aged—"

"Or dead? Yes, it's true. I have lived very quietly for a long time. Why not? I'm an old woman; I have nothing to say."

"I disagree," said Mishko. "I think you have much to tell us all, and this is a time when Old Bolsheviks in particular should be heard."

Aftasia looked up at him appraisingly. Mishko was not a tall man, but he towered over her. "Why this time in particular?"

"It is a time of great change. You know that. I see that your mind is clear, isn't it?"

She said, "There have been a lot of clear thoughts in my mind over the years. I was not the only one to think clearly. A great many of my old comrades had clear thoughts, and spoke them out loud. Most of them have been dead for fifty years now for that reason."

"You are speaking of the excesses of the Stalin years," Mishko said, nodding. "This is a different time."

"Oh? Is Lefortovo empty now? Well," she said, relenting, "yes, the time is different, but old habits are hard to lose. I had a son to raise, Fedor Vassilievitch. He didn't have a father and I couldn't afford to let him lose a mother as well. I kept my mouth shut. I had no desire to sit in a camp for thirty years while Simyon had no one to care for him. I learned to be still."

"We all learned that, for the same reasons."

"And yet," she said, smiling, "I suppose I need not fear thirty years in the camps now, isn't that so? Fedor Vassilievitch, we are not strangers. Your father asked me to marry him in 1944, and if he had not been arrested, I would have looked on you as my own son."

"I wish that had happened," Mishko said sincerely.

"Then why don't you speak frankly to me? Is there something you want me to do?"

Milaktiev said uncomfortably, "Perhaps this is not the place to discuss such matters—"

"Oh, spit it out, man," she said crossly. "Didn't you call me an Old Bolshevik? Well, I am. I'm not a delicate flower who can think of nothing but sorrow at her only son's funeral; my son would not want that of me. Why should you?"

"Well," said Mishko, glancing at his partner, "the fact is, a few of us have certain proposals to make. . . ."

Sheranchuk watched idly as the old woman talked to the men from the Central Committee, impatient for the ceremony to begin. A woman in a smart beige suit walked up to him. "I am Dr. Akhsmentova," she announced. "Blood pathologist for Hospital Number Six. I was in charge of typing blood for you and all of the other patients."

"Thank you for a good job," Sheranchuk said politely. "I didn't recognize you out of your whites."

"But I recognized you, Comrade Sheranchuk. I made it my business to know who you were so that I might speak to you before you were discharged. Tomorrow, isn't it?"

"I hope so," said Sheranchuk, startled. "Speak to me about what?"

The woman pursed her lips. "I had hoped your wife would inform you of this matter, but I believe she has gone."

"She was sent back to her regular duty, yes. What matter are you talking about?"

"You see," the doctor said reflectively, "I take a large view of my work. It is not enough to be technically correct, although I am most careful about that. As I view my duties, they oblige me to call any unusual facts I learn to the attention of the parties concerned."

Sheranchuk was getting annoyed at the prissy woman. "And what facts have you learned about me?" he asked, his tone more ironic than he intended; but she regarded that.

"Not just about you, Comrade Sheranchuk. About your wife and the boy, Boris Sheranchuk."

"Yes?" he prompted, definitely irritated.

"You are blood type O, Comrade Sheranchuk. Your wife is type A. The boy is type AB." She folded her hands at her waist as she finished, regarding him in silence.

"Really, Dr. Akhsmentova," he protested, "I know nothing about such matters. If it is dangerous to my son—"

But she was shaking her head. "Not dangerous to his health, no, but that is not the point. I have had experience testifying in such matters. In paternity suits, for example, where the blood types can shed light on the father of an illegitimate child. And I assure you, Comrade Sheranchuk, if your wife had brought a paternity suit against you when the boy was born, you would not have lost."

The funeral oration was long enough to be decent, short enough so that the Second Secretary would not find he had made some embarrassingly overenthusiastic remark at a later date: ten minutes. Then the casket was lowered into the ground. The mourners took turns, one by one, in tossing clods of earth in after it. Then, of course, it was time for them all to go away and leave the professional gravediggers, leaning impatiently on their shovels just out of earshot, to get on with their work.

But no one wanted to leave until the two men from the Central Committee made a move to go, and they seemed in no hurry. They moved around the small group, shaking each hand, kissing every member of the family, exchanging polite words with all. Did these high Party officials have nothing better to do with their time? Sheranchuk wondered, sick with shame and rage. Of course it was not those two men that he was shouting at silently inside his head, and when they took his hand, he managed to respond to their questions about his health, and to be surprised that they actually seemed to know his name. "But of course, Comrade Sheranchuk," smiled Mishko, the older and more dapper of the two. "We have read your statement, and those of others concerning the accident. There is nothing but praise for your work and your courage!"

"It is too early to speak of decorations," Milaktiev added warmly, "but if any has earned one, you surely have."

Sheranchuk succeeded in thanking them. He stared after them in surprise until, fully half an hour after the service was over, Minister Mishko glanced at his watch and said, quite clearly enough to be heard, "Oh, but it is nearly three o'clock, and I have an appointment at Gosplan at three-thirty."

"And I must get back to my office," Milaktiev added. "Can we give any of you a lift? No? Then let me drop you at your office, Fedor Vassilievitch. And let us hope we see you all again, in happier times!"

Happier times had not yet arrived when Milaktiev arrived at his office. He nodded civilly to his secretary, pushed open the door of his private room, and paused, looking at his desk.

There was an envelope on it, a large square one, marked in a bold hand: *For the personal attention of A. P. Milaktiev ONLY.*

Milaktiev left the door open as he moved to the desk and ripped the envelope open, struggling with the triple seals. Then he glanced at the document inside. It had no letter attached. There was no name on it, or on the envelope. There was nothing to say where it had come from, but what it said was very clear. It proposed what it was pleased to call "A Movement for Socialist Renewal" and, although it was couched in formal and impassive language, what it said was astonishing. Each phrase and sentence leaped off the paper:

> Our country has reached a limit beyond which lies an insurmountable lag. . . . The USSR is now on the path to becoming one of the underdeveloped nations. . . . Economic and political reforms must be combined. . . . We require different competing political organizations, with control by the people in free elections. . . . We must

comply with such fundamental constitutional principles of the socialist state as the freedom of speech, press, and assembly, of personal immunity, private correspondence and telephone calls, and the freedom to join organizations. . . .

It was all there, every word.

Milaktiev read it all through, all seventeen closely typed pages, with his secretary glancing curiously at him through the open door. Then he raised his voice in a roar: "Margetta Ivanovna! What is this thing? Where did it come from?"

She hurried nervously to his side. "It was delivered by hand. A soldier; he said it was urgent, and for your eyes only—"

"And did you get his name? Did you make him show identification? What if it had been a bomb, or something infected with a deadly disease? Would you still have let any criminal walk in here and leave anything he chose on my desk while I am absent and you are charged with protecting it?"

He had her weeping in the next minute, not so much from the violence of his attack but because it was such a terrible contrast with his usual gentle demeanor. Well, he thought, he could make it up to her another time. But it was important that she should be aware that he was wholly astonished, even indignant, that this revolutionary document should have appeared from nowhere . . . for when people began trying to find out who had sent it, the last place they would look was among those who had received a copy from a stranger.

CHAPTER 34

Around the ruin of Reactor No. 4 of the Chernobyl Nuclear Power Station, concrete shields are being poured. The demon still rages inside, but the worst of the radiation from the core itself is contained. Cranes with lead-shielded cabs lift slabs of contaminated debris into trucks with lead-lined drivers' seats to be hauled away. In the other buildings, on the grounds, in the town of Pripyat, the surfaces that have not been paved over or covered with fresh earth have at least been washed down, sprayed, or painted with a latex compound. Even the farms within the thirty-kilometer radius of the evacuation zone have been attended to. The farmers are begging to be let back in to tend their crops, for that area north of Kiev is the breadbasket of the USSR. Its winters are milder than Moscow's, and the soil is black or gray, the richest in the world. Moscow grows cabbages and rye. Around Chernobyl they grow wheat and corn, and Private Sergei Konov knows that the Soviet Union needs that food.

So when he was ordered to accompany one of the white-suited technicians through the grain fields, Konov followed without complaint. The sun was hot. The red-and-white stripes of the Chernobyl exhaust tower were visible on the horizon—at least there was no smoke coming from the plant anymore.

The assignment in the grain fields was hard work. Harder,

almost, than plugging drainage sewers with quick-drying cement or shoveling rubble, for Konov carried two oil tanks on his back so he wouldn't have to waste time going back for more, and they were heavy. When the technician's detectors sniffed a patch of radioactivity among the tall stalks, Konov would step up and spray it thoroughly, destroying that square meter of ripening crop so that the rest might grow unharmed—though who was going to eat that grain when it ripened Konov could not guess.

At noon the technician insisted on taking a break—his decision, not Konov's—and Konov asked him what would happen to the wheat. The man pulled the gauze mask away from his mouth to answer. "It's all a matter of radiation levels," he said. "After the harvest they'll measure it. If it's above the danger level, they'll just put it in storage until it cools down." He pulled out a pack of cigarettes and offered one to Konov, but Konov shook his head. It was all very well for the technician to remove his mask if he chose to, but Konov had not forgotten the standing orders.

And that night, back in the barracks, when he took off the gauze mask over his mouth and nose and handed it to the barracks orderly for testing, he heard faint but ominous *wheepwheepwheep* sounds from the snub-nosed radiation detector. "Nothing serious," said the orderly, yawning as he turned off the wand; but there had been nastiness in the dust after all, and Konov was glad he, at least, had kept the mask on.

Dinner was the usual—thin soup, salt fish, potatoes—but to go along with it there was a rumor: after thirty days the troops were to be relieved, for then the summer intake would provide new Army recruits in plenty.

"Good," said his friend Miklas, dipping his bread in his tea. "Let the rookies fry their balls."

Konov ate silently for a moment. Then he said offhandedly, "I think I would like to stay on here."

Miklas could not conceal his astonishment. "What are you saying? What is it, Seryozha?" he demanded. "There are no girls here to make you want to stay!"

"There are no girls back in Mtintsin, either, just pigs," said Konov, calmly folding his second slice of black bread in half to bite into it.

"The pigs in Mtintsin at least speak Russian. There's not even anything to drink here!"

"And if you go on drinking what they sell you in Mtintsin you will be blind."

"It is better to be blind than to have your balls fried," Miklas said seriously. "How do you know you won't be the next one to find a hero's grave?"

To that Konov had no good answer. As a matter of fact, he had given that prospect a lot of thought. His conclusion was that, for once, the Army orders made a good deal of sense. Therefore Konov meticulously followed the instructions about what he touched and breathed and did. He had never been cleaner. He showered at least six times a day. When off duty he stayed in the old stable with the windows nailed down that was their barracks.

He washed his clothes—his own uniform, not the coveralls that were issued every time he went outside—every time he wore it. Outside, he never removed cap, mask, or gloves, no matter how sweaty. And every other day he would line up at the medic-point at the end of the barracks to let them draw blood, and every time when the report came back it said that his blood still contained plenty of those little white things that the radiation killed first.

In three and a half weeks Konov had worked at a dozen different tasks in the cleanup of the Chernobyl explosion. Scariest was to run out onto the roof of the dead power plant itself for lumps of graphite, where you could feel the heat from the sun on one side of you and that other heat still smoldering out of the great graphite and uranium core warming the other. He had done that three times now, but that particular job was over.

The work was not all scary. Some was simple drudgery, sandbagging the dikes around the plant's cooling pond, diverting the flow of the little streams that led to the Pripyat River, standing guard in the lonely nights at the thirty-kilometer perimeter of the zone, between the hastily erected watchtowers, to keep the foolish ones from trying to return to their lost homes.

What Konov liked best was to be assigned some kind of work in the deserted town of Pripyat. Any kind of work, from spraying liquid rubber on the abandoned cars to shoveling debris into trucks to be hauled away. He had come to think of Pripyat as his town. He knew it as well as he knew the Leninskaya Prospekt by his home in Moscow, from the little children's amusement park (where were those children now? And would anyone ever get into the little red and white cars of that Ferris wheel again?) to the churned-up earth along the main boulevard, where rosebeds and greensward alike had been bulldozed up and carried away.

He even liked the long nights of guard duty in the town, carrying his rifle over his shoulder against looters, with the sorrowful baying of abandoned dogs coming from nowhere under the full moon. But whatever the job was, Konov did it all, and never complained, and arose bright and eager the next morning to do more.

His lieutenant hardly recognized the new Private Sergei Konov anymore.

The next morning was piss-in-a-bottle day. Before breakfast every soldier in the barracks was lined up to urinate into a specimen jar, one by one. The radiation technician would gingerly sniff at that with his radiation detector; but, so far, none of those wheeping little poison bullets seemed to have got into Konov's body. So, Konov thought, there really was no reason not to stay on if he chose. And he did choose, though he didn't like the idea of sharing the zone with a thousand raw recruits who would not understand what it had been like in the first frightening days after the explosion.

He wondered soberly what would happen with new officers on the scene. The present crew had become quite easygoing; Senior Lieutenant Osipev had even stopped ordering him to get his hair cut. But new ones from outside might change all that around, and it could be as bad as the training base again.

Still, he knew he wanted to spend the remaining—what was it, just thirty days? Less than a thousand hours?—of his enlistment right where he was: in the evacuated zone, helping to clean up Chernobyl's deadly mess.

When Konov had picked up his breakfast that morning and taken it to a corner of the barracks, the lieutenant came over and sat down next to him, lighting a cigarette. "Go on eating, Konov," he ordered. "This is not official. Just a little chat, if you don't mind."

Konov said, "As you wish, Senior Lieutenant Osipev."

"I would like to ask you a question, Konov. Why did you volunteer to stay on here?"

"To serve the Soviet Union, Senior Lieutenant Osipev."

"Yes, of course," grunted the lieutenant, "but you have not always been so eager. You have puzzled me for a long time, Konov. You're not an asshole. You have some education, after all. You could have become a lance corporal. You could even have gone to a training battalion to become a sergeant. Why were you such a fuckup?"

Konov looked at him consideringly and decided to tell the truth. "The fact is, all I wanted was to get out of the Army as fast as possible, Senior Lieutenant Osipev."

"Um," said the lieutenant, who had expected no better answer. "But actually, Konov, being in the Army is not altogether bad. As a private, of course, it is one thing. But you could consider applying for one of the service academies—even the Frunze, which is where I myself trained. As an officer the life is entirely different."

"I am grateful for the lieutenant's consideration," Konov said politely, finishing the dark bread and porridge, and saving the one slice of white to savor with his tea.

"The Soviet Union needs good officers, Konov," the lieutenant pointed out. "The Great Patriotic War was not the last that will ever happen, you know." Konov nodded courteously, and the lieutenant went on. "Our country was in great danger then. Great battles were fought in this area. Hitler's Germans, in 1941, came through right here, and these marshes of the Pripyat were our best defense."

"But still they broke through?" Konov offered.

"Not through the marshes. Tanks could not do that, then. There was heavy fighting in Chernigov, a hundred kilometers east of us, and around Kiev, down to the south. It was a bad time, Konov, but where did the Fascists get to in the end? They got as far as Stalingrad, and there they learned how to retreat. Why? Because of the brave men and officers of the Soviet Army. You could be one of them. No," he said, getting up, "don't give me an answer now. I only want you to think about it."

When the lieutenant was gone Miklas came over from his own bunk. "What'd he want?" he demanded.

"To invite me to tea at the officers' club, of course," said

Konov. "What did you think? Now let's get to work. We're going back to Pripyat today."

When the armored car had let them out by the empty radio factory, Konov ordered, "Hand it over."

Miklas made a sarcastic show of reaching into his white coveralls and taking out the sack of leftover food Konov had reclaimed from the kitchen garbage. "Your dinner, your honor," he said obsequiously. "May your honor dine well."

Konov disregarded him. He took out his own sack, heavy with crusts of moldy bread and the pork bones from the officers' evening meal and looked about for a likely place to leave them for Pripyat's abandoned pets. "They're all going to die anyway, you know," Miklas offered.

"Sooner or later so are we," Konov said cheerfully. "I will put it off a little longer for the dogs if I can."

Miklas sighed. "Are you still determined to volunteer to stay here?"

"Why not?"

"A thousand reasons why not! If you must volunteer, why not to work on one of the new villages they are building for the farmers? At least there would be people there."

"And work fourteen hours a day to dig foundations for their houses? Not me," Konov said, though that was not the real reason he had rejected the idea.

"But at least from that you may come away without two heads," Miklas grumbled.

"For you," Konov said, "another head would be a very good thing. Pick your building."

"Oh, I think the factory needs to be guarded most closely," Miklas said at once.

"Then do it," said Konov, knowing that what Miklas most wanted to guard there was the dozen cases of canned kvass and Coca-Cola the first soldiers had found in the radio factory's canteen. Now they were more than half consumed. He debated warning Miklas against taking off his mask to drink a Coke, but he knew that would be no use. Anyway, he consoled himself, the inside of the factory was fairly clean.

Almost a quarter of Pripyat was fairly clean, in fact—well, *nearly* fairly clean. On the best of its blocks there were pockets of intractable radiation—soaked into the paving or trapped in the cracks of a building—that would take a demolition crew to remove. You marked those with the warning signs, and you hurried past them. But there were whole buildings where the radiation level was barely above background.

On the surface, though, the town of Pripyat had hardly changed in three weeks. It was like some lifeless geological formation. No doubt it would weather and perhaps erode away, but only over long periods of time. Nothing else would change. Doors that had been left open remained open. The skis and baby carriages and bicycles on the balconies stayed untouched. Cars that had been left behind by their owners, pulled up under a tree with their canvas coverings protecting them against the elements, were still unmoved. The winds and the rains had wrapped some of the washing around the lines so that the garments no longer danced in the breeze; some garments had danced a bit too passionately and torn themselves free, and now lay crumpled in a gutter or draped across a dead rosebush. Konov stopped at a corner, hesitated, then entered the six-story apartment building on the right.

These were good new buildings, put up for the workers at the Chernobyl plant, and although they had been erected in haste, someone had seen that the concrete was solid and the fittings worked. Of course, there was no power in these buildings now. The little elevator was there on the ground floor, its door open, but Konov hardly glanced at it as he began to mount the stairs.

Most of the tenants of the building had locked their apartments carefully when they left. On the top floor, Konov tried each door with a firm twist and a solid shake, but all four were locked. That was all he was required to do, but he took a moment to put his ear against each door in turn. It was not looters that he expected to find, but there was always the chance that some family had, in its panic and rush, forgotten a cat, a dog, a bird.

There was nothing to be heard. Konov descended a flight of stairs and repeated the process on the fifth floor. Again nothing, but on the fourth floor a family named Dazhchenko—the name was on a card by the door—had been so hopelessly rushed or so foolishly trusting that they had left the door to their flat unlocked. Konov opened it and entered the gloomy hallway for a look around.

He wrinkled his nose in disgust at the air inside. There were some very bad smells in this place. His business, however, was not to smell but to look, and he began his inspection. Just on the left of the entrance was a child's room—no, actually a room for two children, Konov corrected himself; there were clothes for two young girls hanging against the wall. One had perhaps been a four-year-old or thereabouts. The other possessed the skirt and blouse of a teenage Young Pioneer. The next room belonged to the parents, a double bed nearly filling it; it was still unmade, and the drawers of the chest were pulled open, the contents in disarray. There was a picture of Lenin on the wall, but (Konov smiled) there was also an ikon. Both bedrooms were bright in the sun from the windows, but the unpleasant smells remained.

If it had been his own apartment, Konov thought, he would have opened all the windows at once; but it was not, and besides, what was the use? Whatever smelled foul would go on doing so, and an open window would let the rain in next time the weather changed.

And in this place at this time it was not only rot and mildew that the rain might bring.

The stink of decay came from the kitchen. The refrigerator door had been left open. Whatever was inside had rotted thoroughly. Gasping, Konov closed the door; it was all he could do, though he wondered if the gases of decomposition from whatever was in there—a stew? a chicken?—might not blow the door off as they swelled.

It was, he confirmed for himself, a very nice apartment. There were two little doors at the end of the hall; one opened on a sink and tub, the other on a commode; and someone had carefully cut out pictures from some foreign magazine—the language appeared to be Swedish or German to Konov—and pinned them to the back of the door. The pictures were of Lady Di and her husband, the Prince of Wales; so this was where the little girls sat for their private business, gazing romantically at the beautiful royal pair. In the dining room there was a small but quite new television set; it was on the floor, its electrical cords wrapped neatly around it—the father had tried to take it with them, no doubt, and discovered at the last minute that it was impossible to add one more thing.

But there was neither looter nor abandoned pet to be

found in this place, and Konov had other floors to investigate. He fiddled with the lock on the apartment door until he got it to snap in the locked position behind him; so at least when the family returned they would find their home as they left it. Smells and all.

If ever the family returned.

When Konov started on his second building he paused on the step, looking about and listening. It was a warm day, but not a silent one. He could hear bulldozers in some other part of the town, scraping away at the tainted soil so that the worst of it could be hauled away and buried. A nearer rumble was one of the bright orange water trucks, methodically washing down the empty streets of their poisoned dust one more time. (But who would wash the poisons from the roofs, the walls, the windowsills?) Konov started to call to Miklas, who was no doubt smoking a cigarette with his hood off as he loitered in the factory building across the way . . . and then he stopped, listening.

Someone had very quietly closed a door somewhere not far above him.

If it was a looter, it was a very small one. Konov stood out of sight behind the elevator door, listening to tiny, secretive footsteps and the occasional rustle of clothing and panting breath as the person came down. When the intruder was on the last flight of stairs, he stepped out and confronted the person.

"In God's name," he said, staring in astonishment. "What are you doing here, Grandmother?"

The woman was at least eighty, and even tinier than he could have guessed. Her hair, slate and silver, was pulled into a bun, so tightly (and the hair so sparse) that her scalp showed on the top of her head. She wore a grandmother's black blouse and long black skirt, and she carried a gardening trowel in her hand.

She thrust it suddenly toward him, threateningly, almost as though it were a weapon. "Where else should I be, stupid?" she shrilled. "It is my home!"

"Oh, Grandmother," Konov said reproachfully. "Weren't you evacuated with the rest? How did you get back? Don't you know that it is dangerous to be here?"

She asked reasonably, "How can my own home be a danger to me? My name is Irina Barisovna, and I live here. Go away, please. I am very well here; simply leave me alone."

But, of course, Konov could not leave her alone, and, of course, after a spirited ten minutes of argument the old woman accepted the inevitable. Her only other options were either to kill Konov and hide his body, which would only cause a search, or to have him whistle for the rest of the detachment to carry her off. "But please, dear young man," she bargained. "One favor? A small one? And then, I promise, I will go with you. . . ."

When he had delivered her, with her little bag of treasures, to the control post, she kissed his gloved hand. Grinning, Konov went back to his officer to report. Lieutenant Osipev listened with resignation. "These old people!" he sighed. "What can one do with them? They have been told they risk death here. They know that this is true, in one part of their heads they know it—but they come back. What was that she was carrying?"

Konov hesitated, then admitted. "Some things from her apartment. And, yes, also some other things: a religious medal, her wedding ring, a few small things; she had buried them in the ground and I helped her dig them up."

The officer shrugged. Lieutenant Osipev was a reasonably compassionate man but, after all, it was not his concern. "Your pen, then, Konov," he ordered, and when Konov handed over the dosimeter pen, the officer glanced casually through it, then stiffened. "What have you done, you fool?" he demanded. "Get away from me! Have yourself scanned at once!" And twenty minutes later, after the special radiation crew with their counters had run the snouts of the instruments over his entire naked body, Konov stared at the grime under his fingernails.

It did not seem that he would be going back to the 416th Guards Rifle Division barracks in Mtintsin very quickly, after all. He had heard the chatter of the counter shrill loudly as it reached the fingers of his right hand, the hand from which he had taken off the glove in order to help the old babushka scrabble in the ground under the rainspout for her precious oilskin packet of valuables. And when the medical officer looked at Konov's hand, he swore angrily. "If you wouldn't cut your hair, at least you should have cut your fingernails! How long has that stuff been under there?"

"I don't know. An hour, maybe."

"An hour! Well," the medical officer said sorrowfully, reaching for his bag, "those nails will have to come off, at least. If we're lucky, perhaps we can save the fingers."

CHAPTER 35

MONDAY, MAY 19

The Black Sea coast is the Florida of the Soviet Union. It is the only place where the water is warm and the beaches are sunny. The coast is lined with holiday hotels, sanitoria, youth camps, and campgrounds, and they are all filled all the time. Foreign tourists spend hard currency there, but most of the vacationers are Soviet citizens who have deserved so well of their country or their factory that they are given a week or two of luxury. Swimming, snorkeling, windsurfing, fishing, mountain-climbing, strolling, sunbathing—there is so much to do along the Black Sea! And each community has its own special attractions—at Yalta, the place where Stalin, Roosevelt, and Churchill met in World War II, the Nikitsky Botanical Garden, the old house where Chekhov lived and wrote nearly a century ago. Near Sochi, the mineral springs, and the caves at Novy Afon. Sukhumi, Matsesta, Simferopol, and a hundred other communities vie for the tourist, and no one is disappointed.

As Sheranchuk stepped off the IL-86, he saw his wife waiting for him in a knot of people just outside the door of the terminal. He kissed her tenderly, exclaiming, "What do you think of that? A real jumbo jet, three hundred and fifty passengers! When Boris comes back, let us make sure he gets to ride in one like it, shall we?"

"Of course," Tamara said, looking at him anxiously. He returned the look. His wife had been at the resort only a week before him, but already she looked—well, *tropical*. She was tanned. She wore dark glasses, with a gay green and white scarf over her head, and white shorts and a white blouse. She seemed at least ten years younger, except for the strained expression on her face. "Will you have to go back to the hospital?" she asked.

"Never!" he proclaimed. "Complete release! I have even been given permission to go back to work at Chernobyl after our little vacation here—it is all in the medical records, and you can read them for yourself. But not now. Now I want to enjoy this recreational paradise of the workers' state!"

He found his bag quickly and slung it over his shoulder. "How wonderfully hot it is," he exclaimed as they went out of the terminal into the Black Sea sun. "You made a good choice, my dear."

"Are you sure?" she asked anxiously. "It is so hard to know where to go. If we had gone to Sochi instead, there would be the Agur waterfalls and the caves—"

"But isn't it nice," he grinned, "to be so lucky as to be able to choose what we want? And anyway, here we are nearer to Boris at his camp, so tomorrow we will drive over and see him. But today is ours, my dear Tamara, because we have a great deal to celebrate."

Tamara surrendered. "As you wish, my dear," she murmured. "Only, please, you are just out of the hospital. Don't tire yourself."

It could have been, Sheranchuk said to himself, that she was worried about his health. That would account for the slight reserve, the occasional abstraction, the hesitant way she spoke now and then.

It could also be that what was on Tamara's mind was the same thing that was on Sheranchuk's own, specifically, what Dr. Akhsmentova had told him at Smin's funeral.

Although he had had four days to think about it, he had spoken to no one about it, not even his wife—especially not his wife. But for four days he had thought about very little else. He rehearsed every moment of his married life. In particular he cudgeled his memory to try to recall each incident and detail around the time his wife became pregnant. Yes, it was true, he recalled dismally, they had gone through something of a stormy period in their marriage at that time. They had had a number of quarrels. Foolish ones! He had been astonished to learn that she was, of all things, *jealous.*

And foolishly he had tried to make a joke of it. "Oh, yes," he cried with savage humor, "all the girls are after me. It is my steel teeth that make them wild with desire!"

She had said icily, "I don't care what girls are after you. I care that you are interested in the girls."

"But it isn't true!" he groaned. "You're simply being stupid." And that night she had slept in a chair on the other side of their single room, while Sheranchuk tossed sleepless and alone in their bed.

The difficulty was that her jealousy had not been entirely stupid.

There was a woman who interested him. She worked in the personnel department of the peat-fired power plant near Moscow. Sheranchuk had never touched the woman, but he admitted to himself that he had had feelings about her. There was worse than that. Since the two of them worked in the same power plant, they had had their vacations at the same time, in the same place. Nothing had happened—mostly, Sheranchuk conceded, because she had at once taken up with another man—but he had been prepared for an explosion when he came back.

To his surprise, his wife had welcomed him back. In fact, she had been exceptionally loving—it was almost another honeymoon.

The question in his mind now was, what had she been doing while he was away? And with whom?

They spent the afternoon on the beach. Even in May the water was still a little cool for Sheranchuk's taste, but he gladly lay in the warm sun that filtered through the palm leaves overhead, Tamara solicitously replenishing the sunburn cream on his back. When they went back to the airy, clean room in their sanitorium, they made love in the daylight, hardly even speaking as they fell into each other's arms. Not speaking at all of anything important, in fact, because afterward, when Tamara got a serious look on her face and cleared her throat as though about to say some weighty thing, Sheranchuk jumped up and proclaimed that he was starving for dinner.

It was a good dinner, at a seaside restaurant. They took their time over it, talking about Smin's funeral, and their plans for their son, and what was likely to happen at the Chernobyl plant. It was quite late by the time they got back to the sanitorium. "Come, let's enjoy the air a bit," said Sheranchuk, and they found a rocker for two in a quiet part of the broad veranda, looking down a hill and out over the distant water. Sheranchuk had his arm around his wife.

"You are very quiet, my dear," he said at last.

"I've been thinking," she said slowly, hesitantly, and in the dim light he could see that she had that look of being about to speak seriously on her face again.

"If," he said quickly, "what you are thinking about is the future, let me tell you some good news. There is a new personnel man at the plant, his name is Ivanov, and he stopped at the hospital before I was discharged. He promises a job will be waiting for me, actually with more money. He also talked about what sort of place we will have to live in for the next six months or year."

She turned to look at him with a spark of interest. "In Pripyat?"

"Not in Pripyat, no. No one is going to live in Pripyat for a long time. But in the town of Chernobyl. You remember it's beyond the thirty-kilometer perimeter and it is now quite safe. And then there will be a new town that will be built, with good construction. It will be called 'Green Peninsula,' after the place where it is being built. We will have a flat even nicer than our old one, once the new buildings are finished. Ivanov has promised we will be at the top of the list for new housing, and the foundations have already been begun."

He waited for a response. "That sounds good," she said at last, her voice colorless.

"Of course," he said, "without Smin to keep an eye on things, who knows how soon the walls will crack and the doors will come off their hinges? But there is also good news. Ivanov says they will put you on the medical staff at the plant."

"Oh, wonderful," she said, her face lighting up for the first time. But then she withdrew again.

"Are you cold?" Sheranchuk asked solicitously. "Maybe

we should go in and get a good night's sleep. And tomorrow morning we will go to see our son."

She was silent for a long moment. Then she turned to him and said, her voice rapid and almost harsh, "There is something we must discuss. Did Dr. Akhsmentova speak to you?"

He was quite calm. "The bloodsucker? Oh, yes. She was full of some nonsense about blood types; I could not understand such things."

"Leonid," she said sadly, "I don't believe that. You are quite capable of understanding what that bitch had to say."

Sheranchuk shook his head. "What I understand, my dear, is much more important than any blood tests. I understand that we have a fine son who has always been mine. Have you forgotten? I rubbed your back for you when he was still inside your belly, and I walked through every store in Moscow to find rubber pants to put on him, and I fed him and burped him and changed him—not as often as I might have," he admitted justly. "Certainly not as often as you. But often enough to know who is my own dear child, born from my very dear wife. So what is there to say about blood types? And now, my dear, since it seems these mosquitoes are also interested in sampling my blood, perhaps we should go inside and to bed."

CHAPTER 36

The KGB are always thorough, but sometimes they are also meticulously correct. When they are merely thorough in the task of, say, searching a flat, a tornado would be more welcome. Every closet and box and drawer is opened, the contents ransacked and thrown on the floor; pillows and mattresses are ripped open, canisters of flour and salt poured out, the seams of curtains and sheets torn apart; and what the KGB leaves with is always as much as they can carry of papers, books, and whatever else they deem important. When they are being meticulously correct, the process takes longer but leaves less havoc. Then they probe with long needles instead of ripping things apart, they have a city militiaman standing by as required by law, they generally replace what they have taken out of drawers and boxes—well, of course, sometimes not very neatly, perhaps. Sometimes they even present an official search warrant.

They had presented a warrant to Selena, Aftasia, and Vassili Smin before they began on the little flat on the outskirts of Kiev, and the city militiaman, abashed in the presence of so old an Old Bolshevik, was glad to accept a cup of tea while the searchers did their work. But there were so many of them! There were six industrious workers in each room, one of them present only to take notes, one in authority to point to this place or that for special care, the other four to do the actual work, quietly and with great skill.

All the while the Smin family, or what remained of it, chatted politely with the militiaman. "And there is the matter of our water supply," said Selena Smin, rising courteously so that one of the kitchen detail could turn her chair over to examine the bottom of the seat. "One hears that we will soon be getting it from the Desna River as well as from the new wells." For radionuclides had been found not only in the Pripyat River but in the underground aquifers all around Chernobyl, even at Bragin, seventy kilometers to the north.

"They've capped seven thousand old wells," the militiaman confirmed, and then, glancing at the searchers, "or so people say, at least."

"Yes, that is true," Selena nodded, taking her seat again. "Mother Aftasia? When you were at the market this morning, were they taking care about the vegetables from the farms?"

"Oh, indeed they were," said Aftasia enthusiastically. "They were running those what-you-call-them things over all the tomatoes and fruit, and if there was the slightest peep out of the machines, then, snap, into the disposal bin, and no certificate to sell that batch! Our Socialist state is taking excellent care of its citizens! More tea, then?" she asked the uneasy militiaman. He shook his head, frowning. "Ah, but the worst thing," she went on, "was the people. Can you imagine? You could see them walking from stall to stall, looking for farmers with Oriental faces before they would buy. From the eastern provinces! Hoping, no doubt, to get cabbages grown two thousand kilometers away! But I bought only from honest Ukrainians," she finished virtuously.

"Not that our Tatar and Kalmuk brothers aren't honest, of course," Selena supplemented.

"Of course not," Aftasia agreed, and then smiled blandly at the man in charge. "What, are you finished already? And we were having such a nice chat with the citizen militiaman here."

The KGB man eyed her thoughtfully. For one moment it almost seemed he would return her smile. Then he shook his head. "We are removing certain books and documents for study," he said. "Sign the receipt, please."

"If it is a receipt, then you should sign it and give me a copy," Aftasia Smin pointed out. "However, let me see. These letters? Yes, of course you may have them; they are only from my older grandson, who is now back serving his country in Afghanistan. This book? It is written by Solzhenitsyn, yes, but don't you see? It is *One Day in the Life of Ivan Denisovitch,* a quite approved work. Still, perhaps you would enjoy reading it; by all means, take it along." She rummaged through the dozen other books, then pushed them together and spread her hands. "If you need these, then I must not quarrel with the organs of the state. No, don't bother with a receipt; if I can't trust my government, who can I trust? And thank you for your courtesy."

The Chekist folded the paper slowly, regarding her. He was no more than thirty, a pale-haired, plump man with a pleasant face, and very young to be in charge of such a detail. "Comrade Smin," he said, "you are a remarkable woman. A Party member since 1916. Heroine of the October Revolution. And, at your age, so alert and active!"

"Now I am, yes," Aftasia smiled. "Would you believe me, Comrade? Even at my age I feel I have just begun to live."

He nodded, started to speak, then changed his mind. "Perhaps we will meet again," he said, and followed his men out of the flat.

"So," said Aftasia Smin, picking up the cups. "Let's clean up this mess." She headed for her bedroom, but her grandson detained her for a moment.

"Grandmother? Do you think they'll be back?"

Shaking her head, she said decisively, "No. If he had said we would definitely meet again, then perhaps they would return. If he said definitely not, then certainly they would. But he said 'perhaps,' and that means never. Now, help me make this bed!"

On the floor below, the Didchuks were doing their best not to hear the heavy footsteps on the floor above, while they prepared to go to the train station to meet their returning daughter. "But I wonder," Oksana Didchuk said absently, lifting a corner of the curtain to peer out at the street, "if we aren't making a mistake, letting her come home too early. After all, the camp is costing us nothing."

"We discussed that, my dear," her husband said. "She

was simply homesick there, and, really, there's no danger." He glanced at the scrawled chalkmarks on the wall of their room; they had been put there the week before by the radiation-monitor teams, certifying that this apartment was not registering anything above normal background levels.

"I suppose so," Oksana said gloomily. And then, in a lowered tone, "The cars are still there."

Her husband nodded. "Will you pour me some more tea, please?" he said.

"I am worried, though," she said.

She didn't specify the source of her worries, which could have been anything from the behavior of the evacuated couple they had taken in—the husband, now out looking for a new job, seemed a good enough sort, but the wife was still in the room they had given them, sobbing to herself—to what was going on on the floor above. Didchuk chose to interpret it as referring to their daughter. "After all," he said, managing a smile, "if Kiev is safe enough to accept evacuees like our guests, then it really is not sensible that she needs to be evacuated to still some other place."

Oksana sighed. "I suppose we should think about getting your parents back too."

"They're well enough with my sister," Didchuk said. "Let her have a turn."

"But she's expecting a child. And, oh," she said, happy to have thought of a subject to talk about, to drown out the sounds from above, "I read such an interesting article in the magazine *Working Woman*. Did you know that seventy percent of city women, and over ninety percent of those in the rural areas, terminate their first pregnancies with an illegal abortion?"

"An *illegal* abortion? But that's shocking," said Didchuk with indignation, as happy as his wife to have found conversation. "Why illegal, may I ask?"

Oksana Didchuk looked at her husband for a moment. "I suppose you have never been to an abortion clinic."

Didchuk looked startled, almost hostile. "Well, neither have you!"

"No, no," she assured him. "At least, not for myself. But when Irinia Lavcheck became pregnant, she asked me to go with her."

Didchuk didn't scowl, but he came close to it. "The one who is separated from her husband?"

"Her husband beat her, you see. She didn't want to bear his child, she wanted a divorce."

"If she carried his child, he did other things than hit her." He paused, listening to the sounds from the stairwell. There seemed to be faint voices from the landing above. He blinked. "What were we saying? So she had an abortion, and you went along to hold her hand."

"My dear," Oksana said earnestly, "it was not easy for her. It was her child too. Also to get a legal abortion she had to get a special medical permit, so of course everyone knew. And then, when you go to the clinic, do you know what is the first thing you see? A great sign, which says, 'Mother, don't murder your child!' "

"She doesn't have to look at the sign, does she?"

"It is impossible to avoid it. And the operation is, really, quite unpleasant, since often they don't waste anesthetics on a woman who wants an abortion."

Didchuk pursed his lips. "What about the good of our country?" he demanded. "If there are so many abortions, how will the country stay strong for the next generation?"

Oksana didn't answer directly. The only appropriate answer would have been to point out that they themselves had only one child, and if she herself had not needed to abort, the principal reason was that they had been able to get a prescription for the scarce birth-control devices. She was not pleased she had chosen to bring the subject up at all, but she said, "So a silly young girl knows all this, because her older friends tell her. So what can she do? Perhaps she doesn't even want a legal one, because if she is too young, she will have to get her parents' permission. She does what her friends have done. She goes to a midwife."

"And sometimes she dies as a result!"

"Yes, that is true, but—what is it?" she asked, looking at her husband. He had raised his hand, listening.

She heard the sound of footsteps on the stair. Daringly, she opened the door a crack and closed it swiftly. "They are leaving," she whispered.

"Ah," said her husband, sighing. There seemed to be a great many of them and they walked slowly, murmuring among themselves. Oksana peered out of the window cautiously, pulling the curtain just a crack aside.

"They're getting into the cars," she said. "Yes, and now they're all leaving."

"Ah," said her husband again. He blinked at her. "What were we talking about?"

"I don't remember. Well! If we're to go to the train station this afternoon, perhaps I should fix us some lunch!"

While they were getting ready to eat, they could hear the sounds of people moving around on the floor above—lighter footsteps now, and far fewer of them—as the Smins restored order to their flat. The Didchuks didn't discuss it, since there was nothing to be gained by talking about what the organs did, especially while some of them might still be lurking about. Even half an hour later, when there was a knock at the door, both jumped.

But it was only old Aftasia Smin, looking quite cheerful and unconcerned for someone whose flat had just been searched by the organs of the state. "I hope I'm not disturbing you?"

"Of course not," Didchuk said, politely if somewhat uncertainly. "We were just getting ready to go out to meet our daughter."

"Oh, is she coming back today? How wonderful for you. But I'll only keep you a minute." She did not quite brush past Didchuk as he stood at the door, but she moved forward with enough assurance that he got out of the way. "Perhaps you saw that we had visitors," she said gaily. "What a nuisance! They were just doing their job, of course, and, naturally, we were glad to cooperate, since we had nothing at all to hide. The thing is, do you have that present for my daughter-in-law's birthday that I asked you to keep for me?"

"I thought you said it was for your grandson's," Oksana Didchuk said, looking frightened.

"Well, actually it's for both of them," Aftasia smiled as Didchuk pulled a flat envelope out of a drawer. "Is that it? Oh, thank you; I'll take it now, perhaps I'll give it to them a bit early. And one more thing, if I may. The telephone? It's a long-distance call, and I insist on paying for it—an old friend in Moscow." She folded the envelope and tucked it into her bag as she went, without waiting for permission, to the phone. It was a long number she dialed, but it was answered at once.

"Hello," she said pleasantly, not giving a name. "I simply called to wish you happiness on this occasion. We, too, had a party, but I wish we could have been at yours."

The Didchuks could not hear the voice on the other end of the phone, but from Aftasia Smin's expression, it seemed to be a friendly one.

"Oh, yes," she said, nodding. "The article is quite safe; in fact I have it here. Our friends at the party wanted very much to see it, but unfortunately I couldn't put my hands on it at that moment. So. When will we see you again? No? Well then, if you can't come here perhaps we will join you one of these days. Mail the gift? No, really, I think that might not be reliable; one would not want it to get lost. Well, then, all of us send our best wishes. Yes, good-bye."

She hung up and rummaged in her purse for the money to pay for the call. "Wedding anniversary," she explained. "An old Party comrade's son—why, I held him when he was still nursing at his mother's breast and, can you believe it? Now he has a grandson of his own! Well, I won't keep you any longer . . . and thank you for helping with my birthday surprise."

"You're welcome," said both the Didchuks at once. They looked at each other dismally after the old woman left. But they didn't say anything further about the birthday surprise, not then, when one of the visitors might happen to return at any moment, and indeed not ever.

In any case, their daughter's return gave them far more attractive things to think about. They engaged a taxicab for the trip to the railroad station and extravagantly commanded, and bribed, the driver to wait. The terminal was a far happier place this time than it had been three weeks before.

The Didchuks were not the only parents eagerly awaiting a returning child, and everyone was in a holiday mood . . . with somber undertones, to be sure. The official death toll had just been announced again—the number was now up to twenty-three, twenty-one of them men and two women. And everyone was well aware that the number would surely rise. And go on rising, not just this week or this year, but for a long time to come as the slow damage from radiation would produce cells that turned cancerous, or caused babies to abort, or, worse still, let them be born with no one knew what difficulties. The doctors had said that at least one hundred thousand Soviet citizens, perhaps twice that many, had been exposed to levels of radiation high enough to warrant a close watch for decades to come.

The train, of course, was late. After half an hour Didchuk sighed and went outside to pay the taxi driver off, but returned in a glow. "Imagine!" he told his wife, beaming. "He said he would wait for nothing! He, too, had a child who was evacuated, the boy will be back on Saturday, and he said he would be glad to see that our daughter got home in comfort!"

His wife's eyes were suddenly misted with happy, sentimental tears. Then she had a sudden thought. "On Saturday?" For they, like most citizens of Kiev, had been notified that the next few Saturdays were to be devoted to voluntary extra work, helping complete the nine-kilometer aqueduct that would bring water to Kiev if the autumn floods made everything nearer undrinkable with spill from Chernobyl.

Didchuk looked concerned. "Oh, to be sure. I had forgotten. But surely they will give him time off to meet his son," he offered.

His wife wasn't listening. She was looking in surprise at another track, with the waiting afternoon intercity train. An old woman was reasoning with the guard, who finally shrugged and allowed her to march triumphantly onto the platform.

"But that is surely Aftasia Smin," said his wife. "What can she be doing? She didn't mention to us that she was going to Moscow."

CHAPTER 37

The gull-winged TWA airline terminal at New York's Kennedy Airport is not only an architectural spectacle, it is huge. It has its own customs and immigration facilities for passengers arriving from abroad. That relieves crowding, and that's a good thing. The United States is not the easiest country in the world to enter. The customs searches can be very thorough. Foreign nationals must have visas and health cards, and sometimes they are subjected to considerable questioning about their politics and their possible criminal records. Sometimes they are even turned back at the airport and must reboard their plane for its return flight. For many years, even returning American citizens had to spend eternities of time in the long lines, but because so many American voters complained to so many American congressmen, it has now been made easier for Americans to get back into their country; they pass by the immigration desks completely, and even at customs if they say they have nothing to declare they are generally waved through. But not always; and those who are asked to step into another room are sometimes in for an ordeal.

When Dean and Candace Garfield were politely invited out of the line at the customs counter, the shock was nasty. "But we've written everything down on the form," Garfield expostulated. "We haven't even talked to the customs officer yet."

Then he caught sight of his network's New York publicity chief coming toward him with a young woman and a uniformed U.S. Immigration Service official, and Garfield relaxed. "Leave the bags," the man urged, grinning. "Bobbi here will schlepp them through, we've got something else going for you."

The something else turned out to be a little room where a government doctor with a finger-pricking blood sample needle waited for them. Just outside, there were half a dozen newspaper and network people eager to talk, first of all, to celebrities, and, even more, to celebrities who had been near the Chernobyl disaster; and that night the Garfields had the pleasure of seeing themselves on the six o'clock news.

"I should've had my hair done in Paris," Candace fretted.

Her husband, switching channels, said loyally, "You look gor-geous, gorgeous. And, Jesus, he even got us on CBS. Look!"

And there they were. Of course, they got less time than they had been given on their own network, but nevertheless Garfield saw himself once more grinning at the camera and saying, "The doctor says we've got traces of, what do you call it, tellurium and some other 'urium' from the explosion. But so does everybody in the Ukraine. It isn't very much, and we don't have to worry about it. And, yes, the people in Kiev are all doing fine. They've got it all cleared up, far as we could see, though, of course, they're kind of worried about the future. But he— But heck, who isn't?"

"They left out that whole part where I was talking about *Comrade Tanya*," Candace complained as the newscaster switched to a "related subject."

Her husband said, "Hold it a minute, I want to hear this." The "related subject" was a story about a news conference called by the American Association of Nuclear Engineers.

They gave the spokesman more time than they had given the Garfields, as he explained that what had happened in Chernobyl couldn't possibly happen here. Yes, there had been accidents in America in the past—little ones; really, only technical mishaps, if you looked at them impartially and if you weren't one of those antinuclear freaks. And certainly nobody had been hurt in any American nuclear accident. Well, very few people, anyway. Yes, it was true that the Chernobyl reactor did in fact turn out to have a containment shell, despite what had been said earlier, but it was rectangular rather than a dome. Yes, all right, at the time of Three Mile Island the authorities had released no information at all on the accident for several days, too, and maybe the chairman of the Nuclear Regulatory Commission had expressed an irritated wish that sometimes the freedom of the press wasn't observed quite so faithfully in the United States—yes, all right, the man finished, obviously growing annoyed, there were plenty of little nitpicking arguments that could be made against American nuclear power by the Jane Fondas and the people who loved whales. That was certainly their privilege.

But nevertheless it couldn't happen here, and what happened at Chernobyl just showed that the Russians couldn't be trusted with high technology. Their management practices were abysmal. The people in charge at Chernobyl were undoubtedly in bad trouble, and they deserved to be!

"Christ," said Garfield, switching again but getting nothing but the weather report. "I don't like the sound of that. I hope Cousin Simyon's all right."

"I wish I'd worn the blue dress," said his wife.

There was one other "related subject" that didn't get covered on the newscast, although Garfield's clipping service faithfully passed it on to him from the next day's paper. The story came from France, where at the nuclear reprocessing plant in Cap La Hague five workers had received radiation exposure—one of them five times the permitted annual dose— when radioactive liquid leaked from a pipe.

It wasn't much of a story in America. It wasn't even taken very seriously in France, except at one newspaper office, where an enterprising reporter had uncovered something considerably more worrisome. It seemed that earlier that year another French reactor had gone critical when its pumps failed because it lost electrical power on its primary circuits. That was bad enough, but things got worse when they tried to avert total meltdown by switching to the backup diesel generators. The first generator failed. The second was the last resort.

As it happened, the second generator worked. With its electrical power the meltdown was averted. The Frenchmen managed to shut down their errant reactor without catastrophe. They swore a bit, and one or two of them went home to change their underwear; that was all.

That wasn't much of a story, either, because it had a happy ending ... except for the fact (as the reporter told his editor) that it had been really very lucky for France that the accident had happened on a warm spring day. The second generator had also been diesel powered, and in cold weather, the workers at the plant admitted, the diesels generally refused to start at all.

CHAPTER 38

The Chernobyl Power Station is not back in operation, will not be for some time, but optimists are beginning to think that that may sooner or later happen, after all. Even from the air, the plant now looks strangely changed.

Much of the debris has been bulldozed away. The great hole where Reactor No. 5 was meant to go is half filled with radioactive wreckage and excavated soil. Earthen ramps have been thrown up to let heavy machinery into the interior of the plant, the turbine room, and everywhere else they are needed. It is an incredible effort. All the resources of the USSR have been thrown into Chernobyl. Fleets of trucks, trains, and planes are bringing supplies—pipes, drilling equipment, repair and construction materials, etc.—from all over the country; at least forty-five hundred trucks and eight hundred buses are in use.

The working areas of the three surviving reactors are now completely air-conditioned, with triple filters (which are checked for radioactive dust and replaced every two hours). Every exposed surface has been repainted with thick radiation-proof lead paint. The workers come in (on short shifts) in armored cars. Most of the plant is still off limits, except for the antiradiation crews. Water for the generators still comes from the cooling pond, but that water is radioactive now. There is an independent supply of water for toilets and drinking. It is piped in from new wells that have been dug three kilometers away, and there isn't much of it. The plant needs workers even more than it needs water, and they, too, have been provided from sources far away; the nearest place for most of them to live is now the town of Chernobyl.

When Sheranchuk reported for his first day's duty back at the plant, he had to ride the thirty kilometers from town to plant, and the vehicle he rode in was an armored personnel carrier.

Sheranchuk had never been in an armored vehicle before. Nor had he ever met the dozen other workers who shared it with him on the long ride to the power station. Inside the armored carrier they had not bothered with their face masks, but none of the faces meant anything to him. They all seemed to know one another, for they chatted in the manner of people who had worked together for a long time, though Sheranchuk was sure not one of them had been employed by the Chernobyl Nuclear Power Station in that long-ago time—

He stopped himself. Long ago? But it was only, he counted, twenty-seven days since the explosion! Not quite that, actually; Saturday morning at 1:23 would be exactly four weeks.

It seemed half a lifetime, at least.

"Masks on, if you please," the driver of the APC called. Grinning, everyone pulled up the masks as the personnel carrier bumped through the entrance to the plant and stopped. Sheranchuk rose with the others, but the driver put out a polite hand to stop him. "Not you, Comrade Sheranchuk," he said. "Your appointment is with the Personnel Section and they're in the command post twelve kilometers further."

"But I wanted to see the plant!"

The driver hesitated. "Come up and sit beside me," he offered. "It's lead glass in the windscreen; you can see out. Here, I'll take a little run around the plant first so you can get a look; I've got to pick up some others for the command post anyway."

Nobody really "ran" around the Chernobyl Nuclear Power Station anymore. There were too many busy earthmoving machines to avoid, too many areas roped off with signs warning of radiation, too many places in what was left of the roadways, where backhoes and bulldozers had scraped away tainted paving, leaving huge potholes. As the APC bumped and twisted along its obstacle course, Sheranchuk's spirits sank. It didn't look better than the last time he had seen it. It looked far worse. No one had got around to repairing anything yet, it seemed; all the effort was still in demolition. But, of course, Sheranchuk told himself, first the decay had to be cut away before the rebuilding could begin. . . .

And then the armored vehicle turned the corner, and he saw the remains of the ruined reactor itself.

A huge, jointed crane towered over what was left of Reactor No. 4. The remains of its walls had somehow become a blotchy, unhealthy-looking pink—as though it were blushing in shame, Sheranchuk thought wryly. A huge windowless vehicle on caterpillar tracks sat motionless on an earthen ramp, while smaller machines dodged around it. The going was, if anything, worse there than in the relatively undamaged parts of the plant they had just come through, but grimly the driver stepped on the accelerator. They lurched wildly as he sped past the scene, and he seemed to relax when they had the windowless office building between them and the wreck.

"That's all there is to see," he told Sheranchuk. "Now we'll just pick up the next lot, and then we're on our way to the command post."

He blew his horn in front of a sort of canopy of canvas that flapped in the warm afternoon breeze. A moment later six or eight men, unrecognizable in their white or green suits and masks, came hurrying out to board the APC. Sheranchuk looked at them hopefully as the driver closed the door and they began to pull down their masks, but none of these faces were familiar, either.

When they introduced themselves around, shouting over the noise of the armored vehicle, Sheranchuk was surprised to find that the man next to him was an Army general, the one across the aisle one of the trouble-shooters from the Ministry of Nuclear Energy. In the green or white coveralls they all looked alike. The man from the Ministry was quite surprised to find out that Sheranchuk was a senior administrator from pre-explosion times. "Really?" he said. "But I thought they were all—gone," he finished, having rejected either *dead* or *in jail*.

"Some of us remain," Sheranchuk said dryly. "Tell me how things are at the plant."

So for the dozen kilometers he was told. Of the seventy tons of lead shot that had been helicopter-dropped to melt a film over the top of the deadly core ("But still there is so much radiation that the cleanup workers on the roofs nearby can stay there only one minute at a time"). Of the great concrete slabs that were being cast to hoist into place, to make new walls around the core. Of the huge steel tanks that had been assembled to catch the wastewater from the cleanup, so that it would not further pollute the already damaged ground waters around the plant. Of the steel doors that were being welded into all the passageways near the exposed core, never to be opened, part of the "sarcophagus" in which the core would ultimately be entombed forever.

"Forever?" Sheranchuk repeated. "What do you mean 'forever'?"

The man from the Ministry said firmly, "What 'forever' means is *forever*. Through all the rest of your lifetime, and your children's, and your children's children's, for perhaps hundreds of years. Long after the rest of the Chernobyl Nuclear Power Station is decommissioned and torn down and carted away, that sarcophagus will remain."

"And when the other reactors are back in service again, people will be working next to that—sarcophagus?"

"Every day. And watching the instruments inside to make sure that nothing is going wrong. Always. Forever."

The control center had come to a more or less permanent resting place at a Komsomol summer camp. Sheranchuk got out with the others, got the driver's directions, and walked briskly along the graveled paths to what had once been the camp's administration building. He hardly noticed the handsome trees that shaded the barracks and dining halls. He was trying to come to terms with the meaning of the word "forever."

He had not really thought out what was going to be done with the ruined core—dismantled and buried, he had supposed, if he had supposed anything at all. He simply had not realized that it would stay there—still hot, still deadly—forever. The Personnel and Security offices were on the second floor of the rustic, well constructed building. Double doors and double windows had been added to the original plan, and every other window had a bulky air conditioner with triple filters attached; hot as it was outside, it was perfect within. When Sheranchuk got there, the first person he saw, standing at a window, gazing out at the pretty wooded camp, was the runaway operator—what was his name? Kalychenko? The man was standing with his hands clasped behind his back. When he turned and looked at Sheranchuk there was recognition in his gaze, and a certain defensive hostility.

When Sheranchuk had given his name to the secretary, he said, "Well, hello." And then, for lack of something better to say, "You were on duty that night, weren't you?"

"For a time," Kalychenko admitted cautiously.

Sheranchuk looked at him thoughtfully. "We must get together and compare notes sometime soon, if you don't mind," he said. "There are still a lot of questions in my mind."

"Of course," said Kalychenko politely, wishing the man would drop dead. Questions! As if he had not already answered ten thousand questions—with another ten thousand more no doubt coming up as soon as the new First Section Secretary admitted him.

But when First Section Secretary Ivanov came out of his office, he gave Kalychenko only a quick, disinterested glance. It was Sheranchuk he turned to with a welcoming smile. "Yes, please," he said. "Come right in!"

"Thank you," Sheranchuk said politely, "but I think Shift Operator Kalychenko was here before me—"

"No, no! That's quite all right," Ivanov said. "I'm sure the shift operator won't mind waiting for a bit." He turned to the secretary. "No interruptions," he ordered, and swept Sheranchuk into his office, leaving Kalychenko glowering morosely after them.

There was certainly a difference between Khrenov and the new man, Ivanov; one sly and intimate, the other effusive and jolly, but it was the difference between raspberry ice cream and cherry. The inside of both men was at the same temperature, and that temperature was frigid. The fact that on this day Ivanov was cordial, even effusive, as he escorted Sheranchuk inside meant nothing for the future. It meant only that on this day Ivanov wanted the hydrologist-engineer to think of him as a friend.

So Sheranchuk was not at all surprised when, with a wink, Ivanov produced a bottle from somewhere in his desk, and with a twinkle confessed that it was unfortunately only wine, but at least the best Georgian. "Please, Leonid," he said, filling the glass to the brim, "sit down. No, please, not there in the hard chair. Take that couch by the window, and let me pull my chair over to you." He raised his glass. "I drink to the future of the Chernobyl Nuclear Power Station! Like our nation, it weathers all storms and grows stronger through adversity!"

"Of course," Sheranchuk said warily. He sipped at the wine, noticing that the Personnel man had only dampened the bottom of his own glass.

Something had changed.

What it was Sheranchuk could not guess, but there was definitely something in the air that had not been there in his brief meeting with Ivanov in Moscow. The man was not merely welcoming, he was positively beaming. "As I told you, my dear Leonid," Ivanov said, "you are very much needed here. I think I should tell you—it is not official yet, but there is no reason you shouldn't know—the preliminary investigations of the accident show no fault to be laid at your door."

"Investigations?" Sheranchuk repeated warily.

"Very preliminary ones, of course," Ivanov assured him. "And what a rotten mess they are uncovering, as I am sure you can guess! But as to you personally, your actions are beyond reproach. It is clear that you continually warned of deficiencies and worked to correct them when you could. So there is no accusation of any kind against you. Indeed, I think you will wind up with some commendations, at least. There is even talk of a medal."

"I don't want any medals," Sheranchuk growled.

"My dear man! I quite understand. None of us wants such things, really, but nevertheless you behaved admirably, and if the state desires to make its approval public, it will, at least, be an example to many others."

Sheranchuk shook his head. "The man who should be getting the medals is dead."

"Oh? Really? And which man is that, may I ask?" Ivanov asked politely.

"Is there any doubt? Deputy Director Smin, of course."

"Ah," said Ivanov, pursing his lips. "I see. Smin, eh?"

"Of course Smin! You were not here then, Ivanov. You have no idea what Smin did for this plant. There has been talk of inferior materials and poor labor discipline—not untrue, all of it; but it would have been far worse if Smin had not been here. And far better if he had been in complete charge, as he deserved to be!"

"Ah," said Ivanov noncommittally, reaching for the bottle. "Here, let me refill your glass." And when, over Sheranchuk's attempts at polite withdrawal, he had it full to the brim again, he said, "It is interesting that you should mention Smin at this time because, to be truthful, I have much curiosity about him. I never met him while he was alive, you know. I can form an opinion of him only from what the record shows, and from what people like yourself can tell me."

Ivanov paused, smiling at Sheranchuk over his glass as he waited for a response. Ah, thought Sheranchuk, there it was. The subject of the questioning was to be Smin.

He said cautiously, "Deputy Director Smin was a great man."

"Indeed." The Personnel man pursed his lips. "Well, you see, I must rely on your perceptions. Would you mind if I helped make my own estimate of him by asking you some questions?"

"What kind of questions?"

"Oh, various ones. Just to help me form a picture. For example, I understand you shared Smin's room for a time in Hospital Number Six in Moscow. I wonder—what sort of things did you talk about?"

And then the questions stopped being about what Sheranchuk had talked about, becoming about who Smin had seen. Sheranchuk, on his third glass of wine, realized that it was quite clear Ivanov already knew a great deal about Smin's visitors, no doubt from friendly voices among the hospital staff. Still he wanted to know more—for example, if Sheranchuk, as Smin's roommate, had heard anything of Smin's conversations?

Sheranchuk's answers became more and more cautious. There was no doubt that Ivanov had all the official records available to him, so Sheranchuk skated around what he heard, or guessed, of the elder son's drug arrest. Visitors other than

Smin's family? Well, yes, one or two. And two in particular in quite high places, wasn't that right? Ivanov asked with a smile.

Sheranchuk hesitated, suspicious. Still, what was there to worry about? Certainly the fact that he had friends in the highest of places could do Smin no harm. So Sheranchuk was perfectly willing to talk about the two men from the Central Committee—he confessed that he had been very impressed to see them there—but, as a matter of courtesy, he did not eavesdrop and in fact was tactfully out of the room most of the time when Smin had private visitors.

"Of course," said Ivanov courteously. "All the same, there are other ways of communicating with people. Letters, for example. Perhaps a journal? Do you recall seeing Smin writing anything in the hospital?"

Sheranchuk hesitated. He did not like the direction the questions were taking. "Well, yes," he conceded reluctantly, "but I don't know what he wrote. He never showed me any of it. I assumed they were letters to his family, perhaps a will—I don't know, since I had never seen any of it at close range."

"And Comrade Smin's reading? Did you see him reading anything?"

"Reading? No. Hardly ever. You see, it was painful for him to read. I think I saw him with *Pravda* now and then, perhaps once or twice with a book, but never for long."

"I see," said Ivanov. "Only a newspaper, and perhaps now and then a book. Well, there is no harm in that, is there? But, you see, I am thinking in particular of a document that he might have been reading. A sheaf of perhaps typewritten pages, seventeen or so. And you saw nothing like that?"

Sheranchuk shook his head. Ivanov gazed pensively at the wall for a moment. Then he asked, "And have you ever met either Comrade Mishko or Comrade Milaktiev, the two men from the Central Committee?"

"Only in the hospital room—and, oh, yes, at the funeral, but only for a moment."

Ivanov was silent for a while. Then he smiled and poured another glass of wine. "And now," he said gaily, "before you hurry off to your good wife, who is certainly eager to see how you are after your first day back on the job, let us talk about your own future. You have taken a good deal of radiation, you know."

"The hospital released me completely," Sheranchuk said defensively.

"But you have surely exceeded the limits for a worker in a nuclear power plant. Usually anyone with twenty-five rads is sent away. You have at least eighty. You can never enter a reactor room again, I'm sorry to say."

"But that's impossible," Sheranchuk cried in alarm. "How am I supposed to do my job?"

"Simply in another place," Ivanov said kindly. "And in a different job. No, no, we're not sending you away. We need you here for some time, to advise the crews as they complete the job of controlling the damage. Then you will go away for a time, if you're willing, but only to take some courses in nuclear safety. The Ministry has ordered this for all senior administrators. And when you come back to Chernobyl, you will be in charge of training and enforcing the new safety standards on all the operating personnel. It's a very serious job, Leonid. Please accept it."

Sheranchuk stared at his glass of wine for a moment. "I could request a transfer to another power plant. Not nuclear."

"Of course you could. I would not prevent you. But we want you very much to stay."

And there really was no choice, for how could he leave Deputy Director Simyon Smin's plant? "All right," Sheranchuk said at last.

"Very good! Wonderful! Let's see, this is Thursday—no sense in your coming in tomorrow—take the long weekend to get acquainted with your good wife again, eh? Have I told you how pleased I am that she is still with you, after all?" And, as Sheranchuk stiffened, Ivanov added, "And, oh, yes, Comrade Sheranchuk, if you should happen to run into either Comrade Mishko or Comrade Milaktiev again, please be sure to let me know."

When, five minutes later, the secretary told Kalychenko he could go in, his reception was far less amiable. There was certainly no wine; there was, at first, not even an indication that Ivanov knew the shift operator was there standing on one foot before him.

Kalychenko waited patiently enough. He had not expected anything better. The interview with the GehBehs in Yuzhevin had told him what was before him, and Ivanov no more than confirmed it. The circumstances of his running away were permanently on his record. He would be watched carefully. One more misstep would be his last.

Kalychenko stood humble and penitent throughout. He denied nothing. He excused nothing. He acknowledged cowardice, lack of discipline, desertion of his post, unauthorized absence—however many different ways Ivanov discovered to describe the same unforgivable but also undeniable lapse, Kalychenko accepted them all.

It was only at the very end of the conversation that Ivanov said anything that Kalychenko had not expected.

Even that was, when you thought about it, no surprise. It was the logically inevitable next step.

There was no friendly fireman to give him a bunk while he waited to begin his first midnight shift under the new regime, but Kalychenko found a comfortable corner of the canteen not in use. He drowsed over a can of kvass until it was time to report to the main control for the sleeping Reactor No. 3.

He was quite aware that only a few walls separated him from the exploded ruin of No. 4. All of his shift mates seemed a little edgy, as Kalychenko himself was at first. But the monotony of the work was calming . . . and, too, he needed to think over the things Ivanov had said to him.

There was not really much to do, with three of the reactors in stand-down mode and the other permanently out of action. The little that had to be done, however, had to be done most urgently; the temperatures of the slumbering cores needed to be monitored all the time, the pumps and rod mechanisms and circulating water systems checked every day—everything had to be perfectly normal and operational, because no one dared face the consequences if there should be another runaway reactor at the Chernobyl Nuclear Power Station.

Still, the work did not take much of Kalychenko's attention. That was good, because he needed to think of what Ivanov had said at the end. Kalychenko tried to remember the exact words: "There are only two ways you can wipe your record clean, Kalychenko. One is to lead a perfectly blameless existence for the rest of your days. Unfortunately, you can't live long enough for that to work. The other is to perform a great service for the Soviet Union. There are bad elements here, Kalychenko. Not all Ukrainians are as loyal as you—as, at least, I hope you will learn to be. There are rumors of nationalist agitation. Eternal vigilance is needed to unmask them. You can help. See that you do."

Kalychenko winced. It was bad enough to face his comrades as a runaway; what would it be like if they found him to be an informer as well?

When he heard the other people on his shift cry out sharply, it took him a while to realize that a distant alarm bell was ringing loudly, and even longer to recognize that, for some time now, he had been smelling smoke.

Another fire!

It was impossible, Kalychenko thought despairingly. How could it happen that the Chernobyl plant was wrecking itself again? Once more he found himself running in panic . . . but this time, without any conscious decision to do so, he was not running away from the new disaster but straight toward it.

CHAPTER 39

THURSDAY, MAY 22

What Park Avenue once was to New York City is what Gorky Street is to Moscow. People who live there *matter*. The apartments in the buildings on Gorky Street are light and airy. Walls meet each other at right angles, doors close without a body block, and no one tries to enforce the nine-square-meters-a-person rule. Cars, like Johnny Stark's baby-blue Cadillac Eldorado convertible, are not pulled up on the sidewalk and protected with tarpaulins. They are in roomy garages, and it is not only the cars that have plenty of room. The people who live on Gorky Street are ballerinas and film stars, pianists and chess champions, the brothers of members of the Central Committee and the grandsons of great generals. Of course, they all have dachas. Of course, they travel abroad. It is a paradox of Gorky Street that these people whose homes are so spacious occupy them so little of the time.

Emmaline Branford had never been at a party in a Gorky Street flat before. At first she kept very quiet, because she had not been wrong. These people were far out of her league. The skinny uniformed man with the prematurely bald head—all those stars on his shoulderboards surely meant that he was a general. The pretty woman with the plump young man at her arm was, Emmaline was nearly sure, a featured dancer from the Leningrad Kirov, and the man the dancer was talking to was a

Bolshoi opera baritone. As far as Emmaline could see, she and Pembroke Williamson were the only Americans present—not counting Johnny Stark's wife—but the elderly woman with blue hair was something in French motion pictures, and the young couple in hiking boots turned out to be Australian. Emmaline stayed close to Pembroke's shadow until the third or fourth interesting man bore down on her to practice his English or let her work on her Russian. The first had been a film director, another, oh, my God, a cosmonaut!

Then she remembered that her color made her, too, a kind of special celebrity in Moscow.

The red crepe had been, after all, not one bit too dressy, because these other women were at least as stylish as she, and none of their clothing had come from Lerner's. The dancer's pearls were certainly real. And Johnny Stark's wife, the American—well, the *former* American—was really quite modestly dressed, until you looked at the rock on her finger that could not be less than three carats.

Emmaline could not imagine why in the world she had been asked here.

When Pembroke called to say he had been invited by Johnny Stark to the party—though it wasn't really Stark's party, just a friend's—and that she was invited too—"Yes, by all means bring a guest, and why not that very pretty American girl who was at the offices of Mir with you?"—Emmaline had been close to refusing. To be sure, it was an opportunity direct from heaven for a junior dip in Moscow, for such doors were very seldom opened to Americans from the Embassy.

But ten seconds of thought convinced her that she couldn't pass up the chance to be the only American diplomat in Moscow to be a personal guest of the famous (and mysterious) Johnny Stark. So here she was, rubbing elbows with the cream of Moscow's jet set, listening to a short young man with a very nearly punk haircut tell her how much he wanted to sing some of his Soviet rock songs in America.

At least the singer had maneuvered her over to the table with the food, and for the moment she was content to listen to his tortured attempts to define his music—"Not Prince, not the Grateful Dead, perhaps one could say a—a suspicion, is it?—of the Stones, yes"—while she ate as many slices of the perfectly red-ripe tomatoes and loaded thin-crisp toast with as much of the fresh black caviar as she could manage. She had long since lost sight of Pembroke, last seen talking earnestly to the man in the general's uniform through the translation of Johnny Stark's wife. The rock-singer man (at close range he was not all that young) did not require much conscious attention apart from an occasional nod of understanding.

That was welcome to Emmaline, because it gave her time to think about what she was doing here. It was certain that Johnny Stark had not made a point of having her invited simply because she was pretty, or even because she was black.

No. There was surely a reason, she told herself. People like Johnny Stark didn't do things on lighthearted impulse. Did he plan to get her drunk so that she would babble secret CIA plans into a hidden microphone? There was certainly enough champagne around for that, but no one was forcing her to drink to excess. Come to that, Johnny Stark was too sharp an article to expect any secrets from her, because he was undoubtedly aware that she wasn't the kind of person who would know any big ones.

There had to be some other reason for her presence here with Pembroke. Emmaline wondered wistfully if she would ever find out what it was.

She was so wrapped up in her imaginings that she didn't even realize the rock singer had gone off to find a more sympathetic ear until Johnny Stark himself touched her arm. He handed her a fresh glass of wine and said amiably, in perfectly American English, "Are you having a good time among our Hollywood types? I hope so. That's your privilege, being the prettiest girl in the room."

She gave him a diplomat's smile, since he was talking diplomat talk. "I haven't met any Hollywood types yet."

Not counting yourself, she meant. Stark was wearing a black silk shirt open to his breastbone, with a heavy medallion on a heavy gold chain, and he looked like every Russian's image of a Hollywood producer. He said, "Well, that's what Teddy threw this party for, for some of the film people in town for their union congress. But I'm afraid a lot of them are still battling over the elections. Have you heard what they did today? They've thrown over the traces completely, elected that madman Elem Klimov First Secretary of the union."

Emmaline blinked. Soviet trade unions did not "throw

over the traces." Such things never happened. She tried to place the name. "Is Klimov the one who made *Go and See?*"

"Yes, exactly. All rape and bloodshed. I suppose you could call it our equivalent of *Straw Dogs* or *Apocalypse Now.* He's quite mad, you know. Poor fellow, his wife was killed in a car smash—very tragic—and he still talks to her ghost every night. God knows what he'll do with the union." He glanced around. Still smiling, he went on. "Actually, I've been wondering if you'd like to see some of my ikons? I've promised to show them to our honored guest, and I thought you and Pembroke might like to come along. A car? Oh, we don't need a car. My place is just upstairs. What you in America would call the penthouse."

"Well," said Emmaline, trying to estimate what Stark had in mind, "I think I should at least say good-bye to my host—"

"Oh, Teddy's off somewhere. I'll do it for you later."

"Well," she looked around uncertainly, "what about Pembroke . . ."

"Already asked him," Stark grinned. "He was pretty gung-ho. He never expected a chance to spend a little time with a member of the Central Committee."

For Emmaline it was exactly as though someone had touched her with one of those electric tinglers unpleasant people goose girls with at veterans' conventions. She shuddered. Every muscle tightened. She hardly heard the name of the polite elderly man she was introduced to—was it Mishko? —because the reverberations of the words "Central Committee" drowned everything else.

Junior dips never *ever* got to meet members of the Central Committee of the Communist Party of the Soviet Union.

She was only vaguely aware of the elevator Stark bundled the four of them into (though it was at least three times the size of the one for her own flat, and quite noiseless). She noticed that the room Stark led them into was huge and pleasantly air-conditioned, but that was only because she found that she was shivering slightly. She gazed unseeingly at Stark's ikons, though the one from (Stark told them) sixteenth-century Byelorussia was not only as large as the Mona Lisa and crusted in gold leaf, but had track lights discreetly playing on it. She didn't really recover her wits until she found herself sitting on an embroidery-upholstered chaise longue, next to a coffee table with the latest issues of *The Economist, Der Spiegel,* and *The New Yorker,* and Stark began to speak.

His tone was good-humored but rather serious. "And now, perhaps we can have a bit of serious talk, eh? Off the record, as you say. To help us understand each other, so that we can help our countries do so. One moment," he added apologetically, and switched to Russian for Mishko's benefit, while at the same time opening a tiny freezer to pull out four icy glasses and a bottle of straw-colored liquor.

When Mishko replied, Stark translated. "He says this would please him very much. He says that we can speak honestly if not absolutely openly—there are, of course, some things that even candid friends should not say to one another, and let us appoint one another honorary friends for this evening—especially when one of our little circle is in the diplomatic service of the United States."

He smiled at Emmaline tolerantly. So, she thought, I'm here unofficially so that I can report unofficially. But what? Mishko, watching shrewdly, cut in. He spoke in Russian, directly to Emmaline. "You do not have to promise not to report this to your organs. I would not ask for a promise you couldn't keep. In any case, if you do, it will become a classified document in their files which no one will be allowed to read for twenty-five years, and by then it won't matter."

Stark translated swiftly for Pembroke, pouring icy vodka into each of the icy glasses. "I toast the antidrunkenness campaign," he said. "Please don't think I'm mocking it. I approve of it. I now limit my own drinking to two glasses a day, no more than two days a week, except on special occasions. This is one."

When they had all drunk, Mishko spoke. "If we are to speak candidly," he proposed good-humoredly, "let us start with small things. I have a small thing I have wanted to talk to an American about. It is your films. I have seen your *White Nights* and *Moscow on the Hudson.* In one of them, every Russian is evil. In the other, we are all half-wits. Why are there not any American films which sometimes show at least one Russian as a decent human being?"

"Because it would flop at the box office," Pembroke predicted when Stark had translated. "There is only one supreme rule for our American filmmakers. Their films must not lose money. They will be forgiven for anything else, but not that."

"Ah, yes, the capitalist devotion to the dollar."

Pembroke was shaking his head before Stark finished putting the sentence into English. "Yes. But also no. It is the way capitalism works, but that way is not necessarily bad. McDonald's serves better food than the buffet in a Soviet hotel. Why? The people who run McDonald's are better motivated. They know if they don't satisfy their customers, they're out of business. What motivates them is money."

"In fact," Stark put in in English, when he was through with the Russian, "even V. I. Lenin encouraged small private ventures during the period of the New Economic Policy, for just that reason."

"And you could try it again," Pembroke grinned. "Especially in your restaurants. Is it my turn to bring up a small thing? Then let it be this: why do the doormen in every halfway decent restaurant in Moscow work so hard to keep customers out?"

"A good question," Stark applauded. "I have my own answer, but first let's defer to Mr. Mishko." He rapidly translated the question and relayed Mishko's answer. "Mr. Mishko suggests it is mostly because these jobs are given to old people, and old people of any country are likely to be crotchety. I have a different theory. I think it is because of the rule of 'eternal vigilance.' Every Soviet child is educated to be on guard at every moment against enemies of the state—shirkers, black marketeers, drunkards. Oh, and worse than that, of course, but your average ten-year-old child does not encounter many traitors or CIA agents in his playground. To be sure, many of these children themselves grow up to be drunkards and black marketeers. But they never forget 'eternal vigilance.' Then they achieve a position of some authority—doorman in a restaurant, ticket taker at a theater, conductor on a trolleybus. They guard their portals! And they do it ever vigilantly. No trespassers! When in doubt, say no, because to be too vigilant is only an excess of zeal, but not to be vigilant enough threatens the state—so each one is as consecrated as an agent of the KGB itself!"

He was grinning as he elaborated his thesis, and Pembroke and Emmaline returned his smile. But as Stark translated for Mishko's benefit, his own smile faltered before the expression on the face of the man from the Central Committee. There was a rapid interchange which Emmaline could not follow. Then Stark said, with just a touch of strain in his voice, "Our honored guest has rebuked me. He says that I speak of the KGB as Americans do in their spy novels, whereas in fact the organs of the state are, in a sense, the elements which lead us to a more complete democracy."

"Oh, really!" cried Emmaline, unable to help herself.

"Yes, *really*," Stark said firmly. "Mr. Mishko is quite correct. You have the opinion, I am sure, that the Soviet Union has become more 'liberal,' as you would say, in the past ten years or so. And who brought this about? First Andropov, himself a former head of the KGB. Now Gorbachev, Andropov's protégé. You are quite mistaken if you think the KGB are all cold warriors, like your own spies and operatives. They—"

He hesitated, then shrugged, smiling again. He took the bottle out of the freezer again, with four new icy glasses. As he poured, he said, "And so we see how quickly we move from small things to big ones!"

The big things got quickly bigger. Emmaline knew what was coming, and yet was surprised when old Mr. Mishko moved at once to Star Wars. "Since it is my turn, I ask why America is more interested in building new weapons in space than in nuclear disarmament?"

Pembroke turned his empty glass around in his hand. "Does Mr. Mishko think Star Wars will work?" he asked.

The answer came back quickly: "As a 'nuclear umbrella' to protect that pretty little girl we see on American television, no. Of course not. Our scientists say such a total defensive shield is quite impossible, and our scientists are quite intelligent. For that matter, most of your own scientists say the same."

"Then why do you oppose it?"

"Because, first, if it worked even partially, it would be an excellent adjunct to a first strike, made without warning—and your country has always refused to abjure any first use of nuclear weapons. Second, in the course of working on it, you will come up with some very troubling new weapons. These

X-ray lasers with which you propose to destroy our missiles in flight, for example. If they can shoot down a thousand missiles in five minutes, then surely they could, for example, set fire to all of our cities. Is that an effective way to wage a war? Ask the people of Dresden or Tokyo! But," Stark went on, raising a hand as Pembroke was about to speak, "Mr. Mishko asks me to point out that he has answered your questions, but you have not answered his. Why?"

This time Pembroke didn't hesitate. "Americans are afraid of you," he said. "They're afraid that if there's a treaty you'll cheat."

Emmaline's nerves jumped. She had not expected so explicit a word as "cheat." But when Stark translated, Mishko only said, "Yes, we have been accused of cheating. But is it not your rule that even one who is accused is considered innocent until he has been proven guilty?"

Pembroke said stubbornly, "That works only when you have a judge and a jury—and a sentence passed on a person found guilty. There is no international criminal code."

"We have a World Court, which has found America guilty of, for example, mining the harbors of Nicaragua."

Pembroke hesitated. "I'm not in favor of the Contras, and I'm not too crazy about underhanded acts of war. I don't like the CIA much better than the KGB. But that World Court is a joke. It may be biased, as my President claims. It is certainly toothless. It can condemn, but it has no way to punish."

"Because it has no power. Would you give it the power to punish a country such as your own?"

"Would you?"

Mishko took his own turn to think for a moment. "It is not up to me," he said through Stark, "but if it were, I don't think I would. You see, we don't trust Americans, either. You had a treaty that obligated you never to invade the territory of any other American state, but you broke it when you attacked Grenada. You bombed Libya without any declaration of war. Was that any different from Pearl Harbor? You condemn hijacking, but your own Air Force hijacked the civilian plane of a friendly nation over international waters in order to capture the people you blamed for the *Achille Lauro*—that is defined as piracy—"

"Now, wait!"

"A moment, please," said Stark, in the middle of translation. "There was one more thing. Your CIA overthrew the government of Chile, and didn't even have the decency to do it in the open. Now," he said pleasantly, "what was it you wanted to say, Pembroke?"

Pembroke was scowling. "I was going to say that the *Achille Lauro* people were terrorists, but I've got a better idea. Let me run through a little list of my own. Your country has not lived up to the Helsinki declaration on human rights. You built a radar at Krasnoyarsk that violates the Anti-Ballistic Missile Treaty. Your jolly, sweet KGB operates a gulag archipelago that—"

But Stark was holding up his hand. "Can I translate that much before you go on, please? I don't want to get it wrong." And when he had finished, and Pembroke was ready to continue with his list, Mishko grinned broadly and leaned forward to gently slap Pembroke's knee.

Emmaline was astonished to hear Mishko say directly to Pembroke, in slow, thick English: "I speak to you 'Vietnam' and you speak 'Afghanistan.' I speak 'El Salvador,' you speak 'Poland.' I speak 'Bay of Pigs,' you speak 'Hungary.' So for that cause—for cause—" He shrugged and abandoned the attempt at English. He finished in Russian, and Stark translated.

"Therefore, Mr. Mishko says, we might as well stop hurling epithets at each other and talk seriously of problems. He thought the discussion of Star Wars was quite valuable. Have you a question you would like to put to Mr. Mishko?" And before Pembroke could speak, he went on, caressing his gold medallion as he spoke. The tone of his voice didn't change, but there was something in his expression—a tightening of the jaw, a narrowing of the eyes?—that made Emmaline sit up as Stark spoke. "I remember the other day you were asking about some rumors about a secret document. Miss Branford, too, I think, has asked some questions. Would you like to ask Mr. Mishko to comment on it?"

Mishko's demeanor changed too. He didn't scowl. He simply listened very attentively, nodding encouragement to continue each time Stark translated a sentence or two of what Pembroke was saying. "What I heard was a rumor, second-hand at that. Of course, I'd rather not say where I heard it." He went on to describe what he had heard, with particular emphasis on the most revolutionary aspects—the ending of censorship, the free elections with even separate political parties.

When he was finished, he waited while Stark and the man from the Central Committee talked back and forth for a while. Then Stark turned to the Americans. "He asked what I had answered you when you first brought the subject up," he reported. "I told him that I said, as you remember, that I had no personal knowledge of such a thing and wondered if it might be a fake originating with anti-Party emigré elements in the West."

"That's what you said to me, all right," Pembroke agreed. "What does Mr. Mishko say?"

"I'll ask him," said Stark, and reported the result sentence by sentence. "First, Mr. Mishko says that free elections can happen without any change in Soviet laws, and in fact they do. He mentioned what we discussed earlier, Miss Branford, the results of the elections in the filmmakers' union today, where the membership simply rejected the proposed list of officers entirely and elected a whole new opposition slate. So such things do happen in the USSR, though of course they are rare—"

"I'll say," Pembroke grunted.

He got a scowl from Stark for that, but then Stark continued. "Mr. Mishko points out that the possibility that an anonymous document is a fake cannot be excluded. Also, persons in high positions have quite adequate means of arguing cases without resort to samizdat. However, the leadership of the Party and the nation does not wear blinders. It is constantly examining all possible alternatives. All of them can be proposed and discussed. Those that have merit are adopted. But the leadership is not a string of paper soldiers. All sides of a question may be argued, and some people propose projects that are rejected. So, even if the document is a forgery, it is possible that some parts of it do in fact represent the views of certain high officials—but, Mr. Mishko says, not a majority"—Stark smiled—"or else it would have been printed in *Pravda* instead of in samizdat."

As Pembroke waited with Emmaline for her bus, she said thoughtfully, "Johnny Stark knew I'd been asking questions about that manifesto."

"Does that prove he's KGB?"

Emmaline shrugged. What she thought was that it proved two people were KGB—both Stark and Rima, the person she had hinted to about it—but she didn't say that. She only said, "You know, at first I thought it was very indiscreet of him to invite us to talk to this Mr. Mishko—I've absolutely *got* to look him up, first thing in the morning, and find out who we were talking to! But I don't think Stark's ever indiscreet."

"So what do you think was happening up there?"

"God knows! It looked like somebody was trying to score some points off somebody else. About what?" Emmaline shrugged. "Stark was the one who brought up that mysterious seventeen-page document, right?"

"But he didn't say much about it himself."

"Maybe he wanted to see what Mishko would say. Maybe they think Mishko's involved in it. They're both pretty big wheels, you know. The KGB can't just haul Mishko in and interrogate him, so maybe Stark was trying to get a rise out of him." She sighed. "Whatever it was, I don't think you and I will ever find out the score."

"Not even with *glasnost?*"

"There will never," Emmaline told him seriously, "be *that* much *glasnost.*"

CHAPTER 40

Meteorologists who wish to explain the circulation of the Earth's atmosphere sometimes employ an illustration called "Caesar's Last Breath." By an arithmetical coincidence, the average number of molecules of air in a human lung is quite close to the total number of "lungful-equivalents" in the Earth's atmosphere. In the two thousand years since Julius Caesar died of his stab wounds in the Roman forum, there has been plenty of time for mixing, so the molecules of air he exhaled as he perished are now everywhere. Even in your lungs. On average, each time you take a breath, you take in one molecule that Caesar gasped out. This does you no harm. Caesar's last breath contained nothing that can hurt you; but the last huge "breath" from the dying Chernobyl Reactor No. 4 is another matter. It is not as well distributed as Caesar's exhalation. There has not been as much time. Especially in the southern hemisphere, which exchanges air with the north only weakly, through what are called "Hadley cells," only tiny fractions of the Chernobyl gases have yet been circulated. But there was so vastly much *more* of the gases from Chernobyl that every one of us now has in our lungs a certain number of Chernobyl molecules, and this is not only true for all Americans and Russians and Chinese and French and Italians, but for every African, Australian, and Cambodian, and even for all the elephants in Kenya and the Antarctic penguins. We breathe in some of Chernobyl's last breath every day, and will go on doing so all our lives.

By eight o'clock in the morning of May 23 the new fire at the Chernobyl power plant had been puffing additional poisons into the air for half a dozen hours. Leonid Sheranchuk knew nothing about it. He was thirty kilometers away, in the little apartment he and his wife had been given in the town of Chernobyl (only two rooms, and where was Boris to sleep? But what luck to get an apartment immediately anyway!) What Sheranchuk was doing was to discuss with his wife whether they wanted to ask Smin's widow if she intended to sell the plot of land where the Smin's dacha was certainly not now going to be built, and if so whether they should hire a car to go out into the countryside to look at it first.

Then there was the knock on the door and Vladimir Ponomorenko, last living man of the Four Seasons, was standing there, apologetic, worried, insistent.

Was Comrade Sheranchuk going out to the plant in this emergency? If so could he get a ride with him? What emergency? Oh, hadn't Sheranchuk heard? A fire, a big one, a bad one—started only God knew how, spontaneous combustion or something in Section 24 of the plant, now almost out of control because that was the section nearest the deadly core and flooded with radiation so the firemen couldn't get close to it to put it out. "And, please, Comrade Sheranchuk! I have to get out there right away to help!"

And, of course, since Simyon Smin's plant was once again horribly, unexpectedly, in trouble, so did Comrade Sheranchuk.

They found a taxi willing to take them as far as the perimeter checkpoint. They wheedled their way onto an ambulance bringing out a pair of new casualties—firemen again, of course, one knocked senseless by a hose nozzle that got out of control, the other far worse off because his radiation suit had been ripped open when he was breaking through a wall to get at the fire. The medics handled him with caution as they transferred him to another car.

It was bad, all right. The driver filled them in as they bounced along the road to the plant, sometimes circling off the road to avoid a still-contaminated patch of paving.

Sheranchuk knew the layout of the place where the fire started. It was Section 24 of the reactor building, several stories above the imprisoned, dying core. It was a nasty place. Everything in that area had been baked hot and dry from the earlier fires; perhaps some charred rubble had worked itself up to ignition temperature. No one could be sure of that. No one had been there to see. That whole section was sealed off with steel doors welded in place, for it was drenched with radiation. "So they broke through the walls," the driver said, fighting his wheel as he jolted over a series of potholes, "but the fire was higher up. I don't know what they're doing now—look, it's still going, because there's the smoke!"

Smoke there was, black billows of it staining the pretty blue morning sky. Sheranchuk leaned forward, squinting to see what was going on from half a kilometer away.

"What are those people doing on the roof?" he demanded. But the driver didn't know; they hadn't been there when he left. "That's dangerous!" Sheranchuk muttered, peering at the upper stories of the plant.

The core was at least partly shielded by walls on all four sides and the bottom—the solid layer of concrete that replaced the water Sheranchuk had helped remove. But there was nothing over the top of the core but what the helicopters and cranes had dumped there, nothing near enough to stop the flood of radiation. Even in their grotesque rubber and lead suits, those people on the roof were taking chances with their lives.

Then he caught his breath. "The diesel fuel," he said. As the ambulance lurched toward the gateway to the plant he caught a better look at where the firemen were.

"What?" the driver demanded, and Ponomorenko looked at him curiously. Sheranchuk just shook his head. The place where the firemen were struggling with something on the roof was only a few meters away from the fuel stores for the standby diesel generators! And if those went up—

Sheranchuk didn't want to think about what would happen if the fire spread to the diesel oil.

The men on the roof were dangling long lines over the edge for some reason, and firemen on the ground were setting something up below. Sheranchuk and Ponomorenko were out of the ambulance and running toward the building, when a fire major thrust himself in their way. "Do your mother, get out of here!" he snarled. "You don't even have radiation suits!"

"But I'm Engineer Sheranchuk. The diesel stores—they should be drained, or you'll have another explosion!"

The fireman scowled. "Sheranchuk? Yes, all right, I know who you are, but you'll have to go in the bunker. What's this about diesel stores?"

Sheranchuk explained hurriedly, dodging as firemen ran toward them with a limp hose, toward the lines dangling from the roof. "I know where they are," he said. "Let me go up there! You'll need a truck to drain them into; the pipes should be all right—"

"Not you," snapped the major. "You've taken too many rads already. Don't worry, we'll find the tanks—"

"Comrade Major," Ponomorenko said eagerly. "I know where they are."

The fire major glared at him, then shrugged. "All right, off with you to get a suit, then you can show us. But you, Sheranchuk, it's into the bunker for you, and no arguments. It's your life, man!"

So while a hundred firemen and volunteers were fighting the blaze in one part of the plant, Leonid Sheranchuk was fuming in a smoke-filled, stinking underground room a hundred meters away. Once the room had been the barracks for the plant's firemen. Now it was the on-site operations headquarters.

He could not stay there. The thing was, he knew the plant. That whole building was a maze of traps. The corridors were blocked intentionally by steel doors, or simply by heaps of clean-up rubble. And all these firemen were new men, brought in to replace the decimated original crew. Did they know what they were doing? Would Ponomorenko be able to lead them to the diesel tanks? Would they know how to open the drainage valves? Would the pumps work? Had they been able to find a tank truck to drain the fuel into?

Sheranchuk hunted around and found a suit—not one of the good rubber-lead ones, just the compulsory garments everyone in the plant now had to wear, designed to protect against small radiation leaks only. It was at least two sizes too big for him, but he put it on, and when a group of firemen finished a conference and dashed out to put their decisions into action, Sheranchuk ran out with them.

The good thing—the only good thing—was that this time the firefighters seemed to know what they were doing. They even had the equipment to do it with; an oil tanker was parked next to the building wall, its hoses already connected; the tanks were being drained. Everybody was much better at the job now, Sheranchuk thought sardonically, since they'd had the practice. Everybody seemed to take this new fire as a personal affront, too, because everybody had taken it for granted that such a thing could not happen twice.

A sharp explosion overhead made him duck away and stare up in sudden panic.

No, it wasn't the diesel tanks. It was something strange. Someone had dangled an explosive charge from the roof; it had blasted a jagged hole in the wall of the reactor building, and black smoke puffed out.

Sheranchuk was startled to see that already hoses were being dragged up from the ground, and a sort of scaffolding was jerkily lowering from the roof. There were men on that scaffold! Four of them, at least, looking like deep-sea divers, clinging to the ropes as the scaffold swayed—and above them two more men being lowered in harnesses.

Sheranchuk watched unbelievingly as the men reached the gaping hole. They didn't hesitate. One leaped inside, making the platform swing away, then reached out and caught it while his comrades secured the hoses and followed him. Sheranchuk heard a shout. Then the first of the hoses stiffened with pressure, and the smoke pouring out of the hole was joined with hideous yellowish clouds of steam.

He was still standing there, blinking up into the sun, when the fire major tapped his shoulder. "I told you, man, the *bunker*. Otherwise I'll have you arrested and taken away! The fire? Oh, you don't have to worry about the fire anymore— now we've got a fair shot at it, we'll have it out in no time."

And, actually, they did.

It was not really as easy as that.

It wasn't easy at all, in fact, and it certainly wasn't without price. There were twenty-five new casualties, almost all firemen, but the lead and rubber suits had kept the worst of the radiation out, even for the heroes who had jumped into the hole in the wall.

If they had had the same equipment a month earlier, Sheranchuk mused, how many lives might they have saved? Simyon Smin's, for one.

No one was going to die from the second fire. The highest dosimeter reading was less than a hundred rads. There were men vomiting and pale in the assembly area as they waited to be taken away, but most were cursing and joking.

And some, like Volya Ponomorenko, were even proud of the radiation they had taken. "Thirteen rads!" he boasted, waving the pen-shaped instrument. "But we got the fuel out, Comrade Sheranchuk."

"The country's proud of you, Autumn," Sheranchuk said, no more than half jesting. And then, remembering the scene at his cousin's deathbed, "I mean—all of the country. Especially the Ukraine, of course."

Ponomorenko sobered quickly. He fiddled with the dosimeter for a moment before he spoke. "What Arkady said—in a way, he was quite right. You are Ukrainian, too, Comrade Sheranchuk. You know that. But, you see, my cousin was a little bit wrong too. Only a few idiots want an independent country of the Ukraine."

"I don't think much about political questions," Sheranchuk apologized.

"Arkady thought too much of them," the footballer said kindly. "He made me think too. And what I think is that perhaps the Ukraine will have more of a voice on what happens in the Ukraine before long, and that will be worth waiting for." He shook himself and smiled. "Have you spoken to our real hero yet?"

"Real hero?"

"Bohdan Kalychenko. He was here a moment ago, but they've taken him off to hospital, I suppose. They say he was the first one on the roof, even before the firemen. Imagine! He stole a suit from somewhere, they thought he was one of their own!"

When Sheranchuk finally got back to the town of Chernobyl, the little apartment was empty. There was only a note:

I've been called to duty at the hospital. Come and tell me that you're all right!

He poured himself a glass of apple juice, thought of going out to phone the hospital (their luck in getting the apartment had not yet extended to a telephone), decided he might as well go there himself.

As he walked through Chernobyl town's crowded streets, he discovered he was feeling dejected. The adrenaline lift of the fire was gone. He had, after all, been of very little use in that emergency, he told himself. Well, yes, he had pointed out the danger of the diesel fuel, but it was Ponomorenko who had gone into the danger zone to deal with it—and who was to say the firemen wouldn't have dealt with it on their own?

Leonid Sheranchuk was not at ease with his thoughts on that sunny day. The fire was out, yes, but who was to say there would not be another? Or some other sudden emergency, not expected, not planned for—striking without warning to place Simyon Smin's plant once more in mortal danger? Was it as the man had said, that "forever" meant always, every day, remembering how badly things could go and always being vigilant?

He did not allow himself to really think of Simyon Smin. He didn't have to; that pain was always there.

Then there was Tamara. Certainly he had forgiven her in his heart—if indeed she needed forgiving; if what the bitch-doctor, Akhsmentova, had said had anything to do with reality. But would he always remember that she was forgiven? Even if something came up, something perhaps like what Ivanov had said, to remind him that his cuckoldry (if indeed it were true) was known to others than himself ... Not to mention the fact that he could never again do his real job at the Chernobyl plant, or indeed at any other nuclear power station anywhere.

He sighed, crossing the street before the hospital. You can't expect to be happy all the time, he told himself.

Then he revised that. No, he thought, the important thing is to take what you've got, no matter what that is, and find a way to make a happy life out of it somehow.

When he found his wife, flushed and busy in the admitting room, he first assured her that he was all right and then, impulsively, threw his arms around her and kissed her hard.

Tamara was startled. She drew away, then, laughing, returned the kiss. "All of that, my dear," she said, "can wait until later. I'm glad you're all right! Now, please, I'm busy—why don't you go to see Bohdan Kalychenko and let him boast to you of his heroism? After all, he has earned the chance!"

Kalychenko was in hospital pajamas, but he wasn't in bed. He was standing in the hall, in everyone's way, talking reassuringly to the fireman with the broken head. When he saw Sheranchuk, he hesitated, then came to him, grinning. "Poor lad, he's off to the operating room, but they'll fix him up, you can be sure. Me? Yes, I'm fine, but I couldn't find a suit quite tall enough for me. So I took nearly fifty rads, did you know? So they want to watch me for a bit, but that's only their way."

"I see that you just can't help running away from your post of duty," Sheranchuk said, mock severe.

Kalychenko flushed. "But the reactor was down!" he protested. "There was nothing to do there, only to watch the meters—"

Sheranchuk apologized quickly. "I was only making a joke. No, Kalychenko, this time you have covered yourself with honor, up on the roof. And with radiation, too, of course." He hesitated. "It's a pity, but I suppose that means they'll want to send you away. Still, they've made an exception for me. Perhaps they will for you, too."

"No, no," Kalychenko said quickly. "I've already been told that's out of the question, but it's all right. I've had an offer of another job, quite a different kind. Where? In Yuzhevin, the village where we were evacuated." And yes, he said (but silently to himself), all right, it's an "unpromising" village. But the job is good, and Raia likes the idea, and at least there I won't have to report on my comrades.

Sheranchuk couldn't make out the man's expression. "Well," he said vaguely, "I wish you all luck there. And, of course, congratulations on your marriage—have I said that already?"

He tried to think of a way to ease the sudden wariness that seemed to have entered the conversation. Emulating the man who was never far from his thoughts—"Ah, yes," he said. "Do you like Radio Armenia jokes? Deputy Director Smin was fond of them; there's one he told me in the hospital in Moscow, just before he died. It's a twenty-first-century joke. What does the father say then to his little girl when he takes her up a certain hill? He says, 'Don't be afraid, little dove. Under this hill is buried an old atomic power plant, but it's perfectly safe.' And then, when the frightened little girl still doesn't want to climb it, what does he tell her? He says, 'But, really, it's quite all right. Here, if you're frightened, give me your hand. Now give me your other hand. Now give me your other hand.'"

When, late that night, Sheranchuk remembered to tell his wife the same joke, he complained, "Kalychenko was odd, really. He didn't think it was very funny. But it's a good joke, isn't it?"

But Tamara wasn't laughing, either.

AFTERWORD

Because *Chernobyl* is a work of fiction based on fact, it may be hard to tell what in it is to be taken as fact and what the license of the novelist.

To begin with, all of the characters who appear in the novel are fictitious. Some of the things done in the novel were in fact done by real people, as in the case of the three men who donned diving gear and entered into the flooded corridors under the reactor to open the drainage valves—the names of the three actual men are Alexei Ananenko, Valeriy Bezpalov and Boris Baranov—but the characters in the novel are not in any way modeled on them.

The nature and chronology of the explosion and its consequences correspond as closely to reality as has been possible, although I have taken a few minor liberties with timing. The accompanying events have also been drawn from actuality, although in a few cases it is at least arguable what the actuality is.

A special case of this is the "seventeen-page document." The document described does exist. It is a reasoned manifesto that pleads for quite drastic reforms in such areas as freedom of speech, industrial priorities, and political processes. The document has in fact been circulated surreptitiously within the USSR and, after Chernobyl, even abroad. What is not certain is whether this document emanates from high-placed officials, as it claims, or is a fabrication put together by Soviet emigrés in the West. On the other hand, there is good evidence that many of the rather revolutionary changes the document proposes are in fact seriously contemplated by senior officials—though other high-ranking officials oppose them vigorously.

A particularly visible sign of such change is Mikhail Gorbachev's continuing sponsorship of a policy of *"glasnost,"* or candor and honesty both in reporting the facts of Soviet life and in discussing what measures should be taken to deal with them. This policy did not begin with the Chernobyl event, but that disaster is what has made it possible for an outsider to understand the new policy. It was *glasnost* that permitted the publication of Lyubov Kovalevska's savagely critical article on the shortcomings of Chernobyl Nuclear Power Plant in the March 27, 1986, issue of *Literaturna Ukraina,* just a few weeks before the explosion. It was *glasnost* that resulted in the unprecedentedly complete and candid Soviet report on the Chernobyl accident submitted to the International Atomic Energy Authority in Vienna in September 1986 (from which much of the technical background of this novel was drawn). It was also *glasnost* that has since produced the reporting, in the Soviet press and abroad, of stories of riots, accidents, demonstrations, and other Soviet events that were almost never admitted previously—including stories of malfeasance of high Communist Party officials, and even of members of the KGB.

And, on a much smaller scale, I believe it was again because of *glasnost* that I received the great assistance and cooperation that was extended to me when I returned to the Soviet Union to complete my research for this novel. For this I must thank many Soviet officials, but in particular the leadership of the Union of Soviet Writers. They opened many doors for me, and imposed no restrictions on what I might write or whom I might see. With their help I was able to interview scores of people with direct knowledge of the Chernobyl accident, journalists, eyewitnesses, firemen who fought to control the damage, nuclear experts who were on the scene and many others. They did more to help me get this story than I could have hoped, and I am grateful.

ABOUT THE AUTHOR

Editor, futurist and award-winning writer, Frederik Pohl is the author of more than 30 novels and short story collections, including *Jem, Man Plus* and *Gateway*. He has won six Hugo Awards and two Nebula Awards, among others. In 1982, he was elected a fellow of the American Association for the Advancement of Science. He lives in Palatine, Illinois.